# THE PATRIOT GAME

## Ron Culley

Grosvenor House
Publishing Limited

Ron Culley is hereby identified as author of this
work in accordance with Section 77 of the Copyright, Designs
and Patents Act 1988

The book cover picture is copyright to Ron Culley

This book is published by
Grosvenor House Publishing Ltd
28-30 High Street, Guildford, Surrey, GU1 3EL.
www.grosvenorhousepublishing.co.uk

A CIP record for this book
is available from the British Library

ISBN 978-1-78148-808-9

## Previous books by Ron Culley

*The Kaibab Resolution*. Kennedy & Boyd 2010.
*I Belong To Glasgow* [foreword by
Sir Alex Ferguson] The Grimsay Press, 2011
*A Confusion of Mandarins*. Grosvenor House. 2011.
*Glasgow Belongs To Me*. Grosvenor House
[electronic media only] 2012


## Web address

www.ronculley.com

# Dedication

This book is dedicated with love to my four sons, Ron, Campbell, Conor and Ciaran. My grandchildren (currently Arran, Eilidh and Olive) can wait...their time will come.

I'd also like to mention warmly in despatches, my friends Danny Logue who encouraged me to look at this period of history and Tadhg Dennehy from Kerry, just the most wonderful, whip-smart Irishman this side of MacGillycuddy's Reeks! I think it appropriate to mention that Tadhg doesn't necessarily agree entirely with every sentiment expressed in this book.

I'm also grateful to Connie Haag from Konstanz in Germany and Maurice Ahern from Dublin for their help in interpretation and to the various authors whom I mention in a bibliography at the end of the book and whose writing helped me immeasurably – particularly Professor Diarmaid Ferriter of University College Dublin whose book, '*Judging Dev: A Reassessment of the Life and Legacy of Éamon de Valera*' proved invaluable.

Inevitably though, any mistakes are mine. I do deviate slightly from historical fact on a few minor occasions in the interests of improved narrative but these are referred to and explained in my Authors' Notes at the end of the book.

Ron Culley
Glasgow 2013

# Preface

Ireland fascinates me. Its history intrigues, its music inspires and its beauty reminds me so much of my home country of Scotland – perhaps that's why I love it so. I suppose that as a consequence of being a northern European, if someone put a gun to my head and told me I could no longer live in Glasgow, the city of my birth, I'd choose Dublin immediately rather than the sunnier climes of San Francisco or Sydney. I love the fact that, like Glasgow, it experiences four discernible seasons of the year, the rain's warm enough to endure, its pubs are great and its people and their banter are mighty.

I chose to write about this episode in Ireland's history as I believed it not only to have interesting narrative potential but because it seemed to me not an aspect of Irish life which is particularly well known. Éamon de Valera was a politician who divided opinion but most Irish people were behind his policy of neutrality during World War Two and one almost inevitable consequence of that policy was experienced after the war when a number of high-ranking German officers chose to make their home in an Ireland which promised no retribution to belligerents so long as they did not act against the interests of the Irish state.

Certain of those German officers had conducted themselves very badly during the war, escaped the Nuremberg Trials and, in some instances, were fêted in Irish society. This work of historical fiction surrounds these circumstances. I also wanted to explore the matter of 'patriotism' as the title of the book implies. When political and military leaders wrap themselves in the flag of patriotism, they can instruct and connive at behaviours and actions which in normal circumstances would not be acceptable to a responsible public. Churchill thought himself a patriot – but so too did Éamon de Valera, Hitler, Stalin, Truman, Begin and Roosevelt – bringing each, to a greater or lesser extent into conflict one with another.

*Plus ça change plus c'est la même chose...*

# Short Glossary

| | |
|---|---|
| *An Garda Síochána* | Guardians of the Peace of Ireland. The police force of Ireland. |
| Black Stuff | The 'Black Stuff' refers to the famous Irish dry stout, Guinness which is a descendant of an 18th century English porter style ale. |
| Brimmer | Popular wide brimmed hat worn by males. |
| Coaster | Shallow hulled coastal trading vessel. |
| *Craic* | Irish for banter. Chat. Light-hearted discussion. (pron. *crack*) |
| Desperate | A strengthening adjective. Difficult, terrible. |
| Dev | Éamon de Valera, Prime Minister of Ireland during World War Two. His political career spanned over half a century, from 1917 to 1973. |
| Easter Rising | Easter 1916. An insurrection staged in Ireland during Easter Week. Mounted by Irish Republicans, it aimed to end British rule in Ireland and establish an Irish Republic. |
| Eegit | Idiot |
| Emergency | The *Emergency* is a shorthand expression for the period covered by 'The Emergency Powers Act 1939' introduced by the Irish |

|  | Government to take wide-ranging powers in order more effectively to control and protect its citizens during World War Two. |
|---|---|
| Feckin' | A strengthening adjective. A more benign form of 'fuckin'.' |
| Floater | Sea-plane. |
| *Gaelic* | Irish for the native language of Ireland. |
| G-2 | Ireland's Intelligence Services. |
| *Garda* | A police officer. *Gardai*, plural noun. |
| General Army Council | The chiefs of staff of the Irish Republican Army [IRA]. |
| Guinness | A popular Irish stout. Alcoholic beer, 'the black stuff'. |
| Jacks | Lavatory |
| John Bull | International terminology for 'England'/'English' |
| Porter | Irish stout; Guinness. |
| Punt | Pound. Irish currency before the Euro. |
| Shaggin' | A strengthening adjective. Alternative to feckin'/fucking. |
| *Taoiseach* | Irish for Prime Minister. Political Leader of Ireland. |
| Turf | Peat. A main source of fuel in Ireland cut, lifted and dried from the peat bogs. |
| Volunteer | A member of the Irish Republican Army (usually rank and file). |
| Whiskey | Irish spelling of whisky |
| Whisky | Scottish spelling of Scotch whisky. |
| Yous, ye | Frequently used inaccurately as plural word for 'you'. |

# The Patriot Game

*Come all you young rebels and list while I sing*
*For love of one's country is a terrible thing*
*It banishes fear with the speed of a flame*
*And makes us all part of the patriot game*

Dominic Behan 1958

## CHAPTER ONE

# Dublin, Ireland 1944

Dublin slept.

A pencil-thin line of ochre light below a heavy wooden door suggested occupancy in a room situated to the rear of an otherwise darkened and deserted public house. Outside, the city's bars had long surrendered their stumbling clientele to the night. Within, two gunmen watched the street outside from the gloom, an occasional red glow from their cigarettes being the only way of identifying their presence. In an alley to the rear of the pub, a third gunman guarded the back entrance.

In the dimly lit bar parlour, Joseph Kelly sat alone in its silence and felt inside his jacket pocket for his tobacco pouch. Removing it, he began to thumb some of its contents into the chamber of his stubby briar pipe before igniting it with a match whose slight flame he manoeuvred for some moments before satisfying himself that his strands of Sweet Virginia were quite alight.

Further minutes were spent puffing in quiet contemplation before a tapping on the door alerted him to the arrival of his old friend, Con Lehane. Ushered in by one of the men posted outside, Lehane sat down in a whirl of greetings and much wiping of his brow.

Removing his black, broad-brimmed Fedora hat, he placed it atop his briefcase.

"You and I are getting too old for this business, Joe. Would you look at the nick of me? I'm overweight, half blind and in a state of constant fret. I should be retired and home asleep. Instead, I'm flitting between Mountjoy Prison and dark and dangerous places you laughingly call 'safe' to advise on...."

"Con...the quicker you let me know how things stand, the quicker you'll be home safe with herself, so."

Shoving an irritable finger within his shirt collar and tugging at it to relieve his discomfort, Lehane sighed and nodded his acknowledgement of Kelly's sapience.

"Well, Charlie refuses to appeal the guilty verdict of the Military Tribunal. He won't recognise the court. Just *won't*! He wouldn't plead...wouldn't call witnesses... The Free State hasn't been able to show any evidence that he was involved in the shooting of O'Brien. The Thompson submachine gun they found underneath his bed wasn't connected to the shooting...They couldn't produce anyone who saw him at the scene. All they have is a single blurred fingerprint of Charlie's on a bike that was found near where O'Brien was."

Kelly narrowed his lips and exhaled slowly, his pipe smoke causing Lehane to cough and rise in order to pour himself a glass of water.

"You've been workin' hard, Con. Are you bearin' up?"

"Strop the razor, Joe. I'm about ready to top myself. I've just spent three hours with Charlie there up at Mountjoy jail and he's having none of it! The Court

President has denied us leave to appeal and just finished business today by saying, 'Charles Kerins, when you appear back before me on Monday, you're going to have to give this court reasons why you shouldn't hang'! Like I said, Joseph... doesn't look great."

Kelly held his thoughts to himself as he gnawed on his pipe, his silence prompting Lehane to continue.

"Look, Joe. They *know* he's the Chief of Staff of the Irish Republican Army. Too bad they can't prove it... They fail every test of fairness in this trial but de Valera's pulling out all the stops to make an example of our boy. Dev's got most of our Volunteers interned in the Curragh or in Mountjoy Gaol along with Charlie. We've precious few left now and they're hunting down those who remain active. The execution of Charlie Kerins would be an important signal by Dev's government that they have us by the bollocks. "

Kelly inverted his pipe and tapped it against the edge of an ashtray, emptying its contents, inspecting the bowl to ensure it was voided.

"Like you say, Con...not great... and you and me both know that Charlie's as stubborn as they come. Stubborn as a feckin' mule and he'll not bow the knee to the court supposin' they gave him two *years* to mull over his decision instead of two days!"

Lehane met Kelly's gaze.

"Joe, the Irish Free State will hang Charlie Kerins just as soon as they can find a rope."

The stern, grey walls of Mountjoy Gaol were rendered yet more sombre and imposing by the gloom of pre-dawn Dublin. The quiet that had settled over the city was fractured within the prison as small yelps and cries emanated intermittently from within some of its cells whose occupants wrestled in torment with their demons. In the landing of 'B' Wing, the urgent staccato clip of Governor Scallion's segged shoes rose audibly as they approached the door of cell 58. A prison guard and a priest followed, their leather soled shoes making no noise.

"Open it," said the Governor somewhat unnecessarily.

A clutch of keys on a ring jingled brightly and the door opened.

"Thank you. Now leave us."

"Should I maybe wait outside just in case, sir?"

"No thank you. Now leave us and close the door. Don't lock it," instructed Scallion as he and the priest entered the cell.

Sitting on the floor, his back to the wall, facing his visitors was Charlie Kerins, Chief of Staff of the Irish Republican Army. Above him a high window allowed in a pale beam of moonlight immediately obscured by the Governor's hand held lamp. He showed no surprise at being visited at that hour in the morning and bid them welcome.

"Father...Governor. What's the form? I'm honoured. You should both be in your scratchers at this hour."

"That we should, Charlie...that we should. I asked to be notified when your lawyer left and waited until Father O'Driscoll here could join me. If your brief had left at a more Godly hour I'd be in my kip by now."

He perched on the edge of Kerins' bed.

"You've had a long day."

"I have that, Governor. It's been a bit of a week all right."

"Charlie, it doesn't have to end this way. Now I know this is none of my business but I'm a Killarney man and you're a Caherina man from Tralee. We're near enough neighbours. In another time you and me could be suppin' pints in a bar parlour instead of meetin' like this."

"Fair play and the blessings of Jesus upon you, Governor. Just you say the word and I'll go for a glass with you right now!"

The governor smiled. "Sure wouldn't that be great if we could get away with it."

Kerins shrugged his shoulders. "Then maybe in a couple of weeks?"

Scallion ignored the banter, his serious face returning.

"Charlie, they've already sent for Alfred Pierrepoint, the English executioner. There can be no doubt what they have in mind for you. I've not attended the trial but..."

"It's no trial, Governor. They're just going through the motions. This is just a Free State Military Tribunal set up to get rid of a Republican who threatens British rule in the north of our country and de Valera's collaborators in the south. Well, I won't play their game. I won't recognise the court and all I can say is that if the Free State authorities are satisfied that I got a fair trial here, I hope their consciences are clear on that point. If this is an example of de Valera's justice, freedom and democracy, then I would like to know what dictatorship and militarism are. That is about all I have to say."

"Charlie, if those are your words at the court on Monday, you'll swing sure as eggs is eggs."

"All I ask is that the ideals and principals for which I am about to die for will be kept alive until the Irish Republic is finally enthroned."

"Noble words, Charlie. But you have so much to live for. You're an athlete, a leader! People regard you as a good man. A man who inspires others. Why throw everything away for a cause no matter how noble?"

"Like I say, Governor...until the Irish Republic is finally enthroned!"

Governor Scallion eyed the floor of the cell before meeting Kerins' gaze.

"You're an obstinate, headstrong man Charlie Kerins...but God alone knows you're a brave one too. I hope you use the time between now and Monday morning to think again. There's been enough killin' in this benighted island of ours"

He placed his hands upon his knees and made to rise from the small cot. He threw two small packets towards him.

"Here's some cigarettes and matches. I was told you had none. I also brought Father O'Driscoll here to have some private time with you, Charlie. Normally I'd wait until morning but time is short."

Kerins smiled.

"Ah, tomorrow will be soon enough, father. Let's all get some sleep. Sure, I'll more than probably be here when you return."

The three men stood and shook hands. Scallion pushed at the heavy door and he and the priest exited. Outside some paces away, the prison guard stood nonchalantly, leaning against the balcony, moving to attention as the men emerged.

"I just come back to see to Prisoner Killeen in cell 57, Sir. He's been threatenin' to kill hisself so we look in on him every so often."

"Carry on, guard."

Kerins sat back on the cell floor listening to the ebbing sound of the governor's clipped walk along the iron walkway until silence ensued. As it did so, his cell door was locked and the small hatch opened to reveal the scowling features of the guard.

"I was outside listenin' to the governor talkin' his bollocks, Kerins. I thought I'd just let you know that there are more than a few of us in here who hope you rot in hell. One of our guards is related on to Detective Dinny O'Brien; him you shot in cold blood and he's feckin' fit to be tied as you'd imagine. You're a feckin' human disgrace as a man and I wanted you to know *official*, like...that Pierrepoint *is* on his way and that some of us have put our hands in our pocket to ask him a favour for a small consideration."

A row of blackened teeth evidenced themselves as a sneer spread across a face as scarred as many of his charges.

"Have you witnessed a hangin' before now Charlie, have you? Because *I* have and it's a skilled art they tell me. If the rope is too short for your weight, it doesn't snap your neck and you dangle in agony as the breath leaves your body. It's a terrible death...takes maybe twenty minutes. That said, if the rope is too *long* for the weight it carries, you drop so far it just rips the feckin' head off a man. Straight off. I've seen a few of them in my time. Blood everywhere! Me and the boys are tryin' to decide what we'll ask Pierrepoint to do. We'd enjoy both. Now you sleep tight tonight... and don't you go paying no attention to the wise advice of our governor. You just tell the judge what you were goin' to...and let the hangman at you."

Kerins smiled. "You're a man of obvious compassion and intelligence, guard. Now you go on your way and let me sleep the sleep of the just. *An Phoblacht abu!*"

The clang of the slammed metal shutter echoed throughout 'B' Wing for what seemed an eternity.

The rapping on Sinéad O'Grady's front door was insistent. Joseph Kelly eyed his surroundings nervously as he awaited entry. After a few moments the door opened and he was admitted.

"Thanks, Sinéad. At this time of the mornin', the *Gardai* would just presume I was up to no good."

"Uncle Joseph! What brings you here at this hour? Is somethin' wrong?"

She tied a washed-out dressing gown around her waist as she spoke, tugging her unruly curls from her eyes.

"I've just come from meetin' Con Lehane. It's not good. They've found Charlie guilty and it looks like they're goin' to hang him soon enough."

"Sweet Mother of Jesus comfort me this night!" Sinead took her uncle by the arm and guided him into her front parlour. "Can't Charlie appeal?"

"He won't recognise the court so they can do as they please."

Sinéad sat him on a chair as she stabbed some life back into the embers of a turf fire in the hearth. Kelly felt in his pocket for a comforting pipe, talking as he did so.

"The government have put a block on all news and comment about the trial. I was hearin' earlier today that Kerry County Council called for a public meeting at the Mansion House here in Dublin but the *gardai* arrested twenty-six people just for putting up the advertisements of the meeting. They had men in squad cars goin' around tearing down the posters. We've asked politicians to debate the matter but de Valera's threatened their suspension. He's so feckin' cynical that he's told them they can have their debate *after* the execution!"

"The gas is off at this hour so I'll make us some tea once this fire catches. I've no milk, mind...or sugar."

"You're a good girl, Sinéad.

Kelly's pipe was now emitting clouds of smoke and a silence ensued as Sinéad busied herself in the small kitchen, filling a kettle while Kelly contemplated the embers now igniting the cluster of small sticks beneath the dried peat she'd laid on them. By the time Sinéad had returned to hang the kettle on a hook above the fire the flames were licking at the turf, promising warmth and a boiled kettle.

"Sinéad, for the minute I need to put poor Charlie's problems on the long finger. We have a problem."

Sinéad sat and awaited her uncle's further comments while he troubled himself with his pipe until, satisfied with the small furnace that raged in the bowl, he continued.

"We can only have around two hundred Volunteers left in this man's army. Dev has the lot of us interned. How we're expected to take the war to the Brits when we're so poorly off for men and materials escapes me. We've a few cells already in England but they're short of explosives...enough to give their king a black eye now and again but not enough to bring them to heel politically."

He sucked on his pipe as if contemplating the wisdom of continuing.

"Sinéad, over here, we're compromised. Someone... one of our own...grassed off Charlie Kerins. We believe someone told the *Gardai* which phones should be tapped to unearth his whereabouts. Tomorrow I'm to be told who did this. I've been commanded to collect him, soften him up and eventually to execute him. The reason I can trust you..."

Sinéad raised an eyebrow, implicitly challenging her uncle's implication that she might not merit his complete confidence.

"Sinéad, you're my flesh and blood. Of *course* I trust you but my point is...you're a *woman* and I'm informed that our man is just that...a man, so no one could question my judgement in pickin' you. It's a man from County Kerry, I'm told. That's *your* turf. You'll know him. Who better to interrogate him? You'll have the rest of the Volunteers down there to help you. Also, my back's feckin' banjaxed. I'm gettin' too old for this malarkey. Con Lehane was right."

Sinéad met his gaze without comment as her uncle warmed to his theme.

"Sinéad, I've seen you up close. Seen you in shoot-outs with *An Garda Síochána*. You're brave and smart. You'd go a step in the road with anyone. The men respect you and so far, the peelers have no reason to suspect you of anythin'. I need you to travel home to your cottage at first light. I need you to await my identification of this feckin' traitor and I need you to deal with him as we've discussed. Now, what'd you say, girl?"

Sinéad responded immediately.

"I'd much rather be continuin' my argument with the Brits or Dev's *Garda Síochána*. I don't like the idea of gettin' involved in internal IRA politics."

She gazed at the fire as if for guidance before returning to meet Joe's request. "...but I suppose I'll give it a lash."

"Good girl...but be after doin' one more thing for me."

"And what might that be?"

"Well, about four years ago the Germans transported of two of our boys, Sean Russell and Frank Ryan to Ireland after arms negotiations in Berlin. They left Wilhelmshaven on a U-Boat but Sean became ill during the journey. They didn't have a medic on board and he died about a hundred miles short of Galway. He was buried at sea and the mission aborted. That mission was to have provided us with arms...British arms, captured by the Germans. Well, we've been in touch with the Germans and they've agreed to try again. They're sending over someone to help arrange things. We've to meet him off a fishing boat in Drogheda in a week or so's time."

Sinéad folded her arms. "And what would you have me do, Joseph."

"We need these arms and explosives desperate, Sinéad. Once you dispatch our man in Kerry, you come back up to Dublin with a couple of Volunteers and collect this German fellah from the boat and bring him to the safe house here in Rialto. Could you do that, girl?"

Sinéad drummed her fingers on the surface of the table and shook her head in mild vexation.

"You make it sound so simple, Joseph. One dispatch, one collection. I should be workin' for the feckin' post office."

Kelly frowned. "Now Sinéad, I've told you before. I don't approve of your language when you start that cursin'. Your parents would..."

"What, Joseph? Approve of me beatin' a man half to death to extract information then shootin' him but shake their heads just because I speak like my feckin' uncle? Well, don't you fret, when I'm beatin' the livin' shit out of our man in Kerry, I'll make sure I speak like a feckin' lady of the feckin' manor!"

## CHAPTER TWO

# Meinerzhagen, Germany

Lying prone in the undergrowth some distance from a clearing in a pine forest near Meinerzhagen in North Rhine-Westphalia, *Waffen SS Sturmbannführer* Kurt Weber stilled his finger on the trigger guard of his Karabiner 98k Mauser and waited. It was dark now and the ground was still damp from an earlier rain.

Ten minutes passed...fifteen. Gradually Weber heard the distant sound of footsteps mingled with occasional guttural commands coming closer to his hide. Shortly, two men came into the clearing. Stumbling behind them, her hands bound in front of her by rope was a young girl aged around sixteen. The moonlight allowed only limited visibility, improved slightly when one of the men scratched a match noisily against the edge of its box, the phosphorus flaring in his cupped hands before lighting a cigarette. The other man threw kindling on the ground and pouring petrol from a *Wehrmachtskanister*, ignited the cluster of sticks revealing two SS soldiers, one an *Obersturmführer*, a First Lieutenant.

The girl stood dazed and weeping, her strangled moans increasing in intensity when the *Obersturmführer* took the length of rope binding the girl's hands, throwing it over the branch of a nearby tree. He hauled down on it and hoisted the girl's arms skywards until she stood almost on tip-toe before tethering the end of the rope to a lower branch.

Laughing, the two soldiers approached her and ripped her torn and dirty slip until she was naked from the waist up. Holding her terrified gaze, the *Obersturmführer* placed the flat of a large knife beneath the girl's left breast, slowly weighing it before gradually turning it upwards until the razor-sharp blade nestled underneath. A mirthless, rictus grin spread across his features. With his left hand, he grasped the young girl's hair and pulled her head back.

Watching from his hide, Weber tightened his grip on his Mauser, making certain its sights were centred on his target. Content that he was sufficiently close to compensate for any small error in his aim, he eased back his right forefinger; the resulting sharp crack speeding a bullet through the *Obersturmführer's* head just behind his right ear, instantly destroying his parietal lobe and covering the young girl in blood and brain particles.

The German officer dropped where he stood, the light from the fire then revealing his startled accomplice holding an open razor in one hand and his cigarette in such a fashion as suggested that it was not intended for inhalation but for torture. Before Weber had an opportunity to pull the trigger a second time, the second SS soldier made off back down the track crashing into trees and bushes, his eyes trying to re-accustom themselves to the darkness. Weber leapt to his feet and with cat-like stealth, ran tangentially to the path hoping to shorten the distance between them. Now facing the same visual problems as his quarry, he tripped over a small branch and fell headlong before resuming the chase.

In the darkness, his pursuit was informed more by the sounds of the panicked soldier making his way through the forest. *Fool*, thought Weber. *If only he sat down quietly under a bush, I'd never find him in this blackness.* The noise made by the soldier directed Weber onwards until the trees reduced in density allowing him to catch a glimpse of the soldier in a moonlit clearing attempting to leap across a stream. Instantly Weber fell on one knee and raised his Mauser. Taking aim, he fired and the soldier fell forwards into the brook, wounded.

Weber stood slowly, assessing the impact of his shot. He could still hear the soldier moaning as he attempted unsuccessfully to instruct his left leg to propel him from the cold waters.

*Careful, Kurt*, he commanded himself. Slowly rounding a large spruce the better to view the soldier, he could see no weapon. Encouraged, he quietly made his way behind the man until he was but a few yards from him and could see his victim clearly. Disabled by a shot through his pelvis, the soldier was in pain and completely immobilised.

Weber levelled his rifle, waist high.

"*Schüetze*, I hope my bullet buries itself in your soul!"

The soldier turned painfully in the direction of the voice.

"You and your *Obersturmführer* are a disgrace to our uniform. While your comrades are giving their lives for the Fatherland, you prey on young women...young *German* women. The flower of the Third *Reich*. You toy with them and cut and torture them before you kill them. You are nothing but a sadist and have disgraced the *Waffen Schutzstaffel*."

He raised his rifle to eye level and aimed at the prostrate soldier.

"It has been ordered that you must die. *Mistkerl*!"

The velocity of the bullet through his forehead threw the soldier backwards against the bank of the stream. Slowly his body slid down the muddy wall of the bank into the cold, rushing waters until they almost enveloped him.

Before heading back to the clearing, Weber gazed at the semi-submerged form of the dead man for some moments, grappling with the perverted mentality of men who would torture young women for their own base ends.

The fire was low now but by its faint glow he could see that the young girl had succumbed to unconsciousness and was now hanging limply from the tree. Picking up the *Obersturmführer's* heavy hunting knife from his life-less hand, he cut at the rope whilst holding the girl to support her. Lowering her carefully to the ground, he took the knife and cut first the *Waffen* SS insignia from the arm of the *Obersturmführer's* uniform and then the badges of rank from his collar. Dragging the body over to the dying embers of the fire, he picked up the *Wehrmachtskanister* petrol container and poured the remains over the dead corpse. He lifted a piece of lit kindling and paused as if to remember the face of the sadistic beast he'd just killed before casually throwing the stick on to his body. After a momentary pause, during which it appeared that the gasoline vapour was making its mind up whether or not to ignite, it exploded in a *crump* and engulfed the dead *Obersturmführer* in flames.

Satisfied, he removed the jacket of his uniform and placed it over the still naked upper body of the girl and sat back against the tree. For six months stories had reached him about teenage girls being abducted, tortured, disfigured and killed. Normal procedures would have involved an arrest. Normal procedures may have seen the sadist walk free if he knew someone of sufficiently high rank. Normal procedures did not suffice in this instance.

Slowly the girl regained consciousness and started in fear as she awoke to see Weber over her.

"Don't be afraid, *fräulein*. The men who tried to hurt you are dead. I will take you home. Can you stand?"

Painfully, the young girl raised herself unsteadily to her feet. Weber untied the knots that bound her hands and helped her slip the uniform jacket over her arms. Wordlessly, they walked back to the edge of the forest before the girl directed them, pointing towards a cabin in which she lived with her parents. A light was discernible through the window. Carefully, Weber looked inside the cabin. A woman was kneeling on the floor tending the head wounds of a man Weber presumed to be her husband.

Knocking softly on the door and opening it, Weber frightened the woman who rose and screamed as she recognised her daughter, hugging her tightly as she brought her into the small front room.

"The men who took your daughter are dead, *fräu* they will trouble you no more," said Weber. He looked at the man on the floor and stooped to assess his injuries.

"What happened?"

"The two soldiers...they just came in and took our daughter from her bed. She was asleep. When we tried to stop them, the *Obersturmführer* hit father about the head with his pistol knocking him unconscious. I gave chase but one of the soldiers knocked me down and I lost sight of them. I returned to help father...I didn't know what to do about my beautiful daughter. I feared the worst."

Weber finished his cursory inspection and rose.

"Your husband will be fine. He might have a sore head for a while but he's okay. Your daughter is also well. The men were shot before they could do her any harm." He placed a hand on the mother's shoulder as she held her daughter tightly.

"Men...soldiers, perhaps...might ask about tonight's proceedings. It would be in no one's interest for any of this to be known. I ask you to say nothing. Your family is now safe."

He stepped towards the door and lifted a shawl that hung on a hook behind it. Gesturing to the mother, he invited her assistance in retrieving his uniform jacket in exchange for the garment and having put it back on, left them to comfort one another.

A heavy curtain was inched back from a darkened window at *Schloss* Bladenhorst as the increasing roar of Weber's Zundapp motorcycle alerted *Obergruppenführer* Friederike Mencken to its arrival. Looking down from the window to confirm the identity of his visitor, he recognised Weber and returned to the chair behind his desk and waited.

Footsteps outside preceded a soft knock on the door.

"Enter!"

Weber opened the door. Each man saluted the other using the traditional army address, touching their forehead with their fingertips. Neither demonstrated much formality in doing so.

"Well, *Sturmbannführer.* Did you achieve your mission?"

Weber placed the SS insignia and badges of rank on the desk before Mencken.

"Two men. Both SS. One, an *Obersturmführer.* I shot both as they attempted to mutilate a young girl. I returned her to her parents unharmed."

Mencken sipped from his glass and focussed his rheumy gaze on Weber.

"*Schweinehunds!*" he muttered before raising the glass to his lips a second time and finishing its contents. His face contorted slightly as the schnapps hit home. He continued. "Excellent, Weber," he said grimly. "And no one saw you?"

Weber shook his head.

"Then it has been a good night's work. You have been of great service to the *Waffen Schutzstaffel.* Sadists like that disgrace their comrades and their uniform. They deserve to die a coward's death. Even in the face of this horrible war, we must retain some measure of civilisation and permitting two of our men to maim and kill innocent children is totally unacceptable. Totally! The SS has acted in ways certain of us find most unappetising but there is no excuse for our soldiers behaving as these beasts have done."

He took another sip of his *schnapps*.

"You did well...and no paper work. Justice is served."

Rising from his desk, Mencken lifted a file from a cabinet and returned to his chair, signalling to Weber that he should sit as well.

"How long have you been a member of the *Waffen Schutzstaffel...the SS?*"

"For two years, *Herr* Mencken."

"And before that, a professor of history at Heidelberg University before enlisting in the *Wehrmacht* at the start of the war?"

"Yes, *Obergruppenführer* I was in the *Wehrmacht* but for only two years before I was conscripted into the *Waffen SS*. When I enlisted I joined Army Group North under *Feldmarshal* von Leeb and saw action in Poland and Norway."

"You were promoted rapidly."

"I was, *Obergruppenführer.* I was privileged to lead the paratroopers of the 18th Army into Norway under *Obergruppenführer* Nikolaus von Falkenhorst."

"And then into Greece after you were conscripted commanding a battalion of SS troops," he murmured, almost inaudibly.

Mencken studied the file as if for the first time although he'd poured over it on numerous occasions.

"I'm being asked to nominate a member of the Waffen SS for a mission. One that requires intelligence, an excellent command of the English language and someone who has seen battle." He closed the file. "You meet all requirements *Sturmbannführer.*"

"I am at your service, *Obergruppenführer* Mencken."

"You lost your toes to frostbite in Norway?"

"Two on each foot. Many others lost their lives."

"Quite." He consulted the file again.

"You broke your back in Greece following a parachute landing?"

"I was in hospital for a year, *Obergruppenführer*. But I am in good health now although my back pains me from time to time."

Mencken leafed over a page. "And as a result of your bravery in battle you have been awarded the Iron Cross 1st Class, the Wound Badge in Silver and the Knight's Cross with Oak Leaves. You have been promoted three times. On the last occasion to Major?"

"Yes, *Obergruppenführer* Mencken."

The General rose, closing Weber's file and dropping it lightly on a pile of several other similar folders before pouring himself a second glass of *schnapps*, this time decanting one for Weber as well. He placed one of the glasses before the *Sturmbannführer* and continued.

"Kurt, the war is not going well for us in Germany. We have surrendered in Stalingrad and in North Africa. The Allies are massing on the south coast of England under Eisenhower to prepare their landing on continental Europe. *Generalfeldmarshall* Kesselring has done his best but Italy is lost. The Red Army is battering our troops at Sevastopol. No...the war does not go well for us. We suffer reverses across the globe."

For some moments, Mencken stared solemnly into his glass of *schnapps*, saying nothing.

Weber held his glass out of courtesy, disinterested in its contents. Suddenly Mencken was roused from his thoughts and brought the evening's proceedings to an abrupt end. He smiled a smile which did not reach his eyes.

"Still, we have hope."

He gathered himself. "*Sturmbannführer* Weber. You have done well tonight but your country has further need of your services. More specifically, I have a good friend at the *Abwehr* who has need of your services."

He decided further explanation was necessary, answering the question he supposed was resting unasked in Weber's mind.

"Traditionally, our intelligence services do not have good relations with the *Waffen SS* but over the years, *Obergruppenführer* Claus Schäfer and I have become close confidants. He is a good man...and he has a plan to turn the fortunes of war. I want you to meet him. In Berlin. Tomorrow."

"As you command, *Obergruppenführer* Mencken."

## CHAPTER THREE

Mencken's staff car escorted Weber to *Abwehr* Headquarters newly located in Zossen, south of Berlin ever since Allied bombers had begun their daily aerial assault on the capital.

The driver turned in his seat to address his passenger.

"I have been instructed not to wait, *Sturmbannführer*. The *Obergruppenführer* says you will not be returning to the *Schloss* with me."

Weber sighed. "Well, I'm sure that the *Obergruppenführer* will know my fate better than me."

Returning salutes as he passed various security levels, Weber presented himself as requested and awaited the attentions of General Schäfer's staff. Refusing a glass of water, he busied himself reading an old discarded newspaper until he was invited into an office behind which was a further office until, at a third entrance, he found himself in front of *Obergruppenführer* Claus Schäfer.

"*Sturmbannführer* Weber, I am pleased to meet you at last. My good friend *Obergruppenführer* Mencken has spoken very highly of you."

"I am privileged to have his confidence."

"As am I, *Sturmbannführer*. Please have a seat. My secretary will bring us a coffee. It's good stuff...and it's too early for *schnapps*. No?" He smiled as he opened the file that Mencken had Weber bring with him.

"Friederike Mencken and I have looked at a large number of files, *Sturmbannführer*. I have read yours many times because none we read was as compelling as the file I now hold in my hands. You are a remarkable man. A warrior professor!"

"As you please, *Obergruppenführer.*"

"But there was a complaint against you...from the *Gestapo*?"

"It was never pursued. My senior officers intervened on my behalf."

"And what was the basis of the complaint from *Kriminalkommissar*"...He peered at the file before him... "Schmidt."

"I refused to order my men to shoot innocent men and women whose only crime was to live in a village where shots were fired at *Kriminalkommissar* Schmidt's car."

"It also says here that you assaulted him."

"Unfortunately, *Obergruppenführer*. No one could be found to testify on Schmidt's behalf."

"And tell me *Sturmbannführer*, is it your normal practice to assault your comrades?"

"As I say, the charges against me were found to be without merit." He paused, considering the wisdom of continuing further, before deciding to speak.

"*Obergruppenführer*, war is dreadful. If we are not always vigilant, we can become sub-human as we fight our cause. I confess that while I carry the fight to our enemies ferociously, I try to look after my men, try to remember that civilians have no part in these affairs and that, on both sides there are soldiers and officers who do not hold to the ideals I have just uttered. It is difficult... some might say impossible...but I will not allow my ideals to be sacrificed on the altar of the base instincts of lesser men."

Schäfer nodded his satisfaction.

"Well, my friend Mencken told me you were hard enough to make tough decisions but that you had enough humanity to have them keep you awake at night and it is precisely the ideals you describe that some believe have to be the values that must underpin a new Germany...whether we win or lose this war."

He closed Weber's file and threw it casually onto his desk.

"Professor, what we discuss here today is a matter of the highest sensitivity. The full details must remain known only to you, me, my friend *Obergruppenführer* Mencken and one other man...in Ireland, who knows only the broadest information. I must make myself clear on this. There must be no communication whatsoever with any living soul...you must even omit it from prayer if you are a believer."

"Of course."

"Friederike tells me he discussed our analysis of the war with you last night at the *Schloss*."

"He did."

"Did you find his views defeatist, irrational?"

Weber shrugged. "There was rationality to his assessment. But all is not lost."

"Indeed not, *Sturmbannführer* but we must make plans for that eventuality whilst doing all we can to assist the *Fuehrer* in his defence of the Third *Reich*."

He paused as his secretary brought and poured them both coffees.

"Let me explain something of the work of the *Abwher*. As you know, it is Germany's Intelligence Agency and has eleven divisions. I am responsible for three of them; foreign intelligence collection, false documentation and the Anglo-American military. The plan I have evolved with Friederike is located within these responsibilities."

He took out and lit a cigarette, placing it in an ivory cigarette holder as a prelude to drinking his coffee before continuing.

"What I tell you now is top secret. At the start of the war, we developed a plan called Plan Green which involved a full German invasion of Ireland in support of the invasion of Britain, which we called Operation Sea Lion. This plan had two purposes. Firstly, we needed to prepare adequately for the possibility of invading Ireland; England's back door. This was only sensible. Secondly, it was used as a credible threat, a feint that would tie up British forces on their west coast and in Ulster, away from the coastal counties of the south."

A rumbling cough signalled his appetite for nicotine. A sip of coffee allowed him to continue.

"However, over the duration of the war, we have found uses in Ireland's neutrality. We have managed to base our spies there more easily than in England and have developed very productive links with the Irish Republican Army who are as opposed to Churchill and the British King every bit as much as we are. They view the British crime of partitioning their country as evil and unacceptable. But because they are not a belligerent, the cities of Ireland have only a limited blackout at nights due to the absence of power, but this yet renders them clearly visible and this gives our bombers perfect coordinates with which to attack the British western shipbuilding and trading ports of Glasgow and Liverpool. Our agents provide us with reliable weather reports...again assisting the *Luftwaffe*."

"I can see the strategic value in the abandonment of Plan Green but surely the British must have their own Plan Green? They must be aware of how vulnerable they would be if they did not protect their flanks."

"Ah, *Sturmbannführer* you are an insightful man but *you* were a history professor. You will know of the poor relationship between Ireland and England ever since Oliver Cromwell laid waste to Ireland three hundred years ago. If England invaded to protect itself, it would open up at least a guerrilla war on its flank, probably alienate those Irishmen...and there are *many*... in their ranks... and require the use of their precious resources. That is why both they and we respect Ireland's neutrality at present. Now, we know that the Irish routinely intern any German airmen who land on their soil while allowing the British to walk to Northern Ireland unhindered. We know that many thousands of Irish men have joined the British Army just as many of their women have become nurses on their behalf but we accept this. So, the Irish have to be aware of the danger of a British invasion and cannot provoke them. We understand this and it is a small price to pay at the moment."

"And what would you have me do, *Obergruppenführer* Mencken?"

"We require two tasks of you, *Sturmbannführer*. One is defensive, one is offensive. Let's be pessimistic for a moment. If the war goes badly for our nation, many senior officers of the German Army who have the capacity to continue to make a contribution to the glory of the

Third *Reich* in the future will need somewhere to go where the Allies cannot reach them. At present, the Irish Head of Government, what they call the *Taoiseach* ...as well as the general tone of their newspapers...suggests that the population of Ireland is rather more supportive of us than of the English. This may change of course but at the moment we feel confident that Ireland could be a safe haven for many of our senior people. They will require safe houses...places to live and prosper, finance to help them make a living, so our first task is to ensure that we help them fit in with Irish society in a way that permits them to ready themselves for the rise again of the Third *Reich*. We accept that this would require many years of work. Secondly, we require someone who can liaise with members of the Irish Republican Army. We know that for some time they have seen merit in a plan they call 'Operation Kathleen' In this, they propose that the Irish Republican Army would act as go-betweens as well as a fifth column to persuade the Irish Free State to invade Northern Ireland and facilitate the mass landing of German invasion troops at Larne and Londonderry. They would assist us in occupying Northern Ireland as a stepping stone into the rest of the UK as part of our planned invasion. Their plan avoids us invading Ireland in the south and so has its attractions."

"And you think one man can do this?"

"One man and substantial resources, *Sturmbannführer*. This mission could have wide-ranging implications for the future of the *Reich*. The *Waffen* SS and the *Abwehr* have to invest in Ireland. The German nation must speculate against the day when we need to retreat in order to advance."

"This sounds like an expensive speculation."

"It will amount to a sum in advance of seven million pounds sterling. Some will be in Irish Punts, Swiss Francs, some in Sterling but most will be in gold bullion with solid gold Romanian Lei and Tunisian Francs to supplement the ingots and provide for an easier method of exchange. You will require to buy property. You will require to bribe and to pay for services and in support of your new friends in the IRA, we are prepared to take instructions from you to parachute arms, ammunition and explosives captured from the Allies. We have already organised some cash amounts with the German Legation in Dublin under the present control of Dr. Eduard Hempel. You will take the gold with you when you travel to Ireland."

"That sounds like a heavy load."

"It is but we must find a way to get it there with no likelihood of it being lost. We intend to use an *Unterseeboot*, a U-Boat as the English have it. In all probability it will be U-48, our most successful U-Boat. In a moment, one of my assistants will explain in detail how we intend to land you and these resources on the Island of Ireland but in broad terms, you will be transferred to the east coast of Ireland near Drogheda, just north of Dublin. There, you will be taken to the capital where you will find accommodation and support from the German Legation. You report only to me. Dr. Hempel is aware of your mission in only the broadest detail but no one else in Ireland. You have permission from the *Fuehrer* to meet directly with Irish *Taoiseach*, Éamon de Valera and offer to have his military equipment supplemented by captured British guns and ammunition which could be sent to him in neutral ships that we will commandeer."

He shrugged his shoulders and continued. "If de Valera rejects your offer, such is life...but you also have permission to make the same offer to the Irish Republican Army. You can be sure that they will not refuse the generosity of the Third *Reich*...so you will play the role of a double agent. Both de Valera and the IRA must believe you are in total support of their objectives. You will be provided with diplomatic papers, dress as a civilian...and you are to be offered a field promotion as of today. You will serve at the same rank as me ..."

He paused to permit his words to register.

"Congratulations, *Obergruppenführer* Weber. You are now the youngest General in the German Army. You will require this in order to be taken seriously by Prime Minister de Valera or the *Taoiseach* as the Irish call him, but in my view it is well deserved. You are the future of the Reich. Friederike and I are too old and may not survive the war. You will."

He stood and saluted Weber who was sufficiently shocked at his surprise promotion that he sat for a moment clutching his glass of *schnapps* before getting to his feet and returning the salute."

"I don't know what to say, *Obergruppenführer*."

"No longer do you refer to me as *Obergruppenführer*, Kurt. We are now of the same rank. You must get used to calling me Claus."

After languishing in a faded ante-room for some time, Weber was called from outside Schäfer's office in *Abwehr* headquarters and taken along corridors until, somewhat disorientated, he was shown into a room guarded by two soldiers.

An elderly man, slim and wearing an elegant dark suit sat behind a table on which were spread some maps. He stood and offered his hand to Weber as he entered.

"*Obergruppenführer* Weber. I am pleased to meet you. Congratulations upon your promotion."

Weber shook his hand and sat down upon the waved invitation of his host.

"And you are?"

"Ah, *Obergruppenführer*. You needn't know my name for the moment. I am not privy to the purpose of your visit to Ireland and you needn't be privy to my role within the *Abwher*. My job is merely to get you there safely."

Weber nodded as the man picked up the largest of the maps and pinned it to the wall.

"This is a map of the east coast of Ireland, the west coast of England and the Irish sea between them. You will notice the island that lies equidistantly between both coasts. It is called the Isle of Man. The British use the island as an internment camp, a major prisoner of war stronghold just as they did during the First World War. It is home to our boys who have been captured and imprisoned, Italian prisoners of war, enemy aliens whom the British have classified as posing a threat to the United Kingdom, members of the British Union of Fascists and National Socialists and a number of prisoners who belong to the Irish Republican Army. The Isle of Man as you can see is a small island; thirty-two miles long and fourteen miles wide at its broadest point. None of our people have ever escaped from it but we require to assist in the escape of one man, an Irishman called Declan Dennehy."

"Am I to be told who this man is and what is his significance?"

"He held a senior position in the IRA before his capture and I am told that you will have use of him in the second part of your mission."

Weber nodded his appreciation recognising that his instructor didn't have all of the information he sought.

"To do this, we intend landing you on a small, uninhabited islet at the toe of the Isle of Man. You should be quite undetected. The islet is called the Calf of Man and is tiny, only one square mile, but has a concealed quay called Carys Harbour where our U-Boat can dock out of sight at high tide. It will be a precarious docking as the harbour is very small indeed and only the prow of the U-Boat can dock safely but it will be sufficient to unload your cargo, you and your support team."

"Support team?"

"Only for the initial part of the mission. Once safely on the quayside, a fishing boat flying the Irish flag will take you and four SS troops specially selected for the mission over the few hundred meters to the main island where you will make your way a short distance over moorland to the prisoner of war camp in nearby Port Erin. There, you will effect the escape of Dennehy. The SS soldiers will return to the *Unterseeboot* following a rendezvous with the fishing boat but you, Dennehy and your cargo will travel on by the boat to Drogheda, on the east coast of Ireland. A small truck will take you on to Dublin where you will be taken on to the port of *Dún Laoghaire* under cover and presented to their people as just having been delivered from a coaster from Lisbon. Your papers will show you as a diplomat to the German Legation and from then on, you are on your own, *Obergruppenführer.*"

"And when do I leave for the Isle of Man?"

"You have many files to study and memorise as you will understand the need for you to be free of documentation should you be captured by the Allies. It has been decided that you require eight days to do this. *Unterseeboot 48 is* being made ready and its senior command is being briefed. You must leave a week on Friday as the arrangements to assist in the escape of Dennehy must take place at during a particularly high tide at precisely 3.00am on the morning of the following Sunday before he is transferred to another camp, the Peveril Camp, in Peel, some miles away."

"Can I assume that the camp at Port Erin is easier to breach than the one you mention at Peel?"

"Much easier. Port Erin, for the most part, houses women. Dennehy is there only for medical reasons as he has complained of mysterious back problems which are the specialism of the local doctor. The town of Port Erin has been made over almost in its entirety to female prisoners of war, or those whom the English believe to be troublemakers. Having said that, there are very lax security measures in place and other than a couple of reveilles a day, inmates have a pretty free existence behind the wire that surrounds the town. In Peel, they hold the British Fascists and German and Italian prisoners of war. It is a much more secure environment and one that would test us were we to pursue an escape attempt there."

The *Abwehr* officer raised his eyebrows and opened his hands as if to ask Weber whether he had any questions to ask.

"Thank you. I suspect that the sensible thing is for me to look over those files you mentioned and if there are gaps in my understanding, I will alert *Obergruppenführer* Schäfer's office. I am certain they would organise another discussion."

"I am at your disposal *Obergruppenführer.*"

Weber rested in his cramped quarters that night and, unusually for him, consumed more than was sensible from a bottle of *schnapps*. Now, his eyesight blurred, he lifted the five files he'd been given in order to brief him on the nature of the task before him and rubbed his eyes, yawning. One file, containing only one single yellow page, set out his mission. It read;

*Your mission is directed against Allied interests. You are tasked with using resources provided you and gathered in Éire to;*

1) *Secure the escape of senior IRA soldier Declan Dennehy, presently interned on the Isle of Man.*
2) *Consult with the IRA on their perceptions and attitude towards reconciliation between the Irish state and the IRA.*
3) *Direct the military activities of the IRA towards British military targets and arrange for field weaponry and munitions to be supplied them as necessary.*
4) *Report any incidental items of military importance.*
5) *Purchase properties and businesses which might be used in the future accommodation of German officers and private citizens. In this you should establish good relations with the Irish Head of State and support the Legation in this regard.*

*Important.*
*You are being sent to work as a member of the diplomatic core of the German Legation in Dublin reporting to the Head, Dr. Eduard Hempel who should only be made aware of objective five (5).*

Weber had a full day set aside to interrogate the files and so felt able to skim them rather than memorise them in his room. *So I'm being asked to be a double agent? I've to report to two superiors? Tomorrow will be time enough to consider all of this*, he thought.

Just as his thoughts turned to his intense need for sleep, a photograph slipped from between the pages of a file. He picked up a photograph of a young woman wearing a black beret. *Hmmm! Very pretty.* The top of the photograph read, 'Agent Kerry'.

   *I look forward to reading all about her tomorrow. But for now, I sleep.*

## CHAPTER FOUR

# Liverpool

Dr. Hermann Henning finished stitching the jagged wound of the young boy whose elbow had been badly cut by flying glass after a bomb had exploded in nearby Ormskirk Road, in Liverpool.

"You'll be fine, Tommy."

He turned to the boy's worried mother. "Take him home, now. You must both be tired. It's almost three o'clock in the morning. Just try to keep the wound clean. Nurse here will bandage it but he should be right as rain in no time."

He smiled at the boy and ruffled his hair before holding his hand up to the nurse, his fingers spread, signalling a five minute break for a cup of tea, a refreshment he'd come to enjoy since his arrival in England from the University of Greifswald Medical School in Germany some four years earlier.

Entering the staff room, he noticed Dr. McLean, the hospital's chief administrator talking to two men dressed in beige overcoats. Both wore Fedora hats. McLean gestured to him.

"These men are from the police, Dr. Henning. They want to talk to you and I've been telling them what a fine chap you are and how you have been an excellent addition to our medical staff over the past few years."

"Thank you, Dr. McLean."

He turned to the two men. "How can I help you gentlemen? Is it about the drunken man you arrested yesterday after I had set his broken arm?"

The older police officer answered. "No, Dr. Henning. We're here tonight to talk to *you*. Dr. McLean has confirmed that you are Dr. Hermann Henning and that you're a naturalised German Citizen."

"That is correct."

"We're to understand that you've been resident in this country for four years, arriving here in January 1939?"

"That is also correct."

"Our records suggest that you've never been before an Enemy Alien Tribunal."

"That is because I have not been *asked* to attend one. I have merely worked here at the hospital healing the sick and treating the wounded."

The second police officer involved himself. "Quite so, Dr. Henning. But we all 'as to act within the law over here and Parliament has decreed that people like you..."

"And what do you mean by people like me, officer... Doctors?"

"No doctor. I mean *Germans*. There's a war going on and Parliament has decided that all enemy aliens..."

"So you think I am an enemy alien, officer?"

"You might well be, Doctor. You'd be surprised at the numbers of people in senior positions in this country what take advantage of our good nature and turn out to be spies or fifth columnists."

Dr. McLean intervened. "Officer, Dr. Henning is one of my most trusted colleagues. His work here has been invaluable. He is certainly not a Nazi and has become a popular..."

"That's how most of 'em work Doctor. They becomes popular and no one thinks of them as an enemy agent. They'd soon get reported if they was annoying or...not... popular," he finished lamely.

Henning showed his frustration and spoke to the elder of the two policemen.

"Officer. I have been on duty all day. It is now three o'clock in the morning and I am very tired. What would you have me do to prove that I do not intend any harm to England?"

"I'm afraid that you'll have to come with us, sir. We have a Tribunal in the morning and they'll decide what's to become of you."

McLean intervened.

"But this is preposterous, officer. Dr. Hemming has work here. He can't be spared while you tick your little boxes to show that he's been interviewed."

Henning joined in on descant. "So my reward for working all day helping the sick and disabled is to spend a night in a cell?"

"'Fraid so, Doctor. Now, if you wouldn't mind?"

Used to rising early, Weber was dressed when his door was knocked signalling breakfast. An orderly pushed a trolley bearing a selection of foodstuffs into his room and invited the newly promoted *Ober-gruppenführer* to avail himself of his preferences while he poured coffee. More used to eating from a billy-can heated over an open fire on a good day, Weber indulged himself.

Breakfast over, he settled down to a more in-depth reading of the five files, starting with the one that contained the photograph of Agent Kerry. *So she's IRA,* he read...*able to move more freely because she's a woman and less susceptible to search...has killed for her country...not so much pro-German as anti-English and was the operational lead, arranging the attempted but unsuccessful escape of downed airmen under the noses of Irish soldiers in Skibbereen...based in Tralee in County Kerry but often to be found in Dublin.*

He read accompanying papers. *So she's to be my contact in Ireland? Interesting.*

After an uncomfortable night in the police cells, a little of which was devoted to assisting the police deal with a drunk who had cut his ear badly and some of which was spent answering more questions from the two police officers who apprehended him, Henning was awoken by his cell door opening and a police officer bringing him a cup of tea.

"Thanks for your help last night, Doc. That young feller was bleedin' like a stuck pig. Saved us takin' him to the hospital you did."

"Least I could do officer." He took the cup and saucer and sipped. "Look, officer what's all this about? I didn't get too much from your two colleagues last night."

"Them two's worth the watchin' sir, if you don't mind me sayin' so. If they takes a dislike to you, well, they're not nice people in my book."

"They were certainly a bit sharp with me." He sipped again at his tea. "What's this Tribunal all about, officer?"

The police constable leaned against the door. "Well, sir. After war was declared, we rounded up everybody that was German or Italian or that we thought might be an agent-provocateur...fascists and the like...them IRA boys... and we brought them all before Tribunals to see whether we thought they'd be trouble. But don't you worry, sir. Seems you've just bin overlooked, but you'll be alright...a man like you...a doctor."

"I would certainly hope so."

"No problem, sir. They put people in three categories. The 'A' group is them we think might cause trouble. They all go to jail or to one of our Internment Camps. There's a 'B' group. Them, we're not sure about. Mostly they don't go to jail but we keep an eye on them 'case they get up to no good. And then there's group 'C'. That's where you'll end up, sir. Them's people that satisfy the Tribunal that they don't pose no risk to the crown."

"Well, let us hope that you're right, constable. I would take it hard if people like your two colleagues ended up 'keeping an eye on me' while I was working in the hospital."

"Don't you worry, sir. You'll be fine."

Around mid-day, the young officer who had kept him supplied with weak tea all morning opened his door again.

"Right you are, sir. That's you up before the beak. They're ready for you now so if you'll just come with me, I'll take you along."

A dank corridor with cells on either side moaned with complaining, ill or yet inebriated prisoners.

*At least I was in a cell on my own,* thought Henning.

They both walked up stone steps and along another series of corridors until the steps seemed to take on a new elegance signifying their arrival at the public building adjoining the police cells.

"Sit here, sir and I'll just see if the Magistrate is ready."

He returned a moment later and beckoned Henning to follow him through the door and into the courtroom, indicating that he should stand centrally in front of the Tribunal.

Three men sat behind a table on a raised dais. Each was immersed in reading papers Henning presumed were about him. The small man in the middle spoke as if disinterested whilst yet organising his papers.

"Your full name and nationality please?"

"Dr. Hermann Gottfried Henning. I am German."

"Dr. Henning. You are here today before the Liverpool Enemy Aliens Tribunal. My name is Mr. Alfred Stein and I am the Magistrate who will chair this hearing." He shuffled his papers and looked up.

"How long have you been in this country?"

"I have been here for just over four years. I arrived in January 1939."

"And why did you come?"

"Because I was sickened by the behaviour of the Nazi Party, the posturings of the dictator Adolph Hitler and the attitude of the ruling elite towards the Jewish community which has given so much to the world. Certainly my own professor, Dr. Goldstein was a marvellous man of Jewish faith and he did not deserve the persecution he received at their hands."

"Did you leave family behind in Germany?"

"Not directly. I was an only child and my parents are both dead. I have an uncle in Bremen."

The Magistrate shuffled his papers. "The policemen who interviewed you last night report that you know how to make and use invisible ink."

"Henning inwardly cursed his two interlocutors from the previous night.

"I am an intelligent man, Mr. Stein. I am a scientist. I understand how to use human matter like urine or blood to conceal writing. It is no secret."

"Have you ever *used* these fluids to make invisible ink, Dr. Henning?"

"Of course. When I was a student...to see if it worked."

The Chairman didn't seem impressed. Another member of the Tribunal interjected.

"You work as a doctor in Sefton Hospital?"

Henning nodded. "And have done since shortly after I arrived here in Liverpool."

"If this Tribunal directed you to undertake war work against the interests of your native Germany, would you accede to our command?"

"No sir, I would not. I am a doctor. I heal the sick. I would heal the sick if I was in Mexico or Iceland. I am a doctor. I serve here because I left my homeland. It was the Nazi Party that caused me to leave Germany. I do not recognise my country at present. But the country of my birth is Germany and I would not act against it just as you would not act against England"

The Chairman reclaimed his authority. "This Tribunal needs to be clear about your answer, Dr. Hemming. Can you repeat that you would not undertake war work on behalf of the Allied forces?"

"No sir. I would not. Unless it involved looking after the sick. I am a doctor. Not an antagonist...not a protagonist."

"The police report states that you admitted taking photographs of the docks at Liverpool."

"Again, this is true," said Henning wearily. "I take photographs of many beautiful or interesting things... but I took no photographs that would be of benefit to your enemy and certainly did not transmit any. If you were interested I could show you them."

"But how are we to know that you didn't take *other* photographs of value to your Fatherland which obviously you would not show us? Our shipyards have been bombed several times and *some* form of photographic materials must have guided the *Luftwaffe*."

"Well, you would need to trust me as a man of honour."

Again, the Magistrate's right hand man interjected, speaking directly to Henning.

"You are asking us to trust a man who didn't reveal himself voluntarily as an alien, who admits to being aware of the techniques of spying, who refuses war work...a man who takes photographs of a military installation?"

Henning's frustration began to show itself and his voice rose. "I certainly *am* a man of honour! I am a man dedicated to looking after people who are ill."

The Magistrate's tone of voice took on an edge.

"You are a German, Dr. Henning. You..."

"And with a name like Stein, it may be that you are as German as *I* am, Mr. Magistrate...the man you have put in charge of the Allied forces against Germany is called Eisenhower. Are we to assume that both of *you* are fifth columnists?"

The chairman slammed his hand on the table but was beaten to a comment by one of his colleagues.

"How dare you insult this Tribunal! Our Magistrate, Mr. Stein is a highly respected member of our Jewish community here in Liverpool. You and your Nazi friends might like to abuse him and his creed but..."

"What do I need to do to convince you? I am *not* a Nazi!"

"By agreeing to undertake war work."

"I have explained that I will not work against my Homeland nor will I aid her enemies. I just want to continue serving..."

The Magistrate rose to his feet and laid both hands on the table, palms down.

"Dr Henning, I think we have heard enough." Stooping, he consulted his two colleagues in muted tones. He sat again and composed himself.

"We have decided that you are to be classified as an 'A' Category alien. Officer, Take this man down. He is to be transported to the Isle of Man forthwith."

"But...but..."

"Take him down"

## CHAPTER FIVE

# County Kerry, Ireland

In the small farmhouse she shared with her parents just outside the Kerry village of Castlemaine, Sinéad O'Grady finished drying the plate she'd used for a meal of herring and potatoes, placing it on top of four others, none of which were of the same size or design. Putting the drying cloth over the rear of a chair in the small kitchen, she took a damp towel and opened the heavy metallic door of the cooking range within which, golden and crusted brown now, was a rhubarb pie. The old, blackened range was the centrepiece of the kitchen and also provided warmth. It was adorned with copper pans, empty bottles and dried flowers. It was a most efficient cooking and heating system; maintenance free other than the soot which it produced in surprising quantities and on a daily basis.

She lifted the baking tray at each end using the cloth as protection and hoisted it up onto the table. *Looks perfect,* she thought. *The boys'll enjoy this when they arrive.* A sharp outwards tug on a string attached to the bottom edge of the pantry door opened it permitting her to stand on tip-toe and reach up to the top shelf, bringing down an almost full bottle of Paddy's Whiskey which she dusted casually with one hand before placing it next to the sink. Returning to the top shelf she removed a large tub of oats with some difficulty and placed it on the kitchen table. Pulling over a metal basin, Sinéad poured the contents of the box into it, removing a length of fabric which she unwrapped to reveal a Webley Break-Top Revolver and a second pouch with a dozen .455 calibre bullets. The barrel offered little resistance when she held the gun by the handle and opened it, placing six bullets, one in each chamber. A satisfactory clicking whirr resulting from her testing the free movement of the chamber indicated the readiness of the revolver for use. Opening the drawer in which she kept her cutlery, she placed the now loaded weapon towards its rear.

She had a little sugar which she sprinkled over the pie before washing and drying her hands in time to open the door to two cyclists she'd watched from the window above her sink, pushing their bikes along the muddy farm track that led to her door.

"Seamus...Danny. You made it before the rain. Come away in. Come in won't you. I've the tea wet."

The two men left their cycles propped against the wall of the farmhouse and in turn, embraced her.

"*Tá sé go breá tú a fheiceáil, a Shinéid.*" Good to see you, Sinéad," said Seamus. "Are your mother and father away?"

"They're visiting in Tralee. We've the place to ourselves."

Danny Lafferty closed the small door. "*Breathnaíonn tú chomh h-álainn is a bhí tú riamh.* You look as lovely as ever."

"Where's Dub?"

"He's driving up from Tralee. Should be here shortly. Is that a pie I'm lookin' at?"

"Rhubarb. But it's too hot to eat right now. Sit you both down. We'll let the pie cool a bit and maybe Dub'll get here by the time the tea's masked."

After a few minutes of small talk round the kitchen table, a whistling kettle on the range heralded the arrival of a battered black Austin motor car containing a large man whose size required that he had to drive with his head constantly stooped so as to see through the small windshield, despite the commodious character of his vehicle. Moments later, Dub knocked at the door and stepped in without waiting for an invitation in order to shelter himself from the newly pattering raindrops.

"*Tá sé ag éirí stoirmiúil,*" said Dub indicating the storm brewing outside. "I'm glad I didn't cycle up here."

He accepted the cup of tea poured for him by Sinéad and clapped Seamus on the shoulder in friendly fashion before taking the spare chair at the table.

"I have bad news," said Sinéad as she cut into the rhubarb pie, sliced it and plated it for her three guests. "You know that Charlie has been found guilty of the murder of that peeler, Detective Sergeant O'Brien. He's to be executed in Dublin...in Mountjoy Prison? Well, Dev's refused to issue a reprieve. And just to rub it in, the bastard's bringin' over the *English* chief executioner Albert Pierrepoint to string him up because no Irishman will have Charlie's blood on their hands. There's been uproar in the town but Charlie's a dead man."

She forked some pie into her mouth, encouraging the others to do similarly.

"We live in strange times all right. Not six years ago, Dev's entire cabinet was all former Volunteers now he interns us and lets the English execute Volunteers at will so that it doesn't provoke a backlash here if he did it himself. His thinks that because Charlie was convicted in a court of law for shootin' O'Brien and the papers have expressed what they call their revulsion because Charlie shot him in front of his wife, there won't be a reaction in *Eire*."

Seamus spoke, spilling rhubarb from his mouth as he did so.

"Jesus, Sinéad. He was always going to be convicted and they were always going to see him dead."

Dub nodded his agreement. "It's hard to believe that de Valera's the same Republican who was at the heart of our Easter Rising against the Brits. As soon as he's comfortable with the power he has in the land, he outlaws the IRA in '36, then decides that his commitment to achievin' Irish unification by constitutional means requires him to part company with his former comrades-in-arms. Bastard!"

"Yeah, and he's turned the Irish Special Branch into a group of thugs we now hate more than the forces of the feckin' crown!"

Sinéad took control of the conversation.

"Sure, isn't Dev determined that Ireland should remain neutral in the *Emergency?* He knows that us Republicans would never countenance being allied to the crown, and that we'd have another bloody civil war if he tried some form of alliance. But he also knows that, if Ireland is seen as a threat to *English* interests, London might decide to invade. So, we need to shake things up. In recent months we've seen a successful bombin' campaign in London, Manchester, Birmingham and Coventry so we're in the good books over in Berlin at the minute."

There was consensus round the table.

"So Charlie's a goner? asked Danny rhetorically.

"He's a dead man," responded Seamus, repeating Sinead's earlier appraisal.

There was much shaking of heads while more pie was consumed. Sinéad nervously broke the silence.

"Unfortunately, it appears that one of our own informed on him."

Each of the three men spluttered their disbelief on hearing this.

"It's true. We have a man in the *Gardai*. We know who it was, how he informed the *Gardai* and where the information was passed over. What we don't know... yet...is *why* he betrayed the movement."

She rose to her feet and opened the cutlery drawer, removing the revolver.

"Anyone got anything to say?"

"Sweet Jesus, Sinéad. You don't think it was one of us do you? You've known me and Danny since we were in Junior Infants together. And Dub's been our close friend and fellow Volunteer these last ten years."

"I have been given the task of liaisin' with a representative of the German *Reich* who arrives on our shores shortly to provide us with weapons. But I can't do this while there's a traitor in our midst so I've been ordered to get rid of him."

"Holy Mother of God! Have you lost the run of yourself? Put that revolver away, Sinéad. You're scarin' me," begged Danny.

Dub rose slowly to his feet. "It's okay, boys. I suspect it's me she's after. I never liked that bastard Charlie Kerins and he never liked me. Frankly, I'm glad the fecker's goin' to croak. I know he was a Kerry man, like you three. A Tralee man...but himself and me never got on. He always..."

"Sit down, Dub."

Dub regained his seat as if he'd suddenly lost the power of his legs.

She turned the revolver to her right.

"Seamus, this is on behalf of the movement you betrayed... *Go gcoimeádaí Dia slán tú.* May God keep you safe in the palm of his hand."

A loud crash sent Seamus spinning back in his chair as the .455 bullet tore at his chest, penetrating his aorta and ripping at his left ventricle, consigning him to an instant death.

The other two men leapt to their feet.

"Jesus, Sinéad. What have you *done?*" shouted Danny. "You've killed *Seamus*. He's one of *us*."

"Why do you think I volunteered to carry out the sentence of the Army Council?" spat Sinéad angrily, tears welling in her eyes. "If it had been someone else he'd have been tortured first, perhaps for days, before being killed. That was what was asked of me! Would you have done different, Danny? I was told that we'd got sufficient evidence to know for sure that it was him and that because I knew him it might be easier for me to get him to tell me why he dubbed in Charlie. Then I was told to 'break' him then 'dispatch' him. That's what they term it now in the Army Council...'*dispatch*'...almost makes it seem clean and helpful...eh Danny? Would you have done different?"

Danny looked at Sinéad's obvious distress. "No, Sinéad. I'd have done as you done."

With that, he rose and bent over Seamus' lifeless body and hugged it, sweeping hair out of his dulled eyes, talking to the insentient corpse.

"You are one stupid eegit, Seamus O'Leary. You couldn't pour water out of a boot if the instructions were written on the feckin' sole. What the hell did you get yourself into?" He turned again to Sinéad. "We'll need to get old Father Frank to say some words."

Sinéad shook her head.

"That's been forbidden too. We've to take his body to the bog and make sure he just disappears. Father Frank is a good man and one of us, but he has never accepted the need for us to kill our own people. Seamus has just to disappear."

"And what of his wife and two kids, Sinéad. Are they to disappear too?"

"They get no help. They get no hint of his death. They get nothin'."

"That's feckin' unacceptable, Sinéad. They'll need lookin' after." He turned to Dub. "What do you say to this, Dub?"

"Danny, I can't feckin' think straight. As God's my witness I thought Sinéad was goin' to shoot me dead only one minute ago. I'm still feckin' shakin'."

Sinéad shook her head at Dub.

"Dub, you don't get shot in this army just for not likin' someone. If you did, there'd be few of us walkin' the streets for sure. Seamus committed a crime that the Army Council decided was punishable by death. I was called to deliver their verdict. I didn't enjoy what I did. I haven't slept for the past two nights but if I stood back from this, my sweet friend Seamus whom I've known since I was a baby would have been butchered. I couldn't do that to him...just couldn't."

Dub, still standing but holding on to door frame for support was first to call for action.

"Then let's get poor Seamus organised. I'll get a rug from the car and I'll drive him out to the peat bog near Ballycrispin. Yous two don't need to know anythin' more about it. I can handle this on my own. In this rain there'll be no one around."

Ten minutes later, Seamus was wrapped and consigned to the spacious rear seat of the Austin during which time Danny and Sinéad had used the earlier boiled water to remove all traces of blood from the kitchen.

"Right, I'll be off then," said Dub.

"Not yet, Dub. I have more to tell. Come in and finish that pie with me and Danny."

"No offence, Sinéad but I'm now somethin' more than chary about eatin' your feckin' pie. You're a bit too handy with that Webley for my likin'."

"Dub, get in here. That pie won't eat itself and I need to tell you and Danny some information."

Reluctantly, Dub re-entered the small cottage, ducking as he walked slowly through the doorway.

"You're a smooth operator, all right, Sinéad. Sittin' here feedin' us pie not ten minutes after shootin' one of your closest friends in cold blood," remonstrated Danny.

"I'm going to ignore that, Danny. I just want to tell you what I have to tell you then get down to confession at the Chapel."

"That's great. You get to ask for God's forgiveness but poor Seamus gets feck all!"

Sinéad narrowed her eyes. "Good! You understand the situation perfectly, Danny. Now shut up and listen. I'll need your help. Are you with me?"

"As long as you're anywhere near that feckin' revolver I'm doin' exactly as you say, Sinéad," said Dub."

"And you, Danny?"

"I'm sayin' yes right now. But you'll need to give me a couple a days before I actually *mean* it."

"So long as you do, Danny. I can't go tellin' you what's planned if you're not a committed member of the unit."

"So you'd shoot me too, Sinéad?"

"Danny, get your bicycle and go home right now. Dub, thanks for takin' poor Seamus to his grave. Be careful both of you. I'll see you both in a few days. I'll make contact and tell you when... in Boyle's Pub in the village....and if anyone asks, I had to shoot Seamus rather than beat the truth out of him because he went for his gun when I accused him. It was self defence."

Danny's voice dripped with sarcasm.

"Don't you worry, Sinéad. We'll make sure they think you *dispatched* him just as you describe."

## CHAPTER SIX

# Isle of Man

Three days after his being classified as a Category 'A' Internee, Dr. Hermann Henning was alerted by the roar of reversing engines of the docking *Arandora Star* which had sailed that morning from nearby Liverpool with almost two hundred 'A' Class German internees including some one hundred and fifty merchant seamen, forty or so prisoners of war and one very angry German doctor from Sefton Hospital in Liverpool.

"Let's be 'avin' you," bellowed the armed soldier, directing his charges to the upper deck. Ten minutes later, most internees had been marshalled on the quayside at Douglas, Isle of Man. Desks had been set up as military personnel checked the details of everyone before them.

Henning looked at the handsome white edifices that lined the town where it met the Irish Sea. The sun warmed his back and he witnessed the obvious civility of the British soldiers tasked with administering the accommodation of those who had just disembarked. *Let's hope all victims of this war are treated with such courtesy*, he mused. *Difficult to imagine that any of my*

*countrymen would prefer fighting and freezing at
Stalingrad to this.*

Eventually, he found himself at the front of a diminishing
queue in front of an orderly who spoke German.

"*Was ist dein Name?*"

"Thanks, but I speak English."

"Good-oh! Name please?

"Dr. Hermann Henning. I am a medical practitioner
and have worked for the past four years in Sefton
Hospital. Looking after your relatives probably," he
grouched, uncharitably.

"Doubt that, doctor. I'm from Cardiff." He
pronounced it *Caaadiff* as he consulted a list of names
before him.

"Ah, yes. Dr. Henning. Hermann Henning. From
Kaiserslautern in the Rhineland?"

"Yes."

"Excellent. Nice place is it?"

Despite his irritation at finding himself an internee
instead of serving in his hospital, Henning was won over
by the Welsh orderly's inherent decency.

He sighed resignedly. "Yes. It's lovely."

"First class! Now doctor, I see here that we have a
special billet for you because of your medical background. Instead of joining the rest of your countrymen
in Douglas here, you're being shipped off to the south of
the island. Place called Port Erin but don't worry, it's
only twelve miles away by road. The Isle of Man is a
tiny island. Just about thirty miles from top to bottom.
We've a camp there full of women internees and our
local doctor who looks after the place has asked for the
first English and German speaking medical practitioner

we come across. That seems to be you, so if you don't mind taking this piece of paper and going over to that shed there, we'll get you down to Port Erin and you can get settled."

Henning looked at the paper he'd been given. *Well, at least I'm working as a doctor again.*

"Thanks."

The orderly was already preparing himself for the next in the queue. He pointed to the nearby shed.

"Over there, Doctor."

# Zossen, Germany

Newly promoted *Obergruppenführer* Kurt Weber was enjoying his stay in *Abwehr* headquarters. He had been given briefings on all manner of matters to do with Ireland. He had been taught some rudimentary words in Irish; mostly greetings, had been advised of the problems of handling such substantial amounts of gold bullion as was being amassed for his journey and had been taken through the outline of the plan to aid the escape of Declan Dennehy from internment on the Isle of Man. Today he was to be fitted for a suit and other clothes befitting a German General who might well meet with *Taoiseach* Éamon de Valera, the political leader of the Republic of Ireland. A case was provided him as well as documents showing him to be a member of the German Legation in Dublin. Just in case of problems, he was shown how he could access a hidden compartment in his case and retrieve a small Walther P38 side-arm, a knife and two small capsules. The Doctor who instructed him on their use was quite matter-of-fact when describing their effect.

"These capsules, as you can see, are approximately the size of a small kidney bean. They consist of a thin-walled glass ampoule covered in a black rubber coating to protect against accidental breakage and are filled with a concentrated solution of potassium cyanide. It is important for you to note, however, that they are never swallowed whole. Instead, they are first crushed between your molars to release the fast-acting poison contained within. Brain death occurs within minutes and the heartbeat stops immediately thereafter. A suicide pill swallowed without first being crushed in this way would pass through your digestive tract and do no harm."

*He could be describing how most effectively to take a cough medicine,* thought Weber.

"Thank you doctor. Most helpful."

Weber's appointment with *Obergruppenführer* Claus Schäfer was at 9.15am and five minutes prior, he stood outside the inner office in order to present himself timeously.

The door opened and the General appeared in the doorway.

"Kurt. Good to see you."

"*Obergruppenführer...*"

"Claus, remember?"

"Claus, then. Thank you for seeing me. It has been a most interesting few days and I have been treated like a prince by your staff."

"You are comfortable with your briefing?"

"Yes. I've gone over the details several times and have been able to suggest modifications that I hope will prove helpful and might improve the chances of the mission being successful. I was impressed by your technical people. They've dreamt up a most innovative way of transferring the gold from the *Unterseeboot* to the fishing boat."

Schäfer laughed. "I was informed. Ingenious! If it works."

"I watched a trial using rocks as a proxy for the bullion and it worked perfectly."

The General nodded his satisfaction. "You leave soon?"

"When I step from your office."

"And you have everything you need," said Schäfer, more as a statement than a question.

Weber smiled. "A bottle of scotch might make the initial underwater journey more enjoyable."

Schäfer returned the smile. "It would be the least I could do." He took Weber by the arm and led him into his office where he took two bottles of Johnnie Walker Black Label whisky from a burnished oak credenza and handed them to him.

"Kurt, I wish you every success. Yours is an important mission for so many people. God speed."

## County Kerry, Ireland

Dub O'Neill stood over a patch of black gloop in a barren terrain, his hands clasped in front of him. Beside him stood old Father Duggan, a staunch Nationalist priest from the distant parish of Ballyheeda in County Cork. The rain had stopped leaving a misty stillness.

"Am I not to know his name, Dub?"

"No, Father. I'm overstepping the mark as it is. All I can say is that beneath us here in this peat bog lie the fresh remains of a good catholic republican who got caught up in problems he couldn't manage and he paid the price with his life. If some people knew I'd asked you to say a few words over his grave, I'd be joining him, so."

Father Duggan looked thoughtfully at O'Neill for a long moment before bowing his head.

"Lord, for those who believe in your love, death is not the end. The death of a Christian is not the end of life, but rather a transformation in an onward journey towards eternal life with God...."

Lost in his own thoughts...remembering Seamus as he was in life, Dub lost the import of Father Duggan's funeral liturgy until he heard the words, "...for we believe that Jesus died and rose again, and thus it will be the same for those who have died with Jesus. *Dominus noster Jesus Christus te absolvat; et ego auctoritate ipsius te absolvo ab omni vinculo excommunicationis et interdicti in quantum possum et tu indiges. Deinde, ego te absolvo a peccatis tuis in nomine Patris, et Filii, et Spiritus Sancti. Amen.*"

The Priest moved smoothly from Latin to Irish Gaelic to complete his work.

"*Go ndéana Dia trócaire ar a anam dilis.* May God have mercy on his soul."

Dub remained silent for some time. Eyes closed, he waited until he heard Father Duggan's movements before rousing himself.

"Thanks Father. That's grand! Someday, I'll be able to tell his widow that he had a Christian burial."

"Dub...ah, never mind. Just take me back to my parish and let us speak of this no further."

Together they turned and trudged their way across the peat bog back to the single-tracked road that lay just beyond a slight rise which now screened the final resting place of Seamus O'Leary's mortal remains.

# Isle of Man

Alone among the throng of internees on the quayside, Hermann Henning sat in an military General Service Truck more used to carrying the personal equipment of an infantry platoon, guarded only by a uniformed soldier who sat smoking in the seat next to the driver, chatting amiably. After a few minutes, the soldier signed a piece of paper handed to him by the Welsh orderly accepting responsibility for Internee Henning and the truck moved off. Shortly it arrived at the Victorian railway station of Douglas where the soldier beckoned Henning to get off. Together they walked along the platform where he was left alone in an unlocked and unguarded carriage. After some time the soldier rejoined him.

"Are you not afraid that I would escape?"

The soldier laughed. "Doc, this island has been used to keep people locked up in this war *and* the last. There's been some that's got over the wire but no one's ever got off the island. Our C.O. told us that the average time it takes to recapture a prisoner or an internee is twenty minutes. Because everyone knows that, it makes for a more free and easy time of it for all of us."

As he spoke, the small, narrow gauge train began to pull out of Douglas, dragging its passengers slowly up an incline out of the port, following the contours of its river. As he left the handsome town of Douglas, Henning could not but be impressed by the bucolic beauty of the island. Throughout the sixteen mile, one hour journey to Port Erin, he looked on as green field after green field of healthy crops alternated with herds of cattle, flocks of sheep and droves of pigs. He reflected on the fact that on the mainland, the weekly cheese ration had just been reduced to one ounce. *The people of this island must be well fed,* he mused. *I wonder if we internees share in this astonishing bounty?*

## Zossen, Germany

A black Mercedes collected Weber from the *Abwehr* Headquarters in Zossen. He placed his kitbag in the rear seat and joined the driver in the front, keeping the case with its documentation and secret compartment on his lap.

"Bremerhaven is more than two hundred miles, driver. How long will it take us?"

"*Obergruppenführer,* we will have to drive most of the day."

"Then you must tell me when you tire and I will drive for a while." He smiled. "You'll enjoy telling your comrades that you were being driven round Germany by an *Obergruppenführer?*"

The driver looked shocked at the suggestion. "But *Obergruppenführer*, I must drive...what if there was an accident?"

"There will be no accident, *soldat*. But driving all day would be too tiring for you and I want to arrive in Bremerhaven in one piece. The matter is settled."

The car sped west from Berlin as fast as was possible given the poor condition of the roads. Occasional security checks proved little more than cursory when Weber's Waffen-SS silver oak leaf collar tabs were spotted.

It was dusk when, with Weber at the wheel and a very embarrassed *Schütze* in the passenger's seat, the Mercedes drove into the port of Bremerhaven. Its pace had slowed dramatically as Weber picked his way through streets littered with rubble as a consequence of heavy Allied bombing.

Despite himself, Weber mused on how impressive the Allied tactics had been. *They've targeted the Kriegsmarine, but key parts of the port have been left relatively untouched although the city is in ruins. This is no accident. They are now becoming so confident of victory, they're deliberately sparing the port in order to provide a usable harbour for themselves after the war. But perhaps not if my mission succeeds...*

Trying to be helpful, the driver insisted on carrying Weber's kit-bag to *Unterseeboot 48* as it sat at harbour. Weber saluted him, thanked him and bid him a safe journey back to Zossen before turning to the U-boat that would be his home for the next few days.

A small man stood at the end of a gang-plank waiting on Weber navigating the gently bobbing walkway to his boat. The moonlight glinted on his gold braided epaulettes as he saluted his guest.

"*Korvettenkapitän* Hartmann, at your service, *Obergruppenführer* Weber."

Dropping his kit-bag on the decking, Weber retuned the salute.

"Thank you for greeting me. I am honoured to be welcomed by such an illustrious U-Boat Commander. Your reputation goes before you...as does the reputation of your crew."

Hartmann smiled. "No more pleasantries, *Obergruppenführer*. Let's get you aboard and we can have a glass of schnapps once we're underway. We sail with the tide."

"Of course, *Korvettenkapitän.*"

It took more than an hour to prepare the U-Boat and to cast off. Weber took some time to organise his belongings in the tiny room he'd been allocated, to familiarise himself with the internal linear geography of *Unterseeboot 48* and take some air as the vessel slipped from the harbour. After some time, a jarring klaxon sounded the intention of the boat to commence its journey to the depths...and onwards towards its destination of the Calf of Man.

Perhaps ten minutes after the *Unterseeboot* had levelled out underwater, a sailor appeared at Weber's door and invited him to follow him to a specially fashioned wardroom wherein sat *Korvettenkapitän* Karl Hartmann engrossed in carefully pouring two glasses of *schnapps*.

Weber interrupted his concentration by placing two bottles of Schäfer's Scotch whisky on the table. "*Korvettenkapitän,* I have brought you a gift."

"You must call me Karl and I will call you Kurt." He grinned at the munificence of Weber's generosity and held one in his hand, inspecting it.

"Whisky from Scotland? I have not seen a bottle of scotch since this war started."

"Well, Karl. This war will go on for some time so why not finish these two glasses of *schnapps* first, then we can attend to the whisky? Waste not, want not."

"Excellent idea, Kurt."

They toasted each other ostentatiously.

"So, Karl. How quickly will you get me to the Isle of Man?"

"Well, first of all, I'll be putting you ashore on the *Calf* of Man, a small islet of only some six hundred acres. It is only perhaps five hundred metres from the main island but it is uninhabited and has a very small natural harbour that allows me to get you and your equipment ashore without detection."

Both men finished the *schnapps* in one final gulp and smiled at each other as Hartmann unscrewed the top of the bottle of whisky. Hartman continued.

"The underwater top speed of the U-48 is perhaps academic since our batteries would go flat in around forty minutes. Our battery range at top speed is only around twelve nautical miles per hour but we can travel 365 nautical miles if we restrict ourselves to only five knots. Usually we travel at different speeds dependent upon the situation. We'll need to surface regularly at night as we'll be travelling through waters where we'd expect to see enemy shipping. My orders are to land you safely so we won't be at our buccaneering best on this trip...which is why I hope to enjoy this whisky with you on more than a few occasions. The crew is delighted with this mission as it will last perhaps two weeks. Our last patrol lasted six months. During that time, my crew was not able to bathe, shave or change their clothes. This patrol permits me to give some of my men shore leave as our trip should be uneventful and creates space for you and your men although I look forward with interest to discharging our cargo on the Calf of Man."

"I watched your trials from a safe distance, Karl. Most ingenious."

"Well, I hope it works. My orders are to land you safely and to make sure that we don't lose your cargo."

"Were you told what I'm transporting?"

"No. Is it necessary that I know this?"

"I suspect so because of its value and its weight."

Weber raised his glass inviting a refill from his host.

"You are carrying two specially adapted torpedoes full of gold bullion."

Hartmann poured the scotch. "I thought as much. The shells are very heavy but they have been disarmed and only have to travel a short distance. The natural harbour I spoke of permits me to dock only the prow of U-48. You should manage off quite easily by walking towards the prow and stepping on to the harbour. A second reason I selected Carys Harbour is that the shoreline just beyond the harbour is comprised of sand and pebbles on a gently rising beach. This permits me to discharge my torpedoes only yards from the harbour entrance. If I get my trajectory right they should both wash up slowly and gently on the beach, ready to be unpacked. I will then dock and allow you ashore. My men will then transfer the cargo to a shipping boat while you and your four colleagues from the *Waffen* SS take care of your task in Port Erin. Once my men have loaded the cargo, I will retreat and submerge, keeping an eye on the harbour until you return when I will surface and collect your four colleagues. If it all goes wrong and I think it achievable, I will attempt your rescue. If not, dear Kurt, I will leave you and your four men to your fate."

Weber raised his glass in a toast and grinned at Hartmann.

"Such ingratitude after I supplied you with such magnificent whisky."

## CHAPTER SEVEN

# Dublin, Ireland

Three glasses of porter, each three-quarter filled, sat on the stained wooden bar-top in Boyle's Pub in Castlemaine awaiting the further attention of Paddy O'Reilly who, as an experienced barman, would not complete the measures until they had first settled.

"Nearly there, lads....but you're sure Sinéad will be along in a moment? I wouldn't want to serve her a pint that's been sittin' awhile."

"She'll be along in a second, Paddy. She's never late."

Danny paid for the three pints and he and Dub carried them over to a corner table where some privacy was available.

"She's a bold strap, that Sinéad," said Dub. "Are you still sore about what happened to Seamus?"

Danny sipped long at his Guinness. "I am, Dub. And it's only the cause that has me sittin' here tonight. I'll grant you she's good at what she does but she could have protected poor Seamus more...perhaps let him escape to England or somethin'. And thinkin' that he went to an unmarked grave without some religion is hard to take."

Dub shifted uneasily in his chair.

"Danny, if you tell Sinéad, I'm a dead man so I need your solemn word that you'll keep quiet on this."

"Of course, Dub. What's up?"

"The day after I buried poor Seamus, I drove down to Cork and brought an old friend of my father to his graveside; Father Tim Duggan. He's a real long term Republican and he gave him a proper send-off. I even marked his grave with a cross; well two sticks I just laid on the ground so you and me could find it again."

Lafferty's pint-hand had been immobilised, the glass at his lips, as Dub spoke. On appreciating the import of his message he put his pint urgently on the table, spilling it and hugged Dub tightly just as Sinéad entered and sat on the remaining chair at the table.

"What's the *craic* boys?"

Both men, embarrassed, unclinched and sat facing Sinéad.

"Well now, you two seem as thick as thieves. Is that my Guinness?"

"Jesus, Sinéad. You frightened the livin' daylights out of me," said Dub reaching for an excuse. "I was just tellin' Danny... that... my old father has recovered from...a bad illness."

"Excellent news, Dub. And what was wrong with him?"

"Sure he had...the...well...well, let's say it was an embarrassin' illness that men who are younger sometimes get when they have a dalliance with a woman."

"Well, the old goat!" She sipped her pint."And that's news that makes you hug your pal, Danny?"

"I'm quite emotional these days," replied Danny, his face a mask.

"Well, I don't believe either of yous."

"Well, it's true, Sinéad. Plus he caught pneumonia."

"Well, he obviously enjoys his pleasures outside in the rain, then."

"Still, he's better now," said Dub, lamely.

"Well that's grand, Dub. I almost feel like giving you a big hug!"

They settled down to their drinks and spent a moment talking village news with one of the pub regulars who had come over before stumbling off in search of his friends.

"Right, boys. I need your attention now," urged Sinéad. "I've been in touch with Dublin and they need the three of us to head tomorrow for Drogheda."

"Drogheda's feckin' miles away. It'll take two days to get there." Danny was in no mood to be positive.

"Which is why we leave tomorrow. One day to Dublin. We stay with friends and the next day we head for Drogheda. We then wait for a signal to meet a fishing boat that'll dock with a high-ranking German officer who wants to talk to us about arms and money. We're not sure when this fellah'll arrive but we have to be prepared. The Army Council wants us in position early so we're prepared. We've to pick him up in a lorry and transport him and his goods to the estate of Arthur Joyce in Malahide."

"So we have to run around like eejits for two days then sit on our arses for God knows how long until this German appears."

"As ever, Danny, you're being sarcastic but again you've hit the nail on the head. That's exactly what we've been ordered to do and that's what we're going to do. So drink your stout and try to get back into the frame of mind you were in when I arrived."

"I don't know how you can be so feckin' matter-of-fact after shootin' poor Seamus," said Danny quietly but angrily, his face white.

"Well didn't I just *know* we'd have to deal with this tonight," hissed Sinéad in a forced whisper. "I've explained myself once Danny and I don't propose to trawl them seas again. Just get used to being a soldier in the Irish Republican Army. It's quite simple. People higher up than us work out what needs to be done and they order us to do it. We do it. It's called the chain of command. Simple."

She leaned forward and addressed him with barely controlled anger.

"Now is there any part of that you disagree with? Just so's I know what to report back when they ask me if the unit's ready!"

Lafferty's temper was legendary in Castlemaine but he knew to keep it in check this time.

"I understand my orders precisely," he growled through gritted teeth. "And I'll carry them out to the best of my ability."

Sinéad looked slowly away, unconvinced and fixed her gaze on the third member of the team.

"Dub?"

"Me too, Sinéad. I've never been to Drogheda. It'll be nice to see the place, so."

"Right. We travel tomorrow in your car, Dub. We travel unarmed. We'll be given everything we need in Dublin on the way to Drogheda."

# Port Erin, Isle of Man

Doctor John McGregor sat in front of a peat fire in his house in Port Erin and lit his pipe, puffing and poking at the tobacco fill in order to see it ignited. Now an elderly man in his early seventies, he was tired after a day's work attending to his surgery having then had to head off to the camp in Port Erin in order to see to the health of the female internees. The news brought to him by his wife along with a welcome Cognac only five minutes earlier was the news he'd been waiting for. *A locum who speaks perfect English and who has had hospital experience on the mainland? Perfect,* thought the elderly doctor. *Can't wait to meet him tomorrow.*

"Well," he said to his attentive wife as he puffed at his pipe, "perhaps now we can both take it a bit easier around the island. Young Dr. Henning sounds perfect."

"He does, John. Now remember, only one brandy then bed. You can meet Dr. Henning in the morning. The sergeant said he'd bring him to the surgery at ten o'clock."

"Well now. That seems perfect. Now you go on up to bed. I'll finish this pipe and join you in a few minutes."

His wife would have none of it. "No, John. I'll just sit here and talk to you if you don't mind. We both know if you sit alone staring at the fire you'll fall asleep in minutes and won't come upstairs until God knows when."

The doctor nodded his acceptance of his wife's logic. "S'pose you're right."

The request to live in Doctor McGregor's premises having been refused, Dr. Henning was reconciled to spending time in the Internment Camp. Shown to his quarters, he was quite surprised to be shown into a ground floor room in premises close to the harbour in Port Erin. Clearly an established and grand hotel before the war, the room was large, light and airy.

"This'll do you sir. Lap of luxury if you don't mind me saying so," said his escort.

"It certainly is. And I'm the only person using this room?"

"Apparently so, sir. 'Cause you're the doctor."

"Well, it's certainly well appointed."

"Just you get some rest, sir. Doc McGregor wants to see you at his surgery at ten in the morning. He's a nice chap. You'll get along fine with him."

"Thank you very much. I'm tired now. Sleep is overpowering me so if you've no objections, I'll get my head down."

At ten o'clock prompt, Dr. Henning was ushered into Dr. McGregor's surgery which was located only five minutes' walk from his room. The two men shook hands.

"Dr Henning. I was delighted to hear of your arrival even if I'm sure you'd rather still be working in Sefton Hospital in Liverpool."

"I have to be honest. My detention here on the island is disgraceful and I'm very angry about it. I wish no harm to the British state but I would not agree to the twisted logic of the Enemy Aliens Tribunal. So they taught me a lesson, or think they did, I imagine."

"Well, the authorities wouldn't agree to you staying with Mrs. McGregor and me but I hope you're happy with your quarters. You're behind barbed wire but I've ensured your room is comfortable. You'll eat well and I'll ensure that you have occasional evening work to do at my house so you can enjoy the cooking of my wife. Her specialty is fish pie."

"That would be most hospitable of you Dr. McGregor."

"We'd enjoy your company." He paused so as to change the subject. "Now tell me of your experience doctor. Have you dealt much with women patients?"

"During my four years at Sefton I dealt with everything that came through the door although it was mostly minor ailments, cardiovascular problems, slips and spills, back pain and coughs but I also treated allergies, cancers and traumatic injuries. Pretty much the day-to-day illnesses and emergencies we all have to deal with."

"Ever done any operations, dealt with women's health?"

"Usually minor operations, foreign body removals, pre-cancerous and cancerous skin lesions, treatment of burns. I've also had experience in some surgical reconstruction and have become quite accomplished with a scalpel, if I say so myself. As far as women's health is concerned, when I practiced in Germany? ...all of the generic stuff as far as *women* are concerned, perhaps cyclical mastalgia, most gynaecological problems, menopausal issues. I've also had some experience of mental health matters...both sexes."

"You'll do fine, Dr. Henning. Later this morning I'll introduce you to the practice nurse, Nurse Hamilton. She's a bit of a battle-axe but you'll need her around when you're dealing with our female internees. Some of them haven't seen a man in a long time so you'll be faced with a lot of women with imaginary illnesses that they'll argue requires your close attention. Mary Hamilton sees them off if they're not ill. If we have any real problems we have a larger hospital we can refer them to in Hutcheson Square, in Douglas. It's a good system but I'm getting too old for all of this. You'll be a real help around the place."

"Thank you Doctor McGregor. Tell me, is it only women internees we deal with?"

"Almost. I've specialised in back pain over the years so sometimes we are sent someone who is having problems. We have three males in traction right now over in your building. I usually see the men in the evenings after surgery so perhaps I can meet up with you then and introduce you to them. In the meantime, you'll have a queue outside your door and Nurse Hamilton will be getting upset at your tardiness. Blame me but it won't help you."

Henning smiled. "I'll just have to charm her."

"Ten shillings says you won't!"

*Unterseeboot* 48 was making steady progress through the English Channel towards the Celtic Sea before heading north to the Irish Sea and the Calf of Man. *Korvettenkapitän* Hartmann consumed no whisky on this part of the journey. The waters were too dangerous so Weber took the opportunity to get to know the four Waffen SS soldiers who would accompany him on the mission to release Dennehy. He spread a map before him and the four soldiers crowded in to see better.

"Gentlemen, this is a very important mission. To ensure its success we have to engineer the escape of a man called Declan Dennehy. Here is a photograph."

He handed round a monochrome photograph of a handsome, smiling man in his forties. The four soldiers looked hard at it willing the image to their memory.

"He is being held as an internee on the Isle of Man because of his seniority within the Irish Republican Army. As a male internee, he would normally be held in quarters in the capital, Douglas. However, he has complained of serious back pain and has been transferred to another camp in Port Erin some sixteen miles away for medical treatment. His illness is feigned, he knows we are coming but not when. Importantly, the place in which he is being treated is only a quarter of a mile...the last part uphill... from the dock in Port Erin where we will be landed. Under my command, your job is to access his quarters secretly, remove him from his hospital bed and return him to the fishing boat. We must do this without being observed. If we are, we may have to return fire but we want to give the fishing boat time to get out into the Irish Sea without being attacked by British fighter aircraft so stealth is crucial. No one has ever escaped from the island so if they don't see us and have no reports of a boat being stolen, they'll concentrate their search on the island. Dennehy will be in night attire so we'll take warm clothing and shoes for him. The British are using existing homes and hotels on the island as well as camps for internees and these areas are enclosed in barbed wire so we cut here, here and here." He pointed at three lines on the map. The four soldiers nodded.

"When we get Dennehy to the fishing boat, we board it and sail back to Cary's Harbour where we disembarked.

Once we leave, U-48 will dock and pick you up. Dennehy and I remain on the fishing boat unless we're spotted in which case we all board the U-Boat which will submerge as soon as is practicable. We'll work out how to land us in Ireland afterwards...but I'm sure all will go according to plan. You'll be home in no time."

"You make it sound simple, *Obergruppenführer,*" one of the men ventured.

"All the best plans are simple. All we need is perfect weather and everyone on the island asleep except Dennehy."

The four soldiers began discussing the plan among themselves, pointing at various features on the map giving Weber some moments to observe them at a slight distance. *Four brave men,* he reckoned. *Picked carefully, for sure...strong, tall, athletic...obviously bright... committed to the cause. I must ensure they all return safely from this mission.*

## CHAPTER EIGHT

Days passed. *Unterseeboot 48* closed on its destination, Dr. Henning went about his surgery aided by the redoubtable Nurse Hamilton; and Sinéad, Danny and Dub travelled to Drogheda where they settled in a farmhouse outside the town awaiting instructions on how and when to collect their German agent.

It was around seven o'clock in the evening when Dr. Henning paid a further visit to the bedsides of the three men whose back pain was being treated. Dr. McGregor was a man before his time in ensuring that all possible treatments were attempted before considering surgery. He'd seen too many people immobilised because of poor surgery to their spinal column. Two of the men were in obvious and constant pain. The third, Dennehy, protested pain when asked to describe his symptoms but when Henning had observed the patient unnoticed over the last few days since his arrival, he seemed to be able to tolerate his condition quite well. *Either Doctor McGregor is having success with his traction methods or Mr. Dennehy is trying to pull the wool over our eyes. I'll have another word with him tonight.* He crossed the room to Dennehy's bed noticing that his patient seemed red in the face. *Perhaps I was too hasty to think of him as a malingerer.*

"Well, Mr. Dennehy. Still in some discomfort?"

"Terrible pain doctor. The only relief I get is when Dr. McGregor puts on them weights to my legs and takes the pressure off me spine. I swear I'll be two foot bigger when I get out of here." He groaned. "The pain's actually spreading to my stomach as well doctor and I'm feeling poorly."

"Certainly you do look flushed tonight."

He consulted the notes at the bottom of Dennehy's bed.

"Dr. McGregor hasn't given you any oral medication today?" he asked seeking to confirm the notes.

"He hasn't been in." He indicated the two sleeping patients in the next beds.

"Nurse Hamilton gave them two sleeping pills and they're both out cold but not me. I've just lain here feeling sick and sorry for myself."

"Have you vomited?"

"No but I feel like it."

"Sore stomach you say? Is this painful?"

Henning prodded Dennehy's abdomen, and received a low moan in response.

"Let me take your temperature."

He placed a thermometer in Dennehy's mouth and waited for a few moments before extracting it.

"Hmm. You have a fever of 38 degrees. You're burning up."

He sat on the edge of Dennehy's bed.

"You may have appendicitis, Mr. Dennehy. Let's monitor your condition for a couple of hours. If your temperature doesn't come down and your stomach is still tender I may have to operate. The success rates of an appendectomy are excellent but if it bursts and causes peritonitis, we may have serious problems."

"Okay, Doc."

"I'll be back in an hour. It may well be something less serious. Nurse Hamilton will alert me if things take a turn for the worse."

For fully five minutes, *Korvettenkapitän* Hartmann looked carefully at the images he was viewing through his periscope.

"Right full rudder, all ahead flank. Three knots only."

Weber stood silently, only feet away as Hartmann assessed conditions some ten feet above his conning tower.

"Our fishing boat is in position. Wave height less that a metre. No other activity observed." Satisfied, he decided to proceed.

"*Kapitänleutnant*, proceed with caution and elevate the prow ten degrees."

Four more minutes elapsed until final periscope attention satisfied Hartmann. He checked his watch.

"Local time, twenty minutes after one o'clock am. High tide. All engines stop. *Kapitänleutnant* are the torpedoes prepared?"

"Both prepared and the elevation you ordered is achieved."

Hartmann turned to Weber and grinned.

"If I get this bit wrong there will be questions asked. Of that I have no doubt."

He returned his gaze to the viewfinder on his periscope and studied the view outside one more time.

"*Kapitänleutnant*, fire torpedo one."

The submarine shook as the first of Weber's specially adapted torpedoes left the ship and headed the short distance to the shale beach identified earlier by Hartmann, its self-propulsion system tested by the heavier weight it carried on this occasion. For a few anxious moments, Hartmann followed the route of the torpedo before he shouted in delight as a silver bullet-shaped object hit the beach and instead of burrowing into it and exploding, merely slid to the top of the beach aided by the millions of small, smooth stones that characterised the shingled shoreline behind Cary's Harbour.

"A success. First class. *Kapitänleutnant,* fire number two torpedo."

A second disturbance indicated that the second torpedo was on its way. Again Hartmann watched carefully for some moments before erupting in joy once more.

"Perfection! *Kapitänleutnant,* level out and proceed at two knots directly ahead."

After ten more minutes, U-Boat 48 was docked in the small harbour on the Calf of Man, hidden from any prying eyes on its larger neighbour, the Isle of Man. Weber and his four soldiers had disembarked and had occupied sites around the tiny harbour, keeping watch as the crew of the *Unterseeboot* lifted the heavy boxes on to the pier, unaware of their contents.

Twenty minutes later, the heavy boxes containing ingots and coins had been piled alongside the lighter ones containing currency on the quayside awaiting collection by the fishing boat which was still negotiating the difficult currents around the harbour but managing to remain relatively stationary. As *Unterseeboot 48* left the dock in order to submerge and await the return of the four Waffen SS soldiers, the fishing boat *Trinity* occupied its place in the harbour and four men emerged to assist Weber and his soldiers load the cargo.

A further thirty minutes elapsed before Captain Niall Kennedy throttled back and headed his boat towards the slightly larger but still small quayside at Port Erin only seven minutes sailing away.

Weber entered the wheelhouse. "Thank you Captain. I intend that our time ashore in Port Erin will be brief."

"You can't be quick *enough*, my man. The longer you take the more chance we have of being holed below the waterline by a feckin' Brit."

"Just keep your boat out of sight at the old dock and we'll make our way through the main port to the hospital." He changed the subject. "Do you know this man we're going to bring back, a man called Dennehy?"

Kennedy wrestled with his steering. "Know him? I'll say I feckin' know him. The bastard shot my brother Michael."

"That is most unfortunate, Captain. So did you volunteer for this mission or were you *ordered* to take part?"

"I'm just following orders but don't you worry Mr. Hitler, I'll do my job properly. I'm as much a professional soldier as you are."

He fell into a silence and his attention was taken completely by the task of manoeuvring his boat into the old harbour at Port Erin, out of sight from the town but close enough to allow Weber and his men access within three hundred yards of the hospital.

After some further grunting and pulling at the wheel and ropes being thrown, Kennedy's men leapt from the boat onto the quay and began to tie up. Simultaneously, Weber and his men stepped onto the dock. Back in

Zossen, Weber had insisted that they each wear battle-dress, specially adapted to suit the mission. If they were to be captured, he didn't intend that they should be shot as spies. No metal objects were worn, nor were helmets. Green and brown fatigues with German markings would suffice. They would be uniformed but able to move freely. Rubber soled boots to permit them to move silently had been laced up earlier. One Mauser rifle, a Lugar pistol and a knife each were the only weapons they carried other than two wire-cutters which would be used at each of the barbed wire barriers.

Moving stooped and silent, the five men ran along the top of the flat, sandy beach below the promenade wall and covered the yardage to the edge of the harbour in under a minute. Three stepped aside and allowed the two men with wire-cutters access to the barrier. Lying on the ground at the harbour wall, the cutters did their job expertly. As some ten strands were set aside, the five men moved through to the fence at the bottom of the street on which stood Hemming's hotel, now a hospital. No artificial light made their task difficult as Weber had refused to carry flashlights lest their movements be seen. Again the soldiers parted as the two wire-cutters went to work opening up a gap Weber hoped they could close upon their return to disguise the direction they had taken to make their escape. *So far so good*, thought Weber.

His optimism was short-lived.

One of the soldiers caught the glance of Weber and put his finger to his lips, inviting silence.

"*Obergruppenführer* they have a sentry at the next fence," he whispered.

The five soldiers pressed their backs against a wall that sheltered them from view.

"Damn," cursed Weber. He thought for a moment. They were too far in to back off now. He'd hoped for an uneventful mission. *No one sees us...no one gets hurt,* he'd thought earlier when planning the raid.

"Damn," he repeated himself. His eyes locked with the soldier nearest the guard. Weber's head nodded imperceptibly but his meaning was clear.

The sentry hut was inside the wire. Silently the soldier drew his knife, regular issue and razor sharp. Behind him another Waffen SS soldier stood ready to shoot if the guard was alerted. A third soldier moved forward and lay down, placing the cutter blades precisely and gently on the wire. Each cut sounded like a cymbal crash to the anxious Germans but the sentry, quietly humming tunelessly, heard nothing. At last an opening was created and the soldier with the knife slithered through. Getting to his feet, he looked carefully to ensure that there were no other sentries or soldiers within sight of the box. Just as the sentry began a recognisable version of *'The White Cliffs of Dover'*, the knife slid powerfully upwards into his throat, severing his trachea and pressing onwards into the spinal cord, killing him instantly and wordlessly.

Catching him, the soldier dragged the dead man backwards and laid him behind the sentry box hoping that the empty shelter might suggest to any curious colleague that the sentry was on his rounds rather than lying behind it with his throat cut.

Signalling the all-clear to Weber, the four others made their way to the door of the hospital which as they'd hoped, was unguarded, the hospital in darkness. Opening the front door slowly, Weber saw that the black-out curtains had done their job well. Although no light emanated externally from the building, it was clear from the shafts of light showing beneath the internal doors that at least two rooms were illuminated - one of which was the one he'd been advised to expect would contain Dennehy. Silently signalling to his troops, Weber readied himself to open the door. Drawing his Lugar, he placed his left hand on the door handle, turning and pushing at the same time. Inside, Dr. Henning and Nurse Hamilton were tending to Declan Dennehy. The other two back patients were in a drug induced sleep.

He pointed his gun directly at Henning.

"Please be assured we will shoot anyone who resists or makes a noise."

Two strides forward took him close to the two medics and permitted three soldiers to enter the room behind him, one remaining in the shadows at the front door.

"I am a German officer and I have come to remove Mr. Dennehy from this hospital. You can see we are armed so do not test us."

The original three occupants of the room, including Dennehy, held their positions as if statues; stationary in the suddenness of Weber's entrance. Henning was first to react.

"You don't understand. Mr. Dennehy is very ill. He has appendicitis. I was just preparing to operate."

"This is unfortunate but he comes with us now."

Dennehy raised a weak arm. "Officer, it's true. I'm in a lot of pain and he was just going to put me under."

Weber lowered his gun and moved towards Dennehy's bed. As he did so, Nurse Hamilton clutched his arm and tried to pull his pistol from his grasp.

"You Nazi devil. Give me tha..."

Her eyes grimaced in pain and she sighed, falling into Weber's arms, the nearby soldier's knife finding its way upwards through her rib cage, claiming its second victim of the night. Weber took her weight and let her fall slowly to the floor as the soldier withdrew, sheathing his blade before dragging the nurse's body away from Dennehy's bed.

Henning was aghast at the sight of his nurse being murdered in front of him. He spoke harshly to Weber.

*"Was soll das hier? Sie haben meine Krankenschwester umgebracht! Sind sie von Sinnen?"*

Weber turned his gaze on the doctor as he recognised his accent.

*"Sind sie Deutscher? Was führt sie hierher?"*

Dennehy's pain fought for supremacy with his frustration. "For feck's sake will yez speak in English. I might be dyin' here. I want to know what's goin' on."

Weber turned his attention to the patient as one of his soldiers placed an arm across Henning's chest to restrain him.

"Mr. Dennehy. We have been sent to take you home to Ireland. We have warm clothes for you. Come, we must leave immediately."

"But I've been taken not well. The doctor was genuinely going to operate."

"This is true, officer. If his appendix bursts...and I think it will soon... it will cause serious infections and lead to peritonitis, blood poisoning and possibly death. He needs an emergency operation. He also has a problem with his back. Making him move may cripple him."

"Eh...sorry doctor but I was comin' the Mick on that one. My back's fine."

Henning nodded, attempting to convey his hunch that he already suspected as much.

Weber's impatience surfaced.

"Well, we can't wait here. We'll soon be discovered."

He thought for a moment.

"Doctor, you are an Internee?"

"I am. I am a German national. A doctor from Kaiserslautern."

"Then we have no choice. You will accompany us and treat Mr. Dennehy in half an hour's time when we are safe."

"And if I do not want to go?"

"Then your patient dies and either I kill you or I leave you to explain the death of the nurse. The English would hang you. So, doctor, help me lift your patient. You have no choice."

They each held the other's gaze for a long moment; both uncertain.

Two soldiers were preparing Dennehy's clothing as their *Obergruppenführer* and Henning spoke together. Gently but efficiently they began to lift him from his hospital bed eliciting a pained moan from Dennehy that brought Henning to his decision.

"Careful! Let me move him."

Only a couple of minutes later, Dennehy was dressed and was draped over the shoulders of two soldiers, his face grey and pained. Henning left them to prepare Dennehy for his escape and spent the time available first confirming that the nurse's wound was mortal then collecting in a bag, all the equipment and medicines he'd need to deal with the appendicitis and any complications that might set in before he could be treated properly.

Weber opened the door an inch and put his eye to the gap. At the front door, his soldier stood, still in the shadows but untroubled. He turned to those assembled behind him.

"We go now."

Quietly the group stepped out and after checking that the outside remained clear, began to retrace their steps towards *Trinity*. An occasional pained grunt from Dennehy as he was manhandled through the gaps in the wire was the only sound beyond the breaking of the waves on the beach area below the harbour wall. The last soldier through the wire took a few seconds at each breach to use a light cord brought with him to secure the fence and disguise the escape route, however briefly. As an attempt at a diversion, at the final fence, he ran some distance to a nearby road leading into the town and threw the pyjama jacket earlier worn by Dennehy in an attempt to persuade the inevitable pursuers that their quarry had headed inland.

Once they had traversed the beach and made the flat surface of the harbour, three German soldiers merely lifted Dennehy shoulder high and ran quietly but powerfully towards the dock where *Trinity* was berthed. As they closed, Captain Kennedy gave the order to cast off and synchronised his preparations just as the seven men reached the fishing boat.

Hauling Dennehy down into the bowls of the boat and forward to a forecastle bunk, the soldiers closed the hatch as Weber lit a lamp. Henning looked for a place to lay his patient.

"This is far from ideal. I am about to operate on a man and I see nowhere that looks remotely sterile."

Weber understood the import of Henning's appraisal. Blowing out the lamp he'd just ignited, he pulled back the hatch, climbed out and approached Kennedy in the wheelhouse.

"Captain Kennedy, have you any clean sheets?"

"Holy Mother of God! Haven't you eyes in your head to see that this is a feckin' fishin' boat, not a feckin' hotel"

Weber had anticipated his response. "Have you newspapers...recent newspapers?"

Kennedy wrestled with the wheel as he guided the boat back towards Cary's Harbour on the adjacent Calf of Man. He could do without this interference but realised he could be helpful.

"There's loads in a shelf above the nearest bunk down below."

Weber returned, relit the lamp and found the newspapers which he opened and laid out on the bunk, throwing away those most covered in oil.

"Lay him here."

"We must strip him. This will not be so simple an operation while the boat is bucking like this."

Webber nodded but made no attempt to assist, choosing instead to follow his four Waffen SS colleagues up and out of the hold as they prepared to leap on to the dock prior being collected by *Unterseeboot 48*.

"Thank you all," shouted Weber into the wind. "I will make sure your superiors know of your bravery."

The four soldiers made the harbour surface easily. As one man, they turned and saluted Weber who returned the address before the reversing fishing boat had him stumbling backwards. As he staggered he saw the silhouette of the U-Boat preparing to enter the tiny harbour.

*Thank God in heaven. It looks like the first part of my mission will be successful; the men are safe,* he thought as he returned below deck to see to Dennehy. He entered the small cabin to see Henning administer an injection to Dennehy's upper arm.

"How is he doctor?"

"This will see him asleep very shortly. I think I have all that is necessary to conduct the operation but the movement of the boat makes it difficult to stand never mind hold my hand still for an operation. I only hope I don't cut his throat by mistake."

He poured water from a kettle on to his hands and arms and scrubbed them vigorously with soap he'd brought from Port Erin.

"Well, if you do, Captain Kennedy might just buy you some Champagne. There appears to be some enmity between the two men."

"That's *your* job but I'd prefer not to save his life only for the captain to put an end to it."

"Quite."

Dennehy succumbed to the tranquilliser and Henning dried his hands. Taking a scalpel he made a three inch incision in the lower right section of Dennehy's stomach. Weber held the lamp closer to the wound in order that Henning might peer inside the abdomen at those organs he could discern in the dim light and examine them for other disease or abnormalities. After some moments he located the appendix, brought it up into the wound, separated it from all the surrounding tissue and its attachment to the cecum then removed it. He then closed the site where the appendix was previously attached, closed the cecum and returned it to Dennehy's abdomen. Finally he took another needle and stitched the muscle layers and then the skin together. The entire procedure took twenty minutes during which time Captain Kennedy had cleared the island and, satisfied that there was no immediate pursuit, lowered his nets and engaged in midwater pelagic trawling for mackerel such as would be normal for his boat as it made its way to Drogheda, some eighty nautical miles away.

# CHAPTER NINE

# Ireland

Éamon de Valera stopped cleaning his spectacles with a light cloth and pulled gently at the curtain in his office to reveal a day whose weather showed promise. It was still early but a weak sun heralded a quiet, still morning. A knock on his door had him turn and his long-serving private secretary, Miss Kathleen O'Connell joined him with a tray full of papers.

"Good morning *Taoiseach*. I have the overnight correspondence."

"Thanks, Miss O'Connell. In this tray?"

"On the top, sir."

De Valera moved round behind his large oak desk and sitting, placed his round spectacles back on the bridge of his nose, fiddling with the wire earpiece. He narrowed his eyes, the better to focus his failing vision on the paper in front of him.

"So, another epistle from that wind-bag, Mr. Churchill. He's a terrible man for his euphuistic letters. Let's hope he didn't write this note with the help of several large brandies as he has done in the past...D'you remember his last one? 'Now or Never. A Nation Once Again!' You can't fault the old fox for not knowing his Irish history but he backed off quickly enough when he was brought to heel by his political colleagues, telling them that he intended to convey that the *'unification'* he referred to was of the entire British Isles, not Ireland. He was all for leading us down the garden path."

He peered at the note.

"Now what he's on about this time?"

O'Connell had retreated two paces and stood erect holding a notepad and pencil in front of her, alert to her master's next question or command. De Valera read on, silently and emotionless. Finishing it, he laid it before him and pursed his lips.

"D'ye know, Kathleen, I wish that nice Mr. Chamberlain was still Prime Minister over the water. At least when he offered me the self-same offer he did so in a gentlemanly way."

"Another attempt to have us all join the British Army, sir?"

"Indeed so. He'd have us join the Allies by allowing his ships to use our ports. He wants us to arrest our German and Italian civilians, set up what he calls a joint defence council and allow his planes to fly over our sod. In return, we would be provided with British armaments and British forces would cooperate with us should there be a German invasion."

He shook his head as he read further.

"For the love of God!...he still goes on to propose that London would declare openly and formally that it accepts the principle of a united Ireland in the form of a solemn undertaking that the union of Ireland is to become an accomplished fact from which there shall be no turning back. I fear the brandy has influenced his pen right enough. I just wish he'd read the full lyrics of our national song and reached the line, 'And *righteous* men must make our land a nation once again.'"

"He seems not to take seriously your avowed intent to maintain neutrality, *Taoiseach*."

"No he does not, Kathleen, but then there are those who'd say he was not the 'righteous man' I speak of when quoting the song. Nor does he seem to understand the mischief he'd let loose north of our border when the Unionists came to hear of the arrangement. Could you imagine? We'd be spending these war years at serious odds with our *own* people for abandoning neutrality, at odds with the northern *unionists* who'd be down here in a flash exploding their bombs as close to Leinster House as they could manage and of course we'd be somewhat at odds with the *Luftwaffe* who'd be dropping their bombs down our chimneys like they did by *mistake* in 1941 as an incentive to us to maintain our deepwater port and not return them to Britain. I've already told him all this four years ago but listening isn't his strong point"

"Quite, sir. Would you like me to fashion a response for your signature?"

"Possibly, Kathleen but leave it to stew for a bit. I might write something in my own hand to the sly old rogue."

He raised the letter again, scanning it and shaking his head once more before returning it to his in-tray.

"What else have you for me today?"

"A number of pressing matters, *Taoiseach*. Your first important appointment is with Dr. Eduard Hempel of the German Legation. He arrives at ten o'clock."

"Ah, poor Eduard. The only participant in this ugliness who seems genuinely to hold the same ambitions as we do. He's a civilised man and no more a Nazi than you or I. He has to implement their foreign policy but I know him to be embarrassed by the antics of these two German eejits Ribbentrop and Veesenmayer who are bent on bringing rebellion to Ireland, while Admiral Canaris masterminds intelligence-gathering and espionage operations here at every opportunity."

"That said, I'm sure he'd love you to sign a similar treaty as that offered by Mr. Churchill."

"That he would, Kathleen but Hempel's a career diplomat and a conservative one at that. He'll want to make sure that nobody rocks the boat. He's as much told me to my face that the German *Reich* diplomacy lacks coherence and is subject to interference from a number of competing military influences within it. We need to keep him onside because he plays it straight as far as I can see."

"Certainly, sir. I'll leave you to your correspondence. Afterwards, at nine o'clock, you propose to attend Daily Mass with your wife and after Dr. Hempel you then have some Warrants of Appointment to sign. After lunch you propose to visit Donal Hegarty in hospital and then have three, thirty minute meetings here with *Teachtaí Dála* later on. The briefing papers are below the correspondence in your tray so I'll bring breakfast in half an hour and I'll be just outside at my desk if you need me."

"Thank you, Kathleen."

As she left the room, de Valera lifted Churchill's letter once again and sighed. *I think this is one reply I'll write myself.*

Forty nautical miles into their journey to Drogheda, dawn had given way to a bright sky and calm sea.

One of Kennedy's men brought his binoculars from his eyes and called attention from the wheelhouse.

"Niall, there's a plane approaching from the west. Too far to make it out clearly but it looks like an RAF Photo Reconnaissance Mosquito. It's heading straight for us."

"We're in international waters, fishing legally. Our nets are out. Get all of the boys on deck and make sure we're all doing things that'll look right on their photographs. Tell our three guests to stay below."

Gradually the form of the Mosquito became clearer as its drone became louder until it overflew the *Trinity* roaring only one hundred feet above its wheelhouse before turning and flying over the boat a second time.

"Stay in your positions, lads," shouted Kennedy. "It'll soon pass."

This time the Mosquito headed directly towards the prow of the boat, flying so low it appeared to be preparing to hit it head-on. It passed low on the port side to provide a good aerial view of the boat. This time the cacophony was such as to rattle both the windows and all on board.

"Hold steady," repeated Kennedy.

After another return manoeuvre the plane headed back towards the boat but this time at a height of two hundred feet.

"It's okay, boys. They're just taking photographs. Go about your business. Don't wave friendly-like...they'll expect you to shake your fists, so oblige them."

Eventually, as Kennedy had predicted, the plane seemed satisfied and climbed away, flying on in a southerly direction.

"Okay, down below. Seems we got away with it. The plane's off but keep yer wits about yous, boys."

"Jesus, Mary and Joseph. Niall, look astern."

Kennedy stepped from his cabin and looked in the direction of his crewman's pointed finger. Lying on a piece of white canvas on the deck, its black outline in sharp relief to its background was a Mauser rifle.

"Jesus Christ Almighty. We may as well have painted a feckin' Swastika on the roof of the wheelhouse."

He thought quickly. "They won't be able to be sure what they've seen until they're back at base. We've time to out-run them... Joe, haul in the nets...Des, you and Paddy get that red tarpaulin out and cover the wheelhouse; it might confuse them for a moment if they return before we're in Irish waters. Let's get a feckin' move on. If these feckers work out that we have a German rifle on board they'll shoot first and ask questions later."

Weber stepped into the wheelhouse. "Sorry Captain, one of my men must have dropped it as he jumped on to the quayside."

"Too late for sorrys now, soldier boy. We'd better hope our engines do us proud and get us back before they have second thoughts. If they *strafe* us, we've no chance. We all go to the bottom along with your feckin' cargo."

"Anything I can do to help?"

"Help the boys pull them feckin' nets in...but first, would you ever get that feckin' rifle off the deck?"

"Of course."

Stepping out and walking unsteadily to the rear of the vessel, Weber made his way to the Mauser, stopping on his way to pick up a wooden boat hook of similar size. He swapped the two items. *A long shot but if they come back to do a visual check, they might just give us the benefit of the doubt.* He took the Mauser down below deck and remonstrated with himself. *Damnation! Once they process the film, British Intelligence will put two and two together and calculate that Dennehy has made his escape on this boat. Still, perhaps they'll just figure it was the IRA who organised his escape...even with the use of one of our Mausers.*

He stepped back up and onto the deck, grabbed the nets and pulled with all his strength.

Sinéad rose from her small cot and looked at her two comrades still asleep in armchairs which had served as their bed for the past few nights. *The sooner I'm back home and can get a proper bath and a change of clothing the better,* she mused, wrinkling her nose. *And it would do those two no harm either.*

Moving through to the kitchen she placed the kettle on top of the hob and wiped the window with the sleeve of her cardigan while waiting for the water to boil. Outside was calm. The previous night a message passed to her in a Drogheda pub had informed them that they should be ready to welcome their guest when he docked at the harbour around noon. She glanced at the clock on the mantle. *Six-fifteen. Plenty of time yet. I'll let that pair sleep another couple of hours if they want to. Better they're refreshed and not grumpy today.*

The boiling kettle had been fitted with a whistling device that sounded, awakening Dub who came through to the kitchen and stretched, his hands easily reaching the ceiling of the small farmhouse.

"Is that a pot of tea ye've on, Sinéad?"

"It is, Dub. Sit down and I'll get some bread for you. Did you sleep well?"

Dub collapsed onto a wooden kitchen chair, still rubbing the sleep from his eyes.

"Sure, I was unconscious from the minute my head hit the pillow. Them pints we had in Clarke's bar down in Peter Street saw me off no problem."

He took a piece of soda bread from a basket proffered by Sinéad and took a bite.

"Ta, Sinéad...so are we all set for our German agent?"

"We'll see. We have our lorry ready and Niall Kennedy's men will help you load this mysterious cargo he's got with him...Your man's a big fish. He's bringing Declan Dennehy with him so he's off to a good start. Our orders are to have you and Danny take his boxes in the lorry to the estate of Arthur Joyce outside Malahide. You're not to unload it. Just leave it with Mr. Joyce and travel to the city. I'm to take our man and Declan to a meeting of two of the Army Council in Dublin. He'll be reunited with his belongings later. If all goes well, the three of us'll meet in the Palace Bar in Fleet Street. If things go badly, we'll see each other in hell!"

"Well, I don't speak a feckin' word of German. I hope he has a few words of John Bull, 'cos I can't see him havin' the *Gaelic.*"

"I doubt you'll see him after today and you'll be dealing mostly with Niall but I'm told this fellah speaks perfect English. We'll see if he can master our version of it."

She poured two cups of tea and held Dub's gaze as she passed across his cup.

"Now I know Danny's out of sorts with me but you two have an important job to do today. I've been told this could be a really valuable thing we're doing. You two stay safe but don't let us down, eh?"

Dub chewed at his soda bread and took the cup in his other hand.

"No trouble at all, Sinéad."

The *Taoiseach* had found Mass sustaining.

*I fear that sometimes the solitude and the opportunity for reflection provided in church is expended more on the sins of my fellow man rather than on the glory of God,* he mused as he walked back to his office, five minutes late for his meeting with the Head of the German Legation.

He entered his outer office and held out his hand, shaking that of Dr. Hempel's warmly.

"My dear Dr. Hempel. It's always a delight to receive you. Please forgive my tardiness but I thought it unwise to leave Mass before it ended. I need all of the assistance I can manage from our Lord at the minute in order to deal with rogues like you and I didn't want to upset Him."

"*Taoiseach,* I was happy to await your return."

"Miss O'Connell will make us a cup of tea."

He waved his hand at an empty armchair. "Please take a seat."

"Thank you for seeing me *Taoiseach*", said Hempel as he sat. "You are a busy man so let me come immediately to the point in hand. I wish to discuss the continuing issue of Ireland's neutrality. The *Fuehrer* receives reports from a range of sources and he advises of his disappointment to learn that you continue to permit captured British airmen to walk to freedom by heading north to Northern Ireland whereas our airmen are interned."

"Well, Dr. Hempel, I fear the Chancellor is misinformed on this occasion. Our policy is to intern *any* airman whom we believe to have been on a combat mission. That is the policy of the Free State and I'm sure you'll want to reassure Mr. Hitler in this regard. In your role as Minister Plenipotentiary and as a civilised man, you have been assiduous in reassuring the German *Reich* of our determination not to become a belligerent in this war. Ireland is grateful to you for the stance you have taken and for the success you have enjoyed in balancing the guidance the Chancellor receives from his countrymen like Ribbentrop and Veesenmayer. Their words would lead us to believe that they would like nothing better than to see Ireland embroiled in internal strife and external aggression."

Hempel considered the *Taoiseach's* words and was about to offer a diplomatically nuanced challenge when de Valera rose and walked to his desk. After searching for a moment he picked up a piece of paper and returned to his chair. Before consulting the script he held in his hand, he allowed himself a momentary flush of self-righteous anger.

"Not six years ago, the British Army was in occupation of our three deepwater ports of Berehaven, Queenstown and Lough Swilly. These were returned to us under the Anglo-Irish Treaty but Mr. Churchill has been vociferous in his demands for their reoccupation, using belligerence if needs be. How can Mr. Hitler have any doubt as to our determination not to show favour in this war? Let me read my last statement to the *Dail* which was relayed on Irish radio so I'm sure your people picked it up..."

"Yes, *Taoiseach* we read a transcript," interrupted Hempel, now attempting to soothe a now clearly irritated head of state.

"Then you'll permit me to remind you for purposes of emphasis and disambiguation, Dr. Hempel...and I quote only the final sentence... '*We may be facing a grave crisis. If we are to face Churchill's aggression, then we shall do it anyhow, knowing that our cause is right and just and that if we have to die defending our ports, we shall die for that good cause*'...Now, Dr. Hempel, does that sound like the weasel words of a nation keen to ingratiate itself with England?"

"No it does not *Taoiseach* and I assure you that your fine oration has already been relayed to the *Fuehrer* along with my continuing reassurances that Ireland is striving hard to maintain its position as..."

"But this is not sufficient, Dr. Hempel. You and I well understand the constant pressures of war that obliges all belligerents to exploit any opportunity to gain advantage; militarily, economically or in terms of propaganda. I cannot taunt the British...our nation has need of the resources they provide; food and coal, cattle feed and oil...all of our foreign reserves are in British securities. Many of my countrymen have volunteered to serve in their ranks. You know this and we have agreed that it would be folly for me to attempt to bring ruin on my nation by declaring a neutrality so severe it would lead to the British invading us...You are well aware that there are opinions so minded across the Irish Sea...just as we discovered *you* did also with the plans we found in the house of your German spy, Stephen Held after he fled leaving behind him plans on possible military targets in the Republic and proposals to side with the IRA in an invasion of the North...So don't come the innocent with me in *this* office, Dr. Hempel. This remains a most delicate matter and we have agreed formally that you accept we have to show a 'certain consideration' towards Britain just as we did you when we uncovered the activities of Mr. Held."

"You make your point with your usual passion and dexterity..."

De Valera was not to be soothed.

"I have seen the flower of Irish youth too often perish prematurely. My dearest wish and avowed intent is to ensure that my country remains apart from the world's violence and as long as I have breath in my body *Éire* shall remain neutral."

Hempel bowed before the intensity of de Valera's withering outburst and his further diplomatic emollients gradually led to the *Taoiseach* and Minister Plenipotentiary sparring rather more gently, reflecting the genuine warmth in their relationship.

"*Taoiseach,* you know that I share your determination that Ireland retains its neutrality. I can assure you my messages are received in Berlin with the same enthusiasm."

"All well and good, Eduard. I trust you completely and thank you for the part you play in maintaining our good relations with the German *Reich*."

"Thank you, *Taoiseach*. Now, before I leave you, I must inform you that Berlin has seen fit to favour my Legation with further support. I am to be joined shortly by General Kurt Weber. He has been a soldier, of course but I am told he is also an academic; a professor. He will assist in general terms but I'm informed he is to invest in Irish businesses as a contribution by the Third *Reich* in Ireland's prosperity and to prepare for the normalisation of relations after the war is over."

"Well," de Valera laughed, "if he brings money to invest he'll be more than welcome."

"With your permission, I'll ensure that he calls on you once he's settled to present his credentials."

"I'll have a pot of tea warming for him, Eduard."

The Trinity's engines pushed the boat through the calm waters of the Irish Sea as fast as they could towards Drogheda, bullied and whipped by Paddy Boylan who had been an engineer on a fishing boat about as long as he had been an adherent to the policies and practices of the Irish Republican Army; man and boy.

In the wheelhouse, Kennedy could begin to see the beginnings of the hazy outline of the Irish coast at Drogheda when he was alerted by a yelp from one of his crew-hands tasked with binocular duty.

"Niall, here's the feckin' Mosquito comin' back!"

The captain stepped outside the wheelhouse and took the glasses, focusing them in the general direction of his colleague's pointed arm. Turning the central calibrator carefully, he peered through the field-glasses and quartered the sky until assured of his identification. Slowly he brought the glasses down and handed them to Weber who had joined him from the engine room downstairs and who then scanned the skies looking for the plane that threatened *Trinity*.

Kennedy shielded his eyes from the sun as he tried to identify the approaching plane.

"That's no feckin' Mosquito...that's a feckin' floater!"

He hailed his crew. "Joe, Des, Paddy...get up here and bring your weapons."

Weber threw the glasses onto the chair inside the wheelhouse.

"It's a seaplane, alright. A Sunderland if I'm not mistaken."

"They've been radioed by the last lot...they couldn't be sure so asked them to come and take a look. Bastards!"

He growled at Weber. "We're going to have to fight our way out of this." His thumb gestured at the conditions behind him. "Look at the sea. It's like a mill-pond there. They'll definitely want to land and take a closer look." He looked at Weber's uniform. "D'ye not think you'd better go below with the doc and Dennehy. If things get nasty, come up with all guns blazing! We'll need to send that seaplane to the bottom before they sink us. Best we can hope for is that they come in close hoping we're just a fishing boat up to some kind of mischief rather than a fishing boat carrying a top German General, an escaped internee and a senior officer of the IRA."

Weber nodded his agreement and went to join doctor and patient.

Closer now, the seaplane circled *Trinity* from some distance out before tilting a wing and banking, reducing height and closing on the boat.

"Keep your guns hidden, boys," shouted Kennedy. "Wait until they try to board us then we let fly with everything we've got. Des, your only job is to get the pilot before he can use his radio. Shoot the feckin' pilot and the feckin' cockpit to feckin' smithereens. Joe, you and Paddy smile at the feckers like they was your own kith and kin arrivin' for your birthday party but no one shoots before I do...but once I do, take out every man jack of 'em!"

As he finished his sentence, the seaplane roared overhead much as did the Mosquito before banking and returning.

"He's throttlin' back, boys", shouted Kennedy. "He's feckin' landing alright. Remember your orders!"

So saying he stepped out and walked the few paces to the prow of the boat, obviously unarmed and held his hand up in what he hoped would be interpreted as a friendly gesture by the aircrew.

Slowing, the Sunderland's floats caught the water until they settled and the plane steered its way towards Trinity a hundred yards to port. A loud-hailer carried their message very effectively.

"Ahoy *Trinity*. Stop your engines. Repeat. Stop your engines. We intend to come aboard."

Weber shouted to Kennedy from just below the sight line of the deck.

"The Sunderland usually has a single Vickers machine gun in the nose turret and four Browning machine guns in its tail. To board us, the pilot will have to position his plane side on. That makes it vulnerable."

Kennedy caught his eye and nodded his understanding while still waving at the seaplane. He stepped into the wheelhouse and turned off the engines as requested before stepping back into the sunlight and holding both hands in the air."

Another blast from the bullhorn. "*Trinity*...bring all hands on deck and have them stand facing us with their arms in the air."

"Okay lads, do as he says but make feckin' sure you're on your toes and your machine guns are at your feet."

Kennedy gave the seaplane the thumbs-up signal and three very frightened, morose fishermen assembled on deck, arms raised. Gradually, the seaplane manoeuvred just as Weber had predicted but as it completed its turn, positioning itself parallel to *Trinity*, a loud rattle signified the slide opening of a wide door on the side of the fuselage above the waterline to reveal a powerful Nash & Thomson FN-13 powered turret hosting a 0.5-inch calibre Browning...aiming right at *Trinity* and the four men exposed on deck.

"Jesus Christ Almighty," cursed Kennedy under his breath. "Shame you didn't warn us about that one, Mr. feckin' General."

## CHAPTER TEN

From his position down in the engine room, Weber edged a cautious eye round the door at deck level but could see little as a consequence of a woven basket used to hold any crustaceans that were collected inadvertently while they were seeking whitefish. Crouching, he stepped up on one step...two steps. Carefully he peered round the door jamb and realised that Kennedy's order, if followed by his crew, would see them cut down instantly by the Browning. *The pilot's not the main target*, he thought... *it's the machine gunner...and when Kennedy makes a move, that's who I must have in my sights.*

Gradually, the sea-plane bobbed closer to *Trinity* and shut off its engines, the Browning holding the complete attention of its crew who still stood, arms aloft, their guns at their feet hidden by the knee-high side of the fishing boat. *Ach*, growled Weber inwardly, *the first man who stoops to pick up his weapon is doomed.*

Slowly he fed his Mauser rifle up to the top of the steps and stepped back on to the floor of the engine room. From his position he could see nothing of the gunner due to the basket. *If I show myself to get a clean shot, I'm as good as dead.* Cautiously he stepped up again and made his calculations. *This had better work*, he thought as he aimed his rifle at the centre of the basket, a light device that would prove no practical impediment to his bullet. Taking a breath and reckoning again the position of his target behind the obscuration, Weber eased his finger back on the trigger releasing his 7.9mm bullet with a sharp crack. Two more bullets followed instantly, each placed slightly to the side of the original shot in order to spread the target area. Quickly he leapt up the six steps to the deck, noticing as he did so that there was no return fire. Kennedy and his startled and frightened crew had collected their guns and were firing blindly into the doorway of the Sunderland. Gaining the deck, Weber saw the Browning gunner sprawled and bloodied over his weapon.

"Stop firing," shouted Weber, repeating himself three times before the *Trinity's* guns fell silent. "We're just wasting ammunition. There will be four men on board. Take cover and await my orders. We'll try to avoid bloodshed"

Kennedy riled at Weber's mutinous intervention. "I'm the feckin' Captain of this boat and..."

"With your permission, Captain. I am a soldier and accustomed to command. You will follow my orders or I will shoot you immediately. We are in peril and you will not argue. Agreed?"

Kennedy scowled but after a few seconds during which Weber pointedly turned his Mauser in his direction, he took one hand free of his gun.

"Okay, okay!"

Weber knelt and shouted across to the crew on the sea-plane.

"We mean you no harm. Show yourselves at the door and leave your weapons on the floor of the plane."

For perhaps ten seconds there was a silence punctured only by gull cry, then a shot from within the gloom of the hold of the Sunderland splintered wood next to Weber's head. Still he persisted.

"You will come to no harm if you show yourselves. We want to avoid bloodsh..."

Another shot, this time finding the arm of crewman Paddy Docherty, knocked him backwards onto the deck and had other hands ducking for further cover. Kennedy raised his Sten gun in reply only to lower it at Weber's barked order to desist. Walking backwards, he descended the steps and without removing his gaze from the side opening of the Sunderland, felt for a flare pistol he'd earlier placed next to where he had been standing. Curling his left hand around its barrel, he transferred the pistol to his right and checked it was loaded just as it was earlier when he had placed it at his own disposal.

"Captain Kennedy, start your engines. Prepare to move but remain stationary for the moment. If this works there just might be something of an explosion!"

Kennedy retreated backwards into the wheelhouse and the *Trinity* shuddered as its twin Napier diesel engines fired.

Weber moved up the steps once again and levelled the Verey Pistol at the gloomy interior of the sea plane. Once more he shouted a peaceful resolution.

"Leave your guns and come to the door of the plane. Your plane will explode shortly. You will not survive the blast."

With no response forthcoming, Weber aimed carefully and calmly pulled the trigger sending a small pyrotechnic containing potassium nitrate, perchlorate and strontium nitrate bulleting into the hold of the float plane causing an immediate inflagration. Flames licked upwards and caught combustible webbing which fell, igniting the floor of the plane. Dense black smoke billowed from the side opening.

"Hold your position, Captain. We'll have men overboard shortly," shouted Weber.

"If it goes up it'll take the feckin' *Trinity* with it," replied a very anxious captain.

"Hold!" ordered Weber as the fire spread with startling speed.

The plane, now fully ablaze, bobbed closer to *Trinity*.

"We have to move," screamed Kennedy. "Their fuel tank'll go up!"

After a few tormented moments, Weber succumbed.

"Move away," he shouted. "Move away!"

Kennedy, his knuckles white on the wheel, gunned the engines and *Trinity* moved...slowly at first, then with greater urgency and just in time to avoid the full impact of a huge explosion which engulfed the plane, sending a plume of water high above the combatants and showering all on deck with fragments of the plane. The blast wave had been strong enough to knock all on deck from their feet and put paid to the boat's strengthened wheelhouse windows.

After a few moments, Weber took in the carnage, even as he realised that all on deck were cut, bruised, but alive. Blood oozed from a deep cut on his own forehead. He stepped down into the engine room and looked into the forecastle bunk-room.

"Are you both okay?"

"We are fine," responded Henning. "Just worried when this will end!"

Weber nodded and returned to the deck in time to see the remains of the Sunderland slowly turn until the bottom edge of its open door met the sea water which poured in, deluging the plane and consigning it quickly to the depths. Seconds after it disappeared, only some floating detritus and an oil slick suggested there had been anything afloat on that area of the Irish Sea other than *Trinity*.

Weber returned to the entrance of the forecastle.

"It has ended," he said to Henning and a still unconscious Dennehy before walking quickly to the wheelhouse.

"Jesus...I've not seen a flare gun do such damage," said Kennedy as he tried to coax extra speed out of his fishing boat.

"Normally a Verey pistol sends a flare so high and it burns so brightly that it can be seen over forty miles away," Weber said. "The chemicals it uses are so hot when ignited it'll burn through anything, even underwater. I knew the plane would burn but expected the airmen to jump free. They must have been killed or immobilised by the volley of bullets after I shot the gunner."

"Why didn't you let us cut loose on them bastards after you shot the airman on the Browning?"

"In war, Captain Kennedy there must be compassion. These boys were there not because they wanted to but because they were caught up in a war not of their choosing. Just as you are here at your wheel. There must be humanity. There has been enough barbarism."

Kennedy reflected on Weber's reasoning but dismissed it with a grimace.

"No matter. The feckers are gone now! Let's just hope that plume of smoke didn't alert the Irish Army or we might have a waiting party when we arrive in Drogheda."

Kennedy's aside drew Weber's attention to the horizon where the coast of Ireland could now be seen clearly.

"Are we in Irish waters yet?"

"Yes. We're safe now unless the Brits break their international agreement...which wouldn't be the first feckin' time!"

"Then I can remove my uniform."

Weber returned to the cramped quarters downstairs where Henning was taking the temperature of Dennehy.

"How's our patient?"

"He's still unconscious but I gave him enough anaesthetic to keep him under until we reach land. It'll be easier for us and less distressing for him if we carry him ashore and permit him to wake up in a bed somewhere."

"Let's hope so doctor. It will also serve to avoid a confrontation between him and Captain Kennedy."

Weber moved aft where the packing cases had been stored by Kennedy's men, pulled on the one which contained his personal belongings and took it through to the forecastle. Dr. Henning showed concern over Weber's cut forehead.

"Let me see that wound *Sturmbannführer*, it might require stitches."

"I hope not. I've now to become a Diplomat and I'm sure it would look strange if I met my new hosts with a scarred and bleeding face."

Henning took a swab and gently cleaned the wound.

"We'll get it stitched when we're ashore. The bleeding's stopped for now. Because we're not sure what hit you and caused the laceration, you might need some sulphonamide as a prophylactic."

"Some of the crew were cut as well."

Henning pronounced himself satisfied with the state of Weber's wound in the meantime.

"I'll have a look at them now."

He began tidying up before heading up to the deck.

"A Diplomat, eh? I can't begin to understand what's going on here but I want no part in it. If England doesn't want to make use of my services, perhaps I can put my medical training to good use in Dublin."

"Perhaps, Doctor. But I'll need to have a discussion with you regarding what you've seen here. I require your word as an honourable man that you will speak to no man about what has happened here. I have given the matter some thought and my proposal is merely that we inform the Irish authorities that you come to Ireland as part of my entourage and that your task is to see to the health needs of the Legation and any German officers or citizens who may have need of your services...perhaps checking our boys detained behind barbed wire as internees?" He shrugged. "I imagine the Irish will take some small umbrage at the implied suggestion that they are failing us but it's the best story I can come up with that explains your position while allowing you to practice as a medic."

"Why, that would be most agreeable *Sturmbannführer*. I'm appalled at the violence I have witnessed but I'm grateful for your thoughtfulness...and you have my word that I will not speak of anything I have witnessed. But if we are to be associates, allow me to introduce myself properly. I am Dr. Hermann Gottfried Henning from Kaiserslautern in the Rhineland."

Weber accepted his hand and shook it warmly.

"And I am *Sturmbannführer* Kurt Weber, previously of the *Waffen SS* but now attached to Dr. Eduard Hempel who is the Minister Plenipotentiary at the German Legation in Dublin. When we dock, I am to be secreted away by individuals who need not be known to you. I will shortly thereafter be presented at the harbour at *Dún Laoghaire* docks as having just disembarked from a Portuguese coaster carrying wheat from Lisbon which is due to arrive today or tomorrow. You will have to come with me. My paperwork will be in order so we'll just have to explain the loss of yours on the journey over."

Weber started to change from his uniform into civilian clothing.

"But what about Mr. Dennehy, my patient?"

"Well, he's keenly awaited by those who will meet us so they'll be happy that you're accompanying us."

He looked at Henning. "It looks like we're about the same size. Perhaps I'm slightly taller." He looked in his packing case. "Here, take this jacket. We'll get you fitted out in Dublin but for your arrival you'll need to look as if you're an international dignitary, not a doctor interrupted during his rounds."

He looked at Dennehy's face. "Will he awaken within the hour?"

"I don't think so."

"Then if he says anything unhelpful, you'll need to diagnose him as rambling due to the powerful medication you've given him."

"I'll do that."

Henning stumbled for words. "*Sturmbannführer,* I can't thank you enough."

"Both of us will have to get used to me being a *Sturmbannführer* only in front of other soldiers. Socially, I'm Kurt and when I'm being a Diplomat, I'm Professor."

"Certainly, Professor...err...Kurt."

"Kurt it is, Hermann."

## CHAPTER ELEVEN

Sinéad O'Grady stepped from the three ton, flatbed Bedford lorry and walked towards the gateman at the entrance of busy Drogheda docks a mile inland from the mouth of the River Boyne. Danny remained in the passenger seat. Behind the lorry, Dub sat squashed in the driving seat of his black Austin car awaiting the clearance that Sinéad was to negotiate.

The green paint-flaked wooden box that served as shelter for port protection staff was large enough for perhaps only three bodies but as Sinéad ducked under the red wooden barrier and approached by prior arrangement, only one man; old Eddie, was in attendance.

"Morning, Eddie. Everything okay?"

Unshaven and dressed in dirty black overalls, Eddie stepped outside wiping his hands on trouser-leg material that could only have made them dirtier. He walked Sinéad back towards the barrier.

"Just be quick, Sinéad. I can't have this go beyond noon. The Harbourmaster's back soon after so everything must be away by then."

He pushed down on the weighted stub which lifted the wooden trunk that formed the security gate.

"Your boat's on the river. It's just outside the harbour,"

"Yeah, we watched it making the mouth of the river."

"Then get movin'. I'll be warned if the Harbourmaster leaves Balbriggan early."

The Bedford's engine spluttered into life followed by Dub's Austin and both vehicles drove to the side of the dock where three giant rusting bollards stood ready to receive Trinity which was now only a few hundred yards downriver from the port.

Sinéad took control.

"Remember now Dub, you take the German, Dennehy and me and we head off straight away to Dublin. Danny, you and Niall Kennedy's men load up the lorry then you and you alone take it directly to the Arthur Joyce estate in Malahide."

Turning and shielding her eyes, she looked north for the large clock on the church across the River Boyne.

"It's just after ten. You've about an hour and a half to unload the boat. Malahide's only ten miles north of Dublin so we should all comfortably make the Palace Bar on Fleet Street by six, okay?"

Both nodded their assent.

"Then let's get to it."

Captain Kennedy reversed Trinity's engines and slowly his craft approached the dockside where Danny and Dub caught his crew's thrown lines and pulled the boat tight to the quay. Nervously looking over her shoulder lest Gardai or Irish soldiers were in evidence, Sinéad awaited the boat being secured before stepping on to the side of the vessel and jumping ungainly on to the deck where she was greeted by the captain.

"Good mornin' to you, Sinéad. We made it in one piece. Your German's fine but we had to bring that fecker Dennehy's doctor with us as the eegit saw fit to be taken ill with appendicitis just as we were gettin' movin'. Stupid fecker!"

"Still carrying a bit of a grudge, then Niall?

"Wouldn't you?"

"Stop this Niall. Introduce me to the German."

"He's down below in the forecastle with Dennehy and his feckin' doctor," said Kennedy angrily, "so why don't yous just introduce yourself."

Holding his gaze for moments longer than was necessary in an attempt to convey her disapproval of his attitude, Sinéad turned and started to descend the steep steps into *Trinity's* lower deck shouting at Dub and Danny as she did so.

"Get a line going with the crew and get this cargo out of here and into the lorry. One of you keep a watch out for any problems."

She disappeared into the gloom and moved forward where two men stooped over a bunk bed.

Realising that it was Dennehy who was bed-bound and that she didn't recognise the other two, she called their attention.

"Allow me to introduce myself. I'm Sinéad O'Grady. I'm in charge of this operation."

Both men stood upright at hearing a woman's voice. Weber spoke first.

"I don't know why it should be so, but I expected a man to greet us."

"I'm more of a man than these people upstairs...and you three as well, for that matter," said Sinéad with more bravado than she felt. "And it doesn't matter anyway. After Declan Dennehy there I'm the ranking officer here so just follow my directions and we'll be fine. Which one of you's the German?"

Weber smiled at her confidence. "Well, we both are. I am Professor Kurt Weber and this..."

"Professor? They've sent us over a feckin' *Professor*?"

"Well, if it helps, I'm also a General in the *Waffen SS*. I understand warfare, Miss O'Grady...and this is Doctor Hermann Henning, my personal physician. He's been caring for Mr. Dennehy."

Henning bowed his head, attempting to convey respect.

"A pleasure, Miss O'Grady."

Sinéad looked at an unconscious Dennehy. "Will he be out long?"

Henning responded. "Long enough. If it's not far to our destination, he'll wake up there."

"It'll be a two hour drive I expect," said Sinéad.

Weber imposed himself on the conversation. "Hmmm, we'd best get started. Can I trust your people to deliver the boxes in this hold to the estate of Arthur Joyce?"

Sinéad looked behind her. "They're loading up already. But it looks like a lot of cases. What's in them?"

"Alas, Miss O'Grady, that I cannot tell you at present. Our bargain was just that you will deliver them. When I meet with representatives of your Army Council, perhaps more will be revealed."

Sinéad was mollified. "Okay, then let's get you and Dennehy away."

"I'm afraid Dr. Henning comes too. He doesn't leave my side."

"Well, that'll be quite the trick, Major. The car only holds four. Us three and a driver."

"Then I'll drive, Miss O'Grady. But Dr. Henning comes too. He also requires to join me when we register our presence formally at *Dún Laoghaire* harbour when the Portuguese coaster docks."

Sinéad wrestled with Weber's demands. "I don't like it when we step aside from our plan. No one planned for a doctor..."

Weber looked at her squarely and folded his arms assertively. Sinéad knew his argument had merit. "But if you insist..."

"Well, I'm afraid I do," he smiled.

She relented.

Weber and Henning wrapped Dennehy in a rough serge blanket and lifted him to the steps where with some difficulty they manoeuvred him on to the deck. Dub had already moved his car so that it concealed much of the conveyancing of Dennehy from ship to shore. Sinéad joined them on the quayside and bundling Dennehy on to the rear seat, Weber and Henning took occupancy of the front two seats leaving the spare seat for Sinéad who was some paces away explaining to an angry Dub that his car was being commandeered.

Shrugging her shoulders at her inability to persuade Dub of the need to surrender his vehicle without protest, Sinéad took her seat, leaving him seething but powerless on the quayside. She spoke to Weber from the rear of the vehicle.

"Okay, drive slowly. Nothing suspicious. Take us to the red barrier over there. The Gateman will let us out without a search."

Slowly, Weber drove the Austin towards the gatehouse. Old Eddie wasn't to be seen, much to Sinéad's irritation.

"Jesus, Mary and Joseph. Where the hell is he?"

Just as she spoke, Eddie appeared from the toilet block and with a wave of his hand, acknowledged the car sitting stationary at the barrier although, with the unhurried patience of the long-serving dockhand, he made no appreciable effort to increase his pace.

Sinéad shifted nervously in her seat.

"C'mon, Eddie. Get a move on," she said quietly, more to herself than to the occupants of the car. Still, Eddie ambled back towards the car exchanging leisurely comments with other dock workers as he did so.

More seconds passed, increasing Sinéad's increasing anxiety levels. As Eddie gained the barrier, a single shot shattered the side window of the car just as it did the left temple of Dennehy's head, showering the other three occupants in a liquid cloud of blood and glass and smearing the interior of the windscreen in a red mist.

Wordlessly, Weber stamped on the accelerator, spurring the car through the light wooden barrier, splintering it, as both Henning and Sinéad screamed in shock.

Henning turned awkwardly in his seat as the car careered round corners and leaned over. He was swaying wildly but managed to pull on the blanket that covered Dennehy's wound. His medical appraisal was instant.

"That head wound is not survivable. He's dead."

He slumped back in his seat as Sinéad, still shocked, her hands still covering her face, looked on in soundless horror.

Weber got straight to business as he drove frantically, looking for further signs of an impending attack. Suddenly, Sinéad saw a horse-drawn cart in front of them just as did a confused Weber. Instantly self-preservation kicked in and she screamed, "Drive on the left...the left. We drive on the left in Ireland."

Weber wheeled the car urgently onto the left of the carriageway and shouted above the noise of the engine.

"Hermann, use something to clear this windscreen. Miss O'Grady what's your assessment. Is my cargo in danger?"

For some seconds, Sinéad remained numb at the carnage before her. Her escaped IRA boss had just been assassinated. She was covered in his blood.

"I...oh...but...I don't...I don't know this place well, she pleaded," her eyes remaining locked on Dennehy's shattered and bloody head wound.

"I must protect that cargo," insisted Weber, careering across the bridge and heading towards the North Strand.

"If we cross the river we can look at what's happening on the dock from the other side." Slowing now, confident that no one was in pursuit, he drove to a vantage point where he could observe *Trinity*. From his pocket he took a pistol, stepped from the Austin and walked across the road to a grassy bank from which he could look down on the harbour. A knot of men stood at the gate speaking animatedly. No police or soldiers were in evidence yet. At its berth, *Trinity* remained serene, other than its smashed windows, looking as anonymous as all of the other fishing boats...but at its moorings, Danny, Dub and the crew worked feverishly to remove all of the boxes from the hold of the boat to the lorry.

Weber walked back to the car. Henning had moved around to the rear seat and was busily confirming his initial appraisal of Dennehy's injuries. Sinéad sat stationary, holding her head in her hands.

Henning sensed his compatriot returning to the car and looked up.

"Shot in the head. Fatal wound. Immediate death."

"Keep him in the car. We have to dispose of the body carefully or the authorities will know the escape from the Isle of Man was successful and ended here, in Ireland."

Henning nodded his understanding as Weber turned to an almost catatonic Sinéad.

"Who do you think shot Dennehy and why?"

Slowly Sinéad awoke from her torpor. "Obviously it was Niall Kennedy. Well, he had a motive, I suppose."

"Yes, he spoke to me of this as well."

Weber stood erect. "Unless we are pursued, we wait here until my cargo leaves the dock safely. We follow it for a while then we dispose of the body and report to your people as planned. We'll let them determine what went on here."

He looked around to ensure he was not being observed and, satisfied, took his pistol and dragged the barrel along the bottom of the window frame, clearing the remaining shards of glass in an attempt to present it as an open window rather than a suspiciously smashed pane.

"Tell me Miss O'Grady. Can I trust your two colleagues to deliver my cargo? That shooting has unsettled me. If one of your trusted people is prepared to shoot a comrade, why might not two others *steal* from me?"

Sinéad, now more composed, shook her head and spoke quietly. "I'll vouch for them. I've known one since we were children and I've worked with Dub for ten years."

"Still, Agent *Kerry*...that's what you're known as in Berlin...You won't mind if we follow the truck all the way to its destination. I gather it's on our route to Dublin and I'm sure your people won't mind waiting an extra hour or so."

"This plan keeps changing from one minute to the next," complained Sinéad.

"Perhaps so. But good commanders know that you have to adapt to circumstances. I cannot lose that cargo so I'm afraid I trust no one until it's in the safe hands of Arthur Joyce in Malahide."

Without waiting for an agreement, Weber returned to the other side of the road and crouched as he watched his precious boxes being loaded onto the lorry. Sinéad and Henning removed Dennehy's corpse and with some difficulty squeezed it into the boot of the Austin then tidied up the interior of the car as much as was possible without water.

After a further twenty minutes, Dub and Danny lifted the tailgate and entered the cabin of the lorry, ready for departure.

One hundred or so yards away, an officer of the *Garda Síochána* had appeared and was busily trying both to listen to the several and varied accounts of what had happened at the gatehouse while writing down what sense he could make of it.

Smiling, Weber watched as Dub steered the lorry out of the eastern gate, far from the gaze of official eyes other than old Eddie who waved them through.

*If only they knew the fortune they carried...if only they knew!*

# CHAPTER TWELVE

Dub drove the lorry onwards to Malahide unaware that some distance behind him, Weber was following in the Austin. After several miles, Danny suggested to Dub that they pull over.

"'*Straight* there,' was what Sinéad said."

"Sure, but I'd love to see what's in them boxes."

"No, Danny. We have our orders."

Danny's voice lowered to a growl. "Stop the feckin' lorry at the side of the road. I need to pee!"

Reluctantly, Dub slowed and pulled over permitting Danny to exit, make his way to the rear of the vehicle and climb up over the tailboard. Just as he gathered himself on the back of the lorry, Weber pulled the Austin up behind the vehicle and stepped out, holding Danny's gaze.

"You were told to take this lorry directly to Malahide. No stopping."

"This is a toilet break," said Danny unconvincingly.

"Not in the rear of the lorry it isn't. Step down and do your business at the side of the road. Conceal yourself from Miss O'Grady."

Danny complied as Weber spoke through the window to Sinéad.

"I am unimpressed by the professionalism of you and your staff. First, one shoots another then a second tries to open my cargo. You vouched for your men."

"And I still do Mr Weber. They are good men. Don't jump to suppositions."

"My dear Miss O'Grady. You are young and naive. Too young to hold the responsibilities you do!"

He turned his attentions to Danny who had reappeared at the back of the lorry.

"We will follow you until you carry out your orders. I can no longer trust you."

Danny glowered at him but retook his passenger seat as the lorry recommenced its journey uneventfully to Malahide where Weber saw the vehicle safely ensconced in a lock-fast garage supervised by estate owner, Arthur Joyce who greeted the German General as if he were royalty.

"I have had cause to be concerned at the professionalism I have experienced since I arrived in Ireland, Mr. Joyce," complained Weber. "I know you to be a faithful supporter of the Third *Reich* and expect you to guard this vehicle with your life until I return tomorrow."

"Have no worries, General. I'll place a trusted guard, my butler Hennessy, outside this door until you return. He will be armed and he knows how to use a pistol as he was heavily involved in our Easter Rising almost thirty years ago."

Noticing an upturn in Weber's right eyebrow and acknowledging to himself that his old retainer didn't appear at first glance to be particularly lithe or menacing, he continued in explanation.

"Hennessy here was very young when he was involved. He can be nasty if the situation warrants!"

Although not persuaded, Weber saw little option but to accept the security measures vouchsafed by Joyce. He turned to Danny and Dub.

"You two must catch a bus to Dublin immediately. You have your own orders but if you deviate from them one more time and attempt to interfere with my cargo I will simply shoot you on the spot. No questions!"

He looked at a crestfallen Dub and a somewhat less contrite Danny.

"Am I clear?"

Both men nodded and began their walk to the road-end just outside the estate.

"We must now meet your senior officers, Miss O'Grady. Let's go."

A further hour saw them arrive in O'Connell Street in the heart of Dublin. Following Sinéad's directions, they drove on to a house in Dolphin's Barn in Rialto on the south-west outskirts of Dublin next to St. Kevin's Hospital which attracted Henning's attention as they passed.

Sinéad took back control. "Leave Dennehy in the boot. We're late enough as it is."

Weber saw a curtain twitch in an upstairs room window. Their arrival had been noticed.

Weber, Sinéad and Henning exited the car, Weber straightening his tie and putting on his overcoat despite the clement weather.

Moving directly from the side of the car to the opened front door of a Georgian house five steps away, the three entered and were called upstairs by a young man standing on the half-landing holding a sub-machine gun.

"Up here!"

Weber took the lead and walked up the stairs to a room within which were three men. Two who were standing wore shabby suits while the other, a burly man in his sixties who sat behind a table, was in shirt sleeves.

No attempt was made to shake hands and no introductions were made until Sinéad entered and bid them hello. Weber sat on a wooden chair directly in front of the man in shirt sleeves. Sinéad and Henning stood behind him.

"Tadhg...Frannie...Joseph," she exclaimed. "This is Professor Kurt Weber..." And then almost apologetically, reading their response to his academic appellation... "But he's also a German General!

"You must forgive us Mister Weber, but we must be very careful. There are many spies around"

"Presumably that's why you have a revolver in your hand below the table, you have a man outside with an automatic pistol and across the road a further two men armed with pistols stand guard."

"We have to be alert and professional, Mister Weber."

"Not so alert and professional to notice that I *too* have a revolver in my coat pocket, and is pointed directly at you, Mister..?"

Joseph Kelly brought his revolver from beneath the table and placed it before him before pushing it to one side, gesturing a truce.

"We'll get to names later on. Where's Dec Dennehy?"

Sinéad intervened. "He's dead, Joseph. When we were leaving the docks at Drogheda someone shot him in the car. We escaped and circled around to see if it looked like the *Gardai* or the Brits or someone but there was no obvious activity."

She looked uncomfortable. "We kind of wondered whether it might not have been Liam Kennedy. The two of them were at loggerheads since Liam's brother was killed and he blamed Dennehy. He was cursing him all the way across the Irish Sea from the Isle of Man."

"Was the shooting witnessed?"

"No, Joseph. But Liam was armed, he hated Declan and would have been able to position himself for a shot while we were making ready to leave the docks."

Kelly nodded and turned to Tadhg O'Brian. "We'd better question him anyway. Phone Drogheda and have him brought to this place so we can ask him some questions."

O'Brian left the room. Kelly sat back in his chair and puffed at his pipe before pointing the mouthpiece at Henning.

"Who's this?"

"My colleague, Doctor Hermann Henning. He is a physician and will care for members of staff at the Legation and German nationals who are interned here in Ireland."

Kelly acknowledged him and returned to the business in hand.

"So you're a professor *and* a general?"

"In the Waffen SS"

"The SS? I've heard that your boys can be a bit nasty."

"War is a nasty business. But I am a fighting man. My troops were disciplined. I can't speak for other commands."

"So now you're over here to help the IRA?"

"Yes. But I'm being attached to the German Legation in Dublin under Dr. Eduard Hempel. He will not be made aware of any relationship I might have with the IRA."

"What'll he think you're doing over here?"

"He'll believe me to be investing in the Irish economy against the day that the war ends. And I'll be doing a lot of that...but I'll also be interested in assisting you gentlemen if you continue your efforts to strike at the heart of England."

"Well, we'll be doing that sure enough, God willing. And you might be in a position to get us arms?"

"If we get on well and you improve your performance. I have been distinctly unimpressed by your soldiers since I arrived. And I did not expect to be met by a woman...certainly not a young and inexperienced woman. In Germany, we believe that it is the *men* who do the fighting"

Kelly smiled. "Ah, but, Professor General...or is it General Professor? We find that that is exactly what the forces of the *crown* think, as well as our own Irish *Gardai*. Sinéad here is tougher than she looks. She's no shy little pickaheen. Recently she was ordered to dispatch a comrade who was informin' on us and I'm told that she took care of this without so much as blinking an eye. So don't you go falling out with her. As well as being a Volunteer, she's also my niece and she'll be your contact over here so I'd be grateful if you'd allow us the benefit of assumin' that we know what we're doing."

Sinéad looked at the floor as Weber sighed. "We'll discuss this later. I have to be smuggled onto the docks at *Dún Laoghaire* to permit my tale of arriving on a Portuguese Coaster to stand scrutiny."

"And so you shall Professor General. But before we attend to that, you need know only *my* name, Joseph Kelly, at your service, and that of my young niece Sinéad O'Grady here who will be our link person. And you and your pal are?"

Weber rose to his feet. This is Dr. Hermann Henning, my physician. And I am *Obergruppenführer* Kurt Weber of the *Waffen SS*. True, before the war I was a professor but I confess I can scarcely remember those days. The man who stands before you today is schooled in the arts of warfare rather than history, which was my discipline. But once I emerge from the docks at *Dún Laoghaire* I am expected to behave as a diplomat, so please bear that in mind if you wonder about my future motives or behaviours. I was briefed in Germany that Joseph Kelly and Agent *Kerry* here were exceptional people so I must trust that information, even if in regard to Miss O'Grady it is with reservations, since my personal survival and the future of the Third *Reich* may depend on it!"

Kelly leaned back in his chair and shook his head.

"Jesus, you can be terrible serious, professor."

He picked up his revolver and put it in the jacket he had draped over the back of the chair as a prelude to ending the conversation.

"The Portuguese coaster, the *São Marcos* isn't due until late tomorrow afternoon, so I suggest you three sleep here tonight. We have plenty of room. I'll need to pay some attention to Liam Kennedy when they bring him down from Drogheda but we've a few hours to kill until then. Tell ye what, Sinéad, why don't we take the professor and the doctor for a pint and get to know one another a bit better?"

He turned to Henning. "Have you the English language, doctor?"

"I speak English fluently, Mr. Kelly."

"Then we're in good shape."

Sinéad interjected.

"I'd arranged to meet Dub and Danny in the Palace Bar for a glass once our business here was done but if they see you walking in they'll imagine they're for the high jump."

"Sign of a guilty conscience, Sinéad. Let's go."

Sinéad's assessment of the reaction of her two fellow Volunteers was proved accurate.

After affectionately embracing the Widow Ryan, the proprietress and ensuring that she, Henning and Weber were served with their drink of choice in the front bar, Kelly stepped first into the back room of the Palace Bar and noted with some satisfaction that upon seeing him, both Dub and Danny held their pints of stout motionless at their lips; frozen in apprehension.

Allowing a smile to his lips only after some moments of blank recognition, Kelly became the life and soul of the gathering as a relaxed air settled on the company.

Weber, used more to sipping at a glass of *schnapps*, accepted Irish whiskey as a substitute and marvelled openly to Henning at the ability of the three Irishmen to quaff pints of dark stout at a bewildering rate. Sinéad, he noticed, kept up the pace of her colleagues if not the quantities consumed by drinking a half pint to each of their full measures. He noticed too, how despite swallowing quantities of beer that would have felled lesser mortals, Kelly managed to ease the events on the dock at Drogheda into the conversation, returning now and again obliquely to ask the same questions in different form, always affably, always exuding empathy for the *travails* of his two men. Repeatedly he stressed the positive, drawing attention to the safe delivery of the 'General Professor' and his cargo.

Sympathising with the demise of 'poor Dec', he managed to have Dub and Danny talk round the circumstances of the shooting several times, probing any inconsistencies and listening intently to their responses; all the time puffing on his pipe like an elderly uncle.

Weber smiled inwardly. *My old professor of philosophy at university told me he never learned anything when it was he who was doing the talking. Seems Mr. Kelly takes the same approach. The man listens well. Not a common ability.*

Where Weber's professor and Kelly differed, however, was the ease with which Kelly managed to flit between concerned questioning, reassuring comments and boisterous storytelling. *I can see why he's a leader, thought Weber. He's smart, even when roaring drunk! And he has a face that keeps secrets well.*

After three hours of enthusiastic drinking which promised to lead to singing, Kelly brought the proceedings to a halt by downing three quarters of the pint he held in his hand in one swallow and indicating to Dub and Danny that they should stay but that the four others had business to conduct elsewhere.

In the presence of Kelly, Dub had forgotten his earlier resentment and was only too quick to dismiss the notion of any *possible* inconvenience if Weber retained the use of his car until he'd safely driven himself to the docks at *Dún Laoghaire* the following day.

Despite feeling somewhat giddy following his whiskey intake, Weber steered the car following Sinéad's directions and returned without incident to Dolphin's Bar at Rialto. On arrival, he again he noticed the two men standing now in shadows keeping watch on the premises at which he and the others were to stay the night.

Kelly barged ahead bellowing to his men as he climbed the stairs.

"Have we that fecker Kennedy here yet?"

Weber, Henning and Sinéad followed on until they entered the same room they'd been in earlier. Kennedy sat slumped in a chair, his arms tied to the rests on the chair, his face cut and bloody where a severe beating had been administered. His chin rested on his chest.

"He's denyin' everythin' Joseph," said Tadhg O'Brian who stood in his shirt sleeves, his hands bloodied.

Despite herself, Sinéad raised her hands to her mouth in horror. Kelly may have praised her casual insouciance in 'dispatching' Seamus only a few days earlier but she still found herself repulsed at violence.

"Let him keep till the morn,"slurred Kelly as the effects of his drinking became evident. "There'll be time enough for chat when we're more possessed of our faculties, eh professor?"

"As you say, Mr. Kelly."

"'Joseph' from now on, Kurt. Don't you think?"

"As you please, Joseph. Now where do we sleep? I'm tired."

Sinéad took over and escorted everyone to sleeping quarters in a manner that told Weber that she was used to being around this place where the senior staff of the IRA did business.

Morning came late as the previous evening's drinking took its toll. After a breakfast of bacon, eggs and sausage that surprised but delighted Weber and Henning who were used to the more basic foodstuffs available to combatant nations, the two men and Sinéad said their temporary farewells to Kelly who was in jolly mood.

"Everything's arranged, Kurt. Sinéad here's a good girl and'll look after the two of yous just fine. Once you're established in the Legation, Sinéad'll want to talk to you about an airdrop of weapons. But in the meantime, you better make good time if you want to be in place for the coaster. I'll have my hands full with Liam Kennedy here and sooner or later we'll find out what went on. My people took the body of poor Dec from Dub's car last night and we'll see that he gets a proper burial as befits a hero of the Republic. At least he didn't die behind English bars."

The three men shook hands as Sinéad stood back from the proceedings. They left for *Dún Laoghaire* and the formal arrival in Ireland of the new member of the German Legation in Dublin.

## Chapter Thirteen

The *São Marcos* docked at *Dún Laoghaire* on time and, with the help of local IRA Volunteers, Weber and Henning were spirited to the dockside where they were presented to the officials present as having just disembarked. Weber looked imposing. Henning, less so. Weber spoke for them both by presenting his credentials and advising that his companion had lost his belongings and papers overboard upon boarding but that he could vouch for him. Some minor head scratching took place but both were shortly acknowledged formally as having arrived in Ireland and were escorted to the same waiting Austin car that had deposited them at the dockside minutes earlier.

Weber drove again. In his view, it was not the done thing for a woman to drive a car.

Shrugging off his misogyny, Sinead mumbled. "I haven't learned to drive proper yet anyway...but I feckin' *will* soon enough"

Back in Dublin, Kelly had released Kennedy from his tethers and was sitting having a cup of tea with him exuding the same fraternal concern he'd exhibited in the Palace Bar the previous evening. He apologised for the behaviour of his men who had beaten him and prompted Kennedy to discuss the events of the previous day from the docking of the Trinity to the shooting of Dennehy.

Kennedy was in tears as he denied any involvement in the murder of his compatriot.

"Sure I hated the fecker, Joseph. Wouldn't *you* if your brother died at his hand? And I can't say I'm sad at his parting but I had nothing to do with the shooting. I went to the toilet block and saw all the commotion when I got back so I can't account for my whereabouts but just because I *could* have done it doesn't mean that I *did* do it. I'm a good Volunteer and have served you well over the piece."

"Sure you have that, Liam. You have that."

The two men talked back and forth, Kelly adopting the same gently inquisitorial approach he'd taken with Danny and Dub until he remembered a meeting he'd agreed to attend, leaving the field free for Tadhg O'Brian who took his jacket off as he entered the room.

In London, a secretary typed a message onto a simple piece of paper. It read, '*Information received that at 15.30hrs on 11 July 1944, Internee Declan Dennehy of IRA shot dead at Drogheda Docks after escape from Port Erin Internment Camp. Escape assisted by Axis Powers. Two senior officers of German Intelligence presumed now at large in Ireland. IRA complicit.*'

She hit the return arm of the typewriter, ringing a bell internal to the machine before drawing the paper from its roller-bed. Reading it again quickly to ensure there were no typing mistakes, she inserted it in a terracotta envelope marked 'Top Secret' and placed it in a basket at the side of her desk awaiting collection.

Half an hour later, at Sinéad's direction, Weber drew up at 58 Northumberland Road, south of the River Liffey, the home of the German Legation in Dublin. Outside the building stood four Irish police officers, obviously tasked with the state's protection of the Legation but also responsible for reporting all of the comings and goings of those who entered the building. A large flag bearing Nazi Germany's Swastika emblem fluttered in the breeze.

Weber entered, allowing Henning to carry his suitcase and was ushered in to meet Dr. Eduard Hempel, the Head of the German Legation, a tall man with a military bearing wearing perhaps the most vibrant yellow bow-tie that Weber had ever seen.

"Professor Weber. I trust your journey was not too traumatic."

"These days, Doctor Hempel, it is *Obergruppenführer* Weber. My professorship is long forgotten."

"Nevertheless, you are most welcome. And I am informed by telephone that you are accompanied on this trip by?"

"Doctor Hermann Henning." He waved at the younger, more dishevelled man who stood behind him.

"The *Abwehr* were concerned at German nationals and internees being subject to, and possibly influenced by the medical corps in Ireland. They simply preferred our men to be looked after by a German medic to avoid outside interference. Dr. Henning will care for Legation staff, their families and German internees"

"Most welcome," said Hempel shaking Henning's hand..."if an unusually thoughtful appointment for a nation at war. I'd have imagined that they'd want to have you accompanied by a cypher expert or perhaps a radio communications officer."

"Who can understand the tortuous thinking of our intelligence agency, Dr. Hempel?" smiled Weber, easing past Hempel's raised eyebrow.

The trio moved through to a drawing room where comfortable leather armchairs awaited them.

"I will make arrangements for you to present your credentials to the *Taoiseach* of Ireland, Éamon de Valera. He is a man with a difficult task as he requires politically to ensure that Ireland remains neutral. On the one hand, he requires substantial amounts of coal and animal foodstuffs from England. But again, he has to rebuff Churchill who wants the use of his Berehaven port for instance which would enable their anti-submarine escorts to operate a further two hundred miles out into the Atlantic. However, he is well aware, as are we, that enlistment in the British Army is very popular. Over forty thousand Irishmen have joined the armed forces or have gone to sea in the British Merchant Navy. De Valera's only reaction to this is that when these servicemen return home on leave they have to wear civilian clothes to avoid any embarrassment or he'll intern them as foreign combatants under international law. Thousands have gone to England to work in British munitions factories. Thousands of women have gone to England to work as nurses."

"Not very *neutral* as the word is defined in any dictionary that I've read, Dr. Hempel."

"As I say, *Obergruppenführer,* he has a difficult hand to play and in my mind, plays it very well."

Weber accepted an empty cup from a young woman who proceeded to fill it with a rich-smelling coffee. He savoured the moment.

"The Legation lives well, Dr. Hempel."

"We are indeed most fortunate that Ireland's bucolic traditions permit relatively good provisions of meat, dairy produce, breads and fish. We want for little...even the occasional beer and spirits are available," he smiled.

*Indeed,* thought Weber, not wishing to reveal that he had had partaken of some considerable quantity the previous evening.

"Now you bring some resources with you, *Obergruppenführer?*"

"I do, Dr. Hempel. And I will ensure that they are placed in a good, solid Irish bank shortly. You might guide me as to the most secure."

"Might I ask how much you'll be depositing?"

"Certainly you can ask, but I'm afraid I cannot advise you even of that. My mission here - beyond my cover of assisting you at the Legation - has to remain completely confidential, even from an officer as senior and celebrated as you, *Herr* doctor. I can tell you that the *Abwehr* are concerned to invest in the Irish economy and that I expect to spend a lot of time touring the country buying into businesses and properties that I believe would meet this purpose."

"That much I know, *Obergruppenführer.* And you have been given no further brief beyond that of which I've already been advised?"

"As a matter of fact, I have not but had I been asked to undertake additional tasks and had been ordered to maintain secrecy, you must be aware that I would do so," said Weber somewhat disingenuously.

"Nevertheless, despite our reasonably good relations with the *Taoiseach*, you can be assured that your activities will be closely followed by Irish Intelligence officers and members of the *Gardai*. I wouldn't be surprised if British Intelligence also took an interest in you. There are spies everywhere."

"They'll soon become bored. My business procurements will not be secret. Indeed I would expect them to feature in local newspapers so the Irish people can read of the benevolence of the Third *Reich*. Jobs are important to the Irish people during what they call their Emergency and with some judicious bolstering of the occasional failing business, I would expect us to be looked on as fairy godmothers."

"Quite," said Hempel admitting defeat. "Well, we have to get accommodation sorted out for you both. I have already organised a long term residency at a suite at the Shelbourne Hotel at St Stephen's Green not far from here. You will be looked after well there and can come and go as you please."

He turned to a peripheral Henning. "But you, doctor? I had no knowledge of your arrival."

"Please, Dr. Hempel, do not trouble yourself. I hope to find something near St. Kevin's Hospital out near Dolphin's Barn. It would allow me to maintain easy links with hospital staff there."

"And how would a recently arrived doctor in Dublin know about St.Kevin's proximity to Dolphin's Barn?"

Weber interjected as Henning looked nonplussed. "One of the ship's passengers was an Irish medic and he recommended the hospital. Tell, me Dr. Hempel," he said changing the subject abruptly "is my suite ready? I am tired and would like to bathe."

"Certainly, *Obergruppenführer.* I'll arrange a car to take you there immediately."

"Dr. Henning will stay with me for a couple of days until he can arrange something more appropriate."

"Very well."

The German car pulled up in front of the Shelbourne Hotel and Weber and Henning removed themselves from its rear. The driver stepped from the vehicle to collect Weber's case from the boot.

Satisfied that he couldn't be overheard, Weber spoke softly to Henning.

"Hermann, we have sufficient finances to ensure that you can be installed here at the Shelbourne for the duration."

"Thank you, Kurt, but no. I'm afraid I'm not cut out for your life of adventure and espionage. I would much prefer to stay close to the hospital where I might do some good and might even take up your suggestion, if it still stands, of looking after Germans over here in Ireland."

"Of course. Then you must allow me to pay you a stipend, Hermann. It would complement our little deceit...but the price of this, once again, is your word as a doctor and a gentleman that you will mention this little fabrication to no one and that you describe your work here precisely as I've explained it to Dr. Hempel."

Henning offered his hand to Weber. "I'm enormously grateful, Kurt. You need have no worries on my account. This story will go with me to the grave. Just leave me out of any violence."

Weber shook his hand warmly. "Then let's relax for a while in the hotel before going out to see something of our new city."

Henning looked embarrassed. "I've actually already arranged to meet your agent, Miss O'Grady in the Palace Bar tonight after dinner. She wants to know more about my role and I thought I could ask her about accommodation near St. Kevin's."

Weber smiled. "Why my dear Dr. Henning. I do believe you're interfering with the proper conduct of my duties here in Ireland."

"I...but...I assure you..." blustered Henning.

Weber laughed. "Have no fear, Hermann. You can spend as much time with young Miss O'Grady as you wish. I will see her just as much as my duties require. Otherwise, I think I might strangle her."

He put his arm round his younger colleague's shoulders.

"Now, let's get settled in the hotel."

Sinéad sat on the edge of the bed she'd slept in the previous night, lost in her thoughts when a quiet knock on her door made her jump. Opening the door, she saw it was Kelly and bid him enter.

"You startled me, Uncle Joseph. I was dreamin'."

"I hope you were dreamin' about the feckin' shooting," he growled.

"We're getting nowhere with Liam Kennedy and I'm not going to sanction takin' the life of a good Volunteer unless I can be sure he pulled the trigger. We've spoken to all the dockhands who'll talk to us. Nothin'! We've spoken with the crew of the Trinity. Nothin'!" He sat on a chair next to the curtained window and looked outside where still two men stood guard in the shadows.

"Maybe British Intelligence? Or our very own G-2 Military Intelligence? Maybe *An Garda Síochána* shot him. Maybe it was feckin' *suicide*?"

"Where is he now?"

"In a spare room. He's restin'. Tadhg O'Brian beat him pretty sore."

"Can I see him? Maybe he'll talk to me."

Kelly tugged the curtain closer to the middle of the window and sighed.

"It would do no harm."

Sinéad walked to the spare room and saw Kennedy lying on his back on the bed. His face was still bloody and swollen from the countless blows that had punctuated O'Brian's questioning. The room had a small sink so she wet a cloth and sat beside him on the bed bathing his face as best she could, bringing occasional groans from the semi-conscious sea captain.

*Poor sod*, she thought. *Only my word that it might have been him and he has to suffer this!* She continued mopping his brow, promising to herself that she'd be somewhat more circumspect in the future, when Kennedy opened his eyes. As if understanding instinctively what was in Sinéad's mind, he grabbed at her arm and gripped with a power that surprised her.

"Sinéad...by all that's holy...on the lives of my children...I had no part in any shooting. That's the God's truth. Please tell Joseph. Tell him to stop this. O'Brian's killing me. Please tell Joseph..."

His eyes were wide. Flecks of white mucus formed at the corners of his mouth. His grip on her arm strengthened.

"In God's name...tell Joseph before Tadhg kills me."

Sinéad placed her free hand atop Kennedy's which still gripped her arm.

"Just rest now, Liam. Joseph knows now it wasn't you. He asked me to come through and reassure you," she said, hoping she was not badly mistranslating Kelly's assessment.

Showing no sign of whether he'd understood the import of Sinéad's comments, Kennedy closed his eyes and the grip on her arm eased until unconsciousness took him.

Before heading into Dublin town centre to meet Henning in the Palace Bar, Sinéad watched Weber step from a taxi at the front door of the IRA safe house in Dolphin's Barn. Stepping out to meet him, she handed over the door-keys to Dub's car.

"And where are you going with this?"

"I'm afraid my destination is secret. You'll have the car back in the morning."

"Well, don't you scratch it or Dub will give me all sorts of nonsense."

"You go and see Dr. Henning and enjoy yourself. I'll be back shortly."

Sinéad was indignant. "Sure I don't know what you mean, 'enjoy yourself', General. I'm only going to find out what skulduggery you two are up to. There's no enjoyment in that I assure you."

"If you say so, Miss O'Grady. If you say so."

Sinéad was about to frame a response she intended would be scathing but Weber just smiled and seated himself in the car. In seconds it was at the end of the road and off to its destination before she could muster a retort.

After turning a few corners, Weber stopped, observed the rear-view mirror for some time then consulted the map he'd poured over in the safety of his hotel room. Carefully he traced his finger to ensure that he knew by heart the route he intended taking to the estate owned by Arthur Joyce. He couldn't allow the lorry carrying more riches than anyone might imagine remaining protected only by Joyce's butler Hennessy one moment longer than was necessary. He drove off, stopping, waiting and watching three times to ensure that he wasn't being followed before heading directly for Malahide.

In the genteel community of Ballsbridge on the southern outskirts of Dublin, Captain Giles Carter-Hogg recently appointed to the British Embassy in Ireland as a member of the British Secret Intelligence Service stubbed out a cigarette and set down the photograph of his wife of five months and their newborn baby. Reaching into his trouser pocket, he withdrew his wallet and returned the photograph before picking up the next piece of paperwork.

Rubbing the tiredness from his eyes, he opened the envelope and read a message to the effect that a senior member of the IRA, one Declan Dennehy had been shot in Drogheda. *Hmm*, he thought, *that confirms the report we had from our Gardai sources. Didn't realise he was such a big fish, though.* He lit another cigarette, allowing the smoke to escape from between gritted teeth with a *hissss* and coughed. *Idiot*, he brooded. *Shot the wrong man! Silly chap!*

## Chapter Fourteen

On her own, Sinéad drank less than when in the company of her thirstier IRA colleagues. Sitting in the dark wooded parlour of the Palace Bar with Henning, she sipped at her glass of stout while Henning attempted to manufacture a taste for the black ale that seemed to be consumed so ubiquitously in Ireland.

"I confess, it's an acquired taste," said Henning with a smile.

"Ah, drink enough and you'll soon be lovin' it as much as the boys. It's grand stuff!"

The two spoke softly. The shooting...the car chase. Sinéad was obviously interested in Henning's involvement in the German mission and a number of times probed on the issue of his spontaneous decision to throw his lot in with Weber.

"So you were just a normal doctor in Liverpool and the Brits interned you because you were cheeky to some magistrate?"

"That's about it. I just wanted to serve the needs of the ill and these fools decided I should spend my days in an internment camp rather than look after their sick and elderly. A very foolish decision."

"And that's what you want to do now, is it?"

"But certainly. I'm not cut out for the kind of life that you and Kurt Weber have. I'd like to help at the hospital if it's possible and Kurt has asked me to look after the health of a few nationals at the Legation. That would take no time at all and would bore me senseless. Perhaps there's more to do looking after those German nationals who are interned in Ireland although I doubt I'd provide better healthcare that the Irish Army."

"But that's it? You're a medic. Not a soldier. Not one of Weber's spies?"

Henning shook his head. "Well, I don't think I should be discussing Kurt's work here in Ireland. Besides, I know really nothing about it." He sipped again at the pint of Guinness, grimacing as he did so.

"My next drink is your Irish whiskey. I'm afraid your stout is defeating my taste buds." He changed the subject to one of his choosing.

"So, tell me Miss O'Grady, can you help find me accommodation and have you any way of introducing me to the hospital?"

"Well, there's a small place I have in Kilmainham, not far from the place the Volunteers use in Dolphin's Barn. My Uncle Thomas owns it...owned it...he died last year and I stay there when I'm up in Dublin and I've a spare room. You could rent that."

"Miss O'Grady, that would be marvellous...and I can pay well. Kurt has offered me a stipend so you could have some extra cash for everyday needs."

"Just the usual will be fine, Dr. Henning. All of my needs are met by the farm I have in Tralee and my out-of-pocket expenses are taken care of by the Army Council."

"And the hospital?"

"I know people. I'm sure they could use an extra pair of hands - especially if they're not paying for your services."

Henning raised his pint of Guinness in a toast and smiled.

"Well, if you're to become my landlady, perhaps I'd better learn to drink this foul concoction and you could start calling me Hermann."

"You drink what you want and Doctor Henning will suffice, thank you. As will Miss O'Grady. We hardly know one another and it would be improper to become too familiar."

Normally shy in the company of ladies, Henning's face fell as his timid advance was rebuffed by his new landlady. Nevertheless, he ignored the rebuke and raised his glass in acknowledgement of his good fortune.

*"Ein Toast!...Prost!"*

Sinéad lifted her glass in response.

*"Slàinte!"* Good Health!"

Hennessy the butler stood erect as the headlights of Weber's car illuminated the hedgerow that followed the contour of the single-track road that led from the main thoroughfare to his master's grand manor-house.

Stepping behind a carved stone pillar, he awaited the arrival of the vehicle which crunched onto the gravel at the front of the mansion and stopped only feet from his hide. Nervously, he cocked the ancient pistol he'd been given to protect the unimaginable wealth which, unknown to him, was loaded in boxes in the rear of the lorry.

A dark shape emerged from the car which appeared to resemble that of the German officer he'd been told to expect. Taking no chances, Hennessy challenged him.

"If you take one more step, I'll blow your feckin' head off," he said in a very unbutler-like fashion.

Weber stopped and raised his hands. "Now might that be Mr. Hennessy, Mr. Joyce's butler? If so, you have no need of the weapon I assume you're holding. I am Kurt Weber. You are guarding my lorry."

"Step into the light," said Hennessy switching on a lamp.

Weber stepped forward and opened his palms, shoulder high to show he was not carrying arms.

"Has my lorry been interfered with?"

"No, sir," said Hennessy, returning to a tone and a role with which he was more familiar.

"Then please take me to Mr. Joyce. Then return here until I come back."

"Certainly sir."

Weber grasped Hennessy by his elbow and spoke to him earnestly.

"And thank you, Mr. Hennessy. You are every bit the warrior that Mr. Joyce promised you would be. I am in your debt." He bowed his head respectfully.

Hennessy grew some inches in stature as he led Weber up the steps of the mansion to meet Arthur Joyce. *Aye, please God, I've still got what it takes. Still got it.*

In Ballsbridge, Captain Giles Carter-Hogg lit another cigarette from the one he was about to extinguish. He read from another note he'd been passed. *So the bastards killed a nurse and a sentry in Port Erin?* He dragged at the cigarette. *And there's now two of them over here in cahoots with the IRA and one of them's got a lorry full of something or other hidden away in the estate of Arthur Joyce just outside Malahide?* He paused and lifted his pen. *What do we know and what do we not?*

He wrote a series of notes in a column on a sheet of paper in front of him, pursed his lips in contemplation and coughed gloriously.

Kurt Weber shook the hand of Arthur Joyce and bowed his head in salute. Joyce waved him to an armchair and both men sat.

"I am in your debt, Mr. Joyce. Your butler, Hennessy informs me that my lorry remains as I left it."

"Nothing has been touched, *Obergruppenführer*. I am only too pleased to be of assistance to the Third *Reich*. I am a great admirer of the *Fuehrer*. He is a great man. Tell me, have you met him?"

Joyce's face fell somewhat as Weber told him that he had not and the two men continued to engage in small talk until some minutes later, Weber called attention to his time constraints having first established formally that no one knew of his visit that night except Hennessy.

"I must apologise, Mr. Joyce. You have been of great service but I must now take the contents of the lorry to the place you have guaranteed to my superiors is more safe even than here. My contacts in the IRA have told me that there are spies everywhere so the sooner this is moved, the sooner I can begin to behave as a normal diplomat."

"Of course, *Obergruppenführer*. I have a map which I drew myself. The property was purchased a year ago and is possessed of a large barn which will hide the lorry with ease. It is also off the beaten track and never receives any visitors. The farmers round about are all sympathetic to the IRA and are aware of my purchase of the land. No one will trouble you." He handed over a pencilled sketch of a map which gave directions to a farm some twenty miles away.

"I'd burn it after memorising it."

Weber read the map and consulted the large scale map he'd used earlier to find the Malahide estate in the dark. After a few moments he indicated his satisfaction and put the sketched map inside his coat feeling for the pistol he'd placed in his inside pocket. He looked at Joyce who seemed to gaze upon him almost in reverence, and considered the orders he'd been given;

*Upon receipt of the map giving directions to the second location, shoot Joyce and any others who might be aware of the proximity of the gold. No one must be aware of the location of the gold except you.*

Thumbing the trigger on the pistol in his coat pocket, he glanced again at Joyce who still looked on him with innocent trust and admiration.

"Excuse me, Mr. Joyce. May I make use of your facilities before I leave?"

"Of course, *Obergruppenführer*. Back through the door you came in and it's just on the left."

Weber left and entered the bathroom. When inside, he took the pistol and checked it. Satisfied, he placed it in his coat pocket and returned to the drawing room. Joyce stood, hands clasped in front of him, head slightly bowed, every pore trying to convey deep respect. Offering his hand to Joyce, Weber shook it one more time.

"Mr. Joyce. I am in your debt."

Turning on his heel, he left the room and made his way down the steps where a still vigilant butler stood guard over the lorry."

"Thank you once again, Mr Hennessy. You are a match for any of the young troops I have commanded!"

Weber stepped up into the cab of the lorry which started immediately he tugged at the Bakelite ignition pull-switch. He waved at the butler as he reversed. *I'm not sure if I'm cut out for this espionage business. My first order and I've broken it already. Shooting good men? I'd rather wager that my trust in them is justified!*

He waved again...*But perhaps some precautions?*

An hour later, Weber peered ahead where the dim headlights picked up a sign which read, 'Dunboyne Farm'. He consulted the map once more. *Found it!*...and drove along the farm track to the barn which was located exactly where Joyce had shown on the map. But instead of driving the lorry under cover, Weber took a flashlight from the cab and walked past the farm buildings. After stumbling about in the field for some time, he came upon a small pool which was still being used by some quacking ducks and had evidently been used by cattle in those days when the farm was a working entity.

Returning to the vehicle, he drove carefully as close to the pond as possible and reversed to the edge of the nearby small track, grateful that the dry weather permitted him to do so without leaving tyre tracks. Upon drawing the hand-brake, he stepped out and removed his coat. Pulling at the buttons, he removed first his shirt and jacket, then his shoes and socks and finally his heavy twill trousers. *Now we see if I've lost any of my strength over the past weeks drinking schnapps and eating rich food.* Naked, he took the first case from the rear of the lorry and grunted as he lifted it...*One*...he counted to himself as he walked across the field and waded into the shallow pond up to his groin, depositing the gold in its middle with a splash. He returned to the lorry. *That wasn't too difficult!*... He lifted a second box...*Two...*

After forty minutes during which the boxes were removed increasingly slowly as he tired, Weber put his hands on his knees and caught his breath. He gently arched his back and stretched his aching muscles to relieve his pain then stepped up into the lorry and counted the cases remaining, reassuring himself that he had counted the nineteen boxes in the pond accurately. He placed two suitcases full of paper currency in the cabin and left two cases of gold, each containing four gold ingots, on the bed of the lorry before climbing back into the driver's seat and slowly driving the vehicle back to the barn. Five more minutes covering the two boxes in the rear with hay and he was spent. He looked at his watch. *Three-thirty. Perhaps a few hours sleep and then a walk into the village.* He nodded agreement at his own proposition and climbing back into his dry clothes, lay on the hay atop the most expensive bed in Ireland. His infantry experience of resting anywhere when an opportunity presented itself came into its own and in a few minutes he was asleep.

Carter-Hogg blinked wearily at his handwritten notes and asked himself whether matters could wait until morning. The information he'd been given was usually reliable and if he moved now, he might be able at least to observe the two German agents and perhaps have a look at the contents of the vehicle they were using. However, he'd not had had time to establish any kind of a plan and would be flying by the seat of his pants. Wait, however and they could disappear into the ether. Another long drag on his cigarette persuaded him at least to do some further research. He reached into a drawer, took a map of Ireland from its rear and flattening it on his desk with his palm, opened it. *Malahide...Malahide...*Still unfamiliar with local geography, his nicotine-stained index finger traced communities around the edge of Dublin until he came across the village he was looking for. *Other side of Dublin,* he thought. *Perhaps an hour away.* He reflected further and, picking up the map, walked along a corridor to the night-watchman, the senior officer on duty.

"Sorry to trouble you, old chap but I've received a transmission about that killing in Drogheda. We've had it confirmed by our man 'Valiant' that it was a senior officer in the IRA. Chap called Declan Dennehy. Know him?"

Edward Timpson took the note from his junior and read it, sipping from a glass as he did so. Although it was the middle of the night Timpson was known to enjoy regular consumption of red wine through until dawn. 'Helps me think,' he'd say to the junior officers who remarked upon his appetite. His superiors knew both his talents and his limitations and had given him the night shift in order to keep him out of harm's way. Edward Timpson had been kept out of harm's way for five years now and although he was regarded first as a depressive and now as a functioning alcoholic, he served a purpose. He knew Dublin. He knew Dubliners and had a web of informants with whom he'd shared drink over the years. He was worth the problems he caused occasionally.

"Know Joyce well. He's a Nazi sympathiser, a Republican and hates England with a vengeance. Funds the IRA. Very wealthy man, right enough. All inherited. Never done an honest day's work in his life." He sipped again at his glass. "I attended a function at his manor house once as a guest of another chap. Must say, the man has a very impressive wine cellar," he said, almost as if to permit his other characteristics to be overlooked. "I also know Dennehy. Good man of strong convictions... unfortunately, not ours. Shame he's gone. We could have worked with him."

"So, do we take a wander out there and see if we can't nab those two Germans and see what's in their lorry?"

Timpson laid his wine glass gently on his desk.

"My dear boy. They could have the place surrounded by Volunteers. They could have field guns trained at the entrance. We can't just stroll up and ask for an audience with Mr. Joyce. If it went sour on us I'd have a lot of explaining to do to your new wife and baby back home in Windsor."

He looked out of a darkened window for some moments before deciding.

"No, Captain. Write this up as a report for me. Do some work on the layout of the Joyce estate. Handwritten. I'll add to it at seven o'clock and we'll have it typed up for the Division Head for the nine o'clock meeting."

"No chance they'll escape, sir?"

"Every chance, my dear boy. But our first duty is not to embarrass His Majesty, King George so we don't go blundering into situations we haven't thought through. Now, be a good chap and bring me through a bottle of that delicious red that I've laid down in the kitchen before you start on your report. I've allowed it to breathe long enough".

## CHAPTER FIFTEEN

As might have been predicted by the experienced if inebriated Timpson, Britain's secret service merely determined to 'keep an eye' on the Joyce estate in the hope of seeing something which might encourage further attention. Very aware of the suspicion in which British forces were held in Ireland, His Majesty's Government took some care not to offend their hosts. None of the staff employed in the British Embassy in Ballsbridge would ever admit to being a secret agent of the crown but no one in de Valera's administration was under any doubt that Britain had a network of spies and 'n'er do wells' who would take such action as they deemed necessary against the Irish state should they believe it to be in Britain's interest. However, there was no point in acting precipitately and British Embassy officials agreed that a watching brief might be all that was necessary at present. So they placed a man in the grounds of the estate, just behind the tree line but by the time he'd taken up his position, he had nothing to observe but the rather mundane existence of an ageing Irish landowner and his staff caring for a tired and rather dilapidated mansion and its gardens.

A tired and dishevelled Weber had earlier walked to the nearest village and caught a daybreak bus back to

Dublin. Before leaving, he'd hidden the two suitcases in the loft of the barn for later collection but in the absence of a shovel had left the canvas bags of gold coins strewn on the bed of the truck covered in hay. *If ever I have need of resources to make my escape, these might assist in persuading others to help,* he thought.

Weber marvelled at the clear air and the gentle landscape as the old bus bumped and swayed its way back in the early morning light to the city. Sitting in the rear of the vehicle with only an old man and woman for company, he noticed the considerable number of farmsteads that were up for sale; hotels, too and pubs. Many of the unoccupied public houses seemed not to have been missed terribly as several others were open and situated in the same single thoroughfare which constituted the village. However, one or two appeared to have been the only watering hole in the place, might well benefit from some investment and could reasonably expect to enjoy some local custom. *I must keep these in mind as possible acquisitions. I'll soon need to turn my attention to these matters.*

It took him until around ten o'clock to arrive back at his hotel and a further hour to bathe and shave sufficient to allow himself to view the man in the mirror as being ready to undertake his first day's work in the Legation. The mild air permitted him to walk very comfortably to the Legation where his first task upon greeting Dr. Hempel was to ask for the Legation's car.

"I'll only be a couple of hours, Dr. Hempel. But I would be happier if the cash resources with which I've been entrusted are secured first within these walls and then in a number of solid Irish banks."

"I'm sure you'll be very popular, *Herr* Weber."

His inquisitiveness got the better of him.

"Are they currently quite secure? You don't need the assistance of any other member of the Legation?"

"Thanks, but no, doctor." He nodded respectfully as he stood to leave.

"I will return shortly."

Driving to Dunboyne Farm, Weber again stopped and waited several times to ensure no one was following him. Initially, a car had taken the same road as he had but upon reaching the edge of the city, it peeled off and headed in another direction. After an hour's driving, he pulled up outside the barn where the lorry remained hidden. A cursory check was all that was needed to establish that the gold coins still lay untouched beneath the hay. Stepping down, he retrieved the two suitcases and opened each of them to ensure that there had been no tampering of the monies contained within. A rusty shovel, he'd acquired from the Legation permitted him to bury the gold coins remaining in the soft earth next to the barn. He returned and locked the vehicle.

A noise outside caused him to freeze and listen carefully but after some moments he decided that a bird or perhaps vermin had disturbed something. Nevertheless, as he rose to investigate, he held his pistol in his hand ready for action. Checking the barn and its surroundings, edging round corners and peering into some outhouses satisfied him that only his imagination had been troubled and placing the two suitcases in the rear seat of the Legation's car, he began the return journey back to Dublin.

Shortly after lunch, Weber, with the permission of Dr. Hempel had commandeered seven of the staff of the Legation and under the stern supervision of a close functionary of the Head of the Legation, they counted and sorted the money, splitting it into Dollars, Sterling, Pesetas, Swiss Francs and other currencies until around six o'clock in the evening, a value of some three million Irish Punts had been determined.

Hempel was anxious. "But, *Herr* Weber, this is a fortune. I am most anxious about money in these quantities being held here in the Legation."

"Well, the banks will be shut *Herr* Doctor."

"Then I insist that you remain here tonight and stand guard over these two containers. I will not accept responsibility for these amounts."

"I'm perfectly happy to do that, doctor. And in the morning, perhaps you'll escort me to three Irish banks and we'll deposit a million Punts in each of them."

Weber's reasonableness won Hempel over and his thoughts turned to other matters of a practical nature.

"I assume that I'll be a joint signatory on these monies?"

"No, Dr. Hempel. You will not. However, in the event of my being unable to access these funds though death or injury, I have prepared a letter and will tonight make two others which I will hand to the manager of each bank transferring my responsibilities for the accounts to you. I'm sure you'll agree that that arrangement permits me to carry out my mission without hindrance while also providing comfort to you that the funds will not be open to misuse or sterility if I am unable to complete my task."

Hempel nodded his agreement.

"That will be satisfactory."

Doctor Henning was a happy man.

His new landlady, Miss O'Grady had that day arranged for him to meet a senior doctor in St Kevin's Hospital who, Henning assumed, was not uninvolved in Irish Republicism and after a half hour chat over a cup of tea, he had been informed that even in the absence of written proof of his credentials, he was obviously a fine doctor and could assist Dr. Fitzgerald in his work at the hospital. Acknowledging his work for the Legation and for German nationals, Dr. Fitzgerald agreed that his responsibilities need only be addressed on three days a week.

A timid knock on his bedroom door admitted Sinéad who wanted to know of the outcome of his meeting with her Dr. Fitzgerald. Excitedly, Henning told her of his success.

"Good. I thought as much. And what of your room here? Is it worth the rent I'm charging you?"

Henning looked round at the somewhat bare room which contained nothing but a bed, a chair and a small set of drawers presently empty of contents. A fireplace contained some sticks; unlit.

"Every *pfennig*. I'm so very grateful."

Sinéad softened. "Well, if you're that grateful, perhaps you can buy me a glass in the pub round the corner tonight; the Patriot's Inn…it's not as grand as the Palace Bar in the city but it has a big log fire and will save me heating this place up this evening."

Henning stood mouth agape and said nothing leading Sinéad to anticipate a rejection and to further enhance the attraction.

"There's good music as well. Fiddle and whistles."

At last some connection took place between Henning's brain and his vocal chords.

"But...but...Miss O'Grady. I should be delighted. Simply delighted!"

"Then that's good. First, I'll stick on some soup for us to sup before we go out. You should know as a medical man that you shouldn't drink on an empty stomach."

She entered the small kitchen and shouted from its interior.

"We've only use of the gas cookers for six hours a day. There's a Government man sent around to check the use of the gas we're makin' in our homes ever since the Brits restricted our supply. We call him the Glimmer Man because we try to leave the gas on the 'glimmer', the pilot light, to keep the pot of water hot for tea or a slow cook but we'll chance our luck, eh, Doctor?"

"Of course, Miss O'Grady. That would be wonderful."

"And don't get any big ideas Dr. Henning, we're meeting Danny and Dub tonight before they head back to Tralee so this is just us saving some heat."

She smiled. "I'm just being desperate nice, d'you see?"

As he watched her make preparations in the kitchen through the open door, Henning could but appreciate her slim build, dark hair and impossibly pretty face. *She has such a lovely smile,* he told himself. *She should smile more often.*

◆ ◆ ◆

As the doctor and his landlady prepared to eat then step out for a drink in the local pub, on the other side of Dublin, Weber bit on some bread and pushed his chair back from the table before resting his feet on its surface. Underneath were two suitcases filled with money to the value of three million Punts. *I will be relieved when we get that amount into the banks tomorrow*, he thought. *And then I can get down to the serious business of spending it on properties and businesses that one day might be run by officers of the Third Reich.* He mused further on his task and pursed his lips as he swayed between personal preference and practical consideration. *Hmmm, I might have to make use of young Miss O'Grady. I expect that some businesses will be easier to deal with if it's she who fronts the purchase instead of me. I'll speak with her once the money's safe.*

Danny and Dub were surprised when Sinéad brought Henning into the small bar.

"Why's the German here?" asked Danny uncharitably.

"Well, for starters, he's my new tenant for the minute. And he's working at St. Kevin's looking after the great unwashed of Dublin so don't be giving him a hard time. Try and be a decent person for once in your sad life."

Dub stood up. "Sure, you're very welcome, doctor. Now let me get some pints in. We're nearly done here. Is it two pints of Guinness then?"

Henning waved his hand and forced a smile. "Thank you, Dub, but I've decided I'm a whisky man now. And I've a preference for Scotch over your Irish whiskey if you don't mind."

"And I'll just have a glass of porter, Dub", said Sinead, using the Irish expression for half a pint.

Dub moved off to the bar and Henning sat next to a log fire awaiting his whisky. *Life is strange, indeed,* he thought as he observed Danny and Sinéad chatting, Dub organising the drinks midst laughter and banter in the small pub. He warmed his hands at the fire and considered his lot. He'd found a comfortable enough billet with a landlady who was not entirely the most unattractive or uninteresting woman he'd ever met, he'd fixed a job with the local hospital and was being paid handsomely...better than he could ever have imagined for looking after the health of his interned countrymen and those in the Legation. He could see the war out comfortably without compromising his principles. *And Weber seems a nice person too,* he mused. Most of all, he wasn't being held against his wishes in a British Internment Camp.

A man in a rough tweed jacket and a flat cap stood alone at the end of the bar and raised his pint shoulder-high in a toast to the world in general. He closed his eyes and spoke a poem loud, slurring his words;

> "And what, says Cathal Brugha,
> If the last man's on the ground,
> If he's lying weak and helpless
> And his enemies ring him 'round;
> If he's fired his last bullet,
> If he's fired his final shot,
> And they say, "Come into the Empire."
> He should answer, "I will *not*."

The dozen or so regulars at the bar whooped their appreciation, few more so than Danny, Dub and Sinéad. Shouts of 'Up the Republic' assailed Henning's ears and he was slightly taken aback by the spontaneous show of support.

"Give us a stave, Paddy! The Foggy Dew."

Paddy obliged and song followed upon song until gradually the pub fell into a more muted hubbub. Dub collected yet another round from the bar. Grasping a pint of Guinness and a whisky glass in one huge hand and a second tumbler in his second, he turned from the bar and awkwardly handed Henning the Macallan whisky. He toasted his thanks as he lifted the glass to his lips.

After an evening where again Henning left impressed by the sheer quantities of beer that his male companions consumed, Sinéad constraining herself to half their intake - *but still a lot,* thought Henning, he and Sinéad made their way home having bid farewell with the two Volunteers who staggered back towards a dance they'd read via a poster on the wall of the pub advertising a 'hooley', was taking place in Rialto.

"Your two friends seem very nice, Miss O'Grady."

"Well, I've known them a long time but I found out recently that you just never know the minute when you find yourself surprised by how you really don't know people at all well - even people you've grown up with."

Despite having consumed a much greater quantity of spirits than would normally be the case Henning was still sufficiently astute to notice that Sinéad slurred her words as she spoke - and that she uttered them with less guardedness than normal.

"Were you let down by a friend recently?" asked Henning empathically.

"You could say that, doctor. You could say that."

"It seems obviously to pain you even yet."

Sinéad stopped abruptly on the pavement and faced Henning, tears forming in the corner of her eyes. She raised her head in an unsuccessful attempt to pool her tears, trapping them so as not to reveal her emotions.

"And what would you know about feckin' pain, mister doctor? Have you ever had to kill a friend? Have you?" She folded her arms across her chest. "Tell me!... You're a doctor! Have you ever put someone in an unmarked grave that you loved...that you grew up with...that you went to school with...but who you were ordered to *dispatch*?"

She spat the last word out.

"Miss O'Grady, I had no intention..."

"No, of course not. *You're* the man who *saves* people's lives. I'm the woman who *takes* people's lives. We're different, aren't we doctor?" She began to weep uncontrollably.

Henning raised his hand to sweep the raven locks of her hair tenderly from Sinéad's eyes but resisted the movement lest it be construed as an affectionate gesture, placed it on her shoulder instead and gently pulled her towards him. Instead of hugging her as he so wanted to do, he found himself patting her on the shoulder as if she were an elderly relative.

"You're upset, Miss O'Grady. But we all have to remember that we live in troubled times. War is horrible. That's why I'm content to work here in Ireland far from the conflict. But you...well you have to deal with whatever's on your doorstep."

Sinéad leaned her forehead on Henning's shoulder and continued crying until she had recovered some of her composure. She took the handkerchief offered her by Henning and wiped the tears from her eyes.

"I'm sorry doctor. I had one too many glasses of stout. It sometimes makes me emotional."

Henning accepted the handkerchief back and turned her towards their house. Tentatively he escorted her homewards by placing his arm behind her back so lightly that it almost hung loosely, some inches from her coat.

Henning saw himself as a gallant and polite man but would never consider himself worldly in the affairs of male and female relationships. As a doctor he could be direct and assertive but as a man, he was shy and tongue-tied. Even the surfeit of whisky he'd consumed that night was insufficient to have his arm guide his distraught landlady onwards towards her destination.

Shortly they arrived at Sinéad's home and she opened the door, gesturing for him to enter first so she could lock up.

They each removed their coat and Sinéad put the light on in the front room.

"I'll put the kettle on doctor for a cup of tea...or coffee perhaps, unless you'd like to join me in a whiskey before bedtime. I've only the Irish stuff here, mind."

"You have coffee?"

"Well, its chicory, actually but we could pretend?"

"Thank you Miss O'Grady but a cup of tea would seem more sensible...for me at least," he stumbled. "Please, you have whatever you wish."

"And I should bloody think so, seeing it's my house," she said with more belligerence that she'd intended.

She left the room and reappeared few minutes later with two cups, each in a saucer.

"I've no milk and no sugar."

A grandfather clock on an old oak sideboard ticked metronomically; the only audible sound in the room. She sat and sipped at her tea, eyeing her tenant nervously.

"I really should apologise for my behaviour out there."

"No need," said Henning almost too quickly.

Sinéad ignored him. "I've had to deal with matters as a loyal foot soldier of the IRA, a good Volunteer... things I'd never countenanced myself doing. Things I'm ashamed of."

More sips of her tea punctuated her next spoken thoughts.

"D'you know doctor. Perhaps I've been a bit prim with you. You seem like a really nice man. You spend your life helping others and here's me insisting that we remain all formal. What d'you say we start again as Sinéad and...I'm sorry doctor, I've even forgotten your first name...What am I like?"

"It's Hermann...and I'd be delighted if we were to be friends."

"Well, I'm not saying *friends*, like...I mean I just thought we could stop the Doctor and Miss thing... I mean it's not that I don't want to be friends...Och, I'm talking like an eejit...*sure* we're friends...Jesus, we're living under the same roof. Just as long as no one out there gets the wrong idea about us. The priest would have kittens."

"Why of course...Sinéad." They both smiled.

Doctor Hermann Henning sipped at his tea. Truly, he was a happy man.

## Chapter Sixteen

A large car pulled up outside the offices of the German Legation. Two burly men in coats stepped out and stood tall, one holding the rear door open, the other opening the main door of the building, gesturing to those inside that the vehicle had arrived. During his night vigil, Weber had further disaggregated the bank notes into roughly equal amounts and had separated them into currency groupings in order to make it easier for the banks to deal with. On seeing the door open, he lifted the first batch of large parcels of money wrapped in anonymous brown paper and made towards the car.

Twenty minutes later, he found himself standing in the oak-panelled office of the manager of the Bank of Ireland in O'Connell Street.

"Please pass on my regards to Dr. Hempel, Professor Weber. And be sure to thank him for recommending our services to you. Your money will be safe here. We have some documents to sign but I have them all prepared."

"I am most grateful, Mr. Shaugnessy. I'll be making occasional withdrawals in much smaller amounts. Dr. Hempel would have advised you that my task is to invest the monies of the German Reich in the Irish economy against the day when this war is over and we can all return to normality."

"He told me that, certainly...and if I may be so bold... we bankers have always a few ideas about how you might invest."

"Well, I'm sure that your suggestions would be most helpful to the Legation. I'm looking for large businesses which have prospects as well as farms, hotels and inn-houses, that kind of thing. I want to make many *smaller* purchases, not one or two national acquisitions. And I'm not interested in any lame ducks you might have and of which you're interested in divesting yourself. I'll do my homework."

"I understand completely, professor. And you're contactable at the Legation?"

"Unless I'm visiting properties at distance from Dublin or until I'm removed from my command."

"Excellent."

"Now, Mr. Shaugnessy. If I was able to put an occasional ingot of twenty-four carat gold your way, you'd pay me the market price and place money to that value in my account?"

The bank manager stroked his beard. "But of course, professor. Twenty-four carat gold is ninety-nine percent pure. It's most unusual for this quality of gold to be available. Precious metal of this quality does not need to be alloyed. Tell me, have you much in the way of gold? It's such a comforting commodity in these times of strife."

"Now and again I might wish to lodge some with you...if the Third *Reich* provides the Legation with the resources."

"We would be delighted to receive investment from you...whether in the form of bank notes or precious metals."

"Then I expect to return to your offices here on a regular basis."

Following a further two visits, to the Allied Irish Bank and the National City Bank, Weber returned to the Legation where Hempel awaited his return. He showed Weber into a drawing room.

"All went well, professor? You were expected and the transactions were completed to your satisfaction?"

"They were, doctor...and I furnished each of them with a letter nominating you as the person who will have legal rights to the three investments should I be unable to fulfil my obligations to the Third *Reich*."

Hempel gestured Weber to take a seat and sat opposite him.

"Professor, I have worked here in Ireland for some time and have developed excellent relationships with most sectors of their society - especially with those in authority. I must confess, your appointment to the Legation has come as something of a surprise to me, particularly as it was made clear to me that you should have unfettered control of these investments and that you would not report to me on any matter."

He drew his fingers together stiffly, forming a tent.

"However, I find myself forced to the conclusion that you have been given orders that you have been instructed not to share with me. I accept this, obviously... but do feel that you might have a better chance of achieving anything you've been charged with if we had an accommodation...a mutual understanding that we might assist each other in our duties. All I have been told is that I'm to preserve the understanding that I'm head of the mission here in Ireland but that in all aspect, I have no ability to guide or assist you in your task - which I must assume is completely commensurate with my own."

Before responding, Weber allowed a small silence as Hempel, although embarrassed, said his piece...*a piece,* thought Weber, *that he's been rehearsing ever since he received my orders.*

"Dr. Hempel. Let me say immediately that I was honoured when our superiors back in Berlin informed me of the esteem in which you were held. You have been a diplomat representing German interests here in Ireland for a long time..."

"Professor," interrupted Hempel intemperately, "as you say, I have been involved in this business for a long time. I well understand the need for secrecy but you will agree that if you are the senior officer as I am, it is most unusual not to be advised of all aspects of a mission. I have forged an excellent relationship with the Irish *Taoiseach* and I do not wish to see it diminished as a consequence of any adventurism in your part."

Weber smiled as he shook his head, still attempting to mollify an outraged senior officer.

"Dr. Hempel..."

"I don't want to hear your polished words, professor. I want to know what is going on under the roof of my Legation. Specifically I want to know what duties you have been given beyond those of your investment portfolio...which, I must say on the face of it, is a very forward-looking proposition from Berlin." His face reddened. "Now, you will *tell* me...between you and I... what else have you been asked to accomplish?"

Weber hovered between proposing that Hempel contact Berlin asking for clarification of his brief and simply saying nothing. After a pause for thought he responded in compromise.

"Very well, Doctor Hempel. Let us agree that the Third *Reich* would have its interests best served if each of us managed to achieve our objectives. I will share my orders with you, such as I can but we must agree in advance that if and where these conflict with what you may be trying to achieve here in Dublin, my tasks must prevail. You have been ordered to maintain Ireland as a non-belligerent and to advance Germany's interests. You have also been asked to ensure that Ireland does not throw its lot in with Allied Forces. Is this correct?"

"That and looking after and German nationals who pre-existed or now find themselves in Ireland."

"Then I suspect that we have compatible objectives."

Casually, Weber placed his left leg over the arm of his chair as he readied himself to share what he deemed necessary.

Hempel stiffened at the gesture. *This man has no feel for protocol. He thinks he is in his own front lounge.*

"It is true that my main objectives surround buying into the Irish economy. After the war is over, Germany may seek opportunities to house and provide for senior staff who might otherwise fall foul of occupying forces." He hesitated. "You appreciate of course, that I am not being defeatist, merely pragmatic lest the *Reich* does suffer an ultimate reverse."

"Of course."

"Now I must commence by telling you that I was specifically instructed not to advise you of any of my orders other than my investment duties so anything I tell you now could see me shot for breaking orders. You will appreciate the risk I am taking *Herr* Doctor."

"I do indeed, Professor Weber although it pains me to hear of Berlin's attitude to my work here in Dublin."

"I suspect that Berlin is only protecting you so you might face de Valéra with indignant, innocent outrage if anything transpired which might embarrass your relationship."

"To be a diplomat is to be an actor, professor. I would expect to handle these eventualities comfortably."

Weber nodded but determined to share only a portion of his orders. *There's no innocence like actual innocence,* he thought...*and he's likely to find out soon enough that I was instrumental in bringing Dennehy to Irish soil.*

"Very well. My orders were to assist in the escape of one Declan Dennehy from an Internment Camp on the Isle of Man and deliver him here to Ireland. Unfortunately he was shot at the docks at Drogheda."

Hempel's face was a mask.

"I am permitted to maintain good relationships with the IRA leadership but nothing more," he lied.

"Dennehy was to represent a friendly gesture, nothing more, as to engage further might expose us to criticism by both Irish and Allied interests. Beyond that, I am asked to report on any matters that might assist the *Abwehr* in supplementing their intelligence on the Republic."

Weber sat back, still casually swinging his left leg, both hands clasped around his knee, as he awaited Hempel's reaction. It wasn't long coming.

"I can see why you were chosen for this task professor. You are very articulate, very persuasive and, if I may say so, *Obergruppenführer* clearly a man of action. However, I believe you are not disclosing your brief fully to me. I cannot believe that *Abwehr* would commission such a risky venture as causing a member of the IRA to escape whilst also expecting you to carry currency of at least three million Punts."

*If only you knew of the gold,* thought Weber.

"So your arrival here on board a Portuguese coaster is also a fiction?"

"Alas, yes, doctor. I was brought most of the way by *Unterseeboot.* Then by fishing boat from the Isle of Man."

"And how were you to advise Germany of any information you sought to transmit?"

"I am aware that the Legation's transmitter is being held in a bank vault here in Dublin ever since the *Abwehr* had two of their parachutists arrested upon their arrival last December and that the keys are held jointly by you and the Irish, so I have been asked to requisition a short-wave radio transmitter from the IRA...hence the friendly gesture I referred to earlier."

"You play a very dangerous game, professor."

"Perhaps, but I have also been ordered to have you arrange a meeting between me and the Prime Minister of Ireland, Éamon de Valera. Of course it would be helpful were you to attend at my side."

"I would think so, professor. I had presumed that this would be appropriate and have made arrangements for to see him tomorrow at ten o'clock in his offices...and, be clear, I would not permit such a meeting were I not accompanying you. The *Taoiseach* would find it very strange were I not to be present."

Weber nodded and rose from the chair, quietly congratulating himself on telling Hempel everything and nothing. *He still knows nothing of my order to provide the IRA with British arms and I'll make my own judgement about de Valera's current attitude towards the British and the IRA when I meet him.*

Both men went their separate ways, each acknowledging the other with a curt nod of the head. Weber watched as his colleague walked briskly to his next engagement. He drew his forefinger and thumb over his chin thoughtfully...*but first I must meet again with Miss O'Grady and begin making arrangements for my new relationship with her and with the IRA...It does no harm that she's also quite beautiful.*

## CHAPTER SEVENTEEN

A telephone call was all that was necessary to arrange for Weber and Sinéad O'Grady to meet, again in the city centre's Palace Bar. Sinéad was ten minutes late.

Weber stood to attention as she approached his table in the rear of the bar.

"Miss O'Grady. I am pleased to see you again."

"Sorry I'm late. Were you here on time?"

"Teutonic punctuality, Miss O'Grady. I am always on time."

She sat.

"May I buy you a drink?"

"I'll have a glass, thanks."

"Of?"

"Stout, please…Guinness."

Weber approached the bar as Sinéad made herself comfortable at the table. Some minutes elapsed as the barman permitted the stout to settle. Weber removed a note to the value of ten punts from his wallet only to see it handed back with a grimace from the barman along with advice that the denomination was too great.

"Jesus, you could buy the entire pub with that amount. I've not change enough to accept a big note like that"

From her chair, Sinéad overheard the conversation and approached the barman. She smiled as she produced her purse and paid for the drinks. Weber carried them over to their table but had hardly sat down when Sinéad hissed at him through clenched teeth.

"In the name of all that's holy, what the very devil are you doing carrying big notes like that around? Sure, you'll only draw attention to yourself. You've a funny accent and a funny way with money. Ten punts is nearly a month's wages to that barman and you offer it to him for two glasses of beer! Holy Mother of God!"

She looked at him in exasperation. "When we meet, it would be helpful if we didn't bring any attention on ourselves. And the way you dress...you with your posh suit and stiff white collar...you'd be as well standing up in this pub and shouting, 'I'm not the same as you all'...'Would someone please be good enough to phone the *Gardai* or the Brits and have them take a look at us pair...'"

Weber felt as disconcerted as he had been at the bar moments earlier without appropriate means to settle his drinks bill.

"Miss O'Grady...I...I...I'm..."

"You're an *eejit*, that's what you are. You might be a big brave man when you're commanding a squad of your German soldiers but you don't know Ireland."

She looked at him disdainfully.

"And you're the best the Mr. Hitler could *send* us are you? You have the gall to come over here and criticise me and my Volunteers when you can't even buy a round of drinks in a bar? You've a neck as thick as a jockey's arse, Mr. Professor."

In the face of Sinéad's onslaught, Weber found himself smiling as he came to appreciate the truth of her assertions. This infuriated Sinéad even further.

"And what have you to grin about Mr. Professor Diplomat General? You're only bloody likely to get me the jail or killed with your shenanigans and all you can do is sit there and *laugh*?"

Weber's smile morphed into giggles. *Such a pretty face...and here am I being denounced by a strip of a girl...I can see now why the Abwehr held her in such high esteem...she has a steel about her.*

Weber's peals of laughter subsided and he lifted his Guinness in a toast, still smiling.

"Miss O'Grady, you are, of course, perfectly correct in your comments. My laughter was not intended to be insulting or patronising...merely that I am embarrassed at my thoughtlessness. I must tell you that last night I realised that I would actually have to work well with you in order to achieve my objectives and having given it some further thought, came to realise that you'd actually be very *good* for me...and in the first seconds of meeting you again, you have proved it to me beyond peradventure...beyond doubt."

Sinéad slammed her half pint of Guinness on the table causing it to spill and puddle around the base of her glass.

"*Go n-ithe an cat thú agus go n-ithe an diabhal an cat!* May the cat eat you, and may the devil eat the cat!"

"Miss O'Grady. Please forgive my stupidity and let's enjoy our drinks."

Weber raised his glass further in toast but Sinéad's dark look persuaded him that another tack might be wise. His disposition became more serious... "Because tonight I wanted to talk to you about having some armaments dropped to the IRA here in Ireland by the *Luftwaffe*...but of course, if you're not in a mood to..."

Sinéad's demeanour changed...but not immediately. Her temper still dominated.

"Left to your own devices, you'd probably drop the bloody stuff on feckin' Buckingham Palace in London."

She looked steadily at Weber whose right hand still held his Guinness aloft in a frozen toast, his eyebrows arched in question awaiting a response to his offer. Gradually, Sinéad's shoulders relaxed and she sat back in the comfortable leather chair. Noticing the mess she'd made by spilling her Guinness she fished in her pocket for a handkerchief.

"Okay, go...I'm all ears, professor."

Weber sipped at his Guinness, enjoying its bitter taste more than his medical compatriot, and made an offer he knew he would also be making to the Prime Minister of Ireland the following morning. *As long as neither side finds out, it'll be fine,* he'd told himself when calculating the risks...*and as long as Eduard Hempel doesn't find out either, he thought.*

"Well, Miss O'Grady. I am prepared to organise a weapons drop at a place of your choosing in Ireland as long as I can be satisfied that the armaments will be used to strike at England's strategic interests."

"Well, thank you kind sir. It's about time you made a positive suggestion."

"Investing in Irish businesses, is fairly positive, wouldn't you think, Miss O'Grady?"

"I'll grant you that, professor but in our struggle with English imperialism, there are many in our ranks who would just as quickly take up arms against capitalism. We have a fair few communist Volunteers."

"Well, the *Fuehrer* would be most displeased if he thought his weaponry was to be targeted upon anyone other than Churchill's forces."

"On this occasion, I can guarantee you that they will, professor. We'd need rifles, and heavy cannon with all of the necessary ammo."

"Ammo?"

"Ammunition. We'd need the wherewithal to shoot something at them English bastards."

"I well understand, Miss O'Grady. I speak English very well but I haven't come to terms with your colloquialisms quite yet."

"Well, that's what we need and we need it in quantity and we need it soon."

"All very well. But if I arranged this what would you do with it?"

"The Brits have many training camps up north in Ulster. They build warships in Belfast, they've weather stations, airfields, and we can easily cross the Irish Sea just like you did and we have the shipyards at Glasgow and Liverpool within easy reach. There's no end of targets."

"Any one of these would be most acceptable to the Third *Reich*, Miss O'Grady." He paused as if giving the proposition due consideration and held out his hand. Then let us shake on a deal. We can discuss the details of the drop once I've made contact with Berlin...which brings me to my second point...I need a short wave radio transmitter. The German Legation had its taken from it by de Valera when we used it in ways he found undermined Irish neutrality."

Sinéad shook his hand, both of them instantly registering the vastly differing size of the other's clasp.

"Well, I know for certain we can build you one no problem. We have a few scattered around as it is."

Then we have a bargain, Miss O'Grady. You provide me with a short wave radio and I'll arrange a weapons drop so long as you advise me in advance of the targets you have chosen...and that you would be open to me suggesting targets that might suit both the IRA and the Third Reich."

"I'd need to speak with Joseph, but I'm sure he'd be interested in any information you had that would hurt the Brits."

Weber's teeth flashed white in a smile as again he raised his glass to his lips.

"Now you must tell me of Doctor Henning. Have you found him accommodation?"

"Hermann..."

"Hermann?"

"Doctor Henning will be staying in my house in Rialto, not far from the house you were in yesterday when you met Joseph."

"Really?" grinned Weber.

"I knew that was going to be a bad idea. First you. Next'll be the priest. Then my mother will put two and two together and make five."

She leaned over her glass of Guinness and spoke in a low tone.

"The man means nothing to me. I've only just met the bugger. And I'm just trying to be a decent human being giving him somewhere to stay close to St. Kevin's."

Weber sensed her embarrassment and teased her further.

"So you've found him a job as well? He must be very grateful to you."

"He's paying his way, professor. And he's looking after the sick and aged. He's not a murderous bastard like you and me."

Weber opened his palms and gestured reflection.

"Neither you nor I are murderous, Miss O'Grady. War is a dreadful thing. I have killed men in combat and I have heard upsetting reports that many of my fellow SS have also killed women and children... That, I confess, is unforgivable. But in war, people are changed. People commit acts they would not contemplate in normal times. Some of your fellow Volunteers may have found themselves in similar positions."

Sinéad shifted in her seat, eyeing her Guinness, refusing Weber's invitation to respond.

A heavy silence prompted Weber to move the conversation on.

"I am most grateful to you for helping Hermann. He is a good man and cares only for those who are sick and ailing."

Sinéad nodded silently. Weber allowed a further silence as he tried to interpret Sinéad's thoughts.

"You called him 'Hermann'?"

Sinéad's gaze never rose beyond the rim of her glass on the table.

"We had a chat...it seemed silly to continue formalities when we'd see one another every day and when I'd be calling all my other friends by their first name."

Weber permitted a smile - but this time one that attempted to convey understanding.

"So Herman's a friend?"

"Yes...no... Look professor, I'm just trying to be a decent person for once."

"And you are a very *wonderful* person, Miss O'Grady."

Weber placed his glass on the table and placed his hands together, interlocked his fingers and pulling them together until the cartilages crackled.

"Then we must also become friends, Miss O'Grady. Just friends like you and Hermann."

Sinéad looked up at him in surprise.

"I am no ogre, Miss O'Grady. My name is Kurt. Would you call me Kurt?"

Sinéad sighed. "Jesus, Mary and Joseph."

Defeated, she nodded her head.

"Of course, Kurt...and you may call me Sinéad. The priest may as well have a field day."

"The priest?"

"No worries, Kurt. Just an Irish mothers' thing. Kurt and Sinéad it is."

Weber and Sinéad relaxed into several more drinks, the evening becoming more convivial and unhurried as each took turns to describe the culture and backgrounds from which they came. Sinéad bought every round of drinks given Weber's possession only of ten pound notes.

Later, on arriving home, she discovered that Weber had secreted one of the ten pound bills in her coat pocket.

"The man's a special class of an arse." she intoned, before putting the money in her purse. "If I wasn't under orders I wouldn't be within a donkey's bray of him."

# CHAPTER EIGHTEEN

A timid knock woke Weber from his sleep and, upon his shouted response, the door opened to admit a young lady in white livery carrying a tray on which was his breakfast, the plate covered by a silver domed cloche to keep his food warm.

Weber shook his head and placed a knuckle in his closed right eye, rubbing it. *To think there are millions of my countrymen and women who are cold and have nothing to eat...* He thanked the young lady. *Still, I am here and it would not be sensible to refuse such bounty.*

He took an hour to eat and prepare himself for his meeting with the Prime Minister of Ireland. He paused for a moment and examined himself in the mirror. His steely blue eyes looked back calmly. Hempel had asked him to attend the Legation offices by ten o'clock so they could travel together to arrive for eleven, the extra half hour being available for any transport glitches and to permit a brief chat about how to manage the meeting. Punctuality was very important in the world of diplomacy. Neither man expected any difficulty in the half hour appointment that had been scheduled in the *Taoiseach's* diary.

As the antique Symphonium long-case striking clock outside de Valera's office sounded the hour, Miss Kathleen O'Connell, his personal secretary, opened the door from the inside and bid both German diplomats welcome.

"The *Taoiseach* can see you now, gentlemen."

As they rose from the chairs they'd earlier been offered, having arrived ten minutes early to show respect and to avoid the embarrassment of a late arrival, de Valéra was upon them, towering over both men. *Little wonder the Irish call him 'the Longfellow'*, thought Hempel as he offered his hand to the Irish Head of Government.

"Your Excellency... Eduard, you are most welcome."

He turned to Weber. "Ah, *Herr* Weber. I am informed by the Legation that you are both a professor of history and a general in the Waffen SS?"

"*Taoiseach*, I am now but a diplomat under the tutelage of Dr. Hempel here...and I am honoured to meet you."

Turning, de Valera ushered them into his office followed by Kathleen O'Connell who asked how they preferred their tea as they made themselves comfortable.

"Gentlemen. This is indeed a pleasure," said de Valera.

"Don't believe him, Professor," quipped Hempel to Weber. "He always says that...to me at least, then proceeds to abuse me."

The broad smile that each man shared testified to their warm relationship.

De Valera removed his round-lensed spectacles and began polishing them.

"Occupying the position I do, my responsibilities sometimes differ from those of the Legation," he smiled.

"So tell me, professor. Why were you sent over here to assist Dr. Hempel? Has his performance not found favour with your *Fuehrer?*"

"On the contrary, *Taoiseach*. My superiors have made it clear to me that I am very fortunate to work with such a man. No, my work here is intended to compliment that of Dr. Hempel. As I believe you know, I yesterday deposited sums to the value of one million punts in each of three Irish banks. I may be in a position to lodge more as time passes. But my responsibility is to invest in your economy. To create jobs, to create wealth by growing businesses here in the Republic...perhaps training your workforce....building new services in your communities. As I travelled following my arrival, I noticed many farms, inns, hotels, public houses, shops...all closed. I'd like to look at some of them, perhaps some factories, and see whether they might be brought back to life if finance from the Third *Reich* were to be made available."

"Well, Professor Weber, this is indeed most welcome... but what I'd like to turn my attention to is why Mr. Hitler would want to expend some of his much needed resources upon this when there are many other pressing needs in Germany. So, why this, why now and why Ireland?"

"Perhaps you underestimate the esteem in which you are held by the *Fuehrer, Taoiseach. He* appreciates, as do Dr. Hempel and I, the great difficulty you face in maintaining good relations with the British as well as with ourselves. We know you to be a man of peace who sees no advantage in having young Irish men march to their death in Europe. We appreciate your history and your struggles and to be frank, we prefer a neutral Ireland to one which is joined in alliance with those who pit themselves against us."

"Eloquently put, professor and your investment is appreciated, be in no doubt."

De Valera sipped at his tea.

"My secretary tells me you brought a young doctor with you."

"I did. He serves the health needs of the Legation and I must assure you that although we have found the support of your health professionals to be excellent, we have asked him to take an interest in German nationals you have here in interment as well as our small population of some three hundred countrymen who remained after Siemens' building of the power station at Ardnacrusha. As this will not take up all of his time, I understand that he has also found it possible to serve the needs of patients of St. Kevin's Hospital on some days of the week."

"Again, professor, I would have thought that your *Fuehrer* may have had use for someone of his skills in another theatre of war."

"My job is not to question the reasoning of my superiors, *Taoiseach*. But I hope you will accept his services in the spirit with which is intended. Together, our arrival is designed to support both the Legation and the Irish people...medically and economically."

"Some would argue that this gift is too good to be true and that there must be other motives that lie behind your deployment."

"Again, in the spirit of openness and honesty which I gather from His Excellency, Dr. Hempel, characterises your relationship, I have been asked to remind you once again of the offer of the Chancellor to provide you with any weaponry and manpower you might need should you ever take the view that you might wish to join the efforts of the Third *Reich* in acting against England."

De Valera harrumphed. "Perhaps when the German Reich stops acting against the Irish Free State, professor. Perhaps then..." he placed his cup back on its saucer. "I'm trying to protect my people, *Herr* Weber, and this is proving a difficult task. When the war started our nation had but a mere fifty-six ships. Fifteen more were purchased or leased but twenty have been lost. No country has ever been more effectively blockaded because of the activities of belligerents and our lack of ships, most of which had been sunk by *you* lot, has virtually cut all links with our normal sources of supply. Irish mercantile mariners sail unarmed, flying the Irish tricolour. We identify ourselves as neutrals with bright lights on our ships and by painting the tricolour and *Eire* in large letters on our sides and decks, yet twenty percent of our brave seamen have perished thus far as victims of a war in which they are non-participants. Allied convoys will not stop to pick up survivors but our Irish ships always answer SOS calls from whatever side. We always stop to rescue but still we are attacked by both, predominately by *your* Axis powers. Mr. Hitler sending us a doctor doesn't quite balance things up, does it, professor?"

"Your points are fair, *Taoiseach*. Each of us in this room wishes that circumstances were different. But in trying to maintain a neutral stance, you still find it necessary to permit many Allied ships to be repaired in your shipyards. You intern our airmen. Your citizens serve in the British Army. Your womenfolk serve as nurses..."

De Valera raised both of his hands inviting Weber to stop talking. He turned to Hempel who was smiling.

"And your man was doing *so* well, Eduard."

He crossed his long legs and sat back in his chair, lifting both cup and saucer under his chin so as not to spill anything.

"Professor Weber...as you say, we each wish circumstances were different...but they're not. You'll forgive me but I'll take no lessons on the perfidy of the English parliament nor on the steps I need to take to ensure that the people's wish to maintain neutrality is maintained. Each step I take is interpreted by one side in a very different way to the other. Do you think Mr. Churchill will accept your kind offer of investment with equanimity when he hears of it? He'll either try to sabotage your efforts or, with any luck, if I have my way, he'll try to match them. My assessment is that your investment proposition, on balance, is a good thing but my office will want to know through Eduard here each and every business you buy in to."

He placed the cup and saucer on the small table in front of him.

"Your offer of weaponry is rejected. Your medical help is inconsequential."

He turned his head to Hempel. Eduard, perhaps as you return to the Legation you'll explain to your man here some of the political problems we navigate."

He faced Weber in explanation. "While I'm dedicated to complete neutrality during these straitened times, I have to face up to the fact that about a third of my countrymen want to see England badly beaten by Germany. Another third want to see them *nearly* beaten and a final third want to see Germany down. By a substantial majority, our people want to maintain their distance from the war. We wish no part in it but we understand that we are not unaffected. Steering a political route through those realities *can* keep me awake at night."

He smiled at both of his guests. "We had allocated thirty minutes for our chat but I'm afraid that Miss O'Connell would have me see Mister David Gray whom *Herr* Weber here will get to know better as the United States' Ambassador to Ireland even though he prefers to be known as America's Envoy Extraordinary and Minister Plenipotentiary. Trust me Eduard, the man's a pompous arse. He'll have heard of the arrival of the professor here and will want to know what's going on. I'll tell him about the investment portfolio because it'll soon become public knowledge, but nothing of your offer of armaments and your young doctor fellah."

He clapped his hands, signifying an end to the meeting.

"However, as we all know, our women folk are the real powers behind the throne so if Miss O'Connell so instructs me, I must away."

He stood, followed by Hempel and Weber. They shook hands again and left his office.

Outside, Hempel turned to Weber as each man positioned his brimmed hat on his head in preparation for departure.

"Well, professor, I'll grant you, you didn't make a *complete* fool of yourself this morning. But you must remember that your job isn't to pick an argument with a head of state, particularly if he's the one providing you with diplomatic immunity and more than all the comforts of home."

"He's certainly bright and capable."

Hempel raised his eyebrows.

"Bright and capable, you say?..*Herr* Weber... professor...you damn the *Taoiseach* by faint praise. Éamon de Valera was every bit the warrior you are today in *his* day. He has an almost impossible task to accomplish in his present role and, in my view, he's doing it very well. Fortunately for us, he's agreed the most important part of your mission. We both knew he'd reject the offer of armaments but it was worth reminding him of our position. All in all, I'd say it was a successful meeting in that he's no closer to forming an alliance with Churchill."

He folded his arms and bowed his head slightly so it was closer to Weber's ear.

"Perhaps we'll make a diplomat of you yet!"

Weber decided that after a morning's diplomacy, an afternoon walking round his new Dublin environment would be a sensible use of his time. He could take the air and see something of the city. He might also use the time profitably to think.

After some walking and thinking, Weber decided that some phoning might be sensible and called the number he'd been given for Sinéad at the safe house in Rialto. A broad Dublin accent informed him that Sinéad wasn't there. Weber replaced the phone without leaving a name or a message.

*Don't know who I can trust in Ireland yet,* he thought. *I'll call later.*

Sinéad had been sitting in the front room of her small house not far from the Rialto base when the first call had been placed. Seated across from her was Doctor Hermann Henning who was giddily recounting to her his first day's work at St. Kevin's Hospital.

"Sinéad, it was just wonderful. Just like Sefton in Liverpool. I set broken bones, dealt with a number of minor spills and falls and resuscitated an old man who'd had a heart attack. It felt wonderful to be back helping people. I can't thank you enough for helping me find my vocation again."

Sinéad smiled despite herself.

"Doct...Hermann," she reminded herself, "I'm pleased to have been able to help you. I can see in your face just how much it means to you."

Henning gathered himself. "Sinéad, would you consider having a drink with me tonight? We could go to that small pub where we went last night. Sitting in front of that roaring log fire..."

"It was peat...the fire...the fuel was turf, not logs..."

"Yes, yes...the *peat* fire. But sitting there talking with you and Dub and Danny...well, it was just...it just made me very happy. Just as long as I didn't need to drink your ale."

Sinéad's smile hadn't left her face following her earlier remark.

"Well, I suppose that sittin' round the corner in the pub havin' a gargle would be better than sittin' here staring at you in front of an empty fireplace."

She clasped her hands round her knees.

"Will I make us some soup before we go round?"

"That would be lovely. And while you do this, perhaps I could organise my medical bag. The hospital gave me a parcel of medical equipment and a bag to use in case I required to make use of my medical skills outwith the hospital."

"Then you go on right ahead, Doct....Hermann," she corrected herself again. "I'll fix us some soup."

## CHAPTER NINETEEN

Weber was in a foul mood following another fruitless phone call to the safe house - this time from the offices of the Legation. On a third occasion he'd asked if Joseph Kelly was there.

"And who wants to know?"

"Tell him it's the big man from Drogheda."

After a minute's pause while the message was transmitted and decoded, Kelly answered the phone himself.

"Now before you say anything, my man, remember the walls have ears. These days, you can't even trust the phone system. If you want to talk to me we'll do it face to face."

"It's not necessary. I just wanted to talk to that young lady of yours who's looking after me and I can't track her down."

"She's not been in here today," said Kelly.

"Do you know her address?"

"I do not share information over the telephone."

Weber mumbled an imprecation under his breath.

"To be honest, at this time of night, you're more likely to find her at the Patriot's Inn. It's a pub not far from here where I'm speaking' from. If she's in town, she usually looks in there for a pint or two before bedtime. If she's not there, phone me back."

"The Patriot's Inn?"

"Yeah. In Rialto. Any Hackney man'll take you there."

"Thank you Joseph. I'll speak to you about our common interests when next we meet."

"*Go raibh an Tiarna leat*. May God go with you,"

Weber replaced the phone. *Perhaps it wasn't wise to have phoned Kelly from the Legation. Phone calls could be listened into,* he rebuked himself...*and all because my IRA contact has seen fit to go into hiding, apparently...* He admonished himself once more...*What am I doing, getting hot and bothered about a foolish woman?...and one who has a tongue in her...*He allowed his chastisement to abate. *Well, I suppose I am a stranger in town...and his Excellency, boring old Eduard Hempel has gone home to his wife in Dún Laoghaire. I have little option other than to spend time with someone I've got to know...even if she has the very Devil in her!*

Weber walked back to his hotel but before he left for the Patriot's Inn, he changed into an old brown suit in order not to stand out so much. He looked out of the window and decided that the weather would remain fine for the rest of the evening and so decided that a woollen pullover under his jacket would suffice rather than his coat. A flat cap bought earlier that day replaced his brimmer and completed the outfit. Checking himself in the mirror he decided that he looked sufficiently like a local to avoid Sinéad's wrath if he managed to meet her. A taxi was called by the hotel's *concierge* and in a matter of half an hour, Weber was standing in the small bar, holding a glass of Talisker Scotch Whisky up to the light, to all the world looking like a whisky *aficionado* checking his drink for colour and tone, but in reality inwardly cursing Kelly for giving him hope that Sinéad would also be in attendance. Resignedly, he sipped at his whisky mulling whether to make a night of it and consume more than was wise for him. *It's been a while since I've just cut loose and drank myself stupid,* he thought. He finished the glass in a second single swallow, giving the lie, should he have wished to perpetrate it, that he was indeed something of a Scotch whisky *connoisseur*. He showed the empty glass to the bartender.

"Another, please. And make it two whiskies in a single glass. No water."

The generous measure was placed in front of him and Weber took care again to pay the man in small coins more in keeping with the value of the drink. As he lifted the whisky to his mouth, the pub door opened and Sinéad and Henning walked through, both laughing. Weber's glass remained positioned at his lips as his mood fought with contradictory emotions of pleasure and confusion at seeing them together.

Sinéad was first to react seeing him standing at the bar.

"Well now, if it isn't a local farmer I see. Remind me... is it Patrick now...or is it Sean..." she teased, smiling at his less formal attire.

Henning looked at both parties, bemused at the exchange. He couldn't understand how his mentor was standing in an obscure Irish pub and was completely flummoxed by Sinéad's banter.

"Why doctor...Sinéad...This is a happy accident."

"Happy accident, my arse, professor. You must have *known* we'd be in here tonight."

Weber pretended to be offended.

"But Sinéad, I thought that we were in future going to refer to each other by our *given* names."

He turned to Henning, including him in the conversation.

"Certainly, that was what Hermann and I agreed on board the *Trinity*..."

He resumed his conversation with Sinead.

"And you and I agreed only last night!"

"Then, happy accident, my *arse, Kurt.*"

She removed her coat and threw it over the back of a chair next to the fire.

"Well, it seems you've the means to pay for your round tonight so why don't you get me a glass of stout and Hermann here'll take a whisky...but not one the size of yours or he'll be singing before the night's out. We'll sit here at the fire for a warm. In Ireland even the summer nights are bloody freezin' sometimes."

Henning was still confused at the scene before him but took his seat next to the fire with Sinéad as Weber purchased another two drinks. Bringing them over he placed them on the table and sat, before lifting his glass in a toast.

"To serendipity!"

"Would you just use words I understand, Kurt? Don't make me feel a bigger fool that I really am. What the feck does *serind*...whatever...mean."

Henning interjected. "It means 'happy accident'...it derives from a Persian fairy tale called *The Three Princes of Serendip* whose heroes were always making discoveries by accident of useful things they did not seek."

Weber smiled and raised his glass to his fellow national.

"I've learned something new tonight, Hermann. I was a history professor, not an expert in children's literature."

Henning looked embarrassed. "It's what comes of being a boring person who reads anything he can get his hands on. You pick up lots of nonsense along the way."

"Well, I'm teasing, anyway," said Weber. "I had some business to conduct with Sinéad tonight and was informed by our Irish friend, Joseph Kelly that she might be found here...but I didn't expect to be interrupting a tryst," he said mischievously.

Both Henning and Sinéad reacted abruptly to Weber's comment, speaking over each other in their joint denial that the visit to the pub was anything more than a sociable way of keeping warm.

Weber laughed at the reaction he'd caused.

"Sorry." He shrugged his shoulders. "Just now that you're living together..."

As he'd anticipated, this caused even more of a reaction permitting him further guffaws at their expense.

"I apologise. I'm just teasing. I'm sorry."

"And I should bloody think so," said a still angry Sinéad.

"As it happens, I *do* have need of a discussion of a military nature with you tonight, Sinéad," he lied. "But Hermann and I have agreed that he will not be party to any of what he calls 'my adventures' and I think this is sensible, so unless you two had other plans, which you both seem determined to persuade me that you don't, why don't we have another few glasses and Hermann can tell me how he's getting on in the hospital."

He lifted his whisky to his lips, hoping that his next suggestion to Sinéad wouldn't meet with rejection.

"Then perhaps you and I can have a more discrete talk for a few minutes in his absence."

Sinéad turned to Henning. "Would that be alright with you, Hermann? You could leave for home in a while and put the kettle on while me and mister serendipity here have a chat about business. I wouldn't be far behind you."

"And is it safe for you to walk the streets on your own?"

Weber spoke first. "Oh, don't worry about that, Hermann. If the house is close by, I would be happy to walk Sinéad home. If not, we can call one of these Dublin taxis."

Another sip.

"One way or another, I'd see that she didn't come to any harm."

"Well, what a pair of gallant gentlemen you both are. But let me remind the both of you that I have been walking the streets of Dublin for all of my twenty...somethin'... years and I have yet to come across anything I couldn't handle. So don't be worryin' about me."

The evening fell into easy conversation and a further four drinks were taken, all of which were bought by Weber due to Henning reminding him that arrangements hadn't yet been made to pay him his stipend."

Alcohol was beginning to have its effect.

"And you make sure you fix that, Kurt," said Sinéad. "Or he'll be thrown out on the street for not paying his rent before he's had a chance to use the jacks at the bottom of the garden!"

"What's the jacks?" asked Weber and Henning in unison.

"Just fix his money, mister moneybags."

The mention of money reminded her of earlier discovering the ten pound note in her pocket.

"And while I'm at it, what was that trick you pulled last night by stuffing ten pounds in my pocket when I wasn't looking?"

"A small gesture after you'd been so kind to point out my several inadequacies..." He tugged at the pullover under his suit jacket as evidence... "From which I learned...and bought me drink all night."

"Then I owe you some shrapnel!"

"You certainly don't. Please don't make me embarrassed."

Henning found himself confused again. *Sinéad has spent ten pounds buying Kurt drink?*

"I'll maybe give you your change later," said Sinéad leaving matters hanging.

"I should go," said Henning lifting his jacket.

Weber reached to shake Henning's hand as he left.

"I'll make arrangements tomorrow for your stipend, Hermann and I'll see you have a cash advance."

Henning nodded his gratitude and left.

Sinéad approached the bar, ordered two more drinks and returned to the table.

"Right, what's the military discussion you wanted?"

"Thank you," said Weber, lifting his glass. He looked round conspiratorially to check he wasn't being overheard.

"I made contact today with Germany by coded phone call," he lied. "They have approved the weapons drop."

He sat back in his seat expecting Sinéad's enthusiastic delight at his information.

"Is that *it*?" asked Sinéad, a puzzled frown on her face.

"Why, yes...I thought you'd be...I thought..."

"You sent poor Hermann home early just to tell me *that*?" she exclaimed. "Somehow I don't think Christ would have climbed down off the cross for that shaggin' tit-bit! Could you not just have waited till he went to the jacks?"

"What's the..."

"Never mind," said Sinéad. "I'll never understand this business."

Weber recovered his composure and his air of command. He tried to look stern.

"This is important, Sinéad. When I met you at first I must confess I had my doubts over your competency. Since then you have gone up in my estimation but these matters are of the highest importance and it is a small price to pay if Hermann has to go home early so I can share a military secret with you."

"I suppose so," said Sinéad, looking unconvinced.

After one further drink, they left for Sinéad's home, strolling slowly the few hundred yards to her front door.

"I appreciate you taking the time to sit with me this evening, Sinéad. I enjoyed it very much...although, of course, I needed to inform you of military developments."

Sinéad interrupted and nodded at her front door.

"This is me here."

As covertly as he thought possible, Weber privately noted the address, 8 Kilmainham Road, for future reference.

They stopped and faced one another.

"You must ensure that if there are matters from your side that you think I should be made aware of...no matter how small...that you contact me immediately at the Legation or the Shelbourne."

Sinead began to nod her agreement to the proposition but emboldened by his evening's whisky consumption, Weber cupped Sinead's chin with his forefinger and thumb and brought it gently upwards to face him. With the back of the fingers of his left hand he slowly caressed her cheek. Sinéad did not resist.

"You are extremely beautiful, Sinéad." He stumbled for words. "I hope you enjoy being with me as much as I do being with you."

Moments passed wordlessly as their eyes locked. Slowly, Weber removed his hand and resisted the temptation to kiss her.

Sinéad folded her arms and cleared her throat.

"Be *very* clear, General Weber. I'm here with you in Dublin to carry this fight to the British army. I've no time for any nonsense. Not with you...not with anyone. If I need to contact you, I will." She stared fixedly at her feet to avoid eye contact. "I'll see that your information tonight is passed to Joseph Kelly...though why you didn't just tell him when you were asking after my whereabouts, defeats me."

Weber's gaze, momentarily tender, became serious.

"I understand." He bowed his head sharply, as if acknowledging a senior officer. "Until the next time."

He turned and walked off...*in the wrong feckin' direction,* thought Sinéad.

As his form melted into the darkness, Sinéad seated herself on her low garden wall. *What's wrong with me? Why did I just let him hold me and touch my face there, like we were bloody courtin'? I must be going soft.* She raised herself from the wall and knocked the door of her house, having earlier given Henning her only set of keys to let himself in. She sighed. *Jesus, if only my old mother could see me now...I'd be getting another row for givin' another man another chasin'!*

Hermann opened the door and admitted Sinéad who was still in reflective mode after her dealings with Weber.

"Sinéad. I have made us a cup of tea. Did Professor Weber see you home safely?"

Sinéad saw his lips move and heard noises but was too distracted to hear the message. Strong drink also played its part.

"I'm sorry, Hermann. Can you say that again? I must have had too much to drink"

"I've made tea...We agreed in the pub that I'd make tea...would you like...?"

"Eh, sorry, Hermann...I'm going upstairs for a moment...Yes, you pour a couple of cups and I'll be back down shortly."

Henning entered the small kitchen and made for the kettle only to hear a squeal and a crash behind him as Sinéad tumbled down the stairs.

"Sinéad, are you all right?"

Hermann rushed to the foot of the stairs where Sinéad was moaning and holding her right foot.

"I slipped on the second step," she groaned. "I've buggered my shaggin' ankle."

Henning helped her to her feet and assisted her through to the living room where she fell rather ungainly into a chair."

"Let me look at it, Sinéad. I'm going to take your boot off. Tell me as soon as you feel pain."

"I bloody feel pain right now," hissed Sinéad.

"I'll be careful. Is it your right foot? Nothing else is in pain?"

"Yeah."

Carefully, Henning removed the boot by first unlacing it. Placing it to one side, he rolled down her ankle sock until her foot was free. He asked her to wiggle her toes and tested the injury by tentatively applying pressure to the ankle. After some uncomfortable manipulation, Henning offered his assessment.

"Well, it looks like nothing's broken but you've a bad sprain. Probably some ligament damage. Sit still and I'll get some equipment."

He returned with a pail of cold water and some bandages.

"Roll up your trouser leg and place your foot in this bucket, please. It'll be cold!"

"Ouch, ouch, ouch, ouch," exclaimed Sinéad as she lowered her foot. "It's bloody freezin'!"

Well, I'll put the fire on so you're warm but I'll be filling that bucket up with cold water every so often tonight to reduce the swelling in your ankle. Later, I'll strap it up before you go to bed. Tomorrow you rest it, no question... Fortunately you have boots that lace halfway up your calf so that'll offer your ankle good protection. I'll also give you some exercises to do to accelerate your recovery but I'm afraid you'll be indisposed for a couple of days. I hope you hadn't any plans with Kurt."

Sinéad rounded on him.

"Now why in the name of all that's holy would I have plans with Kurt for God's sake?"

Henning was taken aback by the ferocity of her retort.

"I'm sorry, Sinéad. I didn't mean to suggest anything improper...I meant in your role with the IRA..."

"This is gettin' bloody worse by the minute. Listen doctor, you'd better *forget* all about my role with the IRA. I can't be having a lodger here who's blathering on all the time about my role as a Volunteer! It's meant to be a bloody *secret*!"

Again, Henning was nonplussed at his inability to say anything that didn't result in an angry challenge by Sinéad. In a surgery setting or his hospital, he'd have dealt with the matter assertively, but being accosted by a somewhat inebriated, wounded and angry Sinéad in her own home was a different matter.

"I apologise, Sinéad. I didn't mean anything by it."

Gradually, Sinéad relented and they sat by the fire having normal, friendly conversation. Every so often, Henning emptied the bucket and filled it with cold water. In between times, he found himself placing Sinéad's leg on his lap and massaging her calf, asking if it helped before returning it to the bucket.

*Am I completely crazy?* he thought. *What am I doing, manipulating Sinead's calf... which has got absolutely nothing to do with her injury? I'm in danger of abusing the doctor patient protocol...*

Somewhere else in the house, a clock struck one o'clock. Sinéad yawned and stretched her arms.

"I'd better be off to bed, Hermann. You mentioned something about strapping my ankle up?"

"Of course."

Henning dried her leg, took some bandage and began expertly to wind it round the ankle joint until he was satisfied that the dressing had been applied properly. Using scissors, he cut the bandage and fixed it.

"That'll be fine until the morning. Tomorrow, before I go to the hospital, I'll show you how to write the alphabet in the air with your toes to encourage ankle movement," he smiled. "Now, let me help you."

Standing before her, he placed his hands under her thighs and back and lifted her lightly from the chair.

"Jesus, Hermann, you're stronger than you look."

Henning found that carrying her in his arms, her face smiling at him inches from his own, most disconcerting. Embarrassed, he said nothing in response, his emotions confused even further when she put her arms round his neck and squeezed it momentarily.

"Here's me with my very own doctor. If only my old mammy could see me now."

Henning managed a weak smile as he carried her up the stairs to her bedroom and gently laid her on her bed."

"You can undress yourself..." said Henning, colouring as he recognised the clumsiness of his remark. "I mean..."

Sinéad laughed. "Don't bother yourself, Hermann. You're now my bloody doctor, for the love of God. If I'd hurt my arse, you'd have had to fix that, wouldn't you?" she asked rhetorically.

"I suppose..."

"Well, don't trouble yourself. You've been very sweet tonight Doctor Henning and I'm in your debt."

She grimaced as she moved her body in preparation for disrobing.

"I'll scream if I think I'm going to die during the night...but watch out now, I sleep in the nip in the summer...though it would be nothing you hadn't seen before...as a doctor, I mean."

Sinéad's remark sent Henning's brain into overload.

"I...em...I'll be...eh...Goodnight, Sinéad."

He left.

Sinéad struggled with her attire, eventually removed her clothes and slipped into bed pulling the covers over and, even during a Dublin summer's night, shivering.

*What the feck am I doing? My head's in a spin because a German General speaks nice to me...then before you know it, a German doctor is so helpful I end up flirting with the man. Jesus, Mary and Joseph, it's a psychiatrist I need, not a doctor.*

Befuddled by drink, still pained but exhausted, she laid her head on the pillow and in seconds was asleep.

# CHAPTER TWENTY

Ezra Hasofer strode from the bright sunshine into the pungent darkness of a *suq* in Jerusalem, his arms aloft and a huge smile on his face. He waved a piece of paper in the air in the general direction of a girl seated at a table outside a nearby small cafe.

"Rachel, I have been accepted...*accepted*! My application was successful. I'm to study engineering at the *Technion*, the Institute of Technology in Haifa."

The twenty-year old rose from her chair, spilling the remnants of a glass of water she'd been sipping and leapt at her lover, shrieking excitedly. She hugged at his neck and crossed her ankles behind him as he swung her, laughing.

"Ezra, Ezra...how wonderful. Ten years a shopkeeper and now you're to study engineering...we must celebrate. Have you told your parents?"

"Not yet. I came here directly as we discussed. But I told them we'd come over tonight once I heard from the faculty. My father has been insisting that he and mother would help with the fees but they can't afford it without selling the shop so I'll just have to work long hours to earn money as well as study."

"We can deal with that over dinner tonight but for now let's celebrate your success. What a clever young man you are."

"Hardly young! I'll be some years older than any of the other students. They'll all be *your* age."

"Well, you get on well enough with me," smiled Rachel. "Anyway, you'll know so much more about life when you apply your studies to real life situations."

"I'll also have to tell my commander in *Haganah* that I want to resign from *Palmach*. I don't imagine he'll be very pleased with me. He has told me a number of times that he needs me in *Haganah* and I know he feels he is my mentor and guide. I have a meeting with him this afternoon at his invitation to discuss my next assignment and I don't expect he'll be expecting my news. I've kept my career ambitions secret from everyone but you and my parents in case I wasn't accepted."

"Well, if he's such a high opinion of you, I'm sure he'll be delighted at your news."

"Somehow, I think not, Rachel."

"Well, don't you let him talk you out of it, Ezra. You know how long you've wanted to do this."

Hasofer grinned. "He wouldn't try to talk me out of it; he'd just have me shot."

He kissed his sweetheart on her cheek and hugged her again.

"Let's have a quick drink and we'll arrange to meet at my parent's house once I've finished with Menachem Begin"

As he sat waiting his commander's pleasure outside his office-cum-cafe in a noisy *suq* in the Old City of Jerusalem, Hasofer's sense of unease grew. Palestine was undergoing one of its recurring occupations - this time by the British - and Menachem Begin had risen through the ranks to direct the operations of *Haganah*, a Jewish paramilitary organisation in what was then the British Mandate of Palestine. He'd made it clear that Hasofer would play a major part in the resurrection of the Jewish state and that he had every confidence in his abilities. Menachem Begin had some years earlier created the *Palmach*, an elite commando section, in preparation against the possibility of a British withdrawal and Axis invasion of Palestine. Its members, young men and women, received specialist training in guerrilla tactics and sabotage.

*I hope he's not too angry with me,* thought Hasofer. *He has many who would serve as I have. Surely he won't resist my determination to achieve an education...surely...*

After a nervous ten minutes, a curtain concealing a doorway was pulled back. An unshaved face glowered at Hasofer, scanned the room and, satisfied that there was no threat, gestured to Hasofer to join him on the other side of the curtain.

His earlier confidence having deserted him, Hasofer ducked slowly under the string that served to hold up the curtain and entered the room.

Two men sat at chairs behind a desk talking in low tones. One of them, the older man, turned to Hasofer as he entered.

"Ezra. It's good to see you. Take a seat."

"Commander Begin!"

"I called you in today to discuss your next mission. It has been discussed at the highest levels with Eliyahu Lankin, and Shlomo Lev Ami. We are as one in deciding that you are perfect for this task."

He gestured at the second man. "Aryeh Ben Eliezer here has just been apprised of your work with us and the task we have in mind for you. He agrees with our recommendation."

"Commander..."

"You speak perfect English, you are highly intelligent, a dangerous man with your fists, you..."

"Commander...."

Begin stopped talking. It was unusual for him to be interrupted.

"Yes?"

Hasofer took a breath. "Commander, I have been given an opportunity to study engineering in the *Technion*, the Institute of Technology in Haifa. I have discussed this with my girlfriend, Rachel and we believe that a period of study would not be compatible with my continued role in *Haganah*..."

Begin slammed his fist on the table.

"Your *girlfriend?*...Your *girlfriend?*" he repeated for emphasis.

"We are dealing with the very *existence* of the Jewish people. We are engaged in a war to the death. All over the world, we Hebrews are being murdered. The British control our land of Palestine and are refusing entry to thousands of Jews who are trying to escape the *pogroms* in Europe. Your country has great need of your services... But you want to be an engineer? When you don't have a nation to call your own?"

"Commander Begin..."

"Your request is refused, Hasofer.

"But commander, you yourself benefited from an education in Poland! You told me so many times." exclaimed Hasofer, hotly.

"And I also lost my father to the Nazis and my mother and brother are missing. You have been spared that but we have created the *Palmach* precisely to avoid you and your family having to endure what countless thousands of your persecuted brothers and sisters have endured over centuries."

"Commander Begin, I am a member of an elite...a commando section, in case of German invasion of Palestine. I have been proud to serve and I appreciate the specialist training in guerrilla tactics and sabotage which I promise I would put to good use if ever we were invaded but the war is almost over...do you not see how much my education means to me...?"

Begin slammed his fist again on his desk and began to rise to his feet when the other man spoke, quietly placing his hand on Begin's arm.

"Menachem...Menachem. Let us all remember that we are all on the same side. Young Hasofer here has served us well and has an important point of view."

He turned to Hasofer. "Ezra...may I call you Ezra?"

Hasofer nodded silently.

"Ezra. All that Menachem says is true and we all know this."

He clasped his hands together as if in prayer.

"It is now well known that we are receiving troubling reports that the Germans are murdering every Jewish citizen they can lay their hands on. Gassing them. It is a grotesque insult to humanity and we have to face up to it. Now the war is going badly for the Germans and soon we will know the full extent of their evil misdeeds...and soon they will be called to pay for them. Most, we know, will be captured by the Allied Forces but others will escape. After the war ends, there will be great confusion and we expect many senior officers even now to be making preparations for their escape. We will not permit this. And it is to you and a few other strong men that we turn in our hour of need."

He placed his hand on Begin's shoulder.

"My friend Menachem. Why not solve the problem in this way...Ezra here dearly wants to receive an education. But Ezra, unless you are independently wealthy, this will require you working many hours beyond your studies in order to pay for them. Is this not so?"

"I am prepared to make that sacrifice."

"Are your parents still alive?"

"They are."

"Then I expect they will themselves seek to make sacrifices to ensure your education."

Hasofer smiled. "That is the conversation I expect to have when I leave here."

"Then why not tell them that *Haganah* have agreed to pay for your tuition for as long as is necessary so you can make a different kind of contribution once the war is over?"

"But...I don't know what to...are you serious...you can do this?"

"Ezra, we have to be creative. We need you and a few others like you. You will provide a great service to your nation. We want to train you further while we await the outcome of the war. It won't be long now. Perhaps months...but only a few. During that time you will be at home here. Afterwards, you will be sent on a mission. That may take a few months, perhaps less. We haven't yet decided the precise location of your mission and can't be sure until the war ends."

"Are you able to tell me what kind of mission you have in mind?"

Begin scowled. "You should think yourself very fortunate that Aryeh Ben Eliezer here has made himself available to you today. I can tell you that I would deal with this matter very differently."

"I am grateful to you both," said Hasofer... "and the nature of my mission?"

"You will be trained to become a very effective assassin on behalf of the people of Palestine, Ezra Hasofer."

## CHAPTER TWENTY-ONE

A full moon displayed the scene below as the plane lined up with the contour of the valley floor some miles south of Killarney, parachutes already descending from its belly. Sinéad stopped counting after ten as the parachutes opened, permitting the boxes they held to float gracefully as they swooped earthwards before crashing unexpectedly heavily in the expanse of Esknamucky Glen below her. Three containers glided into the depths of the nearby *lough* and were lost.

Almost as the *Junkers* banked and flew off at the end of the glen, an old lorry, its lights extinguished, began to make its way across the pasture to where the closest wooden container had burst open, scattering its contents around it. Stopping, six men leapt from the vehicle and began collecting the rifles and smaller boxes of ammunition that had been disgorged, throwing them unceremoniously into the rear of the vehicle.

"Look at Dub, he's working like a man possessed," said Sinéad excitedly.

Weber did not respond but continued to look through his field-glasses at the scene below him. After a few minutes, the lorry moved on to the next container leaving one man behind to gather the spent parachute and carry it to the edge of the field where a freshly dug hole awaited its interment.

Sinéad refocused her binoculars. "That's Danny tidying up," she said to a still unresponsive Weber.

Slowly the lorry moved from container to container as the men busily collected their contents. Danny hurried to and fro picking up the parachutes and carrying them back to the hole he'd dug close to the river that flowed through the glen.

"It's going perfectly, Kurt," said Sinéad.

The words dried in her mouth as from eight points of the wooded perimeter of the field, car headlights lit up the activities of the men. Weber stiffened and removed the field-glasses from his eyes so as to view the entire scene below.

"We've been betrayed," he shouted. "This is no accident!"

Sinéad's hand rose involuntarily to her mouth in horror as she realised the significance of the headlights.

Slowly at first but then more rapidly, the headlights moved towards the lorry. From their vantage point, Weber and Sinéad could hear shouts over a loudhailer but could not make out what was being said.

Although the lorry remained stationary, some of the men started to run towards the greater safety of the woods despite this having them close on the incoming vehicles from which flashes of gunfire could now be seen. One by one they fell.

"They've shot Dub," screamed Sinéad. "Poor Dub."

"They've all been shot. Perhaps not the driver...but look..."

Down below, Danny had dived into the hole upon the lights illuminating the landing site.

"The car has passed him by," shouted Weber. "He can make it to the forest. Run, Danny, run..."

Both now standing, the moonlight permitted them to see Danny follow their injunction to the letter and run the few yards to safety behind the tree line before disappearing into its darkness.

"The driver has survived the shots, look!"

Sinéad followed the direction of Weber's pointed arm to see old Barney Yates descend from the cab, his arms raised. Men could now be seen walking among those shot, checking their condition, but no one who fell, moved.

"That looks like five dead, one arrested and one escaped," said Weber. He turned around checking his rear to ensure that their own position had not been compromised.

"Come, Sinéad. For all we know, we have also been betrayed. It wouldn't do for a diplomat from the German Legation to be caught here."

He considered the terrain.

"We can make our way back to our car through this gorse. Keep low. In this moon, anyone with a view of the hilltop would see us clearly. Do not approach the top of the hill in case someone sees our silhouette against the skyline. Have your pistol ready for use but don't use it unless I'm using mine. One shot and we'd have these cars chasing us. Let's hope that our own vehicle has gone unnoticed."

After a final, long look down at the carnage below, Weber tugged at Sinead's arm and they moved off, moving quickly but quietly. Every so often Weber would signal Sinéad to the ground and hold his finger to his lips indicating silence as he assessed their position. After half an hour's travel they came close to the narrow country lane where their car was hidden.

"Stay here," ordered Weber.

Carefully, with an economy of movement, he picked his way to the edge of a rocky outcrop that provided him with cover yet permitted him a view of his car concealed on a seldom-used farm track beneath the branches of some trees. Stealthily he made his way closer and lay prone for a full five minutes until he was satisfied that no one else was in the vicinity. He returned to Sinéad.

"We have a problem. We don't know how our plan was compromised. For all we know, our car is under surveillance although it doesn't appear to be so." He thought further. "But if we drive away now, we might find that a roadblock has been established some distance from the airdrop precisely to catch anyone who managed to escape. Frowning, he considered his options and looked at his watch, angling it so he could see the time by moonlight.

"It's three thirty. It'll be dawn in about two hours." He decided. "Okay! We wait here until daylight. Let's not take chances."

Surveying the area round about them, he gestured at a yellow thicket of gorse.

"We'll lie over there. I'm afraid the bush has thorns so it won't be comfortable but it'll provide us with good cover."

Both crawled under the edge of the bush suffering some scratches as Weber had predicted.

They lay motionless in hiding for five minutes without speaking before Sinéad whispered to Weber.

"I'm bloody freezing."

"It's cold once you stop moving," he agreed. "No time for niceties, I'm afraid. Move closer!"

Sinéad allowed the thought that perhaps Weber was still harbouring feelings towards her but as his arms encircled her and warmth spread back into her body, she dismissed the notion. Her face was nestling in his chest area but she could still whisper and be heard without too much difficulty.

"Are you thinking about how we were betrayed?"

"I am. And I'm at a loss to understand it. The only people who knew about the drop zone before tonight were you, me and Joseph Kelly."

"That's right."

"Only you and I knew where we'd hide our car or that we'd observe the proceedings from the hilltop?"

"Yeah!"

"Who selected the seven men?"

"Well, me and Joseph. I volunteered Dub and Danny and he provided old Barney to drive and another four men to take care of the collection along with them."

"Did Dub and Danny know the others?"

"Don't think so. It's not encouraged."

"When were they selected?"

"Joseph'll tell us about *his* men but I told Dub and Danny only yesterday although they knew they were travelling up from Kerry to do a job...but they didn't know what it was until I told them in the Palace Bar yesterday afternoon...that's only about twelve hours ago."

"And Joseph cleared Niall Kennedy after Dennehy's shooting."

"Well, I wouldn't quite say, *cleared*. He wouldn't authorise further beatings or sanction his killing, but I suspect it'll be a while before he takes him into his confidence...just in case. He's back fishing now but he's not being trusted with any information so I suspect you can rule him out."

"Well...what do I *know*? asked Weber of himself in a whisper. "I know it wasn't me. I assume...and it's only an assumption...that it wasn't one of the men who was shot. That leaves you, Joseph, Danny and old Barney."

"Well, it wasn't bloody me!" exclaimed Sinéad rather louder that Weber wished.

"Keep your voice down. I'll give you the benefit of the doubt for the moment. I assume you're no *Mata Hari*, although the special characteristic about a seductress is that the man she seduces is unable to believe she could be complicit."

"What the hell are you tryin' to say? I've seduced no one."

Indignantly, she raised her face to see his demeanour in order to determine if he was teasing and was greeted by a smile.

"But you take my point?"

"I suppose so...but you also have to consider the possibility that the Brits were intercepting messages from that short-wave radio we built for you...or that the *Gardai* are maybe listening in to the phone from our safe house, or even the Legation."

"Agreed...but we can test that hypothesis when we get back by leaving false messages and seeing if they're responded to. If they are, we may have our explanation. If not...we're still looking for a traitor!"

Gradually, the talking tailed off and stopped. Sinéad fell asleep in Weber's arms. Initially her thoughts before drifting off were of the men who were shot, particularly Dub...*perhaps he was only wounded*...but these musings were surrendered to the unusual experience of lying in a man's arms...*hmmm*, she thought...*this is quite pleasant as a way of keeping warm.*

Sinéad woke with a start to find that dawn had broken and that Weber had gone although his coat had been wrapped round her as she slept.

*What the hell's going on? Am I meant to stay here or make my way to the car?* She pulled the coat around her. *Thank God it remained dry last night,* she thought.

A twig snapped behind her, causing her to wrestle with the coat so her gun might be freed from its constraints.

"It's okay, Sinéad. It's only me."

"Where the hell were you? I fell asleep..."

"I decided to go back to our hide to see what had happened at the drop zone. Whoever it was has cleared the field. They've left some of the wooden crates but the arms, cars, lorry and bodies have all been removed. They've even taken the parachutes that Danny hadn't managed to collect. Everything's gone and it's like nothing ever happened."

"Is it safe for us to return to the car?"

"I hope so. We'll have a look now that the sun's up."

Again, Weber tentatively approached the car. He followed the same procedure but this time decided that there was no one lying in wait. He returned to Sinéad.

"I'm going to take the chance that there's no one waiting on us returning to the car. I'll go myself. You hold my pistol so I can argue an early morning walk if I'm apprehended. If I'm arrested or worse, make your own way back to Dublin using the bus. If everything's okay, I'll return in five minutes, so be ready."

He tugged at the lapels of his coat, still covering Sinéad.

"I'll need this coat if I'm to be convincing and you'd look pretty silly trying to haul it back to Dublin."

Sinéad shivered as the coat, warmed by sleep, was returned to Weber who set off briskly.

Moments later, she heard the car's ignition firing and the sounds of the car moving off. Several minutes passed before she heard the car returning. Quickly she crawled from within the yellow gorse bush and joined Weber at the roadside. She pulled the door shut and Weber drove off, heading for Dublin.

## CHAPTER TWENTY-TWO

Eduard Hempel placed the palms of his hands on his desk and leaned towards the seated Weber, his face red with anger.

"Not for a *second* do I believe you!" He shouted. "This was clearly an *Abwehr* initiative and was conducted without my knowledge or permission." He raised a piece of paper and waved it in front of Weber. "This is from Éamon de Valera. He commands my presence at noon today. The man is clearly outraged. He firmly believes that it was we who were responsible for that botched arms drop."

"Well, in that regard he is obviously wrong," lied Weber.

"Do not treat me like a simpleton, Weber. I have been a diplomat too long to be patronised by the likes of you!"

"Dr. Hempel. I hold you in the highest regard, I assure you," said Weber calmly. "But consider this. When we were in conversation with the *Taoiseach* recently, he made it clear that he did not expect Mr. Churchill to let our investment initiative go unaddressed. There is no evidence that the plane was German and the arms drop, according to de Valera, was British. Is it not more likely that Mr. Churchill is intent upon damaging our relationship with the *Taoiseach* by conspiring to have him believe us to be acting dishonourably and aggressively than by Britain attempting to match our investment?"

Hempel paused as he considered Weber's proposition. Slowly, he sat down as Weber continued.

"Your Excellency, the British are well known for their ability to deceive. For months they allowed us to think that areas other than northern France would be threatened by their invasion. They led us to believe that the main invasion would be targeted on *Pas de Calais*. They went so far as to inflate canvas tanks, trucks, and landing craft, as well as troop camp *façades* and then the *Luftwaffe* was allowed to photograph them. If they went to those lengths, why would they not arrange to drop a few arms on a field in Ireland to upset our investment plans?"

He leaned forward, his expression earnest. "Let us not turn on each other in this way, Dr. Hempel. I'm sure that the *Taoiseach* is no fool. He will understand the likelihood of British deception...but we must convince him when we meet him at noon."

"The invitation was for me, not both of us."

"But given my hypothesis and the fact that it surrounds the issue of investment, I would be prepared to accompany you should you believe this to be helpful."

Hempel leaned back in his chair and gave thought to Weber's remarks. A still silence was broken by Hempel.

"Very well! We leave at eleven-thirty prompt."

In the IRA house in Rialto, Joseph Kelly frowned and screwed his eyes in anticipation of burned lips, slurping gingerly at a spoonful of very hot vegetable soup. Before him sat Sinéad and Danny.

"Well, we're in a bit of a quandary here, are we not? First, we have one of our most senior people shot in Drogheda and now we have an arms drop discovered and more men shot. Now, I've given this a bit of thought and can see no advantage to General Weber in informin' the authorities either of Dennehy's arrival or of the drop...and I know it wasn't me who told the Brits, so I ask myself, could it have been one of yous two? I've pretty much excluded Liam Kennedy."

Danny angrily stood from his chair. "I feckin' *knew* this was why you wanted to see us and I'm gettin' tired of all these accusations. I put my feckin' life on the line two nights ago. There were people shootin' real feckin bullets at me. I got away 'cause I was feckin' lucky so I don't feel particular happy at bein' hauled up here and accused of bein' a feckin' spy when you should be handin' me a feckin' medal."

"Sit back down, Danny. If you're no British agent, you've every right to be angry. But you'll understand that I can't let you blusterin' away at me persuade me on its own that you're pure as the driven snow."

He sipped tentatively again at his soup. "For all I know you could just be auditionin' for the Lyric Theatre."

"Well, just don't start by supposin' I'm guilty, Joseph."

"Danny, if I started out by supposin' that, you'd be tied to a chair receivin' a beatin' and lookin' forward to a bullet instead of havin' a wee chat with me here. I have to take account of the fact that both of yous were involved in the two operations and good men were shot each time."

Sinéad cleared her throat. "I know you have to do this, Joseph. But I just want to say that I'm as innocent as Danny says *he* is. I swear!"

Kelly slowly pushed the bowl of soup away from him and laid the spoon beside it.

"That stuff is hotter than the Earl of Hell's kitchen."

Sinéad continued. "I was talking to Kurt...to...to General Weber...and we wondered if maybe the Brits had some way of listening into our short wave transmissions or maybe to telephone conversations from this house or the German Legation?"

"We'll give that due consideration but for the next while this morning, I want to speak with yous individually...just to see if I can discount yous from my enquiries. You understand that, don't yous?"

Both nodded.

"Then first I'll chat with Sinéad."

Danny Lafferty left the room and Sinéad closed the door behind him, taking the seat she'd just vacated.

"Before we start, Joseph, I didn't want to say this in front of anyone else but when I was with Kurt...with General Weber..," she corrected herself, "he told me that to make up for the drop going wrong, he wanted to give me forty thousand pounds sterling to do with as we wish as long as it's against the English. If we want we can buy guns from other sources, we can support our people... whatever we want."

"And how do we get this cash? Is it for you to decide, now?"

"Not at all, Joseph. He said he'd get it out the bank and give it to me then I'd pass it on to you."

"Then you tell the General that I'm most grateful"

"Now," asked Sinéad, "does that sound like someone who's a British agent?"

"Well, we'll see about that. But before we talk about the drop going wrong, I want to take you back to the shooting of Seamus I ordered in your farm in Kerry..."

Edward Timpson accepted the offer of a cigarette from Carter-Hogg as they sat in Timpson's office in Ballsbridge.

"When I first started tapping wires," said Carter-Hogg, "it was a simple proposition. I had a headset and I'd clamp the two wires attached to the headset onto somebody's line and that was all there was to it, aside from scribbling down what I heard. But there's a lot more we can do nowadays. If you'd like to know what's being said in a particular hotel room, just rent the room next to it and I can rig up something for you that will bring every whisper right into your room. I've got a very sensitive device that can listen right through a two-foot wall and amplify every sound in the room beyond."

"Is that what you've installed at the Sherbourne next to Weber's room?"

"Yes. We got lucky, although we can only ever hear one side of the conversation because he never has anyone in his room...only uses the phone. Initially, we just listened for anything to do with this investment responsibility he has but it soon became clear he's involved with the IRA as well. He's been seeing a bit of a woman called Sinéad O'Grady recently. We didn't have a file on her but she's also frequenting the house they have in Rialto so we're interested now. She doesn't have a phone at her house close by and we're chary about trying to listen into the conversations in the IRA's place."

Carter-Hogg sucked deeply at his cigarette, allowing the smoke to escape his lips in a smothered cough.

"The boys always have some Volunteers on the look-out outside their place in Rialto so tapping into their telephone is very difficult - which is why Weber's hotel room has been such a bonanza for us."

Timpson nodded his agreement.

"And the *Gardai* made short work of picking up the contents of the air drop...Very good piece of work, Captain. You should be pleased."

"I am...they took out five Volunteers and captured one old man; a driver...but I'm informed that they haven't got much from him. He seems only to have been trusted to drive the lorry on to the field. I probably believe his protestations of not knowing too much about what was going on...and my informant tells me that's the *Gardai* view as well."

"Timpson smiled."You'll soon have as many informants as me."

Carter-Hogg leaned forward and flicked some ash into a cup he'd used earlier for tea.

"We both know that when it comes to informants, you're peerless."

He took another drag on his cigarette.

"You should introduce me to some of them...against the day when you get hit by a bus."

Timpson shook his head slowly and lazily blew a cloud of smoke towards his young colleague.

"Dearest Giles. I have an infinite appetite for strong drink. I'm not unaware of my frailties. My value to His Majesty King George is that I can be relied on to provide information that can, now and again, be very useful to the Crown. If someone else knew my contacts, I'd be out on my ear before you could shout, 'last orders'."

"Then let us hope that you manage to avoid that bus!"

"Indeed!"

Kathleen O'Connell ushered the two Germans into de Valera's office. De Valera was already on his feet walking towards them.

"Gentlemen...or can I still refer to you in that way?"

"*Taoiseach,* you must accept...."

"I accept nothing, Dr. Hempel. An act of war has been perpetrated upon my country. Is there any other way it can be viewed?"

No offers of seating or teas were made.

"If you refer to the air drop we were advised took place recently, then I would accept your assessment. My purpose here today is to assure you..."

"...That it wasn't the *Luftwaffe* that dropped weapons designed to assist the IRA?" said de Valera, finishing Hempel's sentence for him.

"Precisely that, *Taoiseach*. My colleague, Professor Weber and I..."

"Wouldn't that more accurately be *Obergruppenführer* Weber. The German SS General. The battle-hardened soldier who would be quite at home organising air drops of weapons and explosives?"

Weber interrupted de Valera's invective.

"Enough of this nonsense!"

Despite themselves, de Valera and Hempel were quieted at Weber's growl.

"The German Legation under Dr. Hempel has worked assiduously over a period of years to maintain good relations with the Irish government. You would accept that. I was sent here in support of him... to invest in your economy...an ailing economy. Our strategic interests are best served by Ireland remaining neutral. You have our word as officers...yes, and as gentlemen...that there was no complicity on behalf of the Legation in any act designed to diminish that relationship."

Weber's forceful interjection caused a hesitation in de Valera. Hempel remained silent, his diplomatic senses shredded by the relative ferocity of Weber's interruption.

Weber continued. "His Excellency, Dr. Hempel and I have been working hard to understand this act of aggression and our only assessment is that your Mr. Churchill is behind this in an attempt to undermine our work in investing in Ireland and in building an economic relationship for the future. If he can't afford to match the generosity of the Third *Reich*, perhaps he can afford to spend a few pounds discarding some arms and explosives, hoping that it will rebound on the Third *Reich*."

De Valera folded his arms and bowed his head in contemplation. When he spoke it was in a quieter tone.

"I assure you, professor, he's not *my* Mr. Churchill. I am only too aware of the perfidy of which he's capable." He unfolded his arms and gestured towards some armchairs. "Let's sit."

For the next hour, the three men discussed the Germans' allegations of Allied deceit and gradually moved the conversation on to the prospective purchases Weber had investigated. A knock on the door from Miss O'Connell alerting de Valera to his next meeting brought the meeting to a close. They walked towards the door of the office.

"Gentlemen...and I'm now somewhat more comfortable that I can refer to you in that way...this war is both complex and stressful. I apologise for possibly jumping to conclusions but it did appear obvious to me that you might be encouraging the IRA to strike against me as well as the English."

Weber smiled and shook his head disparagingly. "Our ambitions are to forge excellent relations. Mr Churchill has a history of deception towards us and open hostility towards you. I honestly believe the culprits are to be found on the other side of the Irish Sea."

"But you must also believe me, Professor Weber. The *Garda Síochána na hÉireann* are investigating this act and we have one of their men in captivity. We will get to the bottom of his and if it is demonstrated that the German Legation was behind this, there will be merry hell to pay!"

"I am content with that, *Taoiseach*. You will find no duplicitous behaviour by staff of the Legation."

They exited and wordlessly made for the front door. After making the street outside, Hempel turned on Weber.

"You better be right in your assessment, *Herr* Weber. That was a very convincing performance but my instincts still tell me that all is not as it seems in your portrayal of events. If I discover you have been deceiving me, you will have more to worry about than Éamon de Valera."

"You have been too long a diplomat, Dr. Hempel... too long looking for hidden scheming ... for subtle deceits. I am an honourable man and I am as I appear. A German officer here on a mission to support you. I can tell you honestly, I am unaware of any *Abwehr* involvement in that air drop."

Hempel looked long at him. Partly assuaged, he turned and walked towards his car.

Weber watched him go. *Dear God in heaven...I'm becoming too comfortable at lying and misrepresentation. That was a narrow escape,* thought Weber. *I must be more careful!*

## CHAPTER TWENTY-THREE

Having spent the day being interrogated by Kelly, it was a tired and tearful Sinéad who knocked on the door of her house before being admitted by Henning.

"Sinéad, are you alright?"

"I held my ground but I've had a day of it, no question," she snivelled quietly, trying to conceal her emotions as she entered and threw herself wearily onto a chair next to her table.

"I'll have to get another set of keys cut for that door if you're going to stay here for any length of time."

"Well, I hope I am, Sinéad. Has something happened?"

"Nothing I can discuss with you, Hermann. Let me put it this way, if my feckin' bosses wanted to avoid telling me how much they appreciated my work in this shaggin' movement, they succeeded heroically. It's just been a horrible day...but hopefully, it'll be better tomorrow."

Henning was fast learning the resolution to most problems surrounding Sinéad.

"I'll make some tea...or do you want a whiskey?"

Over the past several weeks, Henning and Sinéad had fallen into an easy relationship, sharing confidences, comparing childhoods; Henning learning not to ask questions if Sinéad went missing for a few days. They each took enjoyment from the other, explaining their day's work although Sinéad was always careful not to reveal too much about her work as a Volunteer, limiting herself to news of her parents' farm in Kerry and the emerging poor health of her parents; Henning always quick to offer medical advice.

"Perhaps, you'd consult with them if we travelled down to Kerry?" suggested Sinéad one evening as she worried again about her parents' health. "You might be able to have a look at dad's cough and mum's swollen ankles. She'll probably want to introduce you to all sorts of old gobdaws and shawlies, friends and family, but you'll get by."

Only too eager to agree, Henning had subsequently been taken down and was introduced to both parents, mother nudging her daughter in his absence while he was in another room dealing with her husband's cough.

"Well, he's a catch and no mistake," smiled an indulgent Mrs. O'Grady. "Just the right weight for you!"

"Mother, he's just a friend. But he's also a doctor and I thought it would do no harm to have him come down and have a look at the pair of you."

Mrs. O'Grady wasn't to be put off.

"Quite good looking too!"

"Jesus, Mary and Joseph."

"And he seems such a kind and gentle man."

"Mammy!"

Doctor Henning had become a popular and respected medic in the months after his appointment. Beyond St. Kevin's, his responsibility for German nationals largely centred around the main internment camp in Curragh used to house German soldiers, mainly navy personnel stranded in Ireland. Later, Gormanston Camp, north of Dublin, in Balbriggan was used to accommodate three Germans who were kept there for a short period. Some three hundred Germans, mostly immigrants involved in the building of the giant Siemens' power plant on the Shannon who had met and married local girls were catered for by local providers. The Legation gave him little trouble other than the occasional bout of influenza and one incidence of pregnancy so his hospital duties gradually increased - as eventually did his estimation of his landlady, Sinéad. Nothing gave him more pleasure than treating her sprained ankle, a stubborn sore on her upper lip and most satisfactorily, her stiff neck for which Henning dutifully prescribed massage and for a week caringly applied oils and lotions followed by an hour's deltoid and trapezius manipulation. Initially, Sinéad had insisted that the massage be applied over her clothing but had succumbed to her doctor's advice that oils would provide greater benefit. After her first experience, she'd relaxed and had enjoyed the treatment immensely, sitting on the floor in front of the fire while Hermann sat on the sofa manipulating her shoulder muscles.

"Hermann, this is wonderful. I can't believe how lucky I am to have someone like you looking after me."

Kneading her neck muscles with strong but tender strokes, Henning was as appreciative of the transaction as was his patient.

"I am pleased to help...and it makes it all the more pleasurable when the patient is as lovely as you, Sinéad. When I do this in the hospital, usually I am dealing with a large woman who could carry bags of potatoes under her arms without any problem. This is a delight for me too."

Sinéad smiled bashfully. "You've spent too much time in Ireland already, Hermann. You have the gift of the gab and no mistake...but that's so nice. I've said it before but you're stronger than you look."

Henning was a man transported when allowed an opportunity to hold the woman with whom he was gradually falling in love. But his natural caution and shyness prevailed and other than a gradual increase in compliments and his slightly greater ease in suggesting a few drinks in the local pub, Sinéad was little aware of the feelings he held for her.

Gradually, Sinéad had succumbed to slumber and had fallen asleep with her head in Hermann's lap. Not wishing to disturb her...and appreciating the moment... Hermann considered carrying her upstairs to her bed but decided to allow her to rest as she was in front of the dying embers of the fire in the front room. From time to time when he was sure she was in a deep sleep, he lovingly stroked her dark locks.

After an hour, Sinéad awoke with a start.

"Dear God, have I been asleep?

"Your eyes closed while I was massaging your shoulders. I didn't want to wake you. You looked so comfortable."

"Dear Hermann...you're an absolute angel!"

Henning summoned up courage he didn't believe he had.

"Sit here...sit beside me."

"But wh...?"

"Do as your doctor says," he ordered, but still in a quiet voice.

Sinéad complied and Hermann shifted his position so they were sitting facing one another on the couch. Caringly, he took her hands in his as Sinéad looked on somewhat perplexed at his request, but allowing the contact nevertheless.

"Sinéad, I fear I am in great danger of breaking my Hippocratic Oath."

"And what's *that* when it's at home," she asked, still bemused.

"Well, doctors, when they qualify to practice, have to swear an oath...a promise if you will, that commits us to lead a life of high ethical behaviour and moral rectitude."

Sinéad smiled, "Well, God alone knows that you've upheld your oath to my certain knowledge. I've been treated like a princess."

She gripped Hermann's hands not unaffectionately. "So tell me more about this oath. What does it say?"

Hermann furrowed his brow and looked into the embers, trying to recall the wording.

"Well, it's quite long but it starts, 'I swear by Apollo the Physician and Asclepius and Hygieia and Panacea and all the gods, and goddesses, making them my witnesses, that I will fulfil according to my ability and judgment this oath and this covenant'..."

"This is great, Hermann. It sounds really serious, like."

"It does go on a bit and covers a lot of ground...but there's one part of it I may be failing..."

"Surely not, Hermann. You're the best doctor this side of the Irish Sea,"

Herman smiled humbly. "I do my best Sinéad...but it goes on...and I've also promised...that whatever houses I may visit, I will come for the benefit of the sick, remaining free of all intentional injustice, of all mischief and in particular of relations with both female and male persons, be they free or slaves..."

A gradual realisation dawned on Sinéad.

"Oh!..." she said slowly, "I'm assumin' here that you're not worried about any 'intentional injustices'... You're sayin' that...You're trying to tell me..." She brought Hermann's hands to her mouth, kissed them and brought them to her cheek. "I swear by all that's holy that I had no idea...and now you think that you're a bad doctor..."

Hermann wrestled with his next utterance.

"Sinéad...Sinéad...I just want to tell you that...that I like you a *lot*!"

Sinéad grasped his hands excitedly. "God bless you, Hermann Henning...*Doctor* Hermann Henning...Well, I want you to know that I like *you* a lot too. You're just the sweetest man I've ever met."

"Really?" asked Henning, surprised and delighted.

"You're just lovely, Hermann. You've become a special, special friend."

"Special?"asked Henning, inviting confirmation.

"*Very* special, Hermann," replied Sinéad.

Hermann decided to quit while he was ahead.

"Well, Sinéad O'Grady, I am very pleased to be your special friend."

Spontaneously, Sinéad reached forward and hugged Hermann tightly then sat back so as to speak.

"We live in such a desperate difficult world right now, Hermann. It's wonderful to know that I'm not alone and that there's someone...a *special* someone...who's looking out for me."

Hermann nodded wordlessly, ecstatic at the fact that the object of his affections had just told him he was the sweetest man she'd ever met. *That'll do for now,* thought Hermann.

"Well, I'm off to bed, Hermann. I've to be up early in the morning ...and so have you, so you'd better get your skates on too."

When Sinéad wasn't in the company of her new *special* friend in Dublin, she was travelling with Kurt Weber as he visited farms, hotels and other businesses on whose prospects he consulted her assiduously. Typically, she would lead the discussions and introduce Weber once a relationship had been established.

Over a matter of some months, they bought several public houses, eight farms including a sheep farm in Kildare, eleven hotels and three businesses; some of which had been recommended to Weber by one or other of the banks and still he hadn't scratched the sums of money he'd lodged with them. In most cases, Sinéad accompanied him on his visits and many evenings were spent in lodgings all over the Republic - always in separate rooms even though as the evening's alcohol had its effect, there had been moments when, as they bid one another goodnight, a closeness was evident. More than once, Weber had brought her close to him, placing a strong arm around her waist, inviting a kiss. More than once, Sinéad had resisted.

When Weber hired a team of builders to erect another room at the back of the O'Gradys' cottage at his expense in order to provide more spacious accommodation for the elderly couple, Sinéad's reaction was almost everything that Weber could have wished. That she was grateful could be in no doubt...that she showed him affection, was clear...that she felt indebted at his act of kindness was indisputable. But still Sinéad maintained what she considered a *professional* relationship.

Again her mother was impressed when they met.

"So this one's got money?"

"Another friend, mother. In fact he's more a business associate that I'm helping to buy some businesses. He's a businessman."

"He tells me he's single."

Sinéad couldn't restrain her indignation.

"Mammy, you're impossible. Stop acting like every man I bring home is a prospective husband. I'm happy as I am."

"And this one is *really* good looking...with money to burn," said Mrs. O'Grady ignoring her daughter completely.

Some nights later in a hotel in Kildare, Weber and Sinéad sat, relaxing after dinner with a drink in front of each of them. Both of them were seated comfortably in front of a log fire, Sinéad staring into its heart. Weber took the opportunity to gaze upon her form. *She's remarkably beautiful*, he thought. A white blouse edged a most impossibly pretty face. Her skin, glowing by the light of the fire, was lightly sun-tanned, her arms, bare below the elbows, had a hint of toned muscle as if she was quite used to an active life. Her long beige dress was in itself unremarkable but framing her slim figure, it took on new properties. The high-laced boots she wore to protect her still aching foot served only to accentuate her slim ankles.

Weber broke the silence in mild enquiry.

"You haven't mentioned any activity you've been asked to do as a Volunteer recently. Am I to believe that I'm now your only responsibility?"

Sinéad's eyes dropped and she gazed at her glass of stout without responding.

"Not like you to be short of a few words," he chided.

"It's not easy bein' a woman in the Republican Army."

"Not in *any* army, I'd venture."

She drained her glass and set it down, deciding to explain her almost constant accompaniment of Weber on his trips.

"You're *almost* right, Kurt, when you say you're my only responsibility. Ever since that air drop and after the shooting of poor Declan, I've been told I'm to focus upon the work of *Cumann na mBan*."

"And what's that?"

"It's the woman's organisation that supports the men Volunteers. I've been told to support you in any way you want, take a leading role in organising prisoner relief agencies and canvassing for *Sinn Féin*. Hardly what I was doing before and I'm not stooping to the usual women's role."

"Well, as long as you're supporting me in any way I choose, I'd vote that a welcome change in your role."

"Trust me...*I'll* interpret what is meant by their expression, *'in any way you choose'*. You can report me if you want but I'm fed up with these people in Dublin thinking they know best all the time."

Weber grinned, his white teeth flashing. "Sounds like you don't trust me either."

Sinéad placed both elbows on the table between her and Weber and cupped her chin in her hands.

"I don't know who to trust these days."

"Poor Sinéad. You try so hard but yet they don't appreciate you."

"Exactly," said Sinéad, acknowledging Weber's empathy immediately.

"I've worked hard to support the Republic... *my* Republic. I've commanded Volunteers and I've obeyed commands even where they went against every fibre of my being...but that's not good enough for them over in Dublin. They think there's a chance that me and Danny might be bloody British agents and unless and until they think otherwise, I'm to be put out to grass."

"So I'm something of a backwater in Republican terms?" asked Weber impishly.

"No...of course not. It's just that...it's just...I don't know. Maybe you bloody *are*!" responded Sinéad with an intolerance she didn't feel.

"Sinéad, you are simply one of the most remarkable women I've ever had the good fortune to meet. I'm glad you're on my side and I cannot fathom why your senior people would not ask ever-increasing responsibilities of you."

"Ah, you're just bletherin', Kurt Weber."

"Indeed I am not, Miss O'Grady. And I'd have thought that by now you'd appreciate how strongly I hold personally affectionate views of you."

Embarrassed, Sinéad looked into his shrewd, clear eyes. "Oh, I'm sure you like me well enough."

"Sinéad O'Grady. If only you *knew* the feelings I hold for you...you completely beguile me."

"It's your round, Kurt. Stop talkin' like an eejit and get me another glass of Guinness."

Weber's face creased into a smile and he stepped to the bar to order more drink.

Sinéad's chin remained firmly cupped in her hands. *What in the name of all that's holy is wrong with me?... When I'm with gentle and caring Hermann, I can only think of strong, forceful Kurt...and when I'm with Kurt, I have only thoughts for wonderful Doctor Henning. Jesus, Mary and Joseph, I should get myself to a bloody nunnery...and quick!*

## Chapter Twenty-four

# Dublin, Ireland
# 1945

Captain Giles Carter-Hogg let out a whoop as he read the decoded massage that had been placed in his in-tray. He leapt to his feet.

"We've got the fucker! He's *dead*...Hitler's dead. The war's over...Hitler's dead!"

He took to his feet and ran down the corridor where other offices were occupied with staff who had also just been apprised of the news. Gleeful staff were hugging and even the most shy, mousiest secretary danced. A senior official, normally the most stentorian of men, stood quietly, tears rolling down his face. Timpson was busily twisting a corkscrew into a bottle of red wine. Carter-Hogg found himself standing on a desk screaming at the ceiling. Chaos reigned.

In his home in Dún Laoghaire, Dr. Hempel sat defeated, slumped at a desk in a small office he used when in his residence. For the first time in his career, he'd loosened his tie at the neck. A note he'd been passed had been crumpled and thrown disinterestedly towards an overfilled waste-paper basket. Knocks at his door had gone unacknowledged. For long moments he stared uncomprehendingly at a sheaf of papers that had just earlier consumed him.

The door opened and Weber walked in, having been shown upstairs by Hempel's wife. He sat on a chair opposite Hempel's desk and spoke slowly; quietly.

"So the *Fuehrer* is dead?"

Hempel did not respond. Weber tried again.

"The wire says he shot himself in Berlin."

Sighing, Hempel brought himself back into the present.

"What?" He hesitated. ..."Yes, yes...it would appear so. The war is over."

"What now, Eduard?" asked Weber, immediately more familiar with his superior.

"I suppose we'll have to await contact from Berlin... and it won't be long before the British show up to gloat."

His tearful wife, a handkerchief at her mouth re-entered Hempel's office.

"Eduard, I am informed by Legation staff that the Prime Minister of Ireland, Éamon de Valera is on his way to see you. Should I ask him to wait downstairs until you are ready?"

"Wh...what...de Valera is visiting me...here?" he asked himself, uncomprehendingly.

Weber asked the question Hempel was asking himself.

"Isn't this against normal protocol?"

"Very much so...and just after the news...I can't... Whatever...?"

Weber and Hempel sat together in the silent office, each silent, lost in thought. After some time, *Frau* Hempel returned.

"Eduard, the *Taoiseach* of Ireland, Éamon de Valera."

Hardly had the word *Valera* registered when the tall, lean figure of the *Taoiseach* strode into the room. Both Germans rose, forcing themselves back into the familiarity of their usual roles.

"*Taoiseach*!" Hempel took de Valera's outstretched hand limply. "You must forgive me. At present...we... Professor Weber and I...we are in deep despair..."

"My dear Eduard. I have brought with me my colleague, Joe Walshe, Secretary of the Department of External Affairs, in order to bring the German people, through you, our deepest condolences. We have been informed of the demise of your *Fuehrer* and appreciate the great sadness you must be experiencing."

"I must confess, *Taoiseach*, we are still reeling from the shock of the news but your thoughtfulness is most welcome." He saw his wife still hover around the entrance to his office. "I forget myself. Please...sit. *Frau* Hempel will bring us drinks."

All sat and de Valera came directly to his point.

"Eduard. You have served the German nation well... more than any other human being could have managed. Your leader is dead and no doubt there will be repercussions. The Allies will doubtless seek retribution."

Hempel looked at him blankly, appearing not to be completely conscious of his meaning.

"Eduard. You are an honourable man. I will not have you thrown to the wolves...so I have a proposal. I wish to grant you diplomatic immunity. Protection against perfidious Albion. As a Free State, you would be shielded here from a vengeful opponent."

Neither Weber nor Hempel reacted to his proposal.

"You must open a book of condolences which I will be pleased to sign."

Hempel stirred. "*Taoiseach*...you are more than thoughtful."

"Not at all. To have failed to call upon you as the German representative in Ireland would have been an act of unpardonable discourtesy to the German nation and to you yourself. During the whole of the war, your conduct has been irreproachable."

"You must understand that my immediate concern is not with myself...but with other German nationals here in Ireland."

He gestured at his colleague. "General Weber here would doubtless be someone whom the Allies would love to see in one of their military courts."

"Well, you and Professor Weber have no fear on that account, Eduard. I am head of an independent nation and have little appetite for hunting down the vanquished. To the victors belong the spoils but not here in Ireland, you may be assured of that. You must think of my offer of diplomatic immunity...both of you...indeed, *all* Germans."

Still in shock, Weber realised the import of de Valera's comments. The *Abwher's* plan might just work after all, he mused.

De Valera and Walshe stood and made ready to leave.

"There is perhaps one more last piece of unhappy business, Eduard. I'm afraid I have to ask you to hand me the keys to the Legation offices. I will require to hand these to the Allies who will, I'm sure, seek to take control of your assets."

Hempel nodded resignedly.

"Eduard, I am sorry about your Chancellor, *Herr* Hitler. *Ar dheis Dé go raibh a anam dílis.* May his soul rest with God."

## CHAPTER TWENTY-FIVE

Weber and Hempel sat together in his office in Hempel's house.

"It'll be on shortly," said Weber, sensing Hempel's impatience.

"I do hope he's statesmanlike," said Hempel. "I know he was most upset at Churchill's broadcast implying his magnanimity by saying that he chose not to lay a violent hand upon the Irish even though they 'frolicked' with we Germans to their hearts' content."

As the wireless set continued to emit only white noise, Weber played with the controls, seeking a signal that would permit them to listen to the much anticipated response the *Taoiseach* had promised the Irish people. Hempel continued his monologue.

"He as much as said he'd have come to close quarters with the Irish if he'd taken the view that it was necessary but spared them because of the concerns he had for his friends in Ulster...what a conceited man!"

Intermittently, the wireless provided sound that suggested a speaking voice just out of reach of the hiss. Weber continued to tune and retune until gradually the unmistakable voice of Éamon de Valera broke through. He came straight to the purpose of his message.

"Allowances can be made for Mr. Churchill's statement, however unworthy, in the first flush of victory. No such excuse could be found for me in this quieter atmosphere. There are, however, some things it is essential to say. I shall try to say them as dispassionately as I can. Mr. Churchill makes it clear that, in certain circumstances, he would have violated our neutrality and that he would justify his actions by Britain's necessity. It seems strange to me that Mr. Churchill does not see that this, if accepted, would mean that Britain's necessity would become a moral code and that when this necessity became sufficiently great, other people's rights were not to count... that is precisely why we had this disastrous succession of wars; World War number one and World War number two...and shall it be World War number three? Surely Mr. Churchill must see that if his contention be admitted in our regard, a like justification can be framed for similar acts of aggression elsewhere and no small nation adjoining a great Power could ever hope to be permitted to go its own way in peace. It is indeed fortunate that Britain's necessity did not reach the point where Mr. Churchill would have acted. All credit to him that he successfully resisted the temptation which I have no doubt many times assailed him in his difficulties, and to which, I freely admit, many leaders might have easily succumbed. It is indeed hard for the strong to be just to the weak, but acting justly always has its rewards. By resisting his temptation in this instance, Mr. Churchill, instead of adding another horrid chapter to the already bloodstained record of the relations between England and this country, has advanced the cause of international morality — an important step, one of the most important indeed that can be taken on the road to the establishment of any sure basis for peace....

Mr. Churchill is proud of Britain's stand alone, after France had fallen and before America entered the war.

Could he not find in his heart the generosity to acknowledge that there is a small nation that stood alone not for one year or two, but for several hundred years against aggression; that endured spoliations, famine, massacres, in endless succession; that was clubbed many times into insensibility, but each time on returning to consciousness took up the fight anew; a small nation that could never be got to accept defeat and has never surrendered her soul?" He allowed a short silence. "I will finish here. *Go mbeannaí Dia Eireann.* May God bless Ireland."

Weber listened for a moment to the announcer offering a few words in comment before reaching over and extinguishing power to the wireless.

"Well, your Éamon de Valera seems the equal of Churchill in the power of his speech making!"

"He is an exceptional man," agreed Hempel..."and generous too. His offer of diplomatic immunity not only to us but to *all* of us Germans is an act of great courage. I have no doubt that he will come under enormous international pressure to return the likes of you and me to the Allied courts. He actually telephoned me yesterday to advise me that he would not shut the door on any German who arrived here in Ireland seeking relief."

"Are you minded to accept his offer, Eduard?"

Hempel shifted uneasily in his chair.

"I spoke with *Frau* Hempel last night and she is agreed that our work here is unfinished. I am the Envoy Extraordinary and Minister Plenipotentiary of the German Government, a government that is no more. In consequence, I propose to accept the *Taoiseach's* offer and remain here at my post in the Legation as long as possible. We have enough financial reserves to continue to pay our staff until the Allies withdraw these resources and given the chaos in Berlin, there are no orders emanating from anyone there. In due course, I'll have to conduct myself as a private citizen if I stay and support our countrymen."

He looked at Weber as if almost seeking his approval but not expecting it.

"So, I will remain," he said with as much authority as he could muster.

Weber rose and looked out of the window without responding.

"And you, Kurt?"

Slowly, Weber turned to face his senior officer.

"Well, I'm much in the same position as you. I have clear orders which most certainly carry me beyond the end of the war...indeed, in many ways, they *anticipate* the war ending as it has done and it is evident that the work I have already accomplished in purchasing businesses across Ireland must now be put to good use by insinuating any German national already here as well as accommodating those who find their way to the ports of the Republic."

Hempel nodded. "I agree with you. Now your work... *our* work," he said tentatively..."must take a new course."

Weber acknowledged Hempel's new enthusiasm for partnership.

"Beyond that, Eduard, I have no one back home in Germany. If I returned I'm sure the Allied authorities would install me in a prisoner of war camp for some time and I might even have to fight to clear my name after hearing of the wickedness of some of my fellow SS officers. I could not be sure of doing so successfully and may have to pay a higher price."

"You *must* stay here, Kurt. Your work here is important and you have the respect of the *Taoiseach* of Ireland as well as the support of the Legation, such as it *is* now."

Weber grimaced his gratitude.

"Thank you Eduard. But there are other matters as well. I have grown very fond of some of the people I have met over here in the course of my duties. I am excited about the possibility of actually seeing our businesses grow and prosper...I can see how we will be able to care for any nationals who make it to these shores...so, in short, like you, I will stay. We also have the necessary resources to be able to fund our activities...and it goes without saying that in the absence of the Legation I will be only too pleased to make provision of finance in a way that permits the essential work of the Legation to continue in all but name, as I will if you yourself want to build a new life here beyond your work with the Legation."

"I suspect that we might have to make arrangements with the Irish banks to move some of our resources, Kurt. As I say, it's only a matter of time before I come under pressure to submit to an occupying power, either Britain or America. I suspect that de Valera will feel more comfortable if we deal with the Americans. They'll want access to all of our accounts so I'd suggest we set aside some money where they can't access it in order to continue our work."

"Be assured, I've already done this, Eduard. As it became evident that the war would not end in a German victory, I started moving funds around so when you hand the Americans the details of the fund, they'll only find half a million pounds sterling there. To track down the rest of the funds will take years of work and even then

I'd be surprised if they found everything. We've money, assets and bullion all over the place."

Hempel smiled at Weber's resourcefulness. The two men shook hands, locked in a shared understanding of their new circumstances.

Over the next months, Germans from a military and civil background began to appear at offices Weber had procured to house the work of the Legation, funnelling funds through his Irish millionaire admirer Arthur Joyce as the lease-holder to avoid any assets being removed by the British or Americans.

"We will continue to refer to our work as being undertaken by the Legation until there is a command structure within Germany that over-rides us," said Weber, now carrying more financial and therefore political weight than Hempel.

Weber took it upon himself to interview each individual in order both to establish their legitimacy as Germans seeking relief as well as reassuring himself that any individual presenting themselves was not an agent working for a foreign power.

Some who were referred to him were family groups interned in England and eager to relocate themselves not to Germany where chaos was still in evidence for normal Germans, nor to elsewhere in England but to a country where they anticipated finding less hostile communities. Others were German officers and ordinary foot-soldiers who had escaped and made their way to Dublin. In the year following the end of the war in Europe, Weber began to see his countrymen settle into roles he found for them in various positions. He enjoyed the process of establishing their abilities and finding them positions in factories, farms, hotels and public houses - a major characteristic being their ability to speak English. No one he interviewed had a grasp of Irish *Gaelic*.

One difficulty he found was the presumption held by many officers who arrived was that they would enjoy a seniority over more junior ranks upon gaining employment and there was one much publicised killing when a second lieutenant shot and killed a private whom Weber had placed in a more senior position in a hotel. Following this episode, Weber made more strenuous efforts to ensure that those he placed completely understood that the war was over, that rank no longer mattered and that if they were to forge a new life in Ireland, they would have to do so on merit and hard work rather than on their past glories.

Eduard Hempel, however, urged reflection on this policy. Using all of his diplomatic skills, he would speak sociably in the evenings with Weber, making the point that German society had for many years been based upon uniformed status and that he might be pursuing his 'entirely understandable' goals too enthusiastically.

This point was made particularly forcibly by Hempel upon the arrival of Klaus Marković, a very senior member of the Nazi party, an *Obergruppenführer* in the *Waffen* SS and accused by the Allies of many acts against humanity. De Valera had granted diplomatic immunity much to the fury of the American Ambassador and despite strong representations made by the British.

Hempel implored Weber to treat him favourably, *'perhaps a pension?...he is, after all, your equal in rank, a brother member of the Waffen SS'*, in order to acknowledge the seniority of the man but only received an agreement to interview him with an open mind.

Some days later, Weber sat across his desk from a rather overweight, pompous man in an ill-fitting suit who had yet to make eye contact as he fished a cigarette from a silver case and eased it into a matching cigarette-holder.

"So, *Herr* Marković. You wish to make your home here in Ireland? The notes provided by Dr. Hempel say that you escaped from a Prisoner of War camp - largely because the Allies didn't realise your true identity."

The bull-necked Marković laughed as he dragged on his cigarette and swept cigarette ash from his lap with his free hand.

"These fools! In the final months of the war, it was a simple matter to forge new documents. It was easy to assume the identity of a cook in the service of the *Abwher*." He gestured at his rotund waist.

"I do not think that the Allies would have believed I was a serving soldier carrying this extra weight."

"I see you are not German, *Herr* Marković?"

Gruber bristled. "*Obergruppenführer* Marković when we are in this office. I am your *equal* in rank and demand that I be treated as such."

Weber closed the file he had on his desk and responded calmly.

"*I* will determine your future here in Ireland, *Herr* Marković. The war is over. I am tasked with helping German citizens with relief and I no longer acknowledge rank. You are no longer a serving officer." He pursed his lips and continued. "So you are not German?"

Marković's face reddened.

"I fought courageously for the German Army for five years. I am...*was* an *Obergruppenführer* in the *Waffen SS*...and, yes, I am Croatian."

"And how did you arrive on these shores?" asked Weber more conversationally.

"As I said, I was held in a Prisoner of War camp near Dusseldorf because the Allies thought me a cook but I escaped and made my way to a Franciscan Order in Würzburg in Bavaria."

Weber didn't respond, reading Marković's file dispassionately and bringing an outburst from the Croatian.

"I am a good Catholic, *Obergruppenführer* Weber. I attend mass regularly."

He slammed his fist on the desk.

"I am a *believer* and so the Franciscans helped get me safe passage to Dublin on a boat from Hamburg."

His temper subsided as he met Weber's gaze.

"My papers say I'm a Professor in History."

Weber laughed. "Yes, I read that. I thought I was reading my own file."

Marković looked confused.

"I am...or at least *was*...a Professor of History at Heidelberg University before all of this started." He continued. "And why did you choose Ireland as a destination, *Herr* Marković?"

Marković shrugged."It was all that was available. I'd heard tell that some of our compatriots had been able to reach Argentina but the Franciscans had only relations with Ireland. Also I was told that there were very few

Jewish people in Ireland. I gather that these vile people are not welcome here."

Weber massaged his neck muscles and changed his tone.

"I have been away from the front for some time, *Herr* Marković and it was only towards the end of the war that Dr. Hempel and I heard of the murder of Jews in the extermination camps. I was ashamed of being German when I heard and I know that Dr. Hempel was similarly. We had never heard of a greater evil."

He glared at Marković. "What do you want to do here in Ireland to earn a living?"

Marković's face fell as he tried to understand an attitude with which he'd not been faced during the war and one he'd not expected from a fellow officer in the *Waffen* SS.

"Before I signed up I was a sheep farmer...on my family's land near Zagreb in Croatia. I would return there tomorrow if I could be protected from the wrath of the Allies."

He scratched his jaw nervously.

"One other possibility might be to change my appearance. To find a surgeon here in Ireland who might alter my face so that even my old mother, God rest her soul, might not recognise me."

"I have heard that these operations are performed sometimes...but on soldiers who have suffered facial injury in combat. I am unaware of any such procedure here in Ireland."

Weber pulled another file towards him, opened it and ran his finger down a column.

"We have a sheep farm in County Kildare. Twenty Acres. We have an Irish farm manager." He consulted the file.

"A man called Séamus Macmanus. You would be expected to keep him and treat him well. The Legation would give you tenancy and if things go well, you will be given the title deeds in four years. During that period, you would be given a stipend of three hundred Irish Pounds a year and be expected to run the farm profitably."

Marković's face lit up. "*Obergruppenführer* that would be wonderful."

Weber rose, walked round his desk to face Marković who was still seated. He balanced himself on the edge of his desk.

"My files show that the Allies have now identified you and want you extradited because you are alleged to have ordered the killing of an entire village of Frenchmen and women. Children too..."

Marković bridled at Weber's comment.

"The fortunes of war, *Obergruppenführer*. There were partisans hiding in the village shooting at our troops. We had no option."

Weber rose and positioned his face close to that of Marković.

"You had *every* option, you murderous bastard. Waging war on women and children despoils the uniform you wore. You call yourself a believer yet you shoot innocents."

He stood erect and opened the door.

"Leave me now before I change my mind about the farm in Kildare. Miss Kerrigan downstairs will take care of the administration."

Slowly, unsure of himself, Marković rose and walked ungainly towards the door whose handle Weber held, as if ready to slam it on his agreement.

"And one more thing, *Herr* Marković. If I find that you have not disappeared into oblivion in Kildare...if I find that you have not treated Mr. Macmanus like a prince...if I find that you have not become *beloved* in the local community...I will personally collect my Lugar...I will visit you in Kildare and I will shoot you like the mongrel *hund* you are. You will not be missed." He looked down at Marković.

"Leave me now. Don't give me a reason to meet you again."

Once Marković had left the building, Weber called Miss Kerrigan to his office.

"Could you contact Doctor Hermann Henning and ask him if he'd join me for supper in my hotel this evening, say around eight o'clock?"

Weber walked back to his hotel and changed before leaving his room, descending the wide staircase that led to the dining area. Already seated in the adjacent bar reading that day's Irish Times was his guest, Hermann Henning. Weber moved to join him, signalling to the barman as he did so that he'd like his usual glass of Scotch whisky. Henning stood as he approached and the two men shook hands in greeting.

"Hermann, it's good to see you. I'm sorry I've not been in touch for awhile, but as you'd imagine, I'm being kept busy by Dr. Hempel and the increasing numbers of our fellow nationals who are arriving weekly."

"It's always a pleasure, Kurt and I've been equally busy in St. Kevin's."

Each man enjoyed the company of the other until Weber signalled to a waiter their desire to eat. Bowing before the request, he drew back Weber's chair and invited them to follow him to the dining room.

Small talk predominated as they ordered and made swift work of the poached salmon they were served. Weber soon turned to his matter in hand.

"Hermann, I was much impressed by your dexterity on board the Trinity when you operated on Declan Dennehy."

Somewhat taken aback by Weber's change of tack, Henning muttered some words of thanks for the compliment.

"So skilful. Have you been called upon to do much work with the scalpel?"

"In Germany I was beginning to undertake quite a few different operations before the war. I enjoyed the responsibility. In Sefton, one or two but my role here hasn't required me to lift a knife. Others undertake these tasks. Experienced men. I'm still relatively inexperienced in theatre procedures. Why do you ask?"

"I had a meeting today with a member of the Waffen SS who is now lodged here in Ireland. A hateful man but he raised an interesting matter with me. He asked if I might arrange facial reconstruction on him so that he might return unrecognised to his native Croatia. I thought I would ask if this was something you thought you might be capable of performing?"

Henning finished chewing a small piece of soda bread and sipped at a glass of Sancerre Weber had ordered earlier, rehearsing his response before offering any utterance.

"In my teaching hospital in University of Greifswald Medical School I saw many operations where disfigurement of some part of the body had taken place. Not always very successful. Every severe injury deforms in its own way but medical practice is not yet sufficiently advanced to repair the damage consistently."

"Facial surgery?"

"Often, but there's something uniquely devastating about having one's face burned or torn beyond recognition. The efforts of surgeons here has not been particularly good. Even the best and most experienced of men in Greifswald could not achieve excellent results. However, these failed efforts refer to those where the very shape of their face has been altered by trauma. Performing an operation on a patient where there was no existing damage, merely a requirement to alter appearance could be undertaken with more chance of success..."

"So might you be persuaded to undertake some operations of this nature?"

Henning laid down his cutlery and held Weber's gaze.

"I owe you so much, Kurt. But I will not be able to assist."

"Your reasons?"

"Well, first, I have not performed surgery for some years and you require a consistency of practice to accomplish these delicate operations. Second, it would take time that I might otherwise bestow on someone who has a serious medical problem and third, I won't be party to a medical procedure that is designed to protect someone from lawful challenge. If the trials in Nuremberg showed anything it was that the courts were fair. Many accused were spared the noose. Some walked free. We have nothing to fear from Allied justice."

"But you yourself were sent to a detention camp for nothing more than annoying a petty bureaucrat."

"Few things are perfect in this world, Kurt. But I won't operate on your Croatian."

Weber smiled, his white teeth accentuating his broad grin.

"And I not only accept your reasoning," He lifted his glass in a light toast. "I applaud your morality."

## CHAPTER TWENTY-SIX

The wind blew colder than any previously experienced by Ezra Hasofer as he stood shivering on the quayside in the port of Dublin. His papers showed him as a German named Dietrich Naumann, a shopkeeper from Dresden. Like most other travellers, he possessed only a small suitcase. Fortunately, these were seldom, if ever, checked. This was of advantage as Hasofer's case contained a Luger semi-automatic, recoil-operated Pistole P-08 with sound suppressor and ammunition along with some clothes and photographs of fictitious family members. His orders from *Haganah* had been memorised; masquerade as a German national, find a way of being of use to the German Legation, discover what you can about those Nazis who have escaped justice in Ireland, report back to *Haganah* and assassinate those they deem should die. He had been given two targets in advance of his arrival; Geert Hirsch and Horst Krueger, both senior Nazis based somewhere in Ireland whom *Haganah* had decided must perish.

It took a long time that day for Irish officials to clear his request for entry to the country. His request for immunity was noted and he was directed to the offices of the unofficial German Legation for aid and assistance while due process was instituted. The docks in Dublin were but a short distance from the city centre and Hasofer asked for directions as he pulled his coat tighter to him and walked beside the slate coloured river towards the offices of the German Legation. He brought with him fifty pounds Sterling which he converted to Irish currency at the first bank he came across before finding a room at a small, run-down hotel near the Legation. Describing himself as Swiss, he took a room and paid four weeks in advance with a further sum to be repaid unless the contents of the room went missing or were damaged.

Leaving his weapon and ammunition under the mattress along with forty of his Punts, he washed and left almost immediately for the Legation where, upon arrival, he was given an appointment with Weber the following day.

The solid steel door in the interview cell in Mountjoy Prison closed slowly with a clattering rattle as the lock demonstrated its age. *Jesus, there's no way anyone's walking out that door without the guard's permission,* thought Sinéad as she accepted the offer of a seat on the other side the of table to Sean Casey.

"Hi Sean. Are you well?"

"*Is miar liom cois na tine agus boladh ne móna im' shrón*...I wish I was by the fire with the smell of turf in my nose, Sinéad."

"We all wish that, Sean," she smiled.

The half-hour conversation, witnessed occasionally by the prison warder through a peep-hole, passed uneventfully as Sinéad took notes from Casey on aspects of his family life he wanted dealt with. Some small talk about the current situation following the end of the war in Europe followed amid some joint cursing of the fortunes of the British and Irish governments before the prison guard opened the door again signifying the end of the visit.

Sinéad hugged Casey.

"See you in a month, Sean. I'll look in on Mary and the kids. Now, don't you worry."

Beyond her duties with Weber, Sinéad had had to make some time available for the task allocated her by Kelly to assist in the organising of prisoner relief and found meeting fellow members of the IRA in custody more to her taste than dealing with other Irish women who wished to offer voluntary help via the women's organisation, *Cumann na mBan*.

*Too tame*, was Sinéad's verdict. *Just one step up from flower arranging.*

Outside the prison while awaiting her exit, Hermann leaned against a fence reading a newspaper article about the German *Oberstleutnant*, Matthäus Thalberg who had been entertained by the Dublin business community the evening before as a consequence of his new role as owner of Ryan's Engineering, one of Weber's acquisitions. As Sinéad stepped through the gates he folded the journal and put it in his jacket pocket whilst walking towards her.

"Go okay?"

"Yeah. Poor guy has two kids with rickets and two with tuberculosis. They just can't afford to eat properly. His wife Mary's just recovering from pneumonia and they've only the money that we make over to them...and that's not a lot, believe me."

Hermann, now more confident in his friendship with her, held her arm as he guided her across the road towards a bus stop.

"Would it help if I took a look at them?"

"Would you Hermann? It would mean a lot to Sean. I didn't promise him but I'd hoped that you might offer."

"Be pleased to."

"They live in Arvagh in County Cavan. About seventy miles from here. It'd be a trip of a few days."

"And would you be going as well?"

"Of course! I'd need to give them some money and spend some time with Mary so I can report back to Sean...and anyway, I wouldn't be lettin' you wander about up there all on your own. You'd drown in one of their lakes. There's more water than roads up there."

"Then it would be a pleasure as well as a mercy mission, Sinéad. I'll speak with the hospital about some time off to make the visit. Three days you say?"

"Three days. I'd say so. And I'll speak with Kurt. He's talkin' about goin' to visit some new properties and businesses in Galway and I'm meant to go with him but I'll make sure the dates don't clash. Will we try for next week?"

"That seems fine. I'll try to borrow some medicaments that might assist...and bring some more just in case there are others in Arvagh who might benefit. I can't imagine they'll get as decent a service as the good people of Dublin."

He paused, masking his uncertainty as he looked along the road trying to identify the bus that would take them back to Rialto.

"Kurt seems to have you all to himself these days," he smiled awkwardly. "You must be doing great work for the German people."

"We agreed we wouldn't talk about that, Hermann. And I'm not doin' it for Germany as you say. I'm under orders and as far as I'm concerned, it's all for the Republic, believe me. Now let's leave it at that."

"If you say so, Sinéad but I can't quite make out how the Republic benefits from Kurt buying businesses to house German immigrants."

"Well, you don't know the whole story, Hermann. And with a bit of luck, he'll buy us a car that we can use to get to Arvagh instead of the bus. I've asked him and if he does, you'll appreciate his assistance. That bus journey would give you a sore behind before you get half the way there."

"So Kurt's buying you a *car* now?"

"He's buyin' the *IRA* a car. It lets us have more freedom of movement as well as other members." She grasped Hermann's arm excitedly. "And he says he'll teach me to drive, despite me bein' a woman...He doesn't think women should drive but I gave him a flea in his ear for that."

"Well, I don't think *that's* very gallant, Sinéad", said Hermann earnestly. "There's no reason women can't drive just as well as men."

Sinéad hugged his arm affectionately. "D'you know, Hermann. You're just the loveliest, sweetest man I've ever met. Kurt thinks women shouldn't leave the kitchen...or the bedroom, I'd imagine."

Hermann drew his right arm tight towards his body accepting Sinéad's hug and grinned.

"Then Kurt's a dinosaur but *you*, Miss O'Grady, are the most beautiful and wonderful woman I've ever met."

Her coy smile in response had Henning glowing as the bus pulled up and they boarded, both comfortable in each others' company.

Weber strode into the small downstairs office which he used to meet new German immigrants. His routine now established, he held his hand out to Ezra Hasofer who was seated in the chair across from his desk. He carried a notepad which he placed on the desk as he sat and consulted the slip of paper prepared for him by Miss Kerrigan.

"My name is Kurt Weber. And you are?"...He glanced at the paper he held in his hand..."Dietrich Naumann... and before the war you were a shopkeeper from Dresden?"

"I was. And while in the army I was a prison guard in Leipzig."

"And how did you reach these shores?"

"My family perished in the air attacks on Dresden while I was in the army. But I am very fortunate in that my family had wealth and I managed to obtain some money from an uncle to make my way here."

"Were you imprisoned after the war?"

"Very briefly. I was expected to work clearing debris from the streets of Magdeburg but I bribed an American soldier to take me to Bremen in the rear of his lorry and then made my way to Hamburg where I bought a ticket to London. I took a train to Liverpool and caught the ferry to Dublin."

"You speak English very well, *Herr* Naumann."

"That comes of spending all of my time with English and American airmen in *Stalag Luft* Seventy-seven in Döbeln near Leipzig."

"And your accent? I can't identify your accent."

"Until I was ten years old I lived with my grandparents in German East Africa...in Dar es Salaam, although by the time we left, there weren't many Germans there."

Weber nodded his acknowledgement.

"And tell me, *Herr* Naumann, *why* did you come here?"

"Because I am tired of conflict, *Herr* Weber...and I am afraid of the aftermath of the war in Germany. I was fortunate to miss the fighting and had a very safe war behind the protected fences of a prisoner of war camp but as I said, I have no close relatives, no real ties to Germany and want to build a new life. I want to continue to *feel* German but to embrace a new culture and to make a fresh life for myself. Ireland is a neutral nation and because of my command of the English language, I thought I might do better here than, say, Switzerland or Spain."

"And are you an educated man, *Herr* Naumann?"

"I like to think so, *Herr* Weber. But my learning is self-taught. At night reading books after the shop closed," said Hasofer truthfully. "I have managed a large store having learned how to run a business from my father and believe that I have the ability to be successful in a country not disfigured by war."

"I believe that *every* country has been disfigured by this war, *Herr* Naumann, whether or not it saw military action on any scale."

For the next hour, Weber and Hasofer fell into an increasingly affable and social conversation until Weber's laughter was punctuated by Miss Kerrigan's sharp knock on the door, reminding him of his appointment with Eduard Hempel.

"I am so sorry, Miss Kerrigan. We quite forgot ourselves. I will only be a few moments more."

He turned to Hasofer. "*Herr* Naumann, I have enjoyed our discussion and I am sure we will be able to help you."

He drummed his fingers on the file in front of him while he reflected.

"Your command of language and your general disposition might permit me to offer you a role beyond that normally offered to those who pass this way."

Again he drummed. "I tell you what *Herr* Naumann, can you return tomorrow at the same hour? Perhaps by then I might have worked out how best we can use your talents. Is this acceptable?"

"I am very grateful to you, Herr Weber. I would be happy to undertake any task you would ask of me."

"Then I will see you tomorrow. Same time."

Hasofer left the Legation and walked back towards his accommodation, quite unaware of the distant attentions of Captain Giles Carter-Hogg who had trained his binoculars on him even as he had arrived more than an hour earlier and which now followed him as he left.

*Another German taking advantage of Weber's charity,* thought the British officer as he wrote down the time, date and a description of Hasofer in his notebook for later reference in case the photograph he took of him on his way in to the Legation didn't develop properly as had happened before. *Better safe than sorry,* he thought ruefully.

## Chapter Twenty-seven

Éamon de Valera sat fretting in his office with Joe Walshe, his Secretary of External Affairs reading a briefing note for the third time. His personal secretary, Miss Kathleen O'Connell had just positioned herself discretely to one side of the twosome and had begun taking notes, arriving late to the conversation.

"I see your point, Joe. If the English decide to repatriate all of their Irish citizens to Ireland now that the war is over we'd have maybe a hundred thousand additional mouths to feed within a very short space of time."

Walshe seemed more agitated than his political master.

"How would we employ them, house them? And *Taoiseach*...given their experiences in English factories and on the front line, they might easily return as radicals, placing outrageous demands on the Free State that would be a most heavy and grievous burden."

"You'd better draft a few words on this for us to consider, Joe. I must say, I view it as unlikely because Churchill will have to rebuild his battered cities and care for his wounded and he'll need our people to assist. But who knows Mr. Churchill's mind. Let's hope for the best but prepare for the worst."

"As you wish, *Taoiseach*."

"Anything else?"

"Yes. Eduard and Frau Hempel have both now formally applied for diplomatic immunity. And so, it would seem, has our German benefactor, Kurt Weber. I'm also told that there are quite a number of Germans and East Europeans who've registered an interest with the Legation now that it's re-opened its offices to represent the interests of German nationals unofficially."

"Well, you know our position, Joe. If belligerents from either the Allied or Axis powers wish to settle here in Ireland and pose no threat to the Free State, then they're welcome. We must maintain our role as neutral peacemakers although I imagine Mr. Churchill might have believed me to be taunting him when I wrote intervening on behalf of German officers sentenced to death at the Nuremberg trials."

"Much good it'll do, *Taoiseach*. The Allies scent blood and it seems to me that they'll use the trials as an instrument to punish the senior officers of a defeated Axis state."

De Valera removed his eyepiece and rubbed the tiredness from his eyes.

"I suppose, Joe but as an independent and neutral nation we're honour-bound to question their right to try military and political leaders for actions taken during wartime and for which there was no statute in law at the time the crimes were committed."

He laughed, gently slapping his thigh to emphasise his light-heartedness.

"In my letter I also compared the Nuremberg trials to the British use of the judicial system in Ireland against our *own* nationalists so I can't imagine Churchill being too impressed by any plight we might foresee here if he repatriates our countrymen in one fell swoop. He'll prod us in the ribs if an opportunity presents."

Walshe shuffled his papers.

"We've also had a request from the American Ambassador to accept some of those poor Jewish people who were found in the German terror camps."

"Ah...now that is a horse of a different colour, Joe. I think I'll ruminate on that request. There's a lot of public hostility to the idea."

He waved his hand at his secretary as if patting a dog, a sign he used when he didn't want his comments to be recorded as part of the meeting.

"Our newspapers aren't exactly on side. The Times and the Examiner are opposed and they carry a lot of clout. I mean the poor Jews have suffered terribly but we have a storm of problems we have to deal with and God alone knows how difficult it'll be to deal with them all without complicating matters. Let's just let that one stew for a while."

Walsh shuffled more papers.

"It may affect Ireland's moral authority and credibility with other nations, *Taoiseach*."

"Then so be it, Joe. Now, have we any further business?"

Ezra Hasofer sat in Weber's small office awaiting his arrival. Outside the mild weather had given way to a drizzle so fine that initially he'd ignored it but after a few minutes walking realised that he'd become completely drenched by the smoky mist of rain that had descended and enveloped him. Now he tried to make himself comfortable and prepare himself for his meeting.

Weber entered the room backwards, laughing with the shapely Miss Kerrigan who remained outside. His smile remained as he greeted Hasofer.

"*Herr* Naumann, I apologise for being late."

He became aware of the bedraggled figure sat in front of him.

"You are wet," he said, unnecessarily.

"I will have to get used to the rain in Ireland. It is much softer than in Germany. Here it fools you into thinking that it's almost dry but soaks you in seconds."

"There are many things you will have to get used to, *Herr* Naumann. Wait until you visit their public houses. I used to think we Germans could drink ale but over here it is a national sport and I recommend that you do not compete with the locals. You will surely lose, and lose badly."

"I will remember you told me, *Herr* Weber."

Weber opened the folder he'd prepared holding information on his newest immigrant and consulted his notes.

"I have given your position much thought, *Herr* Naumann. You have a business head on your shoulders and you speak perfect English. I also like your general demeanour."

He raised his head and held Hasofer's gaze.

"You seem able to get along with people."

Hasofer chuckled. "Well, I think I do but I don't know how you worked that out from our chat yesterday."

"I liked your personality. I thought we would get on well together."

"I'm sure we would," grinned Hasofer.

Weber's smile widened.

"I'm sure too, *Herr* Naumann, or can I call you Dietrich?"

"Of course you can."

"Then I would like to offer you a job. One of my responsibilities is to purchase new businesses; farms, hotels and the like and place German nationals in them... people like you...people who want to make a new start."

"I would love to show you how good I am at running a business."

"Perhaps in time, Dietrich. What I need right now is someone to look after the people I've *already* asked to run a business. Every week we put Germans and other nationals who fought with us in the war into businesses all over Ireland. But once they're placed they're on their own. I'm too busy to return to make sure that everything is as I would wish and that the business is running well."

He closed his file.

"Dietrich, I need someone who can do that job for me. I'll pay you well; a sum of twenty-four pounds, fifteen and tenpence each month but you'll travel all over Ireland so I'll pay you a further twenty pounds in expenses so you can stay in accommodation that I can recommend because over the past several months, *I've* had to travel and there are some beautiful parts of Ireland. You would love it and I'm sure that the advice you give our people you met would be of great advantage to them as they try to do what is a very difficult job... making a new business work in a foreign land."

Hasofer could hardly believe his luck.

"Herr Weber..."

"Kurt..."

"Then, *Kurt*. I would be delighted to do this. I can't believe how lucky I am to have met someone as... someone as..." He struggled for appropriate words that would conceal both his internal delight at the opportunity

*Haganah* was being given yet reveal the feelings he wanted to convey to Weber... Fortunately, they coincided..."Wonderful!"

"Then we must set to business."

For the next hour and more, Weber talked to Hasofer about the number of businesses he had purchased all over Ireland, their whereabouts and the individuals who managed them on his behalf. He allowed Hasofer to understand those of whom he approved and those, like Marković, of whom he did not.

Hasofer left and returned to the dank, misty street after two hours of conversation during which he had agreed Weber's proposition, was now in possession of a job paying over six *Punts* as well as expenses each week and, most importantly, in one fell swoop, had been made privy to the locations of the two Germans; Geert Hirsch, and Horst Krueger that he'd been sent to kill.

As was the case the day before, binoculars followed his every step until he turned a corner and disappeared.

Carter-Hogg turned the photograph obliquely towards the window so the enhanced light might better define its content. *A good likeness but I don't recognise him.*

He passed it to Edward Timpson.

"Know him?"

A long drag on his cigarette was necessary before Timpson accepted the photograph. He placed his spectacles on the bridge of his nose and looked over them.

"And where did you take this photograph?"

"Outside the German Legation. He's been there twice in as many days."

"Do we have a new *wunderkind* on our patch or is he a window cleaner from Mulhuddart, I wonder?"

"I had him followed. He's certainly not from Mulhuddart. He has a bed and breakfast place near the docks. We've taken a look inside his room while he was out. He's got forty quid under the bed along with a Luger semi-automatic with a silencer and some ammunition."

"Then we can agree," said Timpson languidly. "He's probably not the window cleaner...but?...I don't recognise him." He squinted at the photograph one more time in final confirmation. "No...Not known to me."

"Well, if you don't know him he's probably a Martian."

"Or a German...probably a German."

"Then let us assume he's a Hun with a gun, eh? And that we should be taking more than a little interest in him."

Ezra Hasofer returned to his lodgings pleased with his day's work. Bidding a silent hello to his landlady by tipping his cap at her, he turned the key in the lock of his door and entered. Removing his overcoat, he hung it behind the door and went immediately to the far corner of the room where he turned and found the eye-level rose-print at the edge of the heavy curtain. Leaning the back of his head against the wall and aligning his eye with the rose on the curtain, he satisfied himself that his gaze was now exactly as it was when he left the room some hours earlier. Scanning the room he checked that the case he'd left under the chair beside the window was precisely as it was before he left. It was and his eyes moved to the open razor and soap he'd left on top of a small bag containing other items for his ablutions next to the wash-hand basis. It hadn't moved a centimetre. His gaze then moved to the jacket he'd left on the bed, the right arm of which had been left folded so that the edge of the cuff crossed it exactly over the corner of the right hand pocket. It was only out of place by a fraction but there was no doubt in Hasofer's mind that it had been moved. He stepped towards the bed and checked that the weapon and cash he'd left under the mattress was still there. Everything was as it should have been. *There might easily be an innocent explanation*, thought Hasofer. *Mrs. Brennan might just have been cleaning but I'll need to check.*

He opened the door and walked down the narrow hallway towards the front parlour where Mrs. Brennan had told him she could be found and hailed her with a smile.

"I'll need to buy an umbrella if I'm to survive this Irish rain, Mrs. Brennan. I got soaked this morning."

"Oh, you poor man. Would you like me to make a cup of tea while you dry off in front of the fire?"

"No thank you, Mrs. Brennan, I'm fine. But I wondered if you found a copy of today's Examiner when you were cleaning my room?"

"Sure I haven't had time to look in your room, Mr. Naumann. And if you recall, I said I'd only give it the once over every Friday, so we've a bit to go yet."

Hasofer lightly thumped the heel of his hand against his forehead in an exaggerated attempt to convey forgetfulness.

"Of course, Mrs. Brennan. That quite slipped my mind."

He turned as if to return to his room but stopped and turned to face her again.

"Perhaps I left it in the hallway and one of your other guests picked it up as they were leaving?"

"Sure, I told you that you were my only resident, Mr Naumann," said Mrs Brennan beginning to question her guest's mental faculties.

Hasofer shook his head in further remonstration of his failing memory.

"Oh, well."

Mrs. Brennan snapped her thumb against her middle finger and her eyes narrowed.

"I'll bet ye it was them bliddy gas men."

"Gas men?"

"Not long after you left, two gas men called because there was a smell of gas reported by someone."

"And might they have taken my newspaper?"

"Indeed they might. One of them walked through to the kitchen with me while the other one stood at the front door to measure the smell of gas there."

"And you were in the kitchen for a while."

"I don't think that's the point, Mr. Naumann. It would be the man on the door! That beggar would have lifted your paper. Them bliddy thieves. Anything that's not nailed down is fair game to them thieving' gets. I'm sorry Mr. Naumann, I'll nip out and buy you a new paper."

Hasofer shook his head.

"Don't you bother, Mrs. Brennan. I'd read it earlier anyway. I just wanted to look at the weather forecast but it seems I won't need to bother. This rain seems to be here for the week."

He waved her a polite goodbye and returned to his room, locking the door behind him. Stooping he lifted the mattress and removed his Lugar along with the other items and laid them on the bed to inspect them closely. Everything seemed normal.

*So I'm uncovered immediately upon arrival?* he mused. *Now who might be snooping around? A thief would have stolen the money and probably the gun. The Irish intelligence service or their police? British Intelligence? Perhaps Weber is checking me out far more thoroughly than I'd anticipated. What's certain is that I need to secure these things far better than I have done.*

He took a small penknife from his suitcase and hauled a sideboard from its position against the wall. Behind it, a wooden baton along the contour of the floor delineated the wall. Carefully, he levered the baton above a nail which held it to the wall until it gave and moved to the next nail until the timber slat was freed. Behind it the lime plaster and wood strapping surrendered easily to the knife until a space was made comfortably to accept his gun, ammunition, silencer and cash. Before re-affixing the skirting baton to the wall, he carefully swept the grains of plaster and dirt from the floor to its edge at the wall and concealed his efforts by wiping the area to remove all indications that he had created a hide.

Satisfied, he replaced the wooden border and sat on the edge of his bed to think.

## Chapter Twenty-eight

Weber had been generous in the sum he'd paid for vehicular support to the IRA in general and Sinéad in particular. Two large Ford Sedans had been purchased, one retained for Weber's use. Vouchers available to the Legation made travel possible as access to fuel was much limited to the general population.

With Henning in the passenger seat and Sinéad peering over the dashboard of the large Sedan, the car pulled in at an awkward angle to the paved walkway on Arvagh's main street and collided sharply with its edge.

"Handbrake, Sinéad. Handbrake!"

Dutifully, Sinéad applied the brake and sat back exhausted.

"Holy Mother of God! If I'd know that driving was so feckin' difficult I wouldn't have bothered to learn."

"You're *still* learning, Sinéad. You've some way to go before I'd willingly fall sleep in the front seat and leave the driving to you."

"I hardly made a single shaggin' mistake!" she said mulishly.

"Well, not if you don't count just missing that cow on the road and the time you nearly hit that old lady back in Kells."

"Well, that makes *two* old cows I nearly hit then. Sure the ditherin' old biddy was clearly drunk, staggerin' about like that!"

"Drunk or not, you're not allowed to knock people over."

Both emerged from the car and stretched to ease their tense muscles before lifting their cases and entering the reception area of the small town's only hotel. Having been shown upstairs to their respective rooms, they met again at the front door where Henning busied himself checking the contents of his medical bag while Sinéad asked for directions to Mary Casey's house.

Only a few minutes later Sinéad knocked on the middle house of a row of terraced cottages, each in an advanced state of dilapidation. The door opened slightly to reveal a woman's skeletal face framed by dark lank hair.

"Yeah?" she asked softly.

"Mary? Mary Casey? I'm Sinéad O'Grady and I'm here with a message from your husband Sean."

She turned and gestured towards Henning.

"...and this is Doctor Henning. Sean asked if he'd take a look at the kids." She raised the straw basket she held in crux of her left arm. "We've also got some food."

Mary Casey's solemn face slowly crumpled, overcome by emotion. Unable to speak she didn't resist Sinéad's gentle push on the door. With her free arm Sinéad tried to comfort Mary by squeezing her forearm and almost withdrew as she touched the emaciated woman.

They entered the small, darkened living room where four young children sat wrapped in blankets. Henning made straight for them and knelt down.

"I can't see, Mrs. Casey. Can we open the curtains?"

Without waiting for permission, Sinéad pulled back on the filthy covering to reveal an equally filthy window.

"Let's you and me go through to the kitchen while Doctor Henning has a look at the kids, Mary."

They sat for some minutes, Sinéad at a loss to know what to say and Mrs. Casey quietly crying but saying nothing. Eventually, Sinéad lifted the basket of food from the floor and placed it on the kitchen table.

"Mary, we have food for you. I've brought money from Dublin and the doctor will take care of the four kids...everything's going to be alright. Mary?" She touched her on the arm once more provoking a tearful nod as Mary began to collect herself before finding a small voice.

"Thanks be to God and His Blessed Mother!" she whispered. "Since Sean,"... She wiped her eyes and started again. "Since Sean was taken we've had no money and precious little food. Only what the neighbours could afford to give us and God knows that wasn't much."

Sinéad, now uncomfortable, was in a hurry to reassure her.

"It'll all be alright now, Mary. And Sean says not to worry. He'll be out before you know it but the top boyos in the IRA wanted you to know that they'll make sure you and the kids are fine."

"Those poor kids. They're all sick as dogs and I've no way of paying for a doctor."

"Well, Doctor Henning is the best doctor in all Ireland in my view and he's going to make sure they're all better soon."

Sinéad rose and started unpacking the basket, giving Mary some bread as she did so.

"Here, eat this, I'll make some soup for the kids."

Silently Mary Casey ate the lump of bread that Sinéad had torn from the loaf and the two women fell into an easier conversation although every so often Mary would turn her head towards the living room seeking confirmation that everything was going well with her children.

After a while, Hermann came through and joined them, nodding appreciatively at the large pot of soup that Sinéad was ministering to.

"The kids have one or two little problems, Mrs. Casey and you don't look so good yourself so I'd like to have a little look at you, too if that's okay?"

"The kids?" Their mother's concern was etched on her face.

"I'll need to do one or two more tests but we should be clearer later today. I suspect that young Sean and little Brendan might require to spend some time in the local sanatorium until their tuberculosis gets better but I can fix that."

"It's in Cavan town," said Mary, raising her clenched fist to her mouth apprehensively. "But I couldn't begin to afford that."

"I have that taken care of already, Mrs. Casey. But we'll make sure that you're all much more comfortable before they go anyway." He began to remove his jacket. "Before I have a look at you, I need a bucket of hot water. Can we do that?"

"Dear God, are you going to operate on my children?"

Henning laughed. "No, not at all, Mrs. Casey. I'm going to clean your windows. It's a lovely sunny day outside and whenever possible I want you and the kids to be breathing fresh air. So the curtains go, we'll keep the windows open as much as possible and we'll let some of the Lord's good light to shine upon our faces through the window when it's closed. We'll replace the curtains later today or tomorrow."

Sinéad looked at him, her mouth agape as Henning put a pot of water on the stove and walked towards the front door to assess the windows from the outside.

"Our local doctor would never do such a thing," volunteered Mary tearfully.

Sinéad smiled and looked at the retreating form of Hermann Henning.

"But *your* local doctor isn't the best doctor in all Ireland."

Sinéad and Hermann walked back to their hotel as the conversation turned to the medical condition of the five Caseys.

"Well, Sean and Brendan both have tuberculosis. I think they each have it in only one lung and I think we've caught it fairly early on so with rest in a sanatorium they should emerge fit and strong. The other two both have rickets and everyone has gum disease but again we can fix this if their diet improves and I'm going to see to it that it does. They're all covered in lice and that can't be comfortable."

"And how will you do all that? We only have enough food for a few weeks. They'll need more than that."

"Before we left I met Kurt and told him that he'd get more praise from the IRA if he invested some of his money in the welfare of the dependants of those in prison. He accepted my argument and proposes to have this discussion with you when we return. For the moment he has given me two hundred Irish Pounds, enough for a complete change of clothing and bedding for the Caseys, I'm going to pay in advance for a year's supply of fish, liver and fuel for those remaining at home and I'm now going to speak with the local doctor about admitting the children to the sanatorium for rest and treatment. I'll have to tell them that I'm a rich uncle or something as Kurt doesn't want the Irish Government thinking that I'm giving succour to the IRA...but he would like the IRA to know, so can you make sure that your Mr. Kelly that we met when we arrived, knows all about his generosity?"

Sinéad threw her arms around Hermann in delight and hugged him tight.

"God! Doctor Hermann Henning, you're a man in a million!"

"I'm glad that you think so," he smiled. "But we have work to do. Before the sun sets we have to burn all of the lice-ridden clothing and bedding in the house and replace them. This will require that we drive to Cavan. I'll speak with the doctor and you use some of Kurt's money to buy clothes and bedding for the family. When we get back to Arvagh, I'll arrange for the supply of food and fuel."

The short distance to Cavan town was uneventful. Henning took the wheel after promising Sinéad she could drive them back to Dublin and reminding her that they would need to be quick to accomplish all of their tasks.

Doctor Ahern was sympathetic.

"Doctor Henning, I'd be happy to assist in the way you suggest. But you must realise that this family are extremely fortunate to have a rich uncle like you who is also a qualified medical practitioner. There are hundreds of children round here who are in exactly the same boat. It's not medication they need. It's good food. The war's been kind to us in Ireland in that while we've had to endure rationing of goods like soap and tea which are very scarce, we have lakes teaming with fish, farms where butter, eggs, chicken and beef are available and if you have a few pounds in your pocket there's a pretty robust black market out there. But there's also poverty and there are families like the Caseys all over County Cavan and they just can't afford the bounty we have all around us."

Henning acknowledged Ahern's plain speaking.

"And what about the sanatorium?"

"That will be no problem if you have the money. I'd be happy to look at the children if you want a second opinion but from what you say, it's evident that the sanatorium would be the best place for them." He picked absent-mindedly at his sleeve. "You say you're Swiss, Doctor Henning."

"I am," responded Henning, uncomfortable at his deception.

"And will you be returning there now that the war is over or will you remain in Ireland to take care of your nephews?"

"I haven't decided yet. I'm very fond of Ireland but if I do return, I will provide for these children and their mother by some means before I go."

"Then they are very fortunate, Doctor Henning."

He rose. "I will make immediate arrangements for transferring young Sean and Brendan to the sanatorium.

You can take care of the paperwork directly with them. I'll give you the address. It's not far."

Henning and Sinéad met back at the Sedan where the rear seat had been filled to overflowing with blankets and clothes.

"The clothes all needed coupons from a ration book but when I suggested that I'd pay double the price instead they magically found it possible to make the sale," said Sinéad.

"I thought as much. And the doctor's agreed to take the two kids into the sanatorium."

He looked at Sinéad. "So far, so good."

They drove back towards Arvagh where just before the edge of the village, Henning took a detour along a farm-track to a farm he'd been recommended by the hotel receptionist. Sinéad sat in the passenger's seat while Henning negotiated a regular supply of food, especially potatoes, carrots, liver and other cuts of beef. The farm had been recommended him due to their owning a large lake, a river and several tributaries in which bream, trout, and seasonal salmon were found in abundance. The farmer also owned a peat bog and had enough turf to warm the hearth-sides of a small city.

And so it was that for the exchange of seventy Irish Pounds, a year's supply of food and fuel was purchased and would be delivered regularly by the farmer to Mrs. Casey. There was to be more delivered than her family could ever consume but Hermann thought that

Mrs. Casey might appreciate being able to help her neighbours as they had helped her.

Shaking the farmer's hand, Henning returned to the Ford Sedan where Sinéad waited patiently to hear the news which, upon hearing it, caused her to throw her arms around the best doctor in all Ireland one more time.

Upon arriving back in the village, Henning drove to the row of cottages and turned the car so it faced the main road.

"Now, *your* job is to take Mrs. Casey and the kids up to my hotel room in the car and make sure they all have a lengthy, warm bath. Dry them thoroughly and dress them in the clothes you bought today - including Mrs. Casey. I'll burn all of their existing clothes and bedding outside and I'll build a good fire in their hearth. Once Mrs. Casey recovers her strength, I'm sure she'll want to give the house a good clean...and Sinéad?"

"Yes?"

"Try not to hit any cows on the way to the hotel."

On another occasion, Sinéad was well aware that she'd have responded scornfully to Hermann's gently mocking jibe but today he was the best doctor in all Ireland and there were few things she could or would deny him. Inwardly she delighted at the assertive, confident doctor who was a million miles from her diffident houseguest.

"I'll be careful, Hermann."

## Chapter Twenty-nine

Weber laughed uproariously and placed his pint of Guinness carefully on the table before him so as not to disturb its contents while he recovered from his amused merriment at Hasofer's comment.

"Ah, Dietrich, you are such an enjoyable companion. I am so glad you agreed to work with me on the work with which I have been entrusted."

"Kurt, without your help, I'd be starving in a Dublin alleyway somewhere. The privilege of working with you is all mine."

Weber lifted his glass in a silent toast to the comment and took a sip.

"Tomorrow you set off for Kildare to visit that *mistkerl,* Marković."

"I can see why he does not meet with your approval."

"He is a murderous thug who deserves little more that the bullet he so willingly buried in innocent skulls."

"But he is under our protection as an officer in the German cause, Kurt so we must dispel thoughts like these," said Hasofer disingenuously.

"You are correct, of course, Dietrich. But I want to be sure he is doing as I told him, treating his people very well and causing us no embarrassment in Kildare."

I will certainly ensure that he understands the seriousness of our intent, Kurt. And when I leave him

I will call on Geert Hirsch in his hotel in Balyhagan before returning to you to report."

"Excellent, Dietrich. Neither is a long journey. One day will suffice. If you leave early tomorrow morning you won't need to stay overnight. You can use the large Sedan, of course. The Legation still has vouchers that allow us fuel that is denied other people."

"Then no more drink for me this evening, Kurt. I'll phone them both in the morning before I leave to make sure they are available."

"I doubt if you'll get that evil *Schweinehund* Marković. I don't think he has a phone installed on the sheep farm, but you'll get Hirsch in the hotel I bought in Balyhagan."

"Very well. But it is almost closing time now and I must sleep."

Both men shook hands and promised to meet once the visit had been concluded the following day.

Hasofer returned to his accommodation, ostentatiously bidding Mrs. Brennan goodnight as he entered his room. As was his practice, he again went through a routine to establish whether anything had been moved. On this occasion all was as it should be. Taking his pen-knife, he loosened the skirting board and removed his Lugar and silencer along with ammunition, all of which he placed in his coat pocket. Turning out the light in his room, he waited a full hour before gently pulling back the curtain to establish the presence or otherwise of anyone outside.

In a stationary car parked underneath the nearest lamppost, Captain Giles Carter-Hogg had fallen asleep. After a long day's work which had meant to conclude earlier when he'd followed Hasofer back from the Palace Bar, he'd remained awake for half an hour before persuading himself that the man on whom he'd been tasked with keeping an eye had enjoyed probably several drinks in the pub and would now be fast asleep while he sat outside to no purpose whatsoever.

His sleep was sound. So too was Mrs Brennan's when Hasofer checked by quietly tip-toeing along the hallway towards the toilet intent upon establishing her state of wakefulness as she slept next door.

Still, Hasofer waited for a further half- hour before silently unlocking the front door. Slowly, he raised a cautious eye over the top of the wall outside the premises and eyed both the car in the street and its passenger. Even from a distance it was obvious that its occupant had surrendered to slumber. He closed the door as quietly as he could and left.

Stooping low, Hasofer moved right to the garden wall that formed the corner of the street in which his car was parked. Deftly levering himself over the wall, he walked swiftly to his car and without turning on the car lights, reversed to the road behind him cursing all the while at the low growl of his engine lest it awaken his monitor. Having performed a three-point turn, he pointed the car in the opposite direction to that of Carter-Hogg's and set off for Balyhagan in Kildare, some thirty miles away.

Consulting his map and quietly thanking de Valéra for keeping one or two road signs in place during the Emergency, his headlights bored a comforting illumi-nated tunnel along the walls of the night, lighting the *Deorini De*, the 'Tears of Christ' as were called the ubiq-uitous Fuchsia hedgerows. He arrived at Balyhagan and took only some minutes to find the hotel run by Geert

Hirsch, the first of the two names on his short list from *Haganah*. Unhurriedly, he screwed the silencer onto the barrel of the Lugar and checked that the pistol was loaded properly.

Now approaching two o'clock in the morning, Balyhagan was asleep as were the occupants of the hotel. The locked front door proved no obstacle to his *Haganah* training and his picking skills soon opened the door noiselessly. A dim light from a small lamp in the hallway allowed him to establish the layout of the hotel as he stood motionless in Reception hoping there were no dogs. On one wall, a diagram showed the location of the rooms and lounge area. Checking these against the doorways in front of him, Hasofer determined that the door leading to his left was to the owner's quarters.

Quietly moving along the passageway towards the door behind which he expected to find Geert Hirsch, Hasofer absent-mindedly tightened the silencer on the barrel. Gently, he pushed down on the handle of the door, relieved that it opened without the need for any work on the lock. Opening the door, he saw a figure sleeping in a small bed next to the window. It was snoring quietly and rhythmically. Closing the door he approached the form.

"Geert," he whispered. Then louder, "*Geert!*"

With his left hand he shook the shoulder nearest him and Hirsch awoke, startled from his slumber. Confused and reaching for his spectacles, he said nothing as he tried to understand his being roused from his sleep in such an abrupt way.

"Geert. Are you awake?"

Hirsch struggled towards consciousness as he attempted to sit up.

"I am awake", he blustered. "Who are you? What is the problem?"

Hasofer rose and retreated a step. Stooping to his left, he switched on a lamp, causing Hirsch to shield his eyes.

"You are Geert Hirsch?"

"*Was ist das?*"

Suddenly the realisation of his predicament became evident as he noticed Hasofer's Lugar. He slumped back on his headboard.

"Ah, you are to be my executioner!" He spoke with a downward cadence, his words more a statement than a question. Hands shaking, he removed the spectacles he had just placed on his nose, placed them on the bed-side table and spoke in a low tone.

"For many months I have waited for this moment. I have committed many sins and I know I deserve to die like many others I condemned to the same fate. I have thought many times about how it would end." He laughed resignedly. "I did not think it would end this way. In my own bed." He took a deep breath and closed his eyes. "My name is Geert Hirsch. I commanded soldiers and gave orders I should not have. I am responsible for the death of a great many people. Many of them innocents." He grimaced and a sob emerged from somewhere deep in his chest. "I am prepared to meet my maker."

Hasofer maintained his posture, his arm outstretched, the Lugar pointed directly at Hirsch.

"Get out of bed."

Hirsch opened his eyes, curious; but obeyed without demur.

Hasofer gestured with his gun that Hirsch should move towards the fireplace which he did, standing and facing his night visitor in his white cotton vest and pants; his arms, somewhat unnecessarily, raised at head height.

With his spare hand, Hasofer pulled the pillow from the bed and threw it on the floor beside the gas fire.

"Now lie down. Place your head on the pillow."

Hirsch realised his fate as the pillow hit the floor and smiled ruefully in the gloom.

"I suppose this is poetic justice."

He leaned a hand on the corner of his bed and knelt on the floor for a moment before lowering himself to the floor and complied with Hasofer's command.

Hasofer stepped round to the window side of the bed and removed its cover. Opening the window an inch, he stuffed a portion of the blanket in the opening, leaving a small aperture through which the outside air could flow. Still pointing the gun at Hirsch, he lay on the bed with his face close to the breathe-hole he'd created.

"Now, reach over and turn on the gas."

Hirsch paused. "You are American? English?"

"I am Jewish and I am here to ensure that you answer for your crimes. Now, I repeat, reach over and turn on the gas."

Still Hirsch remained stilled.

"The alternative is that I shoot you quietly in the belly and cause you great pain before the inevitability of your death. But make no mistake, tonight you die. You may as well die by falling asleep"

Hirsch slowly nodded his acceptance of Hasofer's logic, reached over and turned on the gas fire which immediately began emitting toxic fumes that began gradually to reduce the amount of oxygen his blood carried to his brain.

Hirsch's head was positioned only inches from the gas spout which was normally lit to feed the bedroom fire but on this occasion, the unignited methane, ethylene and ethane gases began inhabiting his lungs and other organs. In minutes he was unconscious. As Hasofer breathed pure air from the small window opening, he observed the increasingly lifeless body of Hirsch. After twenty minutes, he took a deep breath of fresh air, placed a handkerchief over his mouth and moved over to Hirsch's body on the floor, feeling for a pulse in the internal jugular vein on his neck. Checking a second time, he satisfied himself that Hirsch was dead and returned to the window where he took several large gulps of air before removing the blanket and closing the window.

Before leaving, Hasofer felt in his pocket for the yellow fabric Star of David he'd brought with him; a cloth insignia that the Nazis had forced members of his faith to wear to identify them as Jews. Carefully, he placed it on the chest of his victim before throwing the blanket back over the bed and exited the room quietly leaving the gas fire to continue spewing its lethal toxins.

His car remained parked as he'd left it and after dismantling the Lugar and returning the silencer to his coat pocket, he drove back through the blackness towards Dublin.

Weber was shaving when his phone rang.

"I have a Mr. Naumann on the line for you, Mr. Weber"

"Please put him through."

After a few seconds, Hasofer's voice spoke, in an obviously anxious tone.

"Kurt. It's Dietrich."

"I hope you're not going to tell me you are still too drunk to drive after your visit to the pub with me last night," laughed Weber.

"Kurt. Hirsch is dead. He's dead!"

"Wha...what do you mean?"

"I phoned first thing this morning as I told you I would to make sure he'd be at the hotel and the woman there said that Hirsch didn't arrive for breakfast. When they entered his room they found that he'd committed suicide. The *Gardai* are there right now."

"This is incredible! How did he die?"

"The woman told me he'd gassed himself."

Weber took a deep breath and composed himself.

"Where are you now?"

"I'm at a phone box near my lodgings. I phoned Hirsch only a few minutes ago."

"Then we must go there directly. He is a German citizen and I want to speak immediately to the police officers who found him." He thought further. "You have the car with you?"

"Yes."

"Then bring it immediately to the Shelbourne. We will drive together to Kildare."

Hasofer placed the phone on its cradle and assessed the telephone call. *So far so good,* he mulled. *As long as the police are convinced, so too will be Weber.*

An hour later, Hasofer pulled on the handbrake as the Sedan stopped outside the hotel in Balyhagan. Weber emerged first and strode towards its front door. Hasofer hurried after him and they entered together. A police officer stood guarding the entrance to the room in which Hirsch had perished.

"I am Kurt Weber, the Deputy to the Ambassador Extraordinary and Minister Plenipotentiary of the German Legation in Ireland. I am to understand that a German national was killed here last night?" he said, hoping that the *Garda* before him wasn't too knowledgeable about the latest diplomatic niceties.

The *Garda* decided that Weber's bearing required an officer of a higher rank to deal with him. He shouted over his shoulder.

"*Sáirsint*, we've a politician out here from the German Embassy."

Weber didn't bother to correct him but awaited the Sergeant who emerged from the room beyond.

"I'm not a politician, Sergeant. But I *am* a representative of the German Government. This is my assistant," he said, gesturing at Hasofer. "What happened last night to *Herr* Hirsch?"

The *Garda* looked at Weber, appraising him.

"Now, have you identification, Mister Plenipoten-tiary? Two of my brothers fought in the war on the side of the Allies and I thought that Germany didn't have any plenipotentiaries left. I thought they'd all been locked up!"

"Officer, please let us not play games. One of our citizens is dead. If you contact Éamon de Valera directly, he will vouch that the Free State continues to recognise the work I do and that my questions should be answered."

The mention of his *Taoiseach's* name galvanised the police officer, if only slowly. Apparently reluctantly, he answered Weber's questions.

"Very well then. We have the body of one Geert Hirsch, the owner of this hotel and, as you say, a German national. His body has already been personally identified by his staff. He was found this morning lying on the floor of his room with his head on a pillow beside the gas fire which had been switched on. The bedroom smelled heavily of gas. He had obviously committed suicide. His staff confirmed that he had been drinking heavily the night before but also confirmed that this was a regular occurrence."

Weber assessed the information.

"Is *Herr* Hirsch still in the room? Might I see the body?"

The Sergeant shrugged and gestured with a shake of his head and a purse of his lips that Weber should follow him. Hasofer tagged along and the three men entered the room where Hirsch lay, exactly as Hasofer had left him only some hours before although his pallor was now completely grey. The window had been opened and all scent of coal gas had been expunged from the room.

Weber stood and took in the room. Its ordinariness. Its dreariness. He stepped over to the window and checked its catch and its wooden frame.

*No evidence of break-in*, he thought.

"Were his staff unsurprised at his suicide, Sergeant?"

"They told us he kept himself to himself. Didn't socialise much. They didn't seem to have developed much of a relationship with him and frankly were more worried about whether this means the place would close."

Weber nodded at the yellow Star of David on Hirsch's chest.

"What is the significance of this?"

"Guilty feelings, we think. Drove him to suicide probably what was done to them poor Jewish people. No evidence of a break-in. No evidence of foul play."

Weber pursed his lips noncommittally before stepping back into his more usual role.

"Tell them not to worry. There will be another manager arriving shortly. Their jobs and wages are safe."

He looked to the ceiling as if pondering a problem.

"Have the press been notified?"

"Not yet. But I suspect they'll be interested in what's gone on."

"I suppose so."

He tore a piece of paper from a set of old accounts that lay untended on a sideboard and scribbled his name and the phone number of the Legation on it.

"If the press show interest, I'd be grateful if you'd ask them to get in touch with me, officer."

The Sergeant took the paper disinterestedly prompting Weber to remember the fact that he had access to enormous wealth and had a job to do.

He sighed resignedly. "And if you write your name on a piece of paper along with the address of your local police office, I'll see to it that a new billiards table will be delivered in gratitude from the German people."

The Sergeant took more of an interest in his German Plenipotentiary.

"I think the Police Hurling Team would prefer new uniforms and new sticks and balls."

"Then that is what shall be delivered. My colleague Miss Kerrigan will telephone you once all of this unfortunate matter has been disposed with sensitivity."

Both men eyed one another in unspoken agreement that the matter would now be dealt with in a way that would be acceptable to Weber.

"You can count on the *Gardai* of Balyhagan, Mr. Weber. We'll not let you down."

## CHAPTER THIRTY

Mrs. Brennan knocked timidly on Hasofer's door but was still somehow surprised when it was opened briskly by her smiling guest.

"Telegram for you, Mr. Naumann."

He thanked his landlady and closing the door, walked to the improved light from the window to read his telegram...it read:

'XXX XXXX XX XX MASADA STOP

RECORDED ADVICE FIRST PARCEL DISPATCHED STOP

BANK DETAILS FOLLOW STOP BANK CODE 3:5:7: ACCOUNT NUMBER 25, 01, 10, 10, 30, 01, 65, 32, 12, 30, 01, 15, 08, 07, 11, 21. SIGNED SICARII ENDS XXX XXXX XX.'

Hasofer lifted a small copy of the books of the *Tanakh* from within his suitcase and took it to his table along with the telegram. To an untrained eye, the telegram was innocuous. To a professional eye, it was clearly a cypher but without knowing the source book, the Jewish Bible, it was gobbledygook.

*Bank code three...that's Genesis, Exodus, **Leviticus**. Chapter five, verse seven.* He lifted a pencil and, reading the numbers he had before him masquerading as a bank account, counted along the first line in verse seven until he reached letter number twenty-five and wrote down the letter *M*. He continued to check the numbers against the lines of biblical text until he had formed a collection of letters that spelled the words, 'Matthaüs Thalberg.'

He sat back in his chair. *So, now I know the name of my new target. Next I have Horst Krueger, then I turn my attention to Matthaüs Thalberg.*

*So be it!*

Doctor Herman Henning stepped out on to the path that led to the paved walkway he took each morning that he worked in St. Kevin's Hospital. Standing at the door with her arms folded and a wide smile on her face, Sinéad bid him farewell, picking some stray floss from his jacket shoulder as he turned towards the road. To any innocent observer, other than the omission of a farewell kiss, it looked for all the world as if two newly married sweethearts were parting so the man could attend his workplace and the woman could return to her wifely duties.

"*Go raibh an Tiarna leat,* Hermann. Go, heal the sick. I'll cook soup for us tonight when you get home."

Hermann Henning was indeed a happy man. He was doing a job he loved, was living in the same house as a woman he loved, even if she was unaware of his feelings. *Soon I will tell her,* he decided as he strode towards the infirmary. *Perhaps this week...or perhaps next. The time must be right, but soon...soon.*

Sinéad watched him reach the road end. Henning turned and both exchanged a wave before Sinead returned to her front parlour where she took a coat from behind the door and put it on despite the warm seasonal weather in which Dublin had basked for a week now. Rain was never far away, even in the warm season. She looked in the mirror and tugged at her hair before deciding its form required the cover of a headscarf which she tightened under her chin. She buttoned her coat, opened the door and left, walking towards the house used by the IRA high command only some streets away.

"What d'ye make of this?" asked Kelly as he pushed a copy of the Irish Times towards Sinéad.

"They're sayin' that a German called Hirsch who used to be a top boyo in the German Army committed suicide in Balyhagan, in a hotel that he was runnin'."

Sinéad read the copy and folded the broadsheet.

"Me and Kurt Weber bought that place a while back. One of the first. The idea was that Kurt would use it to give a German national a job here in Ireland. I've told you, he's bought loads of pubs, hotels and farms as well as quite a few businesses. He uses me to soften the seller up and give an Irish touch to proceedings before spending his money. Once he buys somewhere he puts in one of his Germans that are over here. *He* decides who goes where. I have no involvement in that side but I know he tries to put more responsible people in higher profile jobs. Like, he wouldn't put an eejit in a job where he'd mess up and embarrass him. In fact, he's recently brought on a German fellah whose job is to go round all of the people he's placed and make sure they're doin' okay."

She looked again at the article which didn't have the benefit of a photograph of the deceased.

"Don't know the fellah."

Kelly held his hand out and took back the newspaper.

"I was just wonderin' whether the Brits had anythin' to do with it. Their secret service boys are everywhere over here and it wouldn't surprise me if their black hands were all over this."

"Like you say, Joseph." She shrugged her shoulders. "Who knows?"

Kelly walked towards the window and looked out, speaking with his back to Sinéad, something she found uncomfortable. *Why can't the beggar look me in the eye when he's talkin' to me?*

"When are you seeing Weber next?"

Sinéad looked at the clock on the top of the mantelpiece.

"At eleven o'clock today," she said to Kelly's back. "I'm meeting him in the McGinn's Tearoom and then he's taking me to a fishmonger's shop out in Bray that he's thinking of buying."

"That man must have feckin' millions! He's spending German money like there's no tomorrow! Jesus Christ Almighty, they're meant to be a defeated nation"

"Well, he has enough to give you forty thousand pounds a few weeks ago and, through Doctor Henning's good work, has offered more to support prisoners' wives."

"He has that," acknowledged Kelly. "Still, see if he's anythin' to say on the suicide thing. I need to keep an eye on the Germans, the Brits and our own fellow Irishmen in G-2 Military Intelligence as well as in *An Garda Síochána*. Sometimes you pick information up from the most unlikely sources."

"I'll do that for sure, Joseph."

Weber was late and Sinéad sat, quite contentedly, in the front saloon of McGinn's in Ambrose Street. Her training had taught her to choose her table in the café with care, giving her an uninterrupted view of the entrance and of the street outside. A secondary door close by would permit a second exit should it be required.

Not one other customer was in the parlour; only the owner was in attendance, busily wiping tables.

*Maybe this cup of tea will do me better than my usual pint of Guinness,* she thought. *I'm drinking quite a lot these days. Most nights with Hermann, every time me and Kurt go off on one of our tours, whenever Danny and Dub come up to...* Prompted inadvertently, she remembered the fate of her friend, Dub. *Poor Dub, he was such a feckin' innocent, such a good man. I'll not be drinkin' with him again after that shaggin' arms drop...*

"Sinéad, you look as beautiful as ever."

Sinéad shook herself from her *aisling*.

"Kurt! I was elsewhere."

"Too much Irish stout last night?"

"Nah, I was thinkin' of poor Dub. He was such a nice man. He didn't deserve to die for the cause. I'm not sure he even understood what we were all about. I think he only raised his arms in anger because his pals Seamus and Danny did."

Weber sat beside her and placed his hand on her arm, comforting her.

"You mustn't have such dark thoughts. There are many casualties of war. The secret is not to become one yourself."

"I thought you were the big, brave German General. A man who'd lay down his life for his brothers-in-arms?"

Weber smiled. "Well, you have me there!"

He took a seat beside Sinéad but didn't order a cup of tea.

"Now that the war's over, perhaps I have a new perspective on life."

Both chatted a while as Sinéad finished her tea unhurriedly.

"Let's walk to the car," suggested Weber as Sinéad wiped the back of her hand across her mouth in lieu of a napkin and placed the empty cup on the table. "I want to get to Bray and back quite quickly. One of the people I placed committed suicide and I have much to do."

"Yeah, I read it in the papers. Desperate! A terrible thing. Are you sure it was suicide and not someone murderin' the poor man? Only, I was talkin' to Joseph Kelly this mornin' and he was askin' me what I thought."

"No, I think it was suicide, alright. His staff talked about him being a loner and a drunk. When I interviewed him earlier I could see that he was trying to confront his demons but I still thought that he'd cope on his own. I think I underestimated the need for companionship that these people have - even those with good English. They're alone in a new land, friendless, worn out after the rigours of war and suspicious of everyone."

He guided Sinéad towards the door. "I must do something about this or we might see more take their lives like Hirsch. I will give it more thought but something needs to be done."

Sinéad turned to face him, her face displaying genuine concern.

"And what about you, Kurt Weber? Aren't *you* alone in a new land, friendless, worn out after the rigours of war and suspicious of everyone?"

Weber's teeth flashed in a broad smile. "Ah, but Sinéad...I have *you*!"

"Don't you go gettin' above yourself, General Weber. *No* one has me. And you've also got Hermann, have you not?"

"Then I'm blessed with *two* great friends," he grinned, ignoring any intended rebuke.

Carter-Hogg sat with Timpson in his office. He offered his senior officer a cigarette, mumbling his question as he tried to ignite the one he'd placed between his own lips

"So, the *Gardai* are convinced it was a suicide?"

"Apparently so," answered Timpson.

He sucked hard on the high-tar cigarette and continued.

"It seems he was found with his head on a pillow in front of the gas fire. The police reckon he was a depressed, lonely drunk." He laughed his way into a rumbling cough and repeated himself. "A depressed, lonely drunk! I'll have to make sure there's a shilling in my gas meter tonight!"

Carter-Hogg smiled at Timpson's identification with the German.

"Well, our *Herr* Naumann was tucked up in bed all that night so at least he didn't get up to any mischief."

"Who's watching him now?"

"I took a call from Kinsella. He followed him yesterday to Balyhagan with Kurt Weber where they checked on Hirsch. Since then he's either been in his room in Pearce Street or in the German Legation's new offices. Looks like he's working with Weber. Assistant of some sort, I'd guess."

"We can probably reduce the watch. Seems he's *here* legally, working with *Weber* legally. Carrying a weapon is hardly unusual in this country although I'm troubled by the silencer I must admit."

He scratched his jaw thoughtfully. "Perhaps the best we can do as good citizens is to inform *An Garda Síochána* anonymously about the weapon and leave it to them. We can save on manpower, give the *Gardai* something to waste their time on and cause the Germans problems at one and the same time."

Carter-Hogg nodded his agreement, more because he'd be spared his night-time surveillance duties.

"Good idea, sir. I'll make the call from a phone box on the street."

"Be a good chap and have Kinsella make the call, would you? He's a local boy and with the greatest of respect, your accent is blue-blood Oxbridge. The *Gardai* would suspect something immediately if you called. They'd imagine that they were being given inside information from someone in Buckingham Palace."

Carter-Hogg smiled. "I thought my attempt at an Irish accent was now almost perfect."

Timpson grimaced his disagreement.

"I'll get Kinsella on the phone and tell him."

"Good boy. You do just that."

# CHAPTER THIRTY-ONE

Horst Krueger balanced his cigarette on the edge of an ash-tray to free his hand and applauded enthusiastically along with the other customers as three fiddlers drew their bows on the last long note of the slow Irish air *Gaftai Baile Buí*.

Although only having arrived in Ireland some seven months earlier, he'd taken credit for Weber's earlier investment in the small mill that ground corn only three streets away from the pub. The mill had provided employment for eight men and three women and Krueger had become quietly popular in the area. Persuading his community of his Swiss antecedents had helped as had his habit of buying a round of drinks for the small number of regulars who frequented the pub he visited each and every night. Acquiring a genuine interest in Irish traditional songs and tunes had assisted as had his ability to absorb the historical background to songs of protest and rebellion when they were explained to him by locals over a pint. The anti-English sentiments that were threaded throughout most of the songs also resonated with him and more than once he had been moved emotionally to a song sung or a tune played.

Horst had long had had his name adjusted to suit the Irish tongue and he had become known generally as

'Horse' with many subsequent drunken inferences in Heraghty's to his presumed comparison to a steed's genitalia with jocular offers of introductions to a number of 'widow-women' who had lost husbands in the war. Horse was popular in Wexford.

Unknown to those who slapped him on the back in friendly manner and who had accepted his generosity, Krueger had also overseen the killing of many Jewish citizens in Warsaw and had had his heavy artillery reduce its ghetto to rubble. Under his field command, on the eve of Passover of April 19, 1943, troops had systematically burned and blown up the ghetto buildings, block by block, rounding up or murdering hundreds. Known as a ruthless adherent to Nazi philosophies during the war, Krueger had also been a favourite of Heinrich Himmler, *Reichsführer* of the *SS* and had met Hitler on many occasions, three times to be honoured.

But Horse was popular in Wexford.

Ezra Hasofer had been given his list of visits for the week. Wexford, Waterford and Wicklow; all the 'W' towns in the south-east of Ireland and had been pleased to see that Krueger's name had featured. All in all, he had fifty-six Germans based in thirty-seven businesses of one description or another for whom he had been given a responsibility to 'support and report' should anyone give him cause for concern. He found on his travels that some of the Germans he met seemed to have integrated well in their community; others less so. Some were glad to see the war behind them. Others, causing him more personal difficulty, took the opportunity upon meeting him enthusiastically to relive their uniformed glories. No one had settled with a family brought over from Germany so all were having to deal with life as a sole male in a foreign land with all of the problems that that presented.

Weber had advised Hasofer prior to his departure that some whom he'd meet were just individuals caught up in a war in which they had been but mere cannon fodder. Others, he had been told, mostly over a drink once alcohol had influenced his tongue, had prosecuted their war criminally. Weber was ambivalent. On the one hand he had been given orders to support these individuals, on the other he detested certain of them as lower order people; animals not fit to wear the uniform of the German nation they had sworn to serve. He had resolved his personal conflict by his angry denunciation to them of their war-time behaviour coupled with threats that if perfect behaviour was not observed in Ireland, all supports would be withdrawn and they would be 'held accountable' although he was never specific about what that meant.

Some weeks earlier, together in a hostelry, Hasofer had volunteered the thought that in some ways, perhaps it had been better that Hirsch had taken his own life by gassing himself and Weber, nodding, had acknowledged the essential truth of his observation. For a second, Hasofer had contemplated a proposition to Weber that he merely provide him with a list of names and he would arrange that they were punished for their war crimes but stilled his suggestion lest it impede him in the mission set him by *Haganah* by having Weber realise he was himself capable of murder.

In consequence, some days later, Hasofer found himself driving the Legation car along the quayside in Wexford and into the front yard of Horst Krueger's mill in his role as Weber's assistant. Walking through the front door uninvited into the noisy gloom, he was pointed in the direction of 'Horse' who was lifting heavy sacks of ground corn and placing them on a wooden, wheeled platform.

Turning, he noticed Hasofer approaching and smiled a shouted greeting.

"You must be Dietrich Naumann, *Herr* Weber's man."

"I am Naumann. It is good that we meet." They shook hands. "Have we somewhere we can talk?"

"Of course. But it's too noisy in here. We'll have our discussion over a refreshment and some bread along the street."

Shouting some instructions to his employees, he placed his hand on Hasofer's back and guided him from the mill onto the sunlit street where he pointed in the direction of Heraghty's bar.

"Over there."

After four afternoon pints of stout and some bread and cheese, Krueger was merry.

"It is wonderful to meet another German who served the *Reich*, even if you were only a prison guard. I commanded many people and although I miss the responsibility, I have found a place here in Ireland where I could not have believed that such contentment could be found."

He counted off the benefits on the fingers of his left hand.

"The people are wonderful. They have no love for the English. The climate is perfect for my business."

He lowered his voice, "The Allies have no idea that I am in Ireland"... *No, but Haganah has,* thought Hasofer as Krueger continued his monologue.

"At night, I come here..." He waved his arm in an arc describing the pub..."to Heraghty's Bar and enjoy the company of some of my employees and of local people. They are easy to talk to...even if it took me some time to understand the particular form of the English language they speak here. They call me "Horse" you know and joke about the size of my *zuckerstange* but I have yet to persuade any of the local women to make a comparison."

He laughed until a coughing fit had him sip more stout in an effort to conquer it..."but it is only a matter of time, *Herr* Naumann."

"But yet, it must be a relief to be removed from the responsibilities of war?"

"Not at all, *Herr* Naumann. We were all involved in a great struggle to secure the destiny of the Third *Reich*."

"But so many people died, *Herr* Krueger."

"Then it was so destined!" replied Krueger angrily. "I did not shrink from my duties when I had to rid Warsaw of its vermin. Many died...but many *deserved* to die!"

"For just being Jewish? For having a different faith to you and I?"

"You know, like me, that they corroded the German state. They are diseased and ate at our vitals. They had to be put down and only the *Fuehrer* was bold enough to accomplish this."

Krueger slowly placed his Guinness on the table and looked at Hasofer suspiciously.

"Do you not agree?"

Hasofer realised he had strayed and smiled his accommodation.

"Of course. The Jews are vermin." He raised his glass in a mock toast. "And fortunately here in Ireland there are so few of them they can be ignored!"

Slowly, Krueger smiled. "But if I saw one on a country road, I would still hit him with my car!"

Hasofer returned Krueger's smile but with different motivation.

"Then let us toast the occasional car accident."

Krueger laughed as he raised his glass.

"To the occasional accident."

Having constrained himself to only two glasses of stout and some bread throughout the meeting, Hasofer signalled his intention to move on.

"I have to visit another German national, in Waterford some forty miles away before the day is out."

"What? There is another German close by me?"

"Three actually. But General Weber decided initially to keep everyone apart in case there was outside interference but now he's coming more to the view that perhaps we might all meet up to give one another companionship. He's back in Dublin today working on a plan to bring everyone together shortly." He looked at the eager anticipation on Krueger's face. "Can I take it that you would be interested?"

"But of course, *Herr* Naumann."

"Then I will make sure that you are invited, *Herr* Krueger."

"Call me Horse!"

Hasofer smiled and shook his hand in departure.

As the powerful car moved slowly along the quayside avoiding the creels, fishing tackle and other equipment that lay being repaired or re-loaded on to the paint-flaked fishing vessels, Hasofer fell to thinking of his plans for Krueger. Initially he considered an accident, perhaps a car accident as being a plausible cause of death but as he reflected upon Krueger's crimes in Warsaw, he determined that the man should be made aware of the fate that would befall him before he died at his hand.

As the car picked up speed on the outskirts of the town, Hasofer had decided. His Lugar and a confrontation would be needed for this assassination. He rolled down the window and placed his right arm on the open frame as he guided the car casually with his left hand, enjoying the warmth of the sun on his forearm.

He passed over a small hump-back bridge and drove onwards to Waterford unaware that only thirty seconds in his wake, a car driven by Captain Giles Carter-Hogg followed behind having trailed him discretely from his accommodation in Dublin.

## CHAPTER THIRTY-TWO

The clock on the church opposite the British Embassy struck its midday carillon as Edward Timpson read the short briefing note that he'd asked Carter-Hogg to prepare. It told him that a second covert visit to Hasofer's room had disclosed that the weapon and ammunition had been removed; that discrete enquiries of his landlady had brought forth the information that her guest's name was Dietrich Naumann; from a place in Germany called Dresden, she thought. Further it reported that he was working with Kurt Weber of the unofficial German Legation and that a number of visits using a Legation car had taken place; always, it transpired, to meet German nationals living and working in towns and villages all across Ireland. Further, it stated that he had also accompanied Weber to the hotel in Balyhagan upon their being made aware of the suicide of Geert Hirsch. A detailed list of Hasofer's visits was attached to the brief.

"Very interesting, Captain."

He placed the document on the desk, pushed back the spectacles from his face onto his forehead and massaged the muscles at the back of his neck.

"If only we knew what he discussed with the people he visits."

"They all appear to be fitting in well with the local communities. All running businesses of one sort or another. They mostly employ local people and as far as we can see are causing no trouble. Our sources in the *Gardai* tell us quietly that they know of each of them but they're no trouble. We assume they're all here under bogus names but we checked their registrations and they all appear to be here legitimately. We have some of our people on the case, checking to see if they have a war history that would interest us but this fellow Naumann appears only to be a sort of emissary from the chaps at their unofficial Legation offices, although we'd love to know why he had a Lugar when we visited his place the first time."

Timpson had moments earlier opened a bottle of French *vin rouge,* a *Bordeaux* and now poured a glass for himself.

"This is to be my *médecine du jour,*" *he* explained to his junior officer as he sipped at it and replaced the glass on the desk.

"I have a meeting with a contact tonight. I'll see whether he might throw some further light on our Mister Naumann."

Sinéad sat opposite Joseph Kelly in the small dark room he used for quiet discussions in the Dublin house. Outside, two armed men stood in the shadows protecting the entrance to the house from positions across the road

"So help me God, Uncle Joseph. I'm as loyal to the cause today as I was when I joined. I know you have to go through this to find out what's going on but I need you to know that I'm *with* you and would never act against the interest of the movement."

"I'm inclined to believe you, Sinéad. You're my niece and you're a good girl. You've served us well. If I *didn't* think that, niece or no niece you'd be sittin' talkin' to someone else in the basement."

He sucked one more time on his pipe before inverting it and tapping out it's contents.

"No." He shook his head and blew smoke from between thin lips. "Today I want to talk with you about them two Germans you keep company with."

"Kurt and Hermann?"

"Yeah, Kurt and Hermann. The professor and the doctor. The ones who were there at shootin' at Drogheda."

"Sure, what do you want to know about them?"

Kelly bit his lower lip nervously. He'd known Sinéad since she was a baby. She was his brother's daughter but questions had to be asked.

"I have no way of putting this other than direct to your face, Sinéad but I want to know right off if you're shaggin' either of them."

Sinéad's face reddened and her outraged retort tumbled from her lips so indignantly that Kelly was forced to raise his hands in surrender and indicate he was persuaded of her declarations of purity.

"Jesus, Sinéad. You curse like a feckin' sailor man when you get hot under the collar. Your poor mother would have kittens if she heard such a mouthful."

"Look, Uncle Joseph. You *told* me to feckin' work with Weber. I've done a good job there. He's given us feckin' money to help prisoners' wives, he organised that feckin' air drop, he's spent fortunes in our towns and villages..."

"Yeah, I know all that...and your doctor fellah?"

"Well, he was picked up by Kurt almost accidentally when he lifted Dennehy from the internment camp. There's no way he could be anything other than an innocent bystander in all this. Now he's working in St. Kevin's and looking after families like the Caseys. If you want my honest opinion, the man's a feckin' saint and we should get down on our feckin' knees each night and thank the Lord that he made one or two *decent* feckin' people on this blighted isle of ours."

"You make your point, Sinéad but they were both there when Dennehy had his head blown off. Weber was there when the airdrop went wrong. Some fecker's at the back of all this and I want to be sure that Weber isn't some kind of double agent. I took a chance on that airdrop. I trusted Weber but I executed our men just as sure as if I'd put them before a firing squad because some fecker is alive to our moves and I'm going to make the bastard suffer once I find out his name."

"Or hers?" said Sinéad.

"Or feckin' *hers*."

Edward Timpson sat in a small, gloomy alcove in The Grapes Bar in O'Connell Street wincing at the taste of the red wine he'd just swallowed. *Bloody Irish! They only understand stout and whiskey! This red wine isn't fit to feed to the pigs of Dougherty.*

He read the *Examiner*, keeping its pages high to reduce his visibility to the few customers in the bar. After some minutes an Irish voice spoke through an ear-level hole in a broken pane in the opaque stained glass window that separated Timpson's booth from its neighbour.

"Anythin' on page eleven?"

"Just an account of *Runrig* winning the two-thirty at the Curragh. Odds of five to one."

"I got him at six to one earlier."

Each satisfied that they both spoke to the person they came to see and that the other didn't feel compromised in any way, the conversation relaxed.

"Congratulations on providing us with information on the airdrop but what on earth happened at Drogheda?"

Through the coloured glass, Timpson could see the outline of a person on the other side raise a glass to his lips but replace it on the table untasted.

"Drogheda was a mistake. Dennehy was hit by accident...still, it's no loss what a friend gets!" said the outline, its voice heavy with irony.

"Dennehy was someone we could deal with. We'd rather the German had been shot as was ordered."

"It was a moving target. What's done is done."

Timpson raised his glance to the ceiling and quoted his favourite playwright.

"Ah, the Bard...Macbeth...Act three, Scene two...' *Things without all remedy should be without regard. What's done, is done*...and can't be undone'," he muttered, going off script.

"Certainly not in this instance."

"Well, there will be other opportunities and I'll advise you of them in due course."

Timpson contemplated having another sip of his red wine and, grimacing, decided that some alcohol was better than none. He swallowed and cleared his throat.

"No problems with the people round about you?"

"We growl at one another sometimes but, so far, I think I'm above suspicion."

"Then let's hope it stays that way."

Timpson changed tack.

"What do you know of a German called Dietrich Naumann?"

A short silence ensued. "Nothing. Never heard of the man."

"Well, keep your ears open. He seems to work for Kurt Weber in their pretend German Legation. We worry that he's armed and dangerous."

"Dietrich Naumann," said the voice, committing the name to memory. "I'll see what I can find out."

"Good. I'll leave now. Your envelope is inside the newspaper I'll leave it here in the booth as I go. There's a bonus for your information on the airdrop but I should really have reduced it because of Dennehy. Fortunately for you, I'm a very forgiving person."

"Well, I'm a very *knowledgeable* person don't forget, so let's not play games. I expect my feckin' money in full. Just leave the word with the barman here to lower the blind half-way on his window if you want another chat and I'll see you the following night as usual unless I'm indisposed."

"Let's do just that."

"And, by the way, I watched you from over the road as you arrived. Next time don't happen along all tricked up like a gypsy caravan at the local horse show. You stand out a mile."

"Back in London they call this *style*."

"Well you're in Dublin now and you're drinking in pubs with more spit than sawdust. Next time look more like the feckin' regulars in here. It's my feckin' life on the line."

## CHAPTER THIRTY-THREE

Dusk was still some hours away in the quiet, peat-smoked village of Enniscorthy, some fourteen miles north-west of Wexford where Hasofer had planned his meeting with the next man on his list. Horst Krueger had earlier been excited to have been invited at short notice by his new German friend, Dietrich Naumann to meet another German national who lived and worked in a village so close to his own.

"I'll be there at seven-thirty sharp, Dietrich. There's a bus I can catch to Enniscorthy. It will be good to meet someone else from the Fatherland...a *Sturmbannführer* in the SS, you say."

"Seven-thirty, Horse."

"Seven-thirty, Dietrich."

Hasofer replaced the telephone on its receiver which sat on a sturdy table in the quiet hallway of the small hotel he'd sought out and looked at his watch. *Only forty minutes to prepare.* Scanning the street on each side of him as he stepped out, he returned to the car he'd stolen from the driveway of a grand house just outside Dublin and positioned himself in its driver's seat. He took his Lugar from his coat pocket and checked its action before laying it on the seat beside him. From his boot, he withdrew a small knife he had earlier strapped in a sheath just above his ankle and ran his finger down its short blade. *Survivable if stabbed in the gut, but in the eye, throat or neck? Immediate immobility and death*, he reassured himself. *But the Lugar is more certain...*

The bus from Wexford could be heard long before it could be seen. When it turned into Abbey Square where Hasofer stood awaiting its occupant, its belching black smoke marked its journey through the village, momentarily obscuring the shops and houses on either side of the road.

Gradually the old bus limped up to the bus stop and Horst Krueger stepped down, his arms open in wide embrace. He shook Hasofer happily by the shoulders in welcome as he looked round.

"Where is our comrade?"

"We are going to meet him now. He has been working on a farm *Herr* Weber bought some time ago."

"And this farm is close by?"

"I have a car," said Hasofer pointing out the large Armstrong Siddeley Open Tourer that stood only yards from the bus stop. "We will be there shortly."

Krueger looked at the car thoughtfully and accepted Hasofer's gestured invitation to sit in the passengers' seat.

"It is only a few miles outside the village," he smiled and turned the wheel towards a roadway identified by a signpost on which was inscribed *Templeshannon 3 Miles*.

Leaving the village behind, Krueger turned in his seat, positioning himself with his back to the car door, facing Hasofer directly as he drove. Mildly uncomfortable at being stared at, Hasofer waved at the countryside outside.

"It's beautiful here is it not? It reminds me of the farms outside Dresden where I come from."

"Very beautiful, Dietrich. Have we far to go?"

"The farm is called Blackwater Farm. It's just a mile along this road now."

A few minutes later, Hasofer steered the car to a halt at a passing place carved into the woodlands at the side of the road. A dry mud track led to the farm he'd earlier identified to Krueger.

"Here we are, Horse. Let's walk up."

Both alighted and walked together towards the farm. Yards from a wooded clearing Hasofer had previously earmarked as the place he'd shoot Krueger, he stopped and pulled at the Lugar he'd placed in the inside pocket of his coat.

Before the Lugar could clear his pocket, Krueger stepped slightly behind and to the side of him raising his arms before him, his hands clasped. A Walther *Pistole* 38 handgun, its hand-cocked trigger function engaged, pointed directly at Hasofer's head. Hasofer froze.

"I thought as much." Krueger took another step back.

"Now...very carefully...throw your gun into those bushes and face me."

Calculating his options, Hasofer decided that Krueger's trigger finger could send a bullet through his brain faster than he could possibly react. There was a slim chance the gun might jam but resignedly, he slowly took his gun by the heel and holding it between thumb and forefinger, threw it half-heartedly as directed.

Krueger's eyebrows rose in unison as he gazed at the discarded weapon.

"With a silencer attached? Why, Dietrich, a lesser man might think you were about to assassinate me...a simple mill owner from Wexford. Now before I shoot *you*, tell me why you'd shoot a simple mill owner from Wexford."

Hasofer forced a smile as he reached for an explanation. Seconds passed. Eventually...

"Horse, you are mistaken. *Herr* Weber asked me to make sure you weren't an informer for British Intelligence. After the murder of Geert Hirsch in Balyhagan recently, we have to make sure that everyone is who they say they are."

Krueger's stance didn't move an inch but his eyes told Hasofer that perhaps he'd bought some time.

"Hirsch was *murdered*?"

"We now believe so. I interviewed his staff personally and he had no reason to commit suicide as the police stated. There was unexplained bruising," he lied. We believe that he was forced to take his own life and that this could only have been accomplished by someone who knew his background and who had a motive to kill him...British Intelligence, perhaps the Americans."

Krueger remained motionless, his pistol yet held in both hands. He gnawed at his lower lip, slowly, uncertain now. Moments elapsed as he weighed Hasofer's explanation.

"I have survived this long only because I am suspicious of everyone and everything. I am a man who is used to deceit and I pride myself that I can smell it a mile away... *ten* miles away." His jaw clenched as if to steel himself in his decision... "And I smell deceit here."

"No deceit, Horse...or do you also believe that *Obergruppenführer* Weber or Minister Plenipotentiary Hempel are also not to be trusted."

Krueger lowered the pistol slightly as he considered Hasofer's question then raised it again pointing it yet more aggressively towards him. He spoke menacingly, shaking his head almost as if to convince himself in his verdict.

"It's the small things, Dietrich...always the small things. Your accent is not proper German, you could have collected me in Wexford but chose not to...you lure me here and describe the scenery as being similar to that of Dresden, a city I know well and it's nothing like the countryside there...you wear a heavy coat on a summer's afternoon to conceal your weapon....but it's the *suppressor* on your Lugar...the suppressor. There can be no conceivable reason why if you were going to merely question me that you could have any use for a cumbersome device like that."

"But Horse," he shrugged, "it's *not* a suppressor!"

Krueger's eyes narrowed as his gaze moved to the gun thrown on the ground moments earlier. The smallest moment of time it took Krueger to assess Hasofer's confident assertion gave the Palestinian the slightest opportunity to act.

Whereas Krueger had had the perfect stance, feet apart, gun centred to shoot at a close object, it was not a posture that enabled swift movement. Hasofer took advantage of this and exercising every sinew in his body moved fast and nimbly underneath Krueger's gun and swept at his legs with his left. Krueger's body lifted and fell backwards to the ground such was the ferocity of the attack.

Hasofer dropped into a crouch and kicked at the hand that still held the Walther. It took two attempts but the second connected and the handgun flew into a nearby bush, close to where his Lugar lay. Each man rose to his knees despite the burning sensations in their limbs as they struggled to gain advantage. Hasofer balanced himself first and Krueger took a heavy blow directly on the bridge of his twice-broken nose but recovered to rush his opponent and bowl him over with a tackle at his midriff. Hasofer rolled away as best he could but Krueger held fast, fighting for his life. Hasofer grasped Krueger's throat and squeezed hard but a soldier's training and several months of heavy labour in the mill enabled Krueger to prise apart his fingers with relative ease. A blow to Hasofer's head followed and his subsequent disorientation allowed the German to scramble towards the two handguns that lay, tantalisingly close at hand.

Hasofer cursed the heavy coat he wore that slowed his reactions, perhaps only by milliseconds, but sufficient to provide advantage to his adversary. Fortunately, the *absence* of a coat was also Krueger's undoing as it enabled Hasofer to grab the German's belt and haul him back towards the centre of the clearing before he could place a hand on a weapon.

A back-handed fist had Hasofer reeling. He recovered to pull Krueger, who twisted round to face Hasofer but his movement was halted abruptly when his nose was slammed by the heel of Hasofer's hand and followed with a chop to his Adam's apple. A finger strike to his eyes blinded Krueger who lay prostrate and moaning as Hasofer scrambled ungainly towards the two pistols.

Grasping the Lugar he turned quickly and sat, leaning against the base of a large oak tree and pointing the handgun at Krueger who still lay on the ground, each of his hands covering his eyes, screaming in pain.

Realising that his adversary had been overcome, Hasofer rose to his feet, in the process stooping to lift the German's Walther *Pistole* 38 and deposit it in his coat pocket. Breathless, he gulped several deep pulls of clear country air as he composed himself. He looked around to ensure that the fight had not alerted anyone and satisfied, turned his attention once more to the defeated German who had managed to move to a position where he had lifted himself upwards on one elbow.

"Horst Krueger. Open your eyes! Open your eyes for the last time!"

"I am blinded," moaned Krueger. "I cannot see."

"Then you must use your ears. My name is Ezra Hasofer. I am Jewish," he said, still out of breath.

"I have been sent to avenge the murders of the innocents in Warsaw whose deaths you ordered. The young women, the elderly, the innocent children...all murdered by you in the name of the evil Nazi *Reich*."

From his pocket he took two sharpened, lead pencils made from Red Cedar, a strong, splinter-resistant wood. He approached Krueger and holding his Lugar by the barrel, smashed the butt across his head, sending him spinning backwards, almost unconscious.

Roughly he pulled at Krueger's collar, tugging him so he lay on his back. Almost immobilised, Krueger lay, eyes closed and mouth agape. Hasofer placed his knee on Krieger's stomach.

"Horst Krueger. The Jewish people have sentenced you to death."

Still insensible, Krueger offered no resistance as Hasofer placed the two pencils inside the opening of each of his nostrils and manoeuvred them upwards.

"This is for Warsaw! This is for your Nazi inhumanity!"

He placed the butt of his pistol beneath the ends of the two pencils and with the heel of his hand, hit it hard, driving the rubbered ends of the pencils powerfully upwards, pushing the slim, deadly stilettos into the brain of Krueger, immediately destroying both his frontal lobe and hypothalamus. He died without opening his eyes.

Slowly, Hasofer stood. Looking round again, he established that no one was looking at the clearing and stooped once more, removing the two pencils from Krueger's nose and placing them in his pocket. A thin trail of blood seeped from Krueger's nose and Hasofer waited until the slight ooze had ceased before wiping his face clean with a handkerchief. He looked at his victim. At first glance, and perhaps even following an autopsy, the authorities might be confused as to the cause of his death.

The wind was faint but cooled Hasofer's face as it brushed past. Taking Krueger by his heels, he dragged him over to the side of the clearing and pulled him further into the dense undergrowth where he left him invisible to passers-by but not covered so he may be presumed merely to have fallen. He lifted a branch which he used to sweep the area in which their fight had taken place until all suggestion of disturbance had been removed. Satisfied that the animals of the night and decomposition would further mystify anyone seeking an explanation of his death, Hasofer started back towards his stolen car.

Before he left the stilled body of Krueger, Hasofer replaced the Lugar in his coat pocket. Stooping, he removed a small piece of yellow cloth cut in the shape of the Star of David and laid it inside Krueger's shirt on his chest.

"As you say, *Herr* Krueger, it's the *little* things, the little things...like the murder of thousands of Jewish men, woman and children."

He turned to go.

"May your soul rot in hell!"

# CHAPTER THIRTY-FOUR

Hermann Henning sipped at a cup of tea in a spartan staff-room as he confided in a colleague, Nurse Deirdre Murphy with whom he'd become friendly since his appointment at St. Kevin's Hospital.

"So you think I should just be brave and ask her?"

"Of *course* you should. You're a real catch, Doctor Henning. If you don't mind me saying so, you're really good looking, you're kind and you have a very responsible job. No sensible woman would say no to a man like you."

"Oh, Miss Murphy, you don't know Sinead. She's headstrong and very independent. I get on so well with her and I believe that I am deeply in love with her but if she says no it will ruin everything. I'd need to move out of our home and the thought of not seeing her again would send me desolate to my grave. I couldn't imagine her not being in my life. Right now, I see her every night she's not away working and every morning when she's home. We laugh together and I look after her. I'm sure she likes me but I can't be sure she'd say yes to an offer of marriage."

"Men!" exclaimed Nurse Murphy, shaking her head in admonishment. "Doctor Henning, just plan the moment and pop the question. Ask her out for dinner instead of eating in your house one night and when you're alone, just ask her. I'm sure she'll say yes without a moment's hesitation."

Henning considered her advice.

"I'll think on it," he said as Nurse Murphy frowned at him.

As Henning drank an indecisive cup of tea in Dublin, the object of his affections sat in the dingy outer office of a scrap merchant's in Kildare. Shortly, Kurt Weber came out of an office where he'd been engaged in some concluding discussion with a local bank manager who had repossessed the business a year earlier. Normally Sinéad would have been involved throughout the discussions but today she'd felt uncomfortably hot and had asked to be excused half way through the meeting.

Weber and the bank manager shook hands, all smiles. Waving farewell, Weber stepped over to Sinéad and asked after her health.

"I'm just feeling slightly off at the moment. It's cooler out here but I think I should go home and rest. It's just a slight headache."

"Of course you should. But let me take you back to my hotel and I'll call a doctor."

"Don't be absurd, Kurt, I don't need a doctor and sure I've the best doctor in the whole of Ireland back at the house if I needed one."

"Of course! Hermann. Of course, he'd be the best choice."

"I just need a cool drink. Why not let's go to a bar and get ourselves somethin' to cool down."

"Is that wise, Sinéad?"

"Not the black stuff, Kurt. Perhaps some apple juice."

"Very well. There's an inn not far from here. I noticed it on the way."

Weber took Sinéad by the waist and guided her towards the car, settled her and drove the short distance to the Kildare Arms Inn before escorting her again into the dark bowels of the pub where he ordered her an apple juice and bought a whiskey for himself.

"Thanks Kurt. You know for a big rough man, you can be surprisingly tender sometimes."

Weber smiled at the compliment before deciding to lean into the speech he'd prepared many times in his head but had never got round to delivering.

He hesitated...then...

"I wish you could see more of that tender man, Sinéad. You only see me when I'm conducting business or discussing your work with your Republican friends."

He grinned. "I'm jealous of Hermann. He sees you every night and you two can discuss anything you wish in the privacy of your home whereas with you and me it's all business."

Sinéad sipped at her apple juice.

"Sure that's bollocks, Kurt. When we're out on the road we've been together in hotels and pubs the length and breadth of Ireland. Night after night we've been together just as much as I've been at home with Hermann."

"But when we are together you always resist my advances. You must by now know how I feel about you. You are very special to me but anytime I want our conversation to become more personal you always shy away and turn the conversation to something, anything, else."

"I'm sorry Kurt..." She covered her face with her hands, shaking her head. "I'm not very good with all this stuff."

"Then let me help you, Sinéad. Let me show you that I'm not always the German General, or the businessman. Sometimes I'm the professor, sometimes just Kurt..."

"It's not you, Kurt. There's times when I'm just a mixed up little Irish girl. I don't understand my feelings. I think you're very special just as I think Hermann..."

Weber sat back in his chair brooding, nodding his acknowledgement of her comment.

"I thought as much. You're in love with Hermann."

"Jeeesus...would the two of yous just get off my back? I like you both, don't you see? I like your authority and your lovely white teeth when you smile. I love being with you. I love your intelligence. I love how you make me feel...you make parts of me stir that..."

"But you don't love me?"

"Kurt, would you feckin' listen to me? I don't know what feckin' love *is*! I'm just a young girl in over her head...dealin' with the likes of you, a feckin Plenipotentiary, for Christ's sake. And as for Hermann? Well I don't think there's a nicer, kinder man on this entire island but as for love? I don't know what that *is*. You're strong...and he's kind. You're rich and he's...well, he's not as rich as you. You're decisive and he's a ditherer. You're such a great gas but I love each of you in your own way and it's drivin' me round the shaggin' bend. When I'm with you I want to be with him and when I'm with him I think about you."

Tears began to pool at the corner of her eyes as her voice quavered.

"Honest to God, if I hadn't committed so many bad sins in His eyes in the name of Republicanism, I'd be off to the nearest convent as fast as my legs could carry me."

She pulled a handkerchief from her pocket and dabbed at her eyes.

"D'you know, right now I'd love to walk out the door and get some peace away from all this but you have the feckin' keys to the car's door or I'd drive it away until there was no more fuel in the thing, even supposin' it took me off the edge of a cliff."

Weber smiled despite Sinéad's outburst.

"But this is why I want to spend my time with you, Sinéad. You're the most wondrous creature God ever put on this planet. Don't be afraid. I won't hurt you."

He put the whiskey glass to his lips and finished its contents.

"Come. I'll drive you home. We'll talk in the car. I have an idea."

They rose, Sinéad still tearful as Weber put a comforting arm around her, bringing her to him. He held her tight, gently soothing her and nuzzled his face into her dark curls. He spoke quietly.

"Presently I'm arranging a weekend where all of the German nationals can come together in one of our hotels to meet one another. What do you say we go up a couple of days early and we can continue our discussion? I'll try to show you that I'm as kind as Hermann, that I'm just as indecisive in affairs of the heart, that I'm not rich, I just have access to a fortune that will stop as soon as I move on from this position... Let me make you feel special, like the Irish princess you are."

Sinéad looked up at him as he held her close. She pursed her lips, wilting before his flashing smile.

"Please?"

Holding his gaze, she relented.

"No one's ever called me an Irish princess before."

## CHAPTER THIRTY-FIVE

Hasofer sat in Weber's office watching him bite into an apple while he read the reports he had prepared on his visits.

"Excellent, Dietrich. Your work is invaluable. It allows me to concentrate on acquiring new businesses." He read on. "And you say that there's universal support for everyone meeting up?"

"Everyone except Albrecht Trommler. He just wants to be left alone. His farm is remote and I think that suits him. He seems a man who is troubled by his past. He was mistrustful of me and has no contact with villagers other than to buy food from time to time."

Weber pursed his lips in a hard line.

"But the others?"

Hasofer's mouth dried as he introduced the matter of his recent covert meeting in Enniscorthy, testing Weber's reaction.

"All very keen, especially Horst Krueger. When I met him last week in Wexford, he was most interested. I mentioned that there were other nationals living close by and he was very anxious to know who they were and how quickly he could meet them."

Weber's demeanour didn't change. "Well, I'm well advanced in arranging a three day meeting in the Curragh Hotel in Portlaoise. We bought it four months ago and it has enough bedrooms to cater for everyone over a weekend. Presently it's empty. I thought that you, me and Sinéad O'Grady might go over to the hotel a couple of days early to warm it up and make sure that everything's in place."

"That would be wonderful, Kurt. We'd all enjoy that. Will you be inviting Doctor Hempel?"

Weber grinned widely.

"Probably not, Dietrich. I suspect that much of the time will be given over to drinking beer. Eduard is more suited to cocktails and elegant conversation. I'll invite him out of courtesy but won't encourage him, 'though I'll invite Doctor Henning. He's been of great assistance to the Legation's interests here in Ireland."

His attention returned to the concluding paragraphs of the report permitting Hasofer to surmise that the death of Krueger five days previously hadn't yet been discovered. Only a matter of time, though. He'll have been reported by his workforce. Soon someone will ask us here.

It didn't take long for Hasofer's prediction to himself to come true. After a lunch of bread and soup he was at talking with Freya Kerrigan at her desk when Weber came through the door holding a piece of paper she'd left on his desk earlier that morning.

"Dietrich, we appear to have lost Horst Krueger. He hasn't been at his work all week and his staff have reported him missing to the *Gardai*. They've done some checking. They found over fifty pounds in a drawer in his room which suggests that he wasn't going away anywhere for any length of time."

"Perhaps a bit early to be worried, Kurt. He may have taken a few days off. He enjoys his beer and he was popular locally as I said in my report. I certainly formed the view that he was missing female companionship. Perhaps he's here in Dublin visiting ladies of the night down in the Catacombs?"

Weber's frown transmogrified into a wide grin.

"You're only just off the boat yet you know already where the brothels are!"

An image of his sweetheart, Rachael, the woman to whom he intended proposing marriage following this assignment, loomed in Hasofer's mind. He'd never besmirch their relationship...but business was business...a deceit was necessary.

"Sometimes a man gets lonely in a new land," he said conspiratorially causing Freya Kerrigan to open her mouth in disbelief at the office banter of her workmates.

Weber's grin broke into a laugh.

"Well, keep an eye on this, would you. If there's no news in a couple of days perhaps you'd ask some questions of the *Gardai* and his workers in Wexford."

"Still think he'll be in the Catacombs," lied Hasofer, continuing his deception.

Edward Timpson sat on a bar-stool in a small bar in Grafton Street where after earlier, wider research he'd eventually found a tolerable brandy. The available red wine in Dublin pubs was undrinkable and out of the question. Several brandies later he'd finished reading the Irish Times and perfunctorily mulled over the crossword clues. Disinterested, his thoughts turned to his work. He was, he realised, a functioning alcoholic and had long ago accepted his fate. He was well aware that his superiors were concerned at his appetite for strong drink but whilst accepting that he'd let the side down once or twice through being incapably drunk, he also knew that if he kept providing a high enough standard of intelligence, he'd be forgiven much.

A boarding school education in Windsor disguised an original Irish accent as thick as Guinness mash due to an upbringing in Mullingar and two Irish parents who came by wealth following the demise of his father's cousin who owned a cotton mill in Lancashire in England. His great advantage over other colleagues in British Intelligence was not just his secretive nature, or that as a single man, he could devote all of his waking hours to his work but that when on the streets, he could lapse back into his native accent, and if necessary, his *Gaelic* tongue, making him indiscernible from any other *indigéne* Dubliner.

*Now what do I know about all these German invest-ments,* he pondered...*and what should I reveal to my superiors? Well, I know who shot Dennehy; they don't...I know of the existence of an IRA safe house and the names of several volunteers of whom they are unaware...I'm conscious that one of them, Sinéad O'Grady is working with the Germans to invest in Irish businesses and to organise weapon drops...I know where she lives...*

He stubbed out a cigarette and blowing smoke softly from between his lips, nodded at the barman, raising his glass an inch from the bar-top to signify another brandy was required.

*Well, I'm presently living off the information I provided that led to the success in thwarting the air-drop. That's still good for a while yet.* Another cigarette was presented unlit to his lips as he scratched a match. *Perhaps I tease them?* he thought. *If I give up the name of the O'Grady girl it keeps me ahead of the pack...it's all money in the bank...information isn't just power,* he mused. *In my case it's survival!*

## CHAPTER THIRTY-SIX

Ezra Hasofer drew back his curtain and, edging forward slowly, looked onto the street outside his room. For some days now the car that had been parked under the street light had not shown up.

*Perhaps they have lost interest in me,* he mused.

He took a chair from beside the table and wedged it under the door handle, locking the door to ensure that it wouldn't be easy to access the room without him having time to replace the Lugar and its noise suppressor that he'd hid behind the skirting board.

Gently he removed the length of wood and took out the contents he'd stowed there, placing them on the bed for oiling. He'd cleaned the weapon so often he could do it blindfold... and in training with *Haganah*, had had to on many occasions. His mind turned to his return to Palestine and to Rachael. *Two dead as ordered and only one to deal with now...Matthaüs Thalberg.* Once his final target was taken care of he'd be on the next boat to Liverpool and on his way back home to those he loved and to a new future as an engineer.

But Thalberg would be difficult. Matthaüs Thalberg, *celebrated* Matthaüs Thalberg, the doyen of the Dublin business community as a consequence of his new role as owner of Ryan's Engineering. Newspaper reports told of new engineering acquisitions furth of Dublin. Presently he was based in lodgings outside Cork...a full day's drive if he used a car. He'd need to use a car. He thought further. *Why complicate things?* Thalberg would be the last assassination. He would need to keep up his pretence no longer. He could merely shoot him and leave directly for Liverpool. No need to deal with Weber's suspicions, no need to return to his lodgings, just head for the docks.

As he sat on his bed, the noise of two car doors closing alerted him. Curious, he approached his window to see two tall *Gardai* placing their police hats on their head, preparing casually to approach the boarding house. With as much haste as possible, Hasofer gathered the weaponry and pushed it behind the skirting board. Normally the nails that held the wood in place required to be tapped in. He always attempted to do this as quietly as possible but it was never without the peel of metal on metal.

Anxious not to alert anyone to his hide, he placed one thumb on top of his other thumb and pressed the nail into the wood. He could feel the tack piercing his flesh as he did so but persevered painfully until it was almost flush. Hearing the front door knocked and the sound of Mrs. Brennan rising from her front room, he moved quickly to the other end where he reversed the position of his thumbs; this time left on top of right. Again he pressed and twisted until the nail was flush. Blood from the first thumb now dripped on the floor and he felt the ooze from his other thumb. Mrs Brennan was now talking to the Gardai. Only seconds now before they'd demand entry, he calculated. He took a handkerchief from his pocket and wiped the blood from the bare floorboards. Satisfied, he tried to stem the flow from his thumbs while quietly removing the chair from under the door handle.

Just as he settled it beside the table, the door resounded to the heavy thump of the knock of officialdom. A deep Irish voice called out.

"Mister Naumann are you *in* there?"

Hasofer looked round the room looking for any tell-tale signs of guilt.

*Too late now, anyway,* he thought as he opened the door with a confidence that belied his feelings.

"Oh, the police," he uttered in mock astonishment. "Please come in."

The two burly officers entered the room, one looking at the apartment, the other confronting Hasofer.

"Your name is Dietrich Neumann?"

"It is, officer."

"Been in Ireland long then, Mr. Naumann?"

"Only a few weeks, officer. I work at the German Legation."

"So you're a German then, Mr. Naumann?"

"From Dresden. If you wish confirmation, you need only contact my seniors at the allegation. I'm sure they'd vouch for me."

"The *craic* is you're in possession of firearms here, Mr. Naumann. That true?"

Hasofer dug his bloodied hands deep into his trouser pockets and shrugged his shoulders.

"Certainly not, officer. I have no use for weapons of any nature. I'm sure that my seniors..."

A back-handed, clenched fist caught Hasofer off-guard as the second of the two policemen knocked him to the floor.

"*Fuck* your seniors. Where have you hidden the gun? We're told it's a Lugar. And that you have a silencer too!"

Without thinking of the consequences, Hasofer leaned on one elbow, raising his back painfully from the floor. Inadvertently, his other hand went to his bruised chin, causing a transfer of blood from his thumb to his face.

"Oh, I am sorry Mr. Naumann. Have I cut your *face*? Sorry 'bout that. Now, if you'll just give us that gun we'll be on our way."

Hasofer realised immediately that two bloodied thumbs might yet be difficult to explain and contribute to his undoing so made a fist with his left hand, moving it out of sight behind his back as he lay on the floor.

"*Garda*, I can only tell you the truth. I am a German citizen and am trying to start a new life here in Ireland. I don't know who might have told you I had a gun but I can only assume that it was someone who has still not forgotten the war years and wanted to get me into trouble."

"Then you'll not mind if me and Sean here have a look round!"

"Of course not."

The second officer who had earlier landed the blow on Hasofer kicked him painfully in the ribs as he lay on the floor.

"Well, just you wait there until we have a look!"

Hasofer doubled over but managed to maintain his left hand behind his back as the two *Gardai* moved his meagre furnishings around the room, throwing his mattress casually from his bed as they searched. In less than three minutes they had trashed his room, drawers upended, his bed scattered.

Hasofer remained on the floor, partly to conceal his wounds, partly because he could hardly breathe from the assault on his ribs.

Eventually the *Gardai* tired of their search.

"Well, Mr. Hitler, it appears there's nothing to be found."

Hasofer spoke from his position on the floor.

"I told you as much, officer. I have always admired Ireland's neutrality and want to become a citizen of your fine country. I have no weapons. I did not *choose* to be German."

If Hasofer expected sympathy for his room being destroyed or an unnecessary assault upon his person, he was to be disappointed as the second *Garda* kicked him obliquely on the left side of his jaw, knocking him immediately unconscious.

Fortunately, one arm was pinned to the floor behind him and the other hand was firmly located in his right pocket, concealing the blood that still oozed from each of his two wounds.

Had he been even slightly sentient, Hasofer would have heard a parting comment from the *Garda* who'd assaulted him. He stooped so as to speak closer to Hasofer's right ear.

"I fought for King and country, despite me bein' an Irish Republican, Mister Hitler. That last kick was for what your pals did at Remagen."

Cold water being applied to his bruised jaw brought consciousness back to Hasofer. His eyes opened to see Mrs. Brennan kneeling beside him, her face taught with concern.

"What have these bad men done to you, you poor man?" she asked rhetorically.

"Ugggh," was the best response Hasofer could muster in a slow groan.

"Them bastards can be fierce heavy-handed," said Mrs. Brennan.

"Ugggh," repeated Hasofer as he slipped back into unconsciousness.

It took a further ten minutes before Hasofer properly regained his senses. Mrs. Brennan had bandaged each of his thumbs while he was unconscious and now sat beside him on the floor holding a cold compress to his forehead.

"Ah, now. You'll be right as rain once you get a cup of tea in you."

Hasofer began an effort to sit upright. Mrs. Brennan helped him.

"You poor man. Did they torture, you?" She nodded in the direction of his two bandaged thumbs. "Did they come at you with the pliers? Try to take off your fingernails, did they?" convincing herself more with every question that the penny novels she was wont to read had been lived out in what used to be her drawing room; excited about what she'd tell the ladies down at the church hall that night.

Hasofer, despite a fogged head, didn't want either to confirm or deny.

"I don't know, Mrs. Brennan. They asked me what I was doing in Dublin then assaulted me and knocked me senseless. I don't think they like Germans."

"I thought you was Swiss!"

"Er, I am...but they thought Naumann was a German name."

"Sure that's all it takes nowadays," empathised Mrs Brennan.

His landlady was accurate in her diagnosis. After a cup of tea, Hasofer felt much better and managed to persuade her that the sizeable bandages she'd wound round his thumbs were superfluous as the bleeding had stopped.

"Still, that's a nasty bruise on your chin, Mr. Naumann."

"It still feels painful but it'll pass, thanks."

He tired of her solicitudes. "I think I might sleep for a while now."

"Of course you must, darlin', said Mrs. Brennan excited at the thought of her church social. I'll let you alone now."

"You've been very kind."

"Not a problem, Mister Naumann. Now if you're feelin' a bit better, before you get some sleep, perhaps you'd see the room tidied up. Then, if you don't mind, could you ever gather your things together and be out of the house by tomorrow evening. I'll need to keep your deposit...for the damage, you understand. It's just I can't have this kind of behaviour in my lodgings, you see. Bad for business. So," she smiled, "if you don't mind?"

# CHAPTER THIRTY-SEVEN

Hermann Henning carefully balanced the small sticks of wood on top of newspapers he'd twisted into a more compact combustible and lit the kindling. He'd come home early from his stint at the hospital and had determined to make a warm fire before preparing a light meal for himself and Sinead who had indicated that morning that she expected to be home around six o'clock. The flames licked at the slight pieces of wood sufficient to persuade Henning that the fire would take. He added some heavier lumps of turf and waiting some further moments, placed a log atop the nascent blaze.

*Now, I have bread bought and paid for. Sausages can wait until she arrives; they won't take but a few minutes. I'll concentrate on my soup.* He scanned the kitchen, identifying the items he'd need to prepare some broth and assembled the leeks, carrots, potatoes and rashers of bacon he'd bought on his way home. *She doesn't eat enough healthy food*, he thought. *Too much alcohol as well. I think I'll have a word with her about her food and drink intake when she comes home.*

"Isn't healthy", he murmured under his breath, quite happy in his domestic chores.

The flat-handed slap to her face sent Sinéad reeling backwards.

The chair to which she had been bound followed the force of her movement, teetered precariously on its back legs, then returned square to the floor in approximately the same position it had occupied moments earlier.

The pain was immense to a twenty-two years old woman who had never had had a glove laid upon her during her young life. Groggily, she tasted a coppery tang in her mouth where her teeth had pierced her tongue. She lowered her head, and held her eyes tight shut despite the constraints of a blindfold, willing away the dull ache that enveloped her being.

A hand grabbed her hair roughly and jerked her head backwards permitting another blow, now to the other side of her face. Again she lurched back, this time carrying the chair to the floor, hitting the back of her head as she fell.

Eyes still closed within the confines of her blindfold, her disorientation was compounded by the pain she felt as she lay on her back coughing blood from her mouth wound, unable to move her tethered body.

Strong hands grasped her hair and shoulders and pulled her slight frame upwards to a seated position. Terrified, she tucked her head downwards towards her chest, shrugging her shoulders upwards, trying to protect it from the next blow.

A quiet voice from behind her stilled the assault.

"That's enough to start with, Mr. Watson. I'll speak with her now."

Sinéad could feel the presence at her shoulders retreat.

"Let's you and I have a little talk, Miss O'Grady."

*Now where did I put the salt?* asked Henning of himself as he moved some pots to search for his missing condiment. Turning, he saw the cellar on the kitchen table and threw it playfully from his right hand to his left, dropping it on the floor in the process. *Damn this left-handedness,* he scolded himself as the salt lay heaped beside the pieces of shattered white crockery at his feet. *This soup needs salt,* he told himself as he scooped some from atop the pile with a tea-spoon on the basis that it hadn't been contaminated by contact with the floor. The rest he brushed into a heap and deposited in a small box. *I'll get more tomorrow,* he decided, pouring the salt into the pot of simmering vegetables.

"Let's not waste one another's time, Miss O'Grady. I know you to be an active IRA Volunteer. I know you to have been complicit in murder. I know you have a role as a special envoy to the Germans in Ireland. I already know of the role you play in supporting prisoners wives as a consequence of your duties within *Cumann na mBan.*"

Slowly Sinéad opened her eyes seeking some visual clues from behind the rag tied round her eyes. Nothing. The voice was behind her.

Her own voice was inside her head, recollecting the orders she'd been given should ever she find herself in this position. *If you're captured, say nothing. Never say anything. Don't even tell them your name. Fix your eyes on something and say nothing. Take your mind elsewhere. If it's the Gardai and you're to be hauled up to court, write a statement condemning British Imperialism to read out in public. That way the Republican cause will be promoted and we'll know where you are when the papers get hold of it. Other than that, not a word should pass your lips.*

Her head hurt. She could still taste the blood that now oozed over her chin, staining the collar of her blouse.

Captain Giles Carter-Hogg sat casually in a chair behind Sinéad. Before speaking, he detached some strands of tobacco from his lips, spitting lightly.

"Let me begin by saying that I find this type of interview most unedifying, Miss O'Grady. You really are extraordinarily pretty. I assure you I would much rather enjoy your company in drink than have my man beat you. But I also assure you that I would have no compunction, no conscience, in ordering him to do just that."

*Close your eyes, Sinéad and say nothing. Take your mind elsewhere.*

"Frankly, Miss O'Grady, I have little interest in your involvement with your rag-bag of gunmen who masquerade as freedom fighters. I couldn't care less about them."

He lit the slim cigarette he'd rolled and inhaled deeply.

"No, I want to know about your Mister Weber...*Herr* Weber...*Obergruppenführer* Weber."

*Don't even listen to the man. Take your mind elsewhere,* she instructed herself.

Moments passed.

Another blow landed on her face, snapping her head to one side and bloodying her nose.

"Feck!" she exclaimed.

"Well, that's a start, Miss O'Grady. You're talking now so let me repeat my question. Tell me what your orders are regarding *Herr* Weber."

Behind the rag that covered her eyes, Sinéad felt salt tears roll down her face, mingling with the blood on her cheek. *Say nothing.*

A large hand covered her entire face. For a moment, nothing happened, then it pushed roughly, driving her backwards to the floor. Her arm bindings prohibited her from mitigating her fall and again the back of her head hit the stone floor with a dull thud, this time rendering her unconscious.

Henning looked at his watch. *That's the soup been simmering now for an hour, it should be ready. I just wish I'd managed to get a chicken. Chicken always makes a more nourishing soup.* Reducing the flame on the gas cooker yet further, he consulted his watch again just to confirm his understanding of the time it had just conveyed. He pursed his lips. *Sinéad's usually home by now. I hope that Kurt hasn't got her involved in something that's going to keep her late after I've made all this soup.* His stomach gurgled, reminding him that he'd had no lunch that day. *I'm starving,* he thought. *If she's not home soon I might just have a spoonful of that soup while I'm waiting.*

An hour passed during which Sinéad had stubbornly refused to speak other than uttering involuntary curse-words which had latterly been reduced to a whisper as her beating took its toll.

Eventually Carter-Hogg rose from his chair.

"This is useless, Watson."

He looked at the semi-conscious form of Sinéad still strapped to the chair.

"She's small fry anyway."

He walked slowly towards a window and pulled back the curtain, giving him a view of the street outside.

"It's quiet. Take her and dump her in a ditch somewhere."

He turned to the larger man who had begun to loosen the ropes that bound her arms.

"And Watson, you'll remember the incident last year when you were left alone with a young lady who was unconscious. My orders today were clear. So now are yours. Do not attempt to molest her. Do not!" he admonished.

Watson met his gaze and nodded his understanding.

"A ditch it is, Captain."

# CHAPTER THIRTY-EIGHT

Ezra Hasofer had made his decisions. His last target was Matthaüs Thalberg who was presently based in Cork some distance from Dublin. The time for caution and discretion was over. He'd merely travel there, shoot Thalberg once he'd informed him of the reason for his assassination and head for the docks at Dublin, perhaps Belfast, and make his way home to Palestine and to his beloved Rachael.

He placed his case on the table he'd righted after the visit by *an Garda Síochána* and took a final glance round the room. Mrs Brennan had been as good as her word and had allowed him to remain until the evening so he might organise other accommodation. Hasofer had found this easy to do given the financial resources available to him and had merely taken a room in another bed and breakfast facility two streets away. He had paid a week in advance but expected to be long gone by then.

Subconsciously he was aware of a knock at the front door of Mrs Brennan's establishment and moments later he started as his own door was tapped timidly by Mrs. Brennan.

He opened it cautiously, half expecting a return visit from the *Gardai* but Mrs. Brennan stood alone holding a note.

"Mrs. Brennan! I was just about to leave. My case is almost packed."

"The blessings of God on you, Mr. Naumann."

She held up the paper in her hand.

"A telegram before you go. In the nick of time, so to speak!"

"Thank you, Mrs. Brennan," said Hasofer, taking the telegram. "I'll be gone in five minutes."

His landlady nodded her agreement and he closed the door, making his way to the table where he removed the Books of the *Tanakh* from his case, opening it at the *Torah*. He spread the telegram on the table. It read;

XXX XXXX XX XX MASADA STOP

NOTE SECOND PARCEL DISPATCHED STOP FOURTH PARCEL NOW REQUIRED SOONEST STOP

BANK DETAILS FOLLOW STOP BANK CODE 2: 39: 21 ACCOUNT NUMBER 106, 46,19, 23, 68, 6, 11, 6, 19

SIGNED SICARII ENDS XXX XXXX XX.'

Hasofer sighed as he realised his plan to expedite matters and head for home was now to be compromised. Turning the pages of the Jewish Bible to Exodus, Hasofer turned to Chapter thirty-nine and drew his finger down the margin of the page until he came upon Verse twenty-one. He read;

*And they did bind the breastplate by the rings thereof unto the rings of the ephod with a thread of blue, that it might be upon the skilfully woven band of the ephod, and that the breastplate might not be loosed from the ephod; as the LORD commanded Moses.*

Taking a pencil, Hasofer spelled out the name sent him as a cypher and sat back in shock as it revealed itself to him....Kurt Weber!

The fire in the hearth had by now been reduced to embers and two bowls of soup had been taken along with some soda bread. It was dark now and Sinéad hadn't returned home. Henning was disappointed but it had happened before. Her work with prisoners' wives took her to distant locations and sometimes transport arrangements let her down. Sometimes she went for a drink after a visit with Kurt and didn't arrive home until later. All that was unusual was that she'd been aware that dinner was being prepared at six o'clock. *She's very much her own woman but she's not thoughtless or rude,* thought Henning. *Most unlike her.*

He shrugged and turned to a collection of patient files he'd promised himself would be written up that evening. *The soup'll keep and the sausages are untouched. I'll build the fire and prepare them when she arrives.*

The stick had been thrown too far and had landed next to the sluggish slate-coloured waters of the Royal Canal just where stood the once grand but now tawdry lodgings of the Apostolic Nunciature of the Holy See in Ireland at Ashtown in the Civil Parish of Castleknock in Dublin.

"Careful, Paddy," cried the dog's owner, one Daniel Logue who had taken his months' old pup for an evening walk.

"Get out of there, Paddy. You'll get wet and I'll get my shaggin' ear clipped from the wife. *Stay* now!"

Too late he shouted his warning as the pup, giddy with excitement, slid on the bank and tumbled towards the canal.

"Here now!" shouted Logue as he chased after it in a forlorn attempt to stop the dog disappearing behind long grass at the edge of the water. Moments later, a series of yelps told him he'd been unsuccessful and carefully, he picked his way down the bank to rescue his pup.

"Jesus, Mary and Joseph! You're a feckin' eejit," he admonished Paddy as he stooped to assist his exit from the murky waters.

Grasping the skin behind its young neck, he tugged sharply and shortly the pup was on solid ground, shaking itself dry.

"I'm for the feckin' stocks when I get you home, Paddy. Look at you all covered in mud and lookin' at me like it was all my fault. And don't you be lookin' at Mrs. Logue like that when we get back or she'll believe you over me any day of the week."

The dim light made available from a nearby gas lamp illuminated a piece of cloth that lay next to Paddy who still looked up at his master, wide-eyed and hoping for more play.

"C'mere you 'till I wipe that mud off you," said Logue holding Paddy by the neck and reaching for the cloth. It took some moments for Logue to realise that the cloth formed an item of clothing and that the dress, as it was, was being worn by the body of a young woman.

"Holy Mother of God!"

Paddy moved forward, nosing at the woman.

"Feck off, Paddy." Logue pushed back the pup and pressed back the small gorse bush that concealed the woman. Hurriedly he pressed his fingers at her neck feeling for a pulse. He found none so took her face in his hand and shook it slightly inviting a response. He tapped her cheek lightly, noticing the bruising as he did so, again willing her to react. From somewhere deep inside, a low moan escaped her lips.

"Thank the Good Lord. She's alive!"

He allowed the gorse bush to fall naturally into place over the woman. Stiffly, he rose to his height and scrambled up the bank. Despite the pain in his ageing hip, he limped along the dark canal path as speedily as his arthritis allowed to a phone box a short distance away.

Three hours later, Hasofer lay in his bed contemplating a new approach. He'd now have to visit Weber one more time and keep up his pretence. He *would* shoot Thalberg but would have to contrive a way to deal with Weber. He was confused as he'd found him to be a man of principal, one who clearly abhorred and found repugnant the cruel and cowardly acts of many of the men he'd been tasked with helping. *But he did it,* reasoned Hasofer. *He is a patriot. He had his orders and he carried them through despite his own reservations.* He struggled with the next logical step in his argument before reaching it with some finality. *Well, I too am a patriot and I must too! Who knows what the Haganah high command know that I don't. I'm a soldier and if ordered to kill Weber, then I must, whatever my own thoughts on the matter.*

At the same time, Hermann Henning lay in *his* bed waiting to hear the reassuring noise of Sinéad's key turning the lock of the front door. *She's never been as late as this before,* he worried. *Clearly, she's been in an accident. She'll be lying hurt somewhere,* he decided before shrugging the notion aside and reasoning that she'd probably be involved in the Irish custom of a 'lock-in' whereby the patron of a public house locks the pub door at closing time but continues to serve selected customers until the wee small hours of the morning.

*She'll be with Kurt,* he thought as unexpected, new feelings came over him; a jealous teasing, leaving him worried more about her feeling for Kurt Weber than any harm to which she might be exposed.

As Hasofer and Henning slept fitfully, Sinéad O'Grady was laid, still unconscious, in a hospital bed in St. Kevin's Hospital in Dublin. The night doctor had examined her and had listed her injuries on a medical card; badly bruised face, nose bloodied but not broken. Two loose molars. Three ribs bruised but not fractured. Probable concussion. Further assessment when the patient awoke but until then, regular monitoring.

Doctor Fitzgerald addressed the nurse who stood beside him as he placed the medical card in a metal receptacle at the foot of her bed.

"Her respiratory rate is fine now as is her pulse rate. Check her blood glucose levels but we can be fairly certain she's received a beating and isn't in a hypoglycaemic coma. Her temperature is now normal so let's just keep an eye on her and we'll see how she is in the morning."

He lifted her left hand in his.

"She's not wearing a wedding ring or I'd have suspected that she'd been beaten by a drunken husband."

He placed her hand gently at her side and turned once again to his duty nurse.

"Let her sleep."

## CHAPTER THIRTY-NINE

Ezra Hasofer reported as usual to the Legation offices half an hour before he was due. Over the months, Weber's arrival had become less predictable, partly because he was often away on trips, partly because when he *was* in Dublin, he was out drinking with others. This morning, he arrived just after nine o'clock to find Hasofer sitting at his desk only feet from Weber's office door.

"Morning, Dietrich."

"Morning, Kurt." He stood from his desk and approached Weber.

"There's still no news of Horst Krueger."

Weber folded his arms and stared at his feet thoughtfully before raising his gaze to meet Hasofer's.

"What do you think?"

"I still suspect it's likely to be an innocent reason but perhaps I should take some time to ask some questions down at the Catacombs before heading off to Wexford if I get nowhere in Dublin."

Weber nodded his approval.

"Try not to take too long, Dietrich. We have the weekend meeting only days away now and I'll need you to help out at the hotel. Everyone's been notified."

"Certainly. I'll need to use the car."

"Of course."

Hasofer had earlier decided to inform Weber of the visit of the police the previous night lest it came to his attention by other means and brought suspicion on him for failing to disclose the matter.

"One other thing, Kurt. Last night I was paid a visit from the *Garda Síochána*. Two officers. They accused me of possessing a weapon and beat me."

Weber's eyebrows rose.

"They found nothing?"

"Of course not, Kurt. I expect it was just someone reporting me on the basis that I'm German and they wanted to get me into trouble."

"Are you injured?"

"Just my pride."

Weber's eyes narrowed. "We have had few problems during the war. The Irish people, their politicians and their newspapers have been broadly supportive but now that there are some of their people returning after serving in the Allied Forces, we might have to think of improving security for our people for a while. Perhaps we'll discuss this when we meet everyone in Portlaoise." He grinned. "So go and find Krueger. And don't spend too much time in those brothels getting into trouble. A few questions and then straight out the door you entered."

Hasofer smiled his acknowledgement and returned to his desk pleased that he'd given himself time to deal with Matthäus Thalberg. *Then I only need to work out a way to deal with Kurt.* He sat at his desk and looked out of the window...*Deal with Kurt... God, will I have the strength to pull the trigger? Only time will tell,* he decided.

Doctor Henning had awoken, alarmed to find that Sinéad's room was unoccupied and that it was evident that she had not slept at home the previous night. He admonished himself for thoughts he now decided were unworthy of him. Of course Sinéad wouldn't have spent a night with Kurt. She was a pure Irish girl. He cursed his inability to ask for her hand in marriage. That would have solved everything. Had they been engaged to be married, he wouldn't let her out of his sight. But where in God's name was she?

His walk to hospital that morning hadn't alleviated his fears for her. Every step along the roads leading to St. Kevin's persuaded him of the dangers that lurked at every moment, cars driving too fast, horses threatening to bolt, signage above shops not affixed properly... anything might have happened. He steeled himself. He'd go back home at lunchtime and if there was no evidence that she was well, he'd phone Kurt and ask him directly if he'd any information on her well-being.

A busy schedule in St. Kevin's that morning occupied his attention as he concentrated on those who presented themselves for treatment of one kind or another. His ward rounds commenced around ten-thirty and he studiously visited those who were abed, consulting the ward Sister and ensuring that the medical notes on each were accurate, up-to-date and being implemented, adding further treatments where he believed necessary.

Entering Ward Five; the women's ward, he noticed that each of the twelve beds had been occupied during the previous night. *A busy night for the ambulances*, he thought. *I was right about all those dangers out there.*

The first two women had each been diagnosed by the night doctor; one with constant vomiting and one with an expected miscarriage. He checked all of the vital signs as had been recorded and satisfied himself that proper treatment was being dispensed.

He stepped across to the third bed and picked up the medical card from its metal container at the foot of the bed and read it. His first observation was that the patient had no name recorded. This wasn't unusual where accidents were concerned. He read the detail; contusions, rib damage, probable concussion, dental weakening. He stepped towards the top of the bed to examine the patient still reading the medical notes when he gasped in alarm as he recognised the swollen and bruised face of the woman he loved. Sinéad O'Grady lay before him, eyes closed. Unconscious.

Henning's detached medical professionalism deserted him as his mouth opened in shock.

"Sister Mahon...Sister...I know this woman. What happened to her?"

"Well I'm sure that I know as much as you do, Doctor Henning! We have what's written in her notes."

Henning managed to stop himself holding his love and trying to wake her. Trying to reassure himself that her injuries were slight, he began desperately to undertake a series of examinations, checking her skull for wounds, opening her unresponsive eyes and looking carefully at them for pupil size and reaction to light. Carefully he manipulated her jaw for any displacement and looked inside her mouth, noting the damage to her teeth and tongue as reported in her medical report. Her skin was pallid and waxy but her breathing was natural. Her temperature was reported as normal as well. Gradually the medical practitioner overcame the worried suitor and his composure returned.

Unintentionally, Henning's inspection of Sinéad's eyes had caused her to awaken from her insensibility. Groggily she whispered, "Where am I?"

Henning moved quickly to sit at her bedside and placed his face close to hers.

"Sinéad. It's Hermann. You're in hospital. You've had a number of injuries but you're going to be alright now. I'm going to look after you."

Sinéad took a moment to absorb the information before turning her head slowly and painfully to focus upon the reassuring voice of her lodger. Her voice remained a low murmur and tears welled up in her eyes as she recollected the violence that had brought her to this place.

"Hermann..."

Henning took her hand and affectionately stroked her knuckles back and forth with his thumb.

"Be at peace, Sinéad. Just rest now. Your injuries will be painful but they are not life-threatening. You'll be fine with rest and I aim to see that you get the best care possible."

Sinéad smiled wanly through swollen lips.

"You're the best doctor in the whole of Ireland."

With that she closed her eyes and was overtaken again by unconsciousness.

Hasofer tidied his desk and as casually as possible made final preparations to leave his office, ostensibly to ask after the health and welfare of Horst Krueger but in reality to hunt down and kill the third name on his list; Matthaüs Thalberg.

Weber entered the room just as Hasofer was patting his pockets, checking the whereabouts of his wallet.

"Dietrich. I caught you just in time. We have a problem."

Hasofer sat on the edge of his desk as Weber closed the door behind him and held out a piece of paper for Hasofer's inspection.

"The *Gardai* in Wexford have just been in touch. They've found the body of Horst Krueger. He was found in some undergrowth near a farm just outside a town called Templeshannon. There's no obvious wound or sign of a struggle...but they found the Star of David on his body...just like Geert Hirsch."

Hasofer, on edge now, exclaimed his *faux* surprise.

"Then Kurt, it is no accident. Someone is killing our people. Someone who knows who they are and where they can be found."

"I agree. And whoever it is, is giving us a sign that we should be aware of their ambitions. Soon, the *Gardai* will put two and two together and newspapers will alert our people who will be put in a state of fear and alarm."

"What can we do, Kurt? What would you have me do?"

Weber chewed thoughtfully on his lips.

"Fortunately we have our gathering this weekend and with some luck we can speak directly to the German community before the radio alerts people in Ireland to a German killer stalking the land."

"Do you still wish me to visit Wexford and find out more about Krueger?"

"Most certainly. I must remain here in Dublin and make myself available to all of our countrymen as well as making sure of the arrangements for our weekend in Portlaoise. Good speed to you. Make sure you keep in touch with me once you have information on Krueger."

Doctor Henning approached Doctor Fitzgerald when their work-spans overlapped as they did most days between noon and one o'clock in the afternoon. They used this time to update the other on patient care but Henning had only one patient on his mind when they met. However, not wishing to seem over-anxious, Henning allowed some niceties and small talk about patients whom Fitzgerald had asked after on his arrival before turning his attention to Sinéad.

"Doctor Fitzpatrick, a patient was admitted last night whom I know. She's my landlady and she's been beaten. There have been some moments of consciousness today but she's still concussed although her vital signs all seem well enough. I wondered if you'd have a look at her. I'm a close friend of hers now and worry that I've possibly missed something."

Fitzgerald accepted the request with equanimity.

"Certainly! I remember her. Noticed she wasn't wearing a wedding ring or I'd have presumed marital disharmony."

"No, she's not married, Doctor."

"Well I'd be surprised if a *woman* gave her that beating. And I don't imagine she's wealthy looking at her garb."

"No, she's not from money."

"Possibly sexual violence?" pondered Fitzgerald before dismissing the suggestion himself; continuing just before a horrified Henning contradicted him..."but there was no bruising, no evidence her clothes had been interfered with..."

Henning could hold his impatience no longer.

"I'd like to discharge her under my own authority Doctor and care for her myself. She's my landlady and I'm sure she'd prefer to recuperate in the comfort of her own home. I'd need to take a few days off, of course but..."

Fitzgerald placed a hand on Henning's arm to stem the outburst. He placed the notes he had been consulting on a nearby desk and gently closed the door.

"Doctor Henning. You're an excellent doctor but you can't sign the patient out of here without either her or my consent. Frankly, given the way you've just expressed your concern, I'm worried that you may have feelings for the young lady that might prejudice your Hippocratic Oath. In this condition, you are not behaving as yourself."

Henning began to bluster his outrage at such a suggestion until his inarticulacy gave way to a defeated admission.

"Doctor Fitzgerald. It was Sinéad who arranged for me to meet you in the first place and secure my position here at the hospital. It was Sinéad who gave me somewhere to stay when I had nowhere to live and over the past several months, it was Sinéad who innocently and unintentionally stole my heart. For some time now I have been trying to find the courage to ask her hand in marriage and now I find her in hospital, beaten unconscious. Of *course* I am not myself. I am worried and upset and...."

Fitzgerald smiled and took Henning caringly by the shoulder.

"Hermann. You are a fine doctor and a good man."

He squeezed Henning's shoulders and stared at the floor as if looking for guidance before meeting Henning's concerned gaze.

"My wife always tells me that I haven't a romantic bone in my body and I suppose she's right. Too many years as a doctor have reduced my ability to see beyond the logical and rational."

He stroked his chin thoughtfully.

"I tell you what. Let us both have another look at Miss O'Grady and if her vital signs are as you say they are and once she regains consciousness and once she gives her *own* permission...to *me*, not to you, then I'll happily discharge her and permit you the time to care for her in her own home."

Henning's smile lit up the small office.

"Doctor Fitzgerald, I can't...I can't thank you enou..."

"There's no need, Hermann. I just want to be able to tell Mrs. Fitzgerald of my newly discovered romantic side. Now, let's go and see if your woman's awake and in sufficient possession of her faculties to agree your proposition."

## CHAPTER FORTY

The slapping rhythm of the car wheels on the cobbled urban streets soon gave way to a quieter journey as the car negotiated the narrower but smoother bucolic roads. Good progress was made despite the ubiquitous pony and traps which hindered Hasofer's journey south from time to time.

Hasofer looked at his timepiece and grimaced as he drove. He'd have to progress quickly if he was to arrive in Cork in time to lure Thalberg to a meeting place, deal with him and make his way to Wexford. Still his pace was hindered by the movement of farm machinery, livestock and people walking the roads. Tempted as he was to increase his speed, he knew that recklessness might see him explaining his driving to a *Garda* in some village police station in Rathdowney or somewhere so he continued his steady progress, taking advantage of any long empty stretch of road to quicken the miles.

Having made himself aware of Weber's commitments that day, Hasofer pulled over to the side of the road at precisely two o'clock at which time he knew Weber would be out of the office meeting with Eduard Hempel. He approached a phone box and dialled the number that would connect him with Freya Kerrigan in the front office.

"Afternoon, Freya. It's Dietrich. Can I speak with Professor Weber?" he asked disingenuously.

"Hello, Dietrich. I'm afraid he's not in the office. He's away seeing Dr. Hempel."

"Oh, then can you tell him I phoned when he gets back? Tell him that the Legation's car has had a puncture. I'm waiting for a lift or I'll try to get it towed to the nearest garage to get it fixed. Not a real problem, just an inconvenience but my schedule will be affected. Tell him I'll phone when I make it to Wexford."

Returning to his car, Hasofer closed the door and wasted no time in steering it from the grassy verge back on to the road before accelerating, setting the wheels spinning and sending stones and mud flying as the car continued its brisk journey towards Cork City.

Henning had phoned Joseph Kelly and asked him for use of the sedan explaining Sinéad's injuries. His request was granted immediately with the rider that Kelly would call round later in the afternoon once she was settled in her house.

Gingerly, Sinéad stepped from the car, Henning fussing around and helping her stand erect before walking her slowly into the house where earlier he'd returned to set a fire in her bedroom. Despite the warm weather, a constant dampness pervaded the interior walls and a fire was almost always necessary to make it comfortable.

"I'm fine thanks, Hermann," said Sinéad holding her ribs as she walked painfully across the threshold of her house.

She squeezed his arm. "You're an absolute saint, Hermann. God alone knows what would have become of me if you hadn't been around to help me."

Henning's face reddened. Being complimented by the woman he loved made him feel quite sublime. He continued to support her to her bedside where she sat.

"Now, you're going to have to take it easy for a few days, Sinéad. I'm your doctor now as well as your lodger..."

"And my best friend in all the world..."

"And your best friend," he repeated, pleased as punch. "But most importantly, right now, I'm your doctor and it's off to bed with you. You need rest, taking care of and a few medicines and you'll be back on your feet in no time at all - but you must rest to let these wounds heal. We can talk about what happened once you feel up to it but I'll leave you now. Get out of your clothes, into some night attire and into bed with you. Shout me when you're ready. I've some soup to prepare and we'll start the process of making you feel a whole lot better."

Tears formed in Sinéad's eyes as she nodded, unable to express the gratitude she felt towards this man who seemed concerned only to care for her.

Hasofer sped towards the outskirts of Cork city, pleased that his navigational skills had seen him arrive without a single missed turning. He braked and steered the car onto the side of the road turning the engine off before lifting a newspaper from the back seat. Blowing on the edge of the pages, he separated them and turned to page eight where an account was to be found of the business success of German entrepreneur Matthaüs Thalberg in Dublin along with the information that he was to speak that night in the Fitzsimons Hotel in Cork on a new engineering venture he planned for the city. A photograph of Thalberg accompanied the story.

*To make sure, I'll need to hear him speak.* He looked again at his timepiece. *Six o'clock. Something quick to eat and then find my way into the audience.* He threw the newspaper behind him and drove towards the city centre.

After some bread and a small pie both of which he devoured hungrily, Hasofer studied the imposing edifice of the Fitzsimons Hotel before striding confidently into the foyer where he joined knots of men who were entering the ballroom to hear Thalberg speak. Taking a seat near the front, he leaned his arms on his knees and stared at the floor, discouraging conversation with other attendees in order to give unimpeded thought to his plans.

A few minutes passed and the hubbub of conversation died as the evening's chairman rose to his feet and introduced Thalberg. Hasofer now sat upright, listening and watching intently to the man he had been sent to kill explain how he had arrived in Dublin only a year earlier and had used funds made available to him by other Irish businessmen who had faith in his abilities. The purchase of a small engineering company led to instant success as new requirements for goods unrelated to the war effort began to predominate, both in Ireland and in England. *No mention of the sole financing of his endeavours by Kurt Weber*, thought Hasofer as Thalberg continued to provide a credible but utterly false account of how he came by his finance and grew his company. Hasofer harrumphed quietly to himself and listened as further stories emerged about the faith Thalberg had in the Irish economy, improving opportunities, the need to put people back to work and the role that could now be played by women who had proved themselves as a gender during the war.

*God in Heaven, he'd be a good politician if he put his mind to it.*

Loud applause signalled the end of his peroration and a further period was spent listening to Thalberg answering questions, all of which bordered on fawning. *No questions about his war record then,* thought Hasofer, suddenly irritated.

Eventually, further applause signified the end of the evening's lecture and the men who had been seated in serried ranks rose and began to make their way towards the hotel bar or the exit. One or two engaged Thalberg in conversation. Hasofer waited until the last one had bid him farewell after languishing yet more praise on him and smiled an acknowledgement as Thalberg turned his attention finally to him.

"*Herr* Thalberg. Your speech was inspirational."

"Why thank you, young man." He hesitated, narrowing his eyes. "Your accent is not of these parts."

"No, I am German like you, *Herr* Thalberg. *Ich bin von der Deutschen Gesandtschaft in Dublin, und reise in einer nicht ganz unwichtigen Angelegenheit.* I am from the German Legation in Dublin and am actually here on a matter of some importance."

He continued, looking around conspiratorially. "I have a message from *Obergruppenführer* Kurt Weber. We should speak somewhere private."

Instead of acting upon Hasofer's request, Thalberg dealt immediately with his unspoken thoughts given his comments earlier in the evening.

"You must apologise to *Obergruppenführer* Weber for my oversight in not mentioning his exceptional support. I did not want to bring unwarranted attention to a system of support we have available to us here in Ireland lest it excites unhelpful interest."

"Of course, *Herr* Thalberg. *Obergruppenführer* Weber would understand completely."

He took Thalberg gently by the arm and spoke quietly into his ear.

"Perhaps we could speak privately. Have you a room here at the hotel?"

"I do indeed. It's immediately above us. Let us go there now and perhaps we could have a drink in the bar afterwards. *Es ist immer ein Gewinn, sich mit einem Landsmann auszutauschen.* It's always good to speak with a fellow national."

Both men walked up the wide carpeted staircase, Thalberg acknowledging the well-wishers who continued to throng the hallway as they did so. On arrival, Thalberg removed a key attached to a large fob and opened the door to his suite.

"Come in, dear boy," he exclaimed throwing the key on a table just inside the doorway. "You haven't even told me your name."

He stepped over to a drinks cabinet and removed two glasses.

"Some schnapps, eh?" he smiled, turning his head to invite confirmation of his suggestion. The smile froze on his face as he saw Hasofer standing side on, his right arm outstretched holding a Lugar complete with sound suppressor.

"Wha..."

"Matthäus Thalberg, you are a *hideous* human being. You spent the war years torturing and killing your fellow human beings. Jews, gypsies, homosexuals...all fell to your doctrine of the Master Race."

He gestured with the pistol. Thalberg followed its direction and sat in an armchair as Hasofer continued.

"It would be easier in many ways just to have shot you in the back when you entered the room but that way you wouldn't have known that the reason you are about to die is because of your evil and wicked ways. You and many like you will be tracked down and disposed of with more dignity than you ever gave your victims."

Thalberg swallowed hard. "But you don't understand. War is a terrible affair. When orders come from above..."

"Orders?" shouted Hasofer. "Orders to shoot, maim and torture children...women...the elderly...just because they are Jewish? These are what you would have me believe are orders that must be complied with?"

"But..."

"Enough! Matthäus Thalberg. You are sentenced to death because of the way in which you conducted your war against defenceless peoples. You committed unspeakable crimes. You have one final chance to acknowledge them and to ask forgiveness of your maker."

A dark stain spread in the region of Thalberg's groin and he started to weep. His words came in a whisper.

"You don't understand. You think it so easy..."

Hasofer shook his head angrily, silencing Thalberg.

"I understand only too well. You have had your last opportunity to make your peace."

A single muffled shot sent a nine millimetre bullet through Thalberg's right eye, destroying its optic nerve, devastating the soft tissue of his occipital and temporal lobes and smashing a three inch hole in the rear of his skull. He slumped back in his chair, his mouth agape.

Hasofer was immediately aware only of the all-enveloping silence and of the smell of cordite. Slowly, he lowered his arm and unscrewed the silencer from the barrel of the Lugar, returning both to his coat pocket. Walking over to Thalberg, he pulled his head forward by the hair and checked the back of his skull to ensure that there was no need for a second bullet. From the inside of his coat he felt for and retrieved a yellow cloth in the shape of the Star of David and placed it conspicuously on Thalberg's chest.

The deep-piled carpet allowed him to move silently to the door. Listening at the jamb for any evidence of human presence outside, he opened the door, exited, locking it behind him and walked down the stairs through a now deserted foyer into the night.

## CHAPTER FORTY-ONE

The knock on the door was insistent.

Henning left the small kitchen in Sinéad's house where he was drying some dishes and walked towards the door where further impatient knocks hurried his progress. Outside stood both Weber and Kelly.

Weber spoke first, clearly irritated as he strode purposefully into the hallway.

"I've just heard. I should have been notified immediately, Hermann."

Kelly stood behind him pursing his lips, shaking his head imperceptibly at the tone taken by Weber.

"Sinéad is meant to be my contact in Ireland. I should have been informed immediately it was evident that she had been injured."

Henning, although taken aback at his mentor's attitude nevertheless stood his ground.

"My first priority is the patient's health, Kurt."

Weber was in no mood to be mollified.

"And where is the patient as you call her?"

"She was sleeping but I've no doubt that you hammering on the door has wakened her."

"Then *good* because we need to find out what happened," he said uncharitably.

Kelly stood, stilled and dignified, awaiting Weber's outburst to recede.

"Let me check on her," said Henning.

As he turned the handle on Sinéad's bedroom door, Weber pushed past him into the room where a still faint and dazed Sinéad lay abed.

"My God, Sinéad. Who did this to you?" asked Weber sitting on her bed and reaching out to touch her still bruised face.

"And sure, it's good to see you too, Kurt," admonished Sinéad. "Hello, Uncle Joseph."

Joe Kelly walked round to the other side of the bed from Weber and raised his chin, looking down over his nose at Sinéad as if better to focus his eyesight on her injuries.

"You've been in the wars by the looks of it. You look like you were hit by a tractor."

"No, Joe. I was beaten."

"Tell me exactly what happened," ordered Weber.

"Would you keep your hair on, Kurt Weber? You're the most impatient man I've ever met."

Henning hovered at the door unsure whether to intervene as Kelly sat on the other side of the bed and asked the same question of Sinéad in an avuncular tone that saw her placated.

Drawing Weber a slow glare she turned her attention to Kelly and chose to answer his version of the question.

"I can't recall everything yet. I remember walking home when someone put something over my head and I felt two people lift me and throw me into the back of some kind of vehicle. I was told to be quiet although I shouted so loud I'm surprised someone didn't hear me all the way over in Galway."

"Accents?" interrupted Weber.

Accepting his question, Sinéad continued nevertheless to report her story to Kelly who sat, his face composed in almost priestly understanding and sympathy.

"The accent was English. Posh English. I was in the vehicle no more than ten minutes and then I was bundled into a building somewhere, my arms were tied to a chair and the hood was removed and a blindfold applied."

"Sinéad," intruded Henning, concerned for her health.

"Look, Hermann. We need to get to the bottom of this," said Weber tiring of his friend's drag on the questioning. "In fact, please leave us. The information we seek is confidential."

Sinéad leapt to his defence.

"Kurt Weber, if Doctor Henning leaves this room, I won't say another word. He's the only person to have shown me the slightest consideration and I won't have you treat him this way."

"It's alright, Sinéad. I'm your doctor and I wouldn't leave you anyway, no matter the attitude taken by Kurt. If this *interview*, as Kurt calls it gets any more invasive, I'll insist that it's called to a halt until you're in a fit state to deal with it."

"Boys...would you stop gettin' all excited and let me ask the questions?" urged Kelly. He addressed his comments to Henning. "I promise I'll be gentle."

"Very well," allowed Henning as Sinéad glowed at his chivalrous behaviour.

"When the hood was removed...before the blindfold... could you make out where you were?"

"High ceilings. Bare walls. A window but the curtains were drawn."

"High ceilings doesn't sound local," ventured Kelly almost to himself. "Probably nearer the city."

"Then?" urged Weber.

"Then I was asked about *you*. I didn't answer and I was punched on the side of my face."

"Me?" said Weber, surprised.

"I can see where you were punched," said Kelly, more solicitously.

"Well, whoever it was, they seemed only to be interested in the work I was doing with Kurt."

She turned, still painfully to hold Kelly's gaze. Don't worry, Joseph. My training was put to good use. I told them nothing. Posh English was behind me questioning me. The other was hitting me when Posh told him to. His name was Watson. I heard him being called that. The English fellah just asked the same questions all the time, all put to me in different ways but I said nothing."

Tears filled her eyes.

"God bless you, Sinéad. You're a champion. You're a credit to your parents and to us Volunteers," said Kelly squeezing her arm gently.

Sinéad nodded her gratitude, trying to stem her silent weeping.

Kelly asked further confirmation.

"And not a *word* you say?"

"Nothing, Joseph. Eventually they tired. I was knocked unconscious when Watson pushed me back onto the floor and banged my head. I've no idea how long I was out. I was pretty groggy but I heard the questioner tell Watson I was small fry and just to dump me in a ditch."

She remembered another morsel. "And one more thing, I heard him say that he didn't care much about my IRA connections...he seemed to know I was a Volunteer.

He was only interested in the work I was doing with Kurt. The Watson fellah also referred to him as 'Captain'."

"Gentlemen, I'm afraid that..."

Kelly held his hands up as if in surrender.

"Now don't you worry, Doctor. Sinéad's given us lots of food for thought and I can see she's tired. We'll go now."

He stood from the bed. "Might we wander round tomorrow for ten minutes, just to see if she's improving? If she remembers anything else she can tell us, if not?" He left his sentence unfinished and shrugged as if to suggest it wouldn't matter.

"If Sinéad's up to it. Why don't I walk over to your place around midday and let you know if she's improving?"

"That would be perfect."

The three men left Sinéad to sleep and gathered together in the small living room. Weber closed the door quietly and took Henning by the shoulder.

"I'm sorry about my outburst in there, Hermann. I was just anxious about Sinéad. I think the world of her."

"And so do I Kurt. I just want to ensure that she recovers quickly and fully. In the early stages that means rest."

"I was hoping she'd come with the rest of us Germans to Portlaoise this weekend to relax with our community. Will she be back on her feet by then? You're invited too," he added as an afterthought.

"Well, it'll be her decision, of course. But her injuries are mostly bruising. I'd expect her body to improve rapidly but she may well have been traumatised by the assault."

"She's a tough cookie, that girl," interjected Kelly. "She's more likely to be traumatised by you two eegits fussin' over her."

Both men coughed their denials in wide-eyed innocence and were met with Kelly's shaking head.

"What a trim pair of feckin' heels will do to a man! You pair have had your heads turned and no denyin'."

He stepped out onto the doorstep.

"In the meantime, I'm away to talk with some people about this man she called 'the Captain'. I can think of only one candidate and we'll have to demonstrate to him that there are consequences for dealing with our people the way he has with Sinéad."

Having left Thalberg's body in the hotel room and then driven over two hundred miles that day to reach Cork City, Hasofer now made his way through the gathering dusk to Wexford, just over ninety miles away. There's safety in the night, he told himself as he took advantage of the quieter roads and the benefits of the earlier warning of his approach to any who walked the byways due to the relative brilliance of his car headlights.

It was late when he arrived in Wexford. Too late to do anything productive but he determined nevertheless to make his presence known to the local *Garda Síochána* so he might have something to share with Weber when he phoned him upon the opening of the Legation offices the following morning.

The clock atop the town hall showed the time to be ten minutes after ten. The *Gardai* would still be about while those who had enjoyed an evening in one of the city's many pubs were afoot. He asked directions and some minutes later found himself outside the offices of the local constabulary. Entering, he was confronted by a large *Garda* who was busy writing in a thick journal so expansive that it covered almost the entire surface of the desk on which he leaned.

For some moments he was ignored.

"Officer?" enquired Hasofer, trying to capture his attention.

"Sir!" responded the *Garda* without raising his eyes from the script he was writing.

"My name is Dietrich Naumann and I have come here from the German Legation in Dublin."

Continuing to avoid acknowledging him, the *Garda* raised his eyebrows as he made the connection between Hasofer's presence and their recent fatality. Still he wrote.

"I have been sent here to ask information about the death of one of our German nationals, Horst Krueger."

The Garda laid down the pen very precisely in the spine of the book and moved it up the page slightly so it was located dead centre.

"Nothin' I can tell you, I'm afraid. We're still lookin' into it."

"Perhaps you could tell me where he was found, whether there were signs of a struggle, were there any clues in his home that might explain this mystery," suggested Hasofer, mildly irritated at the attitude of the officer.

"Like I said, nothin' I can tell you."

Weber had earlier prepared Hasofer for any intransigence he might have to deal with.

He leaned over the desk towards the *Garda* so he could speak in lower tones, initially alarming him.

"Officer, I have been authorised to provide a reward to anyone whether a member of the public or a member of *an Garda Síochána* if the information provided leads us to a better understanding of this dreadful incident."

Holding his gaze, the *Garda* looked to his left where through a glazed panel in a closed door, Hasofer could see another officer reading a newspaper. Satisfying himself that he couldn't be overheard, he now gave Hasofer his full attention.

"And this reward, is it official? Like, would my *Sáirsint* know all about it?"

"It would depend on what the person wanted. I can arrange for credit to be given or I could make it a private arrangement."

"And how much might this reward be?"

"Ten of your Irish pounds."

"Ten *punts* you say. And no one gets to know who told you?"

"If that is what the person wants...and as long as the information was very helpful."

"Well now, that would be important," agreed the large police officer. "Well now, my *Sáirsint* would have kittens if I was to tell you what you want to know, but if I was eligible for the reward like...it's cash in hand I take it?"

Hasofer nodded.

"Then I could probably go out on a limb...but you didn't hear this from me."

He looked again through the glass panel.

"If the boss comes in, start telling me about a dog you've lost...a German Shepherd..." He smiled at his wit. "And I'll tell you all you want to know."

He looked again to his left and turned his podgy hand, palm upwards keeping his hand flat against the surface of the journal so as not to make the transaction obvious.

"That'll be ten pounds, please. In advance!"

## CHAPTER FORTY-TWO

Having slept most of the early evening, Sinéad was feeling more rested and awake. Henning had forced her to eat some of the soup he'd prepared for her and now sat at the edge of her bed holding her left hand at her wrist and looking at his watch to measure her pulse-rate.

"You're doing very well, Sinéad. You'll be back on your feet in no time."

He made to move his hand away but was stopped from doing so by Sinéad who held tight to his.

"Hermann, I don't know how I'd have coped with the last few months without you. You are just the nicest man in all the world."

"And the best doctor in all the world...you forgot that," he chided with a silly grin on his face.

"And the best doctor..." Her face fell and a silence ensued.

"What are you thinking? A penny for your thoughts?"

Sinéad's reticence continued the stillness in the room. After a moment, she raised her eyes and met his.

"It's just...oh, Hermann, it's just that you're such a *perfect* man. You're so good looking, you're intelligent, caring, dependable...you even make good soup!"

Hermann widened the grin that had been fixed on his face since Sinéad had started to compliment him.

"And why is that a problem?"

The tears that hadn't been too far away all day began to trickle down Sinéad's face. She shook her head as if to convey that whatever she was trying to communicate was beyond her.

"Tell me why all these wonderful things you said about me cause you a problem," asked Henning, his face now concerned.

Sinéad dabbed at her eyes with a handkerchief.

"Hermann. You're everything I've said and more. You're *just* the most wonderful man in the world. But I...I...Herman...I've *killed* in the name of Irish Republicanism. I've shot men...fathers to their children... husbands to their wives. And I've killed them because I was ordered to. I've ended life. That's a sacred thing, life and I've stolen it from people just because they were on the other side of an argument."

Henning squeezed Sinéad's hand that held his.

"I think that killing is a terrible thing. You know that I have decided to devote myself to saving lives...to healing the sick..."

"Exactly...that's why I can never really be a part of your life, Hermann...a friend or anything else. We're worlds apart."

"No, we are *not*," exclaimed Henning flatly. "What you're experiencing is guilt...and it's *proper* that you have these feelings. If you felt no remorse you would be a monster and I would harbour no feelings of affection towards you."

Sinéad wiped more tears from her eyes.

"You have feelings of affection?"

"I have feelings of affection, Sinéad O'Grady. Feelings I've never experience before. You've told me of your violent past. But we must both accept that those caught up in the madness of war have to act in ways that they would never consider in normal life. I look forward to the time when all of this violence ends and all of us can build a normal life...a life where feelings of affection can be exchanged without any of these problems."

"I'm just not *worthy* of a man such as you, Hermann. You are such a dear man...and I have a history of which I'm so ashamed." She shook her head. "Ashamed's the wrong word because I'm a patriot and I *believe* in what I'm doing for my country, but...I suppose bitterly regretful. That's it, regretful. Regretful that I've had to end men's lives. Worried that one day, *my* young life will be extinguished like a candle-flame in a gale. Worried that a beating like I received yesterday will become a regular occurrence. Worried that I'll never meet someone like you who can offer me a future... undeserving as I am."

Henning smiled. "Then why do I find you simply the most wonderful woman I've ever met?"

Again, Sinéad shook her head. "But don't you see, Hermann? I'm not fit for normal company!"

"You're fine for *my* company, if you must know."

Sinéad smiled through her tears. "I'm sorry, Hermann, the last few months have played havoc with my moods. One minute I'm so relaxed in your company and the next I'm a bunch of nerves." She massaged the muscles in her neck.

"Let me do that! You're obviously tense...and no wonder after the things you've been through over the last couple of days."

Sinéad reached out and touched Henning's cheek tenderly with the back of her hand.

"You've been sent by angels. My neck is tense where I tried to stop my head hitting the floor."

Henning sat awkwardly on the side of her bed as she manoeuvred her body, still painfully, to permit his hands access to her shoulders from behind.

"This won't do, Sinéad. Why don't you lie on your front under the covers and I'll kneel beside you so I can get purchase on your muscles?"

"Then take these feckin' clodhopper boots off so you don't dirty my nice bed."

Henning complied and took his position to one side of her prone body, leaning into her neck muscles, using his fingers and thumbs to manipulate and knead her deltoid and trapezius muscles, provoking low moans of painful gratitude.

"God, Hermann, that's so...lovely."

After some ten minutes of massage, Sinéad called a halt.

"That was wonderful, Hermann. You're a wizard with those fingers of yours. Now rest for a moment."

Henning returned to his seated position beside her on the bed and Sinéad turned so she was facing him.

"My ribs are still sore."

"Little wonder!"

Sinéad held his gaze. "Do ribs have muscles?"

Henning's medical background prompted an unnecessarily detailed explanation.

"Well, the rib cage muscles consist of the obliques, intercostals and serratus anterior. Whenever you bend sideways or twist your body at the hips, these muscles are used which is why you are in pain when you move. You've suffered trauma to your chest wall during that beating and probably have costochondritis which is the inflammation of the junctions where the upper ribs join with the cartilage that holds them to the sternum."

During his diagnosis, Henning adopted his most professional medical posture, his fingers laced under his chin. He continued, trying to reassure her.

"But it is a relatively harmless condition and usually goes away without treatment."

"I only asked if I had muscles there."

Henning smiled. "Well, you have."

"Then perhaps you'd massage them for me?"

"Well, I think you'll find that massage won't do much good..."

"Why don't you let me be the judge of that?"

She gestured at Henning with her head and spoke in a low voice..."Stand up." ...and pulled at the blankets covering her until she was revealed lying on a sheet wearing a thin cotton chemise which covered her knees.

"Just be tender, I'm still sore."

Henning frowned. "I don't think..."

"Hermann, lie with me..." She patted the bed-space next to her.

Slowly, Henning lay beside her, leaning on one arm and gingerly touched her rib-cage prompting Sinéad to close her eyes and grimace.

"Ohhh, too sore, Hermann."

Henning smiled."Told you. You'll have to listen to what your doctor says more often."

Sinéad smiled weakly. "Here, put your head on the pillow next to mine. You'll comfort me while I fall asleep."

Henning laid his head next to Sinéad's. "Like this?"

"Yeah. Just like that...just like that."

She closed her eyes and smiled teasingly."It's no good...I'm wide awake."...and opened them to hold Henning's gaze only some inches from her face.

Moments passed as they each lay motionless, both maintaining a near distance from one another.

Sinéad leaned her head forward on the pillow and kissed Henning tenderly on the tip of his nose. Speaking now in a whisper she leaned her head so her forehead was on his chin, avoiding his eyes. Henning closed his eyes and nuzzled the dark locks of her hair, breathing in her delicious scent.

"I want to tell you a secret, Hermann."

"A secret?"

"Yes, she breathed. A secret..."

She took her head back on the pillow until she could observe Henning's eyes.

"I've never been with a man before."

"Never been..." Henning's eyes widened as he began to comprehend the import of her revelation.

He swallowed. A long silence passed as they each tried to make sense of the exchange.

"Then I must share my secret with you also."

Sinéad reached forward and ran her fingers through his dark hair.

"And what might that be...?"

"I've never been with a woman before."

"A good lookin' doctor like you?" she whispered. "You'll have had the nurses fallin' all over themselves to be in your company."

"Perhaps, but I can't say I've ever noticed..." he said in a low tone.

Sinead grinned. "D'you know, I believe you actually *wouldn't* notice!"

"Well, I say again...I've never been with a woman before."

Sinéad tightened her grip on Henning's locks and brought his head forward before tenderly kissing the stubble on his chin.

"Well, Doctor Hermann Henning," she whispered... "You're with one *now*. So what are you goin' to do about it?"

## CHAPTER FORTY-THREE

Hasofer stepped into the saloon car and drove to the location described him by the officer of *an Garda Síochána* the previous evening. He parked exactly where he had done when luring Krueger to the site only a few days earlier and noted that the site looked as undisturbed as it had when he'd left the body of Krueger in the undergrowth. In order further to provide Weber with information, he walked onwards to the small thatched croft further along the track, asked of the farmer's wife the same questions as would have been asked by the *Gardai* and received what he presumed were the same answers. He then drove the short distance to Templeshannon and found a phone box, checking that it was after ten o'clock in order to ensure the presence of Weber and called the Legation in Dublin.

Weber snatched at the phone when Miss Kerrigan informed him of Hasofer's call.

"Dietrich, what have you found out?"

"Well, it was murder, plain and simple. I had to bribe a police officer last night to get him to talk but although they're still waiting on the doctor to confirm how he died, the placing of the Star of David on his chest suggests that he was killed by the same hand that took the life of Geert Hirsch. Alternatively, you take the view that both men were each overcome with guilt at their killing of Jews during the war, each committed suicide and both thought to place the Star of David on their chest before expiring."

"Exactly!"

"I'm not far from the site of the killing right now. I spoke with the farmer's wife but neither she nor her husband saw or heard anything. That's what they told the *Gardai* and repeated to me. In my view, Kurt, this is the work of one or more professionals. We have to be on our guard," he said disingenuously.

"Dietrich, our people will panic if this develops further. It is just as well that we're bringing everyone together in three days' time. We can explain the situation to them and have them take precautions."

He thought for a moment. "Has your police contact any idea who might be behind it?"

"None at all. It could be an Irishman but the odds are that it's someone who is himself Jewish or perhaps an agent of the British or Americans. Krueger was more popular locally than Hirsch but neither man was sufficiently unpopular to have brought this on himself by a local...although the way Krueger talked with me when we met, it wouldn't surprise me if there wasn't an angry husband around somewhere...but if he had upset someone locally, he wouldn't have placed the Jewish symbol on his body."

"I agree, Dietrich. Look, I need you to stay down in Wexford for the moment. Where are you staying at the moment?"

"The Slaney Hotel in Wexford."

"Fine. Stay until the doctor pronounces on the cause of death of Krueger then make your way directly to the

Curragh Hotel in Portlaoise. I'm going up there tomorrow and everyone arrives the day after so perhaps by then we'll know more of what's going on. Make sure you keep in regular contact with Miss Kerrigan, she'll be able to get messages to me if I'm out and about."

"I'll do that, Kurt. See you in Portlaoise."

*So far, so good,* thought Hasofer as he replaced the telephone on its cradle, *but there will be hell to pay when the body of Thalberg is discovered in Cork with a bullet in his brain and the same yellow star on its chest.*

Hasofer stepped from the phone booth, seated himself comfortably in his car and drove off to book ongoing accommodation in his hotel. As his car disappeared over a rise on the road towards Enniscorthy and onwards to Wexford, Captain Giles Carter-Hogg left his car and made use of the same telephone booth as had Hasofer. He called Timpson.

"I'm down in the town of Templeshannon. Our friend Naumann has been visiting the place where *Herr* Krueger was killed and has been asking questions of the *Gardai* and the local farmer. It appears that the Germans are as perplexed as we are."

It was later in the day when the telephone call expected by Hasofer was received in the Slaney Hotel. He was escorted to reception by a maid where he tried to muster as much surprise in his voice as possible when Weber told him of the body of Thalberg being found dead in Cork with a yellow star on his chest.

"This is very serious," said Hasofer grimly.

"It is."

"What would you have me do, Kurt? Remain here in Wexford or travel to Cork to find out more about Thalberg?"

"I need you to do both, Dietrich. Cover both the town and the city and report to me regularly. I'm going to try to see Éamon de Valera and demand protection for our people. I also want to have him provide a *Gardai* presence at Portlaoise but just to make sure, I want you and I to have our own weapons in the hotel. We've had three men murdered over the course of several days and it's obviously being done to target high ranking officers. I'll need to check Thalberg's file again but from memory, all three of them were involved with the killing of innocent Jews. Certainly Hirsch and Krueger were. The Star of David seems to point that way anyway...unless it's a double bluff by the British Intelligence agencies. I'd put nothing past them."

"Exactly. But perhaps de Valera might throw some light on matters. He'll be aware of British activity I feel sure. He has his own agents in the military intelligence branch of the Irish Defence Forces who might be able to understand what's going on, that G2 section."

"Perhaps but I expect that we'll have to depend on no one but ourselves in these matters, Dietrich, but I'll try to ask his support anyway. You'll need to travel between both cities and then get back up here to Portlaoise. Did Miss Kerrigan give you enough coupons for petrol?"

"I expect so, Kurt. But I'll just bribe someone if I run out."

"Good. Keep me informed. I'll bring a weapon for you and give it you when you arrive," he said abruptly before concluding the conversation.

Kelly knocked twice on the door and waited while Henning answered.

"Is our patient able to be seen now, Doctor?"

"She's much improved, Mr. Kelly," replied Henning ushering him inside. "To the right, Mr. Kelly, to the right. She's up and about today. In the parlour."

Kelly entered and smiled beatifically at his niece.

"Ah, Sinéad, you're a sight for sore eyes. It's great to see you up and about so soon after that beatin' you took from them thugs the other day. And how are you feelin' in yourself?"

"I'm still a bit sore, Joseph but I've got the best doctor in all Ireland lookin' after me so it's no wonder I'm on the mend."

She beamed at Henning who returned her smile.

"I can manage on my own. I can walk, wash dishes and clean up so I'm just about ready to get back in harness."

"Perhaps you're being a little hasty," countered Henning.

"Nonsense, Hermann. I'm certainly not letting whoever beat me defeat me. I'm back in the saddle tomorrow anyway when I go to Portlaoise with Kurt."

"Don't you think that's a bit too soon?" asked Hermann. "In my opinion...."

"You *know* how much I cherish your opinion, Hermann but I know how I feel and I think the best way of gettin' back at these people is to carry on regardless and show them that I won't be cowed."

"Perhaps the doctor has a point, Sinéad." He changed the subject. "What's all this about Portlaoise anyway?"

"Kurt Weber is bringing all of the Germans he's placed in business together in the Curragh Hotel over the weekend and he's asked me to help him prepare as part of the advance party. Hermann's coming down on Saturday."

"Well, as long as you don't exert yourself. Your mother would give me what for."

"Jesus, Joseph! You don't think she'll be beside herself if she knew I'd been knocked unconscious by someone and ended up in hospital? Helpin' prepare for a get-together isn't quite as fretful for a mother."

"'S'pose you have a point, girl."

Henning shook his head disapprovingly.

"That beating certainly didn't make you any less headstrong, Sinéad."

"Glad you understand that, Doctor. Anyway, it's part of the job that Joseph gave me to do and I aim to do my job to the best of my ability."

Kelly moved to a wooden seat and sat down facing Sinéad.

"Let's take a few minutes while you feel like talkin' to go over again the day you were taken and beaten, Sinéad. I have some more questions."

Eduard Hempel and Kurt Weber were given the immediate appointment they sought with the *Taoiseach* of Ireland. Kathleen O'Connell bid them enter his office. Tall as he was, Eduard Hempel was still dwarfed by de Valera who greeted both men as if old friends.

"Gentlemen, you are both very welcome. Please sit."

As all three found comfort in de Valera's armchairs, the *Taoiseach* continued talking.

"I can imagine why you asked to see me. These murders are most troubling."

"So they've been found to be murders?"asked Weber.

"Not quite yet. Initially there were no suspicious circumstances in respect of Krueger. Hirsch was presumed to have been a suicide but the third killing, that of Thalberg, suggests that the previous two were also caused by underhand means. His was very obviously murder. The *Garda Síochána na hÉireann* are still investigating."

"I'd have thought you might have asked your own security people, G2 to take a look at this."

"I already have, Professor Weber."

Hempel leaned forwards in his seat.

"I'm grateful *Taoiseach* but I'm afraid I must support the sentiments implied by my colleague, Professor Weber. This is obviously an orchestrated attempt to kill German citizens, all of whom are living in Ireland legally, all of whom are contributing materially to the well-being of the Irish community in which they find themselves...all of whom..."

De Valera spread the fingers of each hand, imploring respite.

"Eduard... Eduard...You need have no fear. I am determined that we get to the bottom of this. It is an embarrassment for *Eire* and I'll put all means at the disposal of the authorities so we can find the person or persons who did this, bring them to justice and stop further incidents. I can very easily understand how concerned you must be."

Weber intervened.

"*Taoiseach,* Germany is contributing markedly to the economic growth of your country and we find that those at the forefront of this effort are being murdered. Tomorrow, we begin gathering German nationals in the Curragh Hotel in Portlaoise. It's been planned for some time and was designed to respond to what we thought was a suicide by Geert Hirsch on the basis of his loneliness and his separation from his countrymen. Of course, now, we'll use it to forge stronger relationships between them but also to discuss with them the need to be careful. We don't know who is committing these dastardly crimes, it might be a Jewish organisation, a misanthropic adventure by the Americans or British... like you, we simply don't know...but we have to be suspicious until the matter is resolved."

"That makes sense, professor."

Hempel came to the point of the visit.

"If I may, *Taoiseach*. Might it be possible to have a *Gardai* presence at the Curragh Hotel for the duration of the conference? Friday, Saturday and Sunday? It would make the point to our nationals that you are taking the matter seriously and protecting those gathered at the same time."

"It shall be done, Eduard."

## Chapter Forty-four

In the bathroom of his suite at the Shelbourne Hotel, Weber had had a sleepless night, remonstrating with himself over the preoccupation he was having over the time he intended spending with Sinéad at a moment when someone was on the loose murdering those he was meant to protect. *But,* he reflected, *Dietrich Naumann is covering things for me in the south, we have the support of the Taoiseach in addressing our problems and my job starts when we get everyone together. Today and tonight, I should just focus upon my time with Sinéad,* he persuaded himself. He looked in the mirror and regarded his chiselled mouth, his contoured dark eyebrows and steady gaze. He ran his fingers over his newly-shaved chin. *For someone who has spent many years living rough on the front line, I haven't turned out too badly,* he thought, entertained at musings that had never crossed his mind since he attended dances at his university before the war.

He held his tie between his teeth as he buttoned his shirt then took some time ensuring that the knot sat correctly before satisfying himself that he looked as personable as possible. He put on his suit jacket and admired himself in the mirror. *Well, this is my big chance. I have Sinéad all to myself until tomorrow. If my plans go well, I'll be able to convince her that my feelings for her are both honourable and implacable*. He glanced one more time at his reflection in the mirror. *Here we go!*

Half an hour later Weber was nervous but almost giddy with excitement as he helped Sinéad into the passenger's seat of his car. Some two hours earlier, Henning had departed for the hospital leaving Sinéad to prepare for her visit to Portlaoise. They'd lingered on the doorstep, nuzzling each other, trying unsuccessfully not to be too demonstrative in public view lest the Priest were to be informed of their calumny.

"Careful now," instructed Weber. "We've to look after you."

"I'm fine Kurt. Now stop fussing like an old hen!"

Both arranged themselves in the front of the commodious sedan, Weber behind the wheel.

"I'm really looking forward to our time together, Sinéad. I have so many troubles to deal with but when I'm with you, I can only think of your beauty."

"You're *meant* to be thinkin' how you can help me and mine take our war to the Brits! Not gettin' all gooey on me. I was meant to be comin' down to Portlaoise to spend a bit of time recuperatin' and workin' on how you might help us get our hands on some weapons with all that money you have."

She turned sideways in her seat so as to face him directly as he turned the wheel and set off.

"On a personal basis Kurt, I also wanted to take the opportunity to thank you from the bottom of my heart for the money you've given us for the relief of prisoners. You've no idea how much it's helped so maybe when we're relaxin' we could have a chat about how we might dip into that money bag of yours and slip another few quid towards the assistance of poor women and children Dev has condemned to a life of poverty and loneliness while their husbands and fathers are in jail."

Weber nodded enthusiastically.

"Of course we must discuss that. I was hoping over a glass of Champagne. I've managed to get my hands on several crates of the stuff to welcome our German nationals but I thought that you and I might sample it beforehand."

"Good God, I've never tasted the stuff. Is it as delicious as it's made out to be?"

"Better than that, Sinéad. You'll love it."

"I'll maybe give it a try," she smiled.

Weber looked in the rear view mirror, an automatic reaction now when driving a car to ensure that no one was following. He saw no vehicles behind him and relaxed somewhat turning his attention once again to Sinéad.

"I hope you'll forgive me Sinéad but I wanted to make this weekend special for you and to thank you particularly for all the help you've given me since I up arrived in Ireland," he said disingenuously. He hesitated before continuing.

"I have some gifts for you."

"Gifts?" exclaimed Sinéad.

"Yes. I hope you don't mind but I wanted to do something to thank you so I consulted Miss Kerrigan, Freya Kerrigan who works at the Legation. I asked her to help me. She looks like she's the same size as you and..."

"The same size?" said Sinéad, confused.

"Well, I had an opportunity to acquire some items not usually available in the shops of Dublin these days and wanted to obtain them for you. Freya is the same size as you so I asked her to select items of clothing."

"Well if *that* doesn't take the biscuit. D'you think I'm knockin' about the place like some old trollop? Is that it?"

"Not at all. Of course not. It's just...just... Well, I thought that because you're so beautiful you deserved to dress like a lady. For perhaps the first time you could be dressed in the finest silks and drink Champagne..."

Sinéad stared at him open-mouthed for some moments before starting to giggle.

"Oh, Kurt. Here am I trying to be as good as any man in the Irish Republican Army and you're trying to turn me into a lady." She giggled again. "The finest silks is it?"

Weber stiffened as she laughed.

"Well, if you don't appreciate my efforts, I'll just give all of these parcels in the back seat to Miss Kerrigan. I'm sure she'd be most grateful."

Sinéad turned round to see shopping bags on the rear seat. Her curiosity was tweaked. She turned again to face Weber.

"Well, can I maybe just look at them? No promises!"

Weber had recovered some of his composure.

"Bring them over into the front of the car and open them up if you wish. I was going to give you them at the hotel but if you must..."

"Now then Kurt, you can't tease a young lady like that," smiled Sinéad reaching into the back.

As she looked into opening of the bags, her curiosity got the better of her and she took out a simple yellow dress made of cotton. She played it through her hands and felt the lining.

"God, this is beautiful, Kurt," she said, her demeanour becoming more appreciative. She looked him. "This is lovely."

Weber smiled. Perhaps this might not end in an argument after all.

"Try another bag. There are many!"

Sinéad pulled over a large brown bag within which was a tailored suit in green with a pleated skirt. She couldn't help the cry of excitement as she held it up within the confines of the car.

"Kurt, this is heavenly. It's just beautiful."

"There are several. I told Miss Kerrigan to acquire anything she thought you'd like."

More bags were pulled forward, eliciting further cries of delight until one was opened containing some smaller boxes. Sinéad turned them round so as to read the nature of the contents."

"Jesus, Mary and Joseph, Kurt Weber. Is this the *silks* you were talkin' about?"

She read the boxes once more to be sure of her ground.

"Unless I'm very much mistaken, Kurt, these contain ladies' undergarments."

Weber felt his face flush.

"Miss Kerrigan informed me that it was necessary to purchase these. She told me that you would not feel properly dressed if you were wearing pretty clothes without the accompanying garments to go with them."

Sinéad reverted to her earlier astonished look.

"Well, I'm sure I don't know what to say!"

She looked at the assorted bags, parcels and garments now gathered around her in the car.

"I don't know about this, Kurt. I mean it's very generous of you..."

"Sinéad, these are not purchased so you can wear them when you visit with Joseph Kelly or any of your Republican friends. They are not designed to have you impress the prisoners' wives you visit. They are my way of thanking you and to allow you...for a short while...to forget the horrors of war and misery and spend an evening in my company dressed as if you were the Queen of Sheba."

Sinéad sat quietly, trying to form an attitude. She looked again at the elegance of the clothes, suspected that this Miss Kerrigan, whom she'd never met, might actually have bought the proper sizes and slowly, uncomfortably surrendered to the thrill of delight at the prospect of dressing gracefully. War had blunted her womanliness. All notions of sensitivity, of beauty and kindness had been suppressed, only recently being rediscovered at the side of Hermann.

She looked again at the array of clothes.

"Then I'll tell you what, Kurt. When we get to the hotel, I'll try them on in the privacy of my own room and if I decide to, I *might* wear some of this stuff for dinner. *Might*!" she repeated.

Her voice took on a more confrontational tone.

"But there's every chance I'll decide to come down to dinner tonight dressed like the old trollop you obviously think I am," she joked, now more comfortable at Weber's gesture.

"That's all I could ask, Sinéad," smiled Weber.

The journey to Portlaoise continued in a less fraught atmosphere, Sinéad every so often fingering the garments inside the bags as if to ensure that somehow they didn't disappear.

## CHAPTER FORTY-FIVE

Hasofer sat in a pub close to the police office he'd visited several times now asking for updates. Staring into the middle distance, he pondered his next move. He had but one final task; to kill Kurt Weber, a man he'd come to admire. *Haganah* would be pleased with him, he was certain. Three senior Nazis, all dispatched as ordered...a wave of fear and uncertainty unleashed upon the German community as the murders became known, no evidence pointing to a particular perpetrator although it could be assumed, with no little justification, that the Jewish community had struck back. There would be a realisation that there could be no hiding place for those who had behaved in a bestial fashion during the war years. Indeed, he could also be pleased that he'd managed to persuade the very people he'd been sent to assassinate that he was one of them. *If it wasn't all such a distasteful business, I might well feel very pleased with myself,* he thought.

He finished the glass of water he'd ordered and refused the barman's sarcastic offer of a second, deciding instead to visit the police station one final time. *Whatever they have to say,* he thought, *I'll start making my way back to Dublin. I have enough information known to me to bluff for a short period. That's all I'll need to finish my assignment. With a fair wind I'll get there by later tonight and see if an opportunity presents itself to slay Kurt Weber....if God gives me the strength to pull the trigger. Then I can make for Palestine as fast as a ship can carry me...back home to see my beloved Rachael... back to marriage and a new life as a student engineer... away from this murder and mayhem.*

Timpson had decided that his office for the day was to be O'Shea's pub on the banks of Dublin's River Liffey. He'd adopted his Dubliner persona and was very drunk, loud and gregarious as he sat at the bar, joining in the rebel songs so beloved of the regulars, buying drink for two or three other alcoholics who found solace in afternoon drinking, listening to scraps of information he would later dredge sober from a highly intelligent mind, damaged but not yet ruined by liquor.

The bar door opened slightly and Carter-Hogg peered into the gloom, his eyes attempting to establish the presence of Timpson. He heard him before he could see him.

> *"I passed on my way, God be praised that I met her*
> *Be life long or short, sure I'll never forget her*
> *We may have brave men, but we'll never have better*
> *Glory O, Glory O, to the bold Fenian men."*

A pattering of applause received the ending of the song and Timpson threw his arm around his nearest crony, laughing heartily. Carter-Hogg slipped into the bar and, ignoring Timpson, nodded the attention of the barman to the Guinness pump rather than attempt his *faux* Irish accent.

Paying a shilling allowed him merely to accept his change without any discourse with bar staff about the price of a pint and upon being served, he moved over to a four-seat table where he sat and sipped at his pint awaiting the moment when Timpson would step aside from his revelry and make contact in a way that was consistent with his character. Ten minutes passed before Timpson made his way uncertainly to the toilet.

"Ah, young man," said Timpson loudly. "Have you a spare choker? I'm gaspin' for a fag!"

Carter-Hogg smiled tolerantly at a scrofulous Timpson who sat down, still grinning before lowering his voice and growling softly so only his colleague could hear him.

"Places like this are out of bounds to you," he hissed.

The junior officer ignored the rebuke.

"Need your advice. We've received an urgent signal from one of your contacts. It wasn't encrypted. Just says that the German community are massing at the Curragh Hotel in Portlaoise over the weekend. We need to know if we should take an interest."

"How did the contact sign himself?"

"The message was phoned in but I spoke to him and he told me that when last you met, you quoted Shakespeare at him."

In a low voice, Carter-Hogg attempted the bogus Irish accent earlier ridiculed by Timpson in his mimicking of the message he'd received.

"*Things without all remedy should be without regard. What's done, is done...*"

"That's not how you exclaim the words of the Bard" said Timpson, suddenly animated.

"*Things without all remedy should be without regard. What's done, is done,*" he intoned, his shoulders shrugging, his demeanour resigned as if performing Macbeth at the Old Vic.

"*That's* how you express the words of William Shakespeare. He's trying to convey that you shouldn't cry over spilt milk."

He cupped his hand round Carter-Hogg's neck, pulling him forward as if affectionately.

"The contact can be trusted as can the message. If everyone's gathering at Portlaoise, get some people over there. Quietly. Take cameras. If there's going to be a Nuremberg Rally in my back garden, I want to know who's out there saluting."

He rose to visit the toilet still holding to his character, speaking quietly in a broad Dublin accent.

"And one more thing. Finish your pint quick and leave before people start talkin' to you...because what you call your Irish accent is feckin' useless. It's more Cockney than Cork and that's the truth of it...Now go."

The large sedan crunched onto the front driveway of the Curragh Hotel and braked, sending stones flying. The car settled and its engine chugged to a halt. Weber exited first and moved hastily to open the door for Sinéad.

"Careful now, Sinéad. You're precious goods."

"Not as precious as them silk unmentionables you have in boxes in there now!" she retorted, easing her way out of the passenger seat.

"Let's get you organised in our suit in the hotel and I'll bring all of these things up to your room."

She manoeuvred stiffly so the car door could be closed at which point the import of Weber's suggestion hit home.

"What the devil do you mean, '*our*' suite?"

Weber reddened. "Oh, sorry...just an expression. I've booked a large suite in the hotel. Your room is next to mine. There are public rooms as well as a bedroom in each. The rooms are connected by a door but don't worry, the door is locked and the key is on your side. I insisted upon that!"

He smiled, hoping the explanation both satisfied her and permitted the arrangement to stand.

Kurt Weber had organised the evening at the Curragh Hotel with all of the detailed attention he'd normally pay to an assault on a strategic military objective. Sinéad moving her sleeping quarters from the room next to his was not in his plans.

"There'd better not be any funny business, Kurt Weber."

"On my oath, Miss O'Grady."

"Then let's remind ourselves what this hotel looks like."

They entered the foyer and were greeted by Frank Connolly, the man who used to own the hotel but whom Weber had re-employed to renovate it. Smiling broadly, he shook Weber's hand and bowed his head courteously to Sinéad.

"I hope the hotel is as you'd wish it, Mr. Weber. We've had all the local tradesmen in here for the past two months bringing it back to the state it should have been in when I sold it to you. It's taken a good bit of your cash to do it as you know but I'm hopin' you'll think it worth the time and money."

"Well, it looks good from where I'm standing. What do you think, Sinéad?"

"It looks fabulous, Mr. Connolly. Have you managed to retain all of the rooms?"

"Some we knocked together to make things more comfortable, Miss O'Grady. Still, we have sixty rooms. More than enough supposin' all of your fifty-six invited guests turn up."

He turned to face Weber. "Have you any final number, Mr. Weber. It's just that it's hard to cater for an unknown number of guests"

"I'm afraid we won't know until people arrive tomorrow. Some will arrive tonight and I hope you'll be able to look after them. I've arranged that Miss O'Grady and I will dine at seven-thirty and don't want to be disturbed by arriving guests so if you could look after them that would be most helpful. I have a list of names..."

He fished inside his pocket and took out a piece of paper.

"If their name is not on this sheet of paper they do not gain entry. We expect the *Gardai* to have a presence over the weekend. They should have access to this list as well."

"The *Gardai* have already been, Mr. Weber. They told me all about these dreadful murders. Just terrible, sir. But we'll make sure no one gets in here that's not meant to get in here so just you and Miss O'Grady relax."

He made to pick up Weber's case.

"Thank you, I'll keep a hold of this. Perhaps you could show us to the suite I earmarked and then collect Miss O'Grady's case from the car along with all of the parcels and bags on the rear seat and bring them to her room?"

"Certainly, sir."

"Thank you. And once you're finished, you agreed that one of your men..."

"My brother Thomas, sir, very reliable..."

"That Thomas would return to Dublin tonight and prepare to bring Doctor Hermann Henning out here from St. Kevin's Hospital first thing tomorrow morning. Can you ask him to phone Doctor Henning tonight and confirm arrangements? He's on duty in the hospital until nine o'clock."

"It's all organised, Mr. Weber."

"Then first Miss O'Grady and myself will relax. We will meet in the restaurant at seven o'clock for some of the Champagne I ordered to be brought down."

"It's been chilled within an inch of its life, sir."

Weber smiled. "Chill it some more."

Hasofer made slow progress towards Portlaoise as a caution because of the numbers of ponies and traps sharing the road space. As dusk fell, his headlights brought him more confidence to proceed at a faster pace knowing that his lights would warn other users of his presence.

He used the travel time to consider his options. *I could always say that I shot and missed...or that security was too tight...*He shook his head. *That wouldn't wash*, he remonstrated with himself. The facts could be checked and put my bargain with Menachem Begin in jeopardy. *No, there's no way out of this. I must do my duty and obey the order to shoot Weber.* He felt in his jacket pocket for the gun he knew was there. He patted his other pocket and felt for the silencer. Still ambivalent, he drove on.

# CHAPTER FORTY-SIX

Connolly unlocked the door to Weber's suite and opened it in a grand gesture closely observing his paymaster's face for signs of approval or disapproval.

Weber's gaze took in the spacious room as Sinéad peered round him trying to see how it had been renovated and furnished.

"Why, Mr. Connolly, this is superb. You must have burgled all of the great manor houses of Ireland to acquire this quality of furnishing."

"Your budget was very generous, sir and I know you wanted the hotel to be a showpiece."

Weber strode forward permitting Sinéad access to the room. She turned slowly, gaping at the expensive furnishings.

"Mr. Connolly, you have this place like a palace."

Connolly beamed, satisfied that his work had been appreciated.

"Then, if you wish, I'll retire and get things organised. I'll bring Miss O'Grady's things up and get on with tonight's arrangements. Your apartment is next door, Miss. You can access it from that connecting door or from the next door down in the hallway."

"That'll do me fine, Mr. Connolly."

Connolly left and Weber took Sinéad by her arm, accompanying her the few paces to the entrance of her suite next door. Turning the key in the lock, Weber held the door open for Sinéad who entered to find a room furnished in heavy oaken woods, deep piled rugs and bright curtains.

"This is luxurious, Kurt," she said wondrously.

"That looks like your bathroom over there and this..." He stepped over to the connecting door and removed the key, turning the handle forcibly, demonstrating the strong lock on the door. "This...is the key you were anxious about."

He withdrew it and laid it on top of a dresser. "It'll come to no harm there."

He turned to find Sinéad running her hand down an edge of the velvet curtain, looking at the outside view.

"It's lovely, isn't it? Your bedroom is through there." He gestured towards yet another door.

Sinéad held the velvet to her cheek and spoke quietly.

"Kurt, I don't deserve all this. This is far too far away from the person I am. I'm a girl from the country. From a farm. I'm not used to this finery."

"Then I want you to *get* used to it, Sinéad. I've told you. You're a princess as far as I'm concerned and you deserve only the best. Now, Connolly will be here shortly with your bags. Why don't you take a relaxing bath, have a think about what you want to wear for dinner tonight and I'll meet you in the bar downstairs for some of this Champagne I've been promising?"

Sinéad continued to hold the velvet curtain to her face, still uncertain.

"Shall we say seven o'clock?"

Almost imperceptibly, Sinéad nodded, her eyes still cast downwards.

◆ ◆ ◆

Timpson placed his hand on Carter-Hogg's arm as the approached the town of Portlaoise.

"Slow down now. We're not far from the entrance to the hotel grounds. Drive past slowly so I can have a look."

The car decelerated to a more modest speed and after negotiating a couple of bends in the road, it arrived at the wide, stonewalled entrance to the Curragh Hotel.

"Just drive past slowly," instructed Timpson.

He turned stiffly in his seat as he tried to maintain a view of the entrance as long as possible.

"Two uniformed *Gardai* and one plain clothes chappie. They've obviously heightened security." He thought further. "Drive on into the town. I've arranged to meet our surveillance squad in the Leinster Arms pub on the edge of town. We can discuss our next move there."

Sinéad had luxuriated in a warm bath for half an hour enjoying the sensation of the scented water, sampling the various oils and lotions that had been made available on the marble ledge to the side of the tub. Noticing the skin on her fingertips wrinkling as a consequence of the time she'd spent in the water, she rose and dried herself on a towel which had been warmed on a radiator.

*God, this is Heaven,* she thought as she pulled a towelling robe over her naked body, tied it at the waist and walked through to her bedroom where Connolly had earlier placed the various boxes and bags purchased for her by Weber. She sat on the edge of her bed and lifted the bag she had brought with her and shook her head as she opened it to reveal a long dress made for her by her mother, the hem hanging loose at the rear.

Lifting it clear she looked down on a clutter of white cotton undergarments, all aged.

*Well, at least they're clean,* she thought, turning her attention slowly to the boxes of expensive clothing that lay, tempting her touch only an arm's length away. Softly she stroked the top of the nearest box as if afraid of opening a Pandora's Box of trouble. She turned the box to read the label affixed to the top of the cardboard container.

"Axford Edwardian vintage silk corset with four strap suspenders," she mumbled to herself. "Ideal for evening wear...dear God in Heaven," she breathed.

She set it aside and pulled another box towards her and read the box without opening it. *Axford silk lingerie waist reducing cincher. An under-bust corset designed to offer an hour-glass figure. Fluted panels emphasise the feminine shape...*

"Jesus and Mary," she mumbled.

Her eye caught a large bag she hadn't seen while in the car. She leaned over and lifted the bag towards her. Opening it she removed a light blue, fine satin dress. Pulling it upwards, she found the label and read it to herself. *Fully lined Duchess satin. This fishtail evening dress is modern yet regal...Holy Mother of God...what on earth have I got myself into?*

More exploration uncovered silk and lace lingerie, stockings, scents and cosmetics. Finally she opened a small box which had no markings to hint at its contents. Inside was a necklace which sparkled as she moved it into the light.

Slowly she examined the necklace before placing it back in the box. She closed it and rose from the bed, walking over to a large wall mirror. She untied her robe and let it fall. *Only one man has seen me like this,* she mused. Lifting her chin she regarded her body with new eyes...loose-limbed, not an ounce of fat, toned arms, full, taut breasts. She opened a small bottle which contained a rich, velvety cream she'd tried earlier on the back of her hands. She nosed its subtle scent and began to massage it on her shoulders, moving down, melting it on her chest. She closed her eyes as she thumbed the ointment into the swell of her breasts, remembering the night she'd spent in Hermann's arms. She finishing by fingering some on her face where she smoothed it until the cream had dissolved, leaving her skin glowing. She leaned forward, her hands balancing her on a dressing table and met her own gaze.

*Oh, Mammy. What's become of me? Only a few short weeks ago I was happy to journey this land with a Webley revolver in my waistband, shooting men if ordered. Now I'm no longer the virgin you wanted me to be at marriage, I've a doctor who seems smitten by me and who's the nicest man in the world and a powerful man of war who wants me to dress like a harlot...or a princess. I can't make my mind up which.*

"Harlot bad...princess good," she intoned.

She looked again at her naked body. *Mind you, I do look passable with the light behind me.* She smiled. *D'y know, I'm not exactly an ugly old hag. Some might think I was a catch...*

She picked up a hairbrush and began the task of taming her dark curls. After a few strokes, she looked past her image in the mirror to the reflection of the collection of garments on her bed and then at the bag containing her torn dress and clean white underwear.

*Well, what clothes better befit a murdering, blaspheming, cursing farm girl?...Am I a princess or a harlot?...The Queen of Sheba or the Whore of Babylon? Which one is the real me?*

Timpson swilled the brandy round in his glass, anticipating his first sip whilst at the same time checking that his bar order had been completed and that each of his men had a drink in front of them.

"We don't have much time before the Germans start arriving, gentlemen. So sup up and George, Stan and Bill, your job is to secrete yourself in the woodlands on the approach to the front of the hotel and try and photograph those who arrive, even the car they're driving might be of assistance. No flash bulbs. The gate post is well illuminated, four floodlights...but most should arrive during daylight. Locate yourselves at three different angles. Tom, I need you inside the grounds, same objective but be careful as they may well have people patrolling within the perimeter. Someone's out there murdering their fellow-Nazis. They'll be on their toes. Now, each of you is armed but if anyone has to pull a trigger just make terribly sure that you're nowhere to be found within seconds of the shot being heard. I want no diplomatic incidents thank you very much but if *Obergruppenführer* Kurt Weber shows his face anywhere outside, I want to be informed immediately."

"What would you have *me* do?" asked Carter-Hogg.

"Right now, you stay and ply me with drink at field headquarters which is right here in the Leinster Arms. When field headquarters closes at drinking-up time, we'll be in the car parked at the edge of the town at the precise point where the main Dublin road meets the Rathbrennan road."

"Don't you want someone inside the hotel itself," asked his junior officer.

"I have already taken care of that. We have a man already in place. My main concern is to protect him. That's why we've identified the meeting point I've agreed earlier with our man on the inside. Just in case we need to leave in a hurry. We protect him at all costs."

Carter-Hogg looked round at the group of men who sat listening to their senior officer. Despite his well known dependency on alcohol, Timpson still carried a substantial measure of respect and affection from those who worked with him.

"Is this man known to us?" asked Stan.

"He is *not*."

"Might we know something of him. If there's gun-play you'll want to ensure that he isn't accidentally shot."

"There will be no gun-play. But if someone jumps over their wall and tries to get into our car, it's a safe bet he's on our side."

He lifted his glass of brandy and held it as if in a toast.

"To a successful venture. Now drink up and be off."

The strains of *Beethoven's Clair de Lune; Moonlight Sonata* played using shellac records on a 78 rpm gramophone provided ambience in the Hotel bar. Weber stood alone in the room, leaning on the bar watching the bow-tied, white-shirted barman polish glasses. Awaiting the arrival of Sinéad, he turned and rested his back on the bar, scanning the saloon, acknowledging the high quality workmanship that Connolly and his men had deployed in creating a quite excellent facility. He looked at his watch and noticed with only the slightest irritation that it showed five minutes after the appointed hour. Punctuality was important to Weber but tonight of all nights he couldn't find fault with the woman he hoped to persuade should commit her life to his. He would just have to be patient.

The barman removed the Beethoven recording and began to play the most recently issued recording of 'Sentimental Journey' by Les Brown & His Orchestra which had been purchased at some cost only days earlier from a ship docking at Dublin Harbour.

As the opening bars of a sumptuous brass introduction filled the room, Weber caught sight of movement on the sweeping staircase. Gradually, the form of Sinéad descended, one hand on the banister, the other holding a small purse. She was wearing the blue satin dress and stepping on each tread very carefully in order not to turn her ankle on the high-heeled shoes Weber had purchased.

Slowly she made her way to the bottom of the stairs and pausing to ensure she had retrieved her poise, walked unsteadily towards Weber, biting her lower lip in unsure awkwardness.

Weber was motionless, his mouth agape.

"Well, whatyathink, big boy?" She curtseyed theatrically, putting on an American accent.

Weber took a moment to form his words.

"Sinéad, you are the most beautiful woman in the world."

"Well, maybe in the bar tonight," she responded. "I don't know about these heels. They should give out prizes just for bein' able to walk downstairs with these beggars on."

Weber stooped and kissed her on the cheek.

"I am so glad you decided to wear these garments, Sinéad. You look every bit as enchanting as I'd hoped. I repeat, you're the most beautiful woman in the world... at least in my eyes."

"Well, your eyes must have been affected by that Champagne you were on about. Now am I goin' to get some of this stuff or do I just have to perch all night long on these stilts?"

Weber smiled broadly and bowed formally at her request.

"Of course."

He directed his attention to the barman who was attempting but failing not to pay too much interest in the beauty of a young woman the like of whose style and grace did not normally prop up his bar.

"Henry, might you open the Champagne now?"

Hasofer sped towards Portloise. From his pocket he pulled a time piece and stopped the car underneath a streetlight, consulting it. Eight-thirty. He still had some distance to go but was anxious to arrive at the hotel at a time when Weber might still be about and before too many of the Germans arrived. Still possible, he thought. If I can take care of business tonight and make my escape, I could make Belfast by morning and be on the British mainland by lunchtime, away from the horrors of all this killing.

He steered the wheel towards the road and accelerated towards his destination.

Frank Connolly's brother Thomas managed to have his call to St. Kevin's Hospital answered. It was eight-thirty and he wanted to speak to Doctor Henning about arrangements to collect him early in the morning as ordered.

"Doctor Henning here."

"Aye, hello, doctor. My name's Thomas Connolly. I've to collect you and take you to Portloise early tomorrow morning and I just wanted..."

"Can we change this..Mr, eh, Mr. Connolly. I really have to get there by tonight. Is there any way you could help me out? It's important!"

"Well, sir. I'm already in Dublin. I was intending staying over at a sisters' but you wouldn't be puttin' me out at all if you were to go down tonight. That way, I'd be sleepin' in my own bed alright."

"That would be simply wonderful, Mr. Connolly. I'll be finished here at the hospital by just after nine o'clock. If you were able to collect me we could make Portlaoise by..."

"Certainly by eleven, sir. That would be my guess."

"Excellent. I'll see you at the front. I'm wearing a dark suit, red tie and carrying a brown leather briefcase."

"Then I'll make sure and keep an eye out for you, Doctor Henning."

Henning placed the telephone on the cradle and grinned widely. *I'll be able to surprise Sinéad a day early,* he reasoned. *And rather than stay later here to complete these*...he grunted as he placed a number of thick files into his briefcase...*I'll just work on them while Sinéad's dealing with my other German compatriots over the weekend.*

*This might be quite fun,* he thought as he stepped out of the office to complete his ward rounds. *Quite fun! But,* he remonstrated with himself...*it's also serious business. Enough is enough. This is the weekend I ask her for her hand in marriage.*

## Chapter Forty-seven

The barman's collection of music enraptured both Sinéad and Weber. Such was Weber's attention to detail, the barman had not only been given a range of songs to play on his gramophone but also the order in which they should be played. And so it was arranged that at the elegant commencement of the evening the meal was to be accompanied by songs such as the liquid and sanguine '*A String of Pearls*' by Glenn Miller and Anne Shelton's rendition of, '*I'm Stepping Out With A Memory Tonight*', metamorphosing into higher tempo, more optimistic music such as Tommy Dorsey and his Orchestra's playing of, '*On The Sunny Side Of The Street*'. At a signal to be communicated by Weber, the barman was to play a selection of songs as dinner ended finishing with, '*It's A Lovely Day Tomorrow*' by the popular songstress, Vera Lynn.

"Jesus, Kurt. I've never even *heard* of some of these dishes. *Pâté de foie gras*, now what was that exactly?"

"It's perhaps one of the most exquisite foods in the world. *Foie gras* is synonymous with great taste and unabashed elegance but in essence, it's just fattened goose or duck liver."

He reached over and collected Sinéad's hand in his.

"Did you enjoy it?"

"I did that, Kurt...but then I've always enjoyed simple cabbage and bacon as well. Food's just for the eatin' as far as I'm concerned but..." she held up her empty glass, "I'm fair taken with this stuff...You could well lead a girl astray with this stuff; your Champagne!"

If Sinéad suspected that Weber's motives were exactly as she'd articulated, she gave no hint. He poured her a fifth glass.

"This stuff is so easy to drink, Kurt. It makes me feel like I've no worries. I love Champagne. The bubbles tickle my nose."

"Well, we have enough here to keep us going so you enjoy it as much as you wish."

"I'm dizzy with enjoyment, Kurt. You've been such an angel tonight. The music, the food and drink, your company. You are a very charming man and I've had a simply wonderful evening."

"Well, you make an enchanting dinner companion, Sinéad. These clothes merely act as the picture frame does the Mona Lisa. The real beauty lies within."

"You certainly have the gift of the gab, Professor Weber," smiled Sinéad. "And although I hate to admit it, I absolutely love the clothes you bought for me. They transport me and make me feel like a film star."

"So everything fits?"

Sinéad nodded and the couple continued their discourse, Weber sharing his experiences as a young man in Germany and his academic ambitions before the war started, Sinéad listening intently as she sipped at her Champagne. Gradually, a wave of light-headedness passed over her. Her forehead felt hot and her tongue found certain words difficult to pronounce as she'd wish. She fanned her face with her hand.

"Sorry, Kurt...feelin' a bit woozy here. This Champagne's gettin' the better of me."

She strove to continue. "You mus' thank Miss Kerrigan. One of them corsets had whale bones that hurt my sore ribs but eve'ything else fits pe'fec'ly. And she was right about the unmentionables too." She giggled. "I'd have felt silly wearing a beautiful gown but with rags underneath."

Sinéad's description of her netherwear had Weber raise his eyebrows.

"Oh, Kurt, I'm sorry. Am I 'barrassing you? These bubbles are making me talk like a hussy."

She sat back in her chair, somehow deflated and folded her arms crossly, like a small child.

"I'm talking like a hussy 'cause I *am* a hussy!"

Shaking her head to clear her mind, she leaned forward with her elbows on the table and her head in her hands.

"God Almighty. What am I like?"

"Sinéad, would you prefer a glass of water or perhaps some coffee? We've managed to get some..."

"Princesses drink *Champagne*...isn' tha' wha' you said earlier?"

She fell silent for a moment as she stared at the bubbles in the glass. Quietly she began to breathe along tunelessly to the song being played by the barman on the gramophone.

"*You made me love you... didn' want to do it...didn' want to...*"

Slowly she cast her eyes upwards to meet Weber's steely gaze and rejoined the melody a couple of bars later.

"*...all the time you knew it...guess you always knew it.*"

Her eyes fell again and she lost herself in the glass as Judy Garland continued singing.

*'You made me hap.. sometimes, you made me glad*
*But there were times......made...feel so bad'*

Sinéad shook her head and let her thoughts trail away as Weber reached over and touched her hand again.

*"Jeder hört die musik anders, aber der gemeinsame tanz ist wunderbar."*

"Y' know I don' speak Ge'man, Kurt," muttered Sinéad drunkenly.

"It means, 'everyone hears the music differently, but the dance together is wonderful'."

"Well, I'm in no condition to dance, thank you ver' much. An' I only know our Irish dancin'. None of that modern dancin', thank you ver' much again," she slurred.

Weber realised that the conversation he'd intended having that evening with the woman he loved was slowly slipping from his grasp with every sip of Champagne taken by Sinéad.

"Dearest Sinéad," he smiled despite himself, "Somehow I think the Champagne was a mistake."

"Champagne was the ver' bess part of the night..."

Resignedly, Weber decided that the evening had reached its conclusion.

"I think it would be best if you retired, don't you?"

Skittishly, Sinéad grasped the half empty bottle of Champagne.

"I wanna take my friend here with me." She hiccoughed.

"By all means..."

Gently, Weber took her arm and escorted her to the bottom of the stairs. Sinéad held on to the banister and gestured to Weber to stop. Theatrically, she handed him the bottle conveying to him in gesture that he was to take great care of it. Unsteadily she stooped and removed her shoes, tucking them under her arm before asking wordlessly for the return of her bottle by wiggling her fingers, giggling.

"I'll carry that, Sinéad...just in case you drop it," he explained quickly as her features took on a combative look.

It took a minute but they arrived at the door to Sinéad's suite. Very deliberately, she slowly opened her purse and removed the key to her room.

"Foun' it..."

Her eyelids drooping, she turned to face her host.

"Kurt...you have b'n a perfec' gen'leman. You are very gallan...gallant. But I think I should just go t' my bed now."

She stood on tiptoe and made to kiss Weber on the cheek just as he turned his head and held her in his grasp, kissing her full on the lips. Initially Sinéad struggled to withdraw from his embrace but lingered momentarily... then gave herself to the caress. After a moment, they each pulled back and observed the other .

"I want so much to possess you, Sinéad. I have done almost since we met."

Weber pulled her roughly towards him and kissed her again. This time, Sinéad resisted.

"Mr. Weber...you fo'get yourself, sir," she said, grandly. "Now, if you please?"

She held out her free hand and invited the return of her Champagne.

Grimacing, Weber took the key from her hand and opened the door, handing her the bottle as she stepped into her room.

Steadying herself by holding onto the door handle, she bowed slightly, wishing him goodnight and teetered rather before closing the door on a frustrated and disappointed Weber.

Connolly was closing on Portlaoise. The Legation's spacious saloon carried Henning in some comfort, his thick briefcase lying on the back seat awaiting attention having been thrown there after Henning realised that he could neither see any details using the interior car light or write anything given the car's erratic rolling and surging as Connolly sought to avoid pot-holes.

The field headquarters had transferred to Timpson's car following the closure of the bar at the Leinster Arms.

Carter-Hogg returned to find Timpson leaning on the bonnet of the car smoking a cigarette.

"Unwise, Sir. I'm sure there's a fuel leak in this car. We don't want to advertise our presence by exploding the thing and alerting everyone."

"Young man, I know enough about explosions to know that me sitting out here in the open air having a quiet cigarette presents no prospect of detonation. Otherwise, garage mechanics the length and breadth of Ireland would be exploding themselves every time they filled a gentleman's car with a Player's Navy Cut between their fingers."

"Very well, Sir. Everyone's in position."

"Well, we'll be here for a while. This is a weekend-long event and nothing's surer than it'll be as boring as hell." He looked at his watch. "It's just gone eleven o'clock. We'll give it to around midnight and leave these chaps until morning. We'll come back then and bring a new shift to relieve them."

"And until then?"

"We wait, dear boy. It's a lovely night. Unfortunately, life in His Majesty's Intelligence Services can, on many occasions, be as boring as hell. Tonight promises to be just that. You can check things one more time in an hour, then we'll head back to Dublin. Can't see anything happening when everyone's abed."

In a forested area across the road and slightly forward of the vehicle, Joe Kelly made his way gingerly beneath the branches of a small elm tree and placed his hand silently on the shoulder of Martin McCann who was kneeling beside its trunk.

McCann made no movement of surprise, expecting the arrival of his boss. Kelly stooped beside him, labouring slightly as he lowered himself on one knee.

He whispered. "Are we sure that's him?"

"He's the one sittin' on the front of the car smokin'."

"And we're sure?"

"I've been followin' him since you told me and that's him puffin' away there alright."

"How many strong are they?"

"There's the boss in the car, least I'm assumin' he's the boss. There's that Captain on the bonnet of the car and they've another four men. They all came out of the pub in the village. Three are in the woods in front of us and one's gone over the wall into the grounds of the hotel."

"Armed?"

"The ones in the woods are. I'm assumin' that the two at the car are too."

Kelly ran his hand thoughtfully over his mouth as he pondered his move.

"So if we shoot just now, we have potentially six guns ready to respond."

"Yeah, but it's a black night. There'll be some confusion and we've a car with a lunatic driver on the path not twenty paces behind us."

Kelly held his counsel before instructing McCann. Some moments passed.

"Don't like the odds," he whispered. "They see the gun flash...the car fails to start...you miss...anything could happen..."

McCann patted the butt of his heavy Lee-Enfield Mark V rifle.

"Anythin' bar me missin'," exclaimed McCann in a small voice. "He won't know what hit'm."

"Maybe so...but somethin's up. We have the cream of British Intelligence before us, six of them...armed and ready outside a hotel full of Germans with my young niece, Sinéad, a Volunteer same as you and me inside..."

After further thought he decided.

"Martin, my boy. There's something afoot here tonight. It's becoming more important we wait and find out what's goin' on. If we get a free shot at your Captain later in the night, so be it. There'll be other opportunities if not. But for now, we wait and see why them bastards are so interested in this little German get-together."

◆ ◆ ◆

Hasofer had made his plans.

Back in Dublin, he and Weber, discussing the security of the event, had consulted both a map of the grounds and a plan of the hotel many times. In addition, he knew Weber's suite location and that of his own, lesser accommodation. Indeed, he'd allocated it to himself when placing guests in their rooms. The hotel had been constructed in a square with a large atrium in the middle. He'd chosen a room across from Weber's and one floor up from his. From the plan, it appeared that he'd have a clear shot across the square to his room. What his plan didn't permit, he reminded himself, was any obstruction, finding that the windows of his room didn't open, bad weather or Weber merely closing his curtains.

The car pulled up under the spreading branches of a large oak tree on the road at the rear of the hotel. Hasofer took stock. *Weather's fine,* he reassured himself. If he was to make a clean getaway, he calculated he'd clear the grounds of the hotel more easily if he made his way on foot through the shrubbery and wooded surroundings. If the alarm went up, the security people or the *Gardai* need only close the exit and his car would be rendered useless. This way, he calculated he need only make his way in the darkness to the rear wall, climb it and make off in his car to Belfast.

He checked the fuel gauge before turning the motor off. It was half full. Enough to carry him some considerable distance and Weber had been generous enough to provide him with enough cash to bribe even the most upright and principled garage-hand. He'd make Belfast easily, even if he had to take a most circuitous route if a border-crossing became problematic.

He sat back in his seat and contemplated the concern that had troubled him ever since he'd received the cyphered telegram from *Haganah*...did he have what it takes to shoot a man he liked and respected?

## CHAPTER FORTY-EIGHT

Sinéad sat on the edge of her bed and giggled. *Look at the feckin' state of me,* she chuckled. *I'm dressed to kill, drunk as a lord, bin kissed by one man but smitten by another...*She massaged her neck muscles. *Holy Mary, Mother of God.*

She stood and moved unsteadily towards the wall mirror and contemplated her image.

"Still passable," she decided as she pushed back some untidy strands of hair.

She took a deep breath. *I just know I'll suffer in the morning and I'll give myself what for for kissing Kurt only feckin' days after sleeping with Hermann. Well feck it! That's for tomorrow. I've never known a man proper and now I've two of 'em at my feckin' feet.* She shook her head reproachfully. *One more little taste of this gorgeous Champagne and I'm off to the land of nod.*

She poured a half glass and sipped it. *Some fresh air; that would be the thing.* A few steps took her to the window where she opened it a few inches and breathed in the cool air.

Returning to the mirror, she placed her glass on the dresser and pulled at the buttons on the side of her dress, letting it fall to the floor. Stepping out of it she took time to examine her appearance as she stood wearing her silk corset, suspenders and seamed stockings. *Hmmm, quite revealing,* she thought, smiling, returning to the question she'd posed herself that afternoon. *Princess or harlot?... Queen of Sheba or the Whore of Babylon?* Her giggle returned. *Maybe I'm the Queen Whore of Babylon.* She stood tall in front of the mirror, looking at how her new lingerie fashioned itself around her body like a sheath. "Creates a shapely, hour-glass figure" she repeated, recollecting the words on the box. *I like this look.* She took another sip of her Champagne and began to hum the song she'd been singing at dinner with Weber.

"You made me love you...I didnnn wanna do it..."

Next door, Weber had stripped ready for sleep but sat naked, fretting on the edge of his bed.

*That woman! One minute she's a tough Irish soldier, then she's compassionate, then a wonderful dinner companion, then a tom-boy then the most beautiful woman I've ever seen. Now she's a drunk!* He rose from his bed and stared at the locked door that separated him from the woman he'd just informed he'd wanted to possess. Ambivalent now, he walked over to a table where he lifted a copy key that would open the door and gain him access to his beloved's bedroom. Careful planning had gone into its possession but how could he use it now? She wasn't in a fit state to entertain him. This wasn't how he'd envisaged the evening. Moments passed before he threw the key onto his bed. *What am I, an animal? How could I intrude on her boudoir?*

He walked to the sink next to his bath and waited until the water ran cold before splashing some on his face. He wiped it dry and threw the towel round his shoulders. But what if she'd passed out and was lying ill on the floor of her bedroom? *She isn't used to Champagne,* he reminded himself.

Still in two minds, he walked to a wardrobe and pulled a towelling dressing gown from the rack, covering his nakedness. He looked at himself in the wall mirror completely unaware that on the other side of the wall, Sinéad was engaged in exactly the same activity.

Hasofer presented himself on foot at the entrance to the hotel and was cleared by the *Gardai* and security without much query by presenting his false passport in the name of Dietrich Naumann and having explained that his car had run out of petrol a mile from his destination. Equally, his hotel registration was completed efficiently and he allowed himself to be escorted to his room despite having had the ability to find it blindfold.

"There's three of your companions already here, sir. They're in the bar."

Thanking him, Hasofer entered his room and threw his bag on the bed. He returned to the door and listened to the departing footsteps of the valet before turning his light out again and proceeding to the window.

"*Arschwarze!*" he cursed. A mature fir tree located centrally in the atrium partially obscured the view he had of what he calculated would be Weber's rooms. Two windows were observable without impediment. All were illuminated. He stepped to the side of his window to gain a better view of those he could see.

What he saw shocked him. In the room abutting Weber's, a beautiful young woman dressed only in exotic underwear was sipping from a Champagne flute while standing in front of her window, closing it. Apparently unabashed, she placed her glass on the window sill so as to free both of her hands to lock the window catch.

*"Erst mach' dein' sach dann trink' und lach!"* he murmured to himself as he tried to tear his eyes from the image of the semi-naked beauty. *First take care of business.*

Weber had decided. This wouldn't be an attempt to seduce a lovely young woman, he told himself but a caring visit to ensure that she was not suffering any ill effects from her over-indulgence in alcohol. Persuaded that his motives were pure, he stooped and looked through the keyhole into Sinéad's room. All he could observe was that the room light was still on. Quietly, he placed the key in the lock of the door and turned it. He opened it slowly and peered round. The room was empty. A half open door led into her sleeping quarters. Softly, he left his door ajar behind him and padded across the carpeted room to the bedroom.

Sinéad had squeezed her feet back into her high-heeled shoes and was admiring the full effect of her expensive lingerie in a bedroom mirror whilst her legs, already quite long and slender, were enhanced by the three extra inches of height.

She squealed rather than screamed in surprise when Weber stepped from behind the door. Her hands raced to cover her chest and she staggered backwards against the bed.

Weber was first to speak, anxious to import the altruistic and compassionate nature of his visit. He held his hands out in front of him, fingers spread as if pushing an invisible object, trying to convey that she shouldn't panic at his unexpected arrival in her bedroom.

"Sinéad…please let me explain…"

"Kurt, in the name of all that's holy…what the feck are you doing?"

Weber surrendered all pretence at his rationalised reasoning.

"Sinéad, I'm in love with you. You are a beautiful creature…"

His voice took on a new edge. "And when I kissed you earlier, you kissed me right back."

He strode forward and took her in his strong arms. He kissed her again, roughly this time. As earlier, Sinéad resisted but succumbed for some moments before pressing her hands against his chest.

"Kurt, stop! I'm confused. You don't understand…"

"Dearest Sinéad…I want you so badly. You can't understand how difficult it is for me to see you like this…a Goddess…"

Holding her tightly in one arm, Weber pulled at the tie on his robe and shrugged it off, letting it fall to the ground.

"Jesus, Kurt, what are you doin'?"

"Something I should have had the courage to do some time ago when we were together all those nights in hotels all across Ireland."

Briefly, Sinéad wrestled to no avail as Weber held her hair tightly, pulling her head back to meet his descending kiss.

The lock on Weber's door gave way to a half-diamond pick and a pistol entered the room followed by its owner. Dropping into a stoop, he moved to the centre of the room, all of his senses alive as he sought to detect the presence of Weber, a man known as a fearsome warrior. No chances could be taken. The room was empty and no sound came from the bedroom but noises were discernible through the open door leading to the suite next door.

Taking a deep breath and summoning every ounce of determination in his being. the gunman stepped through the door, holding the pistol in both hands at shoulder level in front of him.

Anticipating pulling the trigger immediately upon entering the room, he was faced by the naked rear of a tall man obviously in a clinch with a semi-naked woman. Instead of shooting, he stepped back towards the window to take stock, keeping his pistol pointed at the couple.

"What the fuck is this?"

Sinéad struggled free from Weber's grasp and tried to focus upon the intruder. Gradually there was mutual recognition.

"Danny?"

"Well if it isn't feckin Sinéad O'feckin' Grady."

Danny Lafferty laughed, despite his intense level of anxiety.

"So what do we have here? My sainted leader. A dedicated Irish Republican maiden shaggin' a German General!"

He gestured with the gun, inviting Weber to step aside from Sinead.

"Look at the pair of you. You, bollocks naked...You, dressed like a prossie. Oh, this is good!"

Sinéad forgot her state of *deshabille* and confronted Danny, hands on hips.

"Danny, what the bloody hell are you doin' here?"

"I'm more interested in *your* explanation right now, Sinéad. I had two things to do tonight, enjoy a cool Guinness and shoot Weber...and I've supped my Guinness not half an hour ago. Now I have to kill you both."

"Danny, have you lost your mind?"

Sinéad froze as a fresh realisation dawned on her.

"Are you the one who's bein' goin' around killin' the Germans?"

"No, Sinéad. I'm only after Weber here. But I *can* tell you now that it was me that set up the tap that had Charlie Kerins captured by the *Gardai* and fixed it so poor Seamus O'Leary was accused of betrayin' the movement and stood and watched as you shot your dear friend in your own cottage...an innocent man. Pleased at yourself, are you?"

Sinéad's hand shot to her mouth in horror at this revelation.

"Yeah, I watched you shoot an innocent man when the bullet should have been meant for me. And the air drop? Bet you wondered how that leaked. Why d'you think I was the only one to escape while your pal Dub got shot at the airdrop? Because I'm the only one who's workin' for British Intelligence. That's why! Workin' to deal with murderin' Nazis like Weber here who thinks he can buy his way into the hearts of the Irish. I thought I'd got him in Drogheda but missed and shot Declan Dennehy by mistake. And then watched Joseph Kelly have Niall Kennedy beaten to a pulp! If it wasn't so serious it'd be hilarious! Bunch of feckin' amateurs!"

Across the quadrangle, Hasofer had screwed the silencer on to his Lugar and had opened the window, looking for an opportunity to find Weber in his sights. The appearance of Lafferty had confused and stalled any action he intended taking until he understood the significance of his appearance.

Sinead sat weeping on her bed as Weber stood naked, every sinew preparing for any chance of overpowering the gunman.

Lafferty laughed again at the scene before him. It was the nano-second in time that Weber needed to disarm his assailant. In an instant, his legs, arms and back muscles shortened in length, developing the powerful tension in his quadriceps he needed to launch himself at Lafferty. A countermovement backward swing of his arms converted the squatting thrust of his legs into a powerful forward motion generated through his core and he sprang forward.

Lafferty merely inclined his pistol downwards slightly at Weber's crouch and pulled the trigger sending a 4.55 calibre bullet in a downwards trajectory through the centre of Weber's chest, tearing at his aorta and lacerating his *vena cava*, propelling him backwards onto the bed next to Sinéad and killing him instantly. Blood splattered on her face and bodice and she screamed, throwing her body over Weber's; comforting a corpse.

In the hallway outside Sinéad's door, Henning was about to tap timidly, anxious lest the woman he loved were to be asleep when he heard the crash of the pistol shot. Alarmed he rattled the door handle and shouldered the door when it proved obstinate to his intentions. He rushed into her public room and seeing nothing made his way to her bedroom where Lafferty still stood, now preparing to shoot Sinéad.

In an instant realisation of the danger in which his lover found herself, he lunged at Lafferty who shot a second time, on this occasion at Henning. The leather briefcase stuffed with the medical files he'd anticipated working on over the weekend saved him as the bullet lodged in the pages within permitting him the trice he needed to make contact with the midriff of the gunman, knocking him over. Lafferty made to manoeuvre his gun while Henning, never before having found himself in a fist-fight, acted instinctively and grasped his assailant's gun-wrist, holding on to it despite the writhings of his adversary. A blow landing on the side of Henning's head dazed him and he retaliated by elbowing Lafferty on the underside of his jaw causing a painful wound to his mouth. Despite his injury, Lafferty grasped Henning's throat with his free hand and squeezed, diverting the German's attention instantly from all other concerns other than maintaining his grip on the gun. Twisting, he screwed his body round and found himself now side by side with Lafferty on the floor. A clumsy punch to the bridge of Lafferty's nose was all it took to stun him and provide Henning with an opportunity to use both hands to prise the gun from his fingers. Kneeling, he quickly rose to his feet followed by a recovering Lafferty. Holding the gun in both hands, Henning pulled the trigger and sent the bullet meant for himself into the top of Lafferty's head as he made for him causing a crimson eruption. Immediately, the Irish agent of British Intelligence fell to the floor, mortally wounded.

Shaken, Henning stared at the gun in his hands scarcely able to believe that he'd taken the life of another human being. In the ensuing stillness as the smoke cleared he turned his attention to the bed whereon Sinéad still lay, now silenced by the horror that had unfolded, her arms still around the naked corpse of Weber. Henning stood immobilised at the scene before him, trying to make sense of it while coming to terms with the near-death struggle he'd just had.

Moments passed before he found words. He spoke slowly.

"You're with Kurt...with Kurt."

Sinéad nodded tearfully.

"And you're in a state of undress..."

Sinead could only nod tearfully as she gazed upon the strangely peaceful countenance of Kurt Weber who lay in her arms.

"I have to ask this, Sinead...I thought...I was going to..." He gathered himself. "Have you been intimate with Herr Weber? Have you kissed him?"

Sinead's face crumpled as tears flowed freely down her cheeks. Slowly, she nodded once.

Henning dropped the gun on the floor and stood immobilised, his face a mask.

Outside, the *Gardai*, having been alerted by the hotel staff, had hurried up the driveway and were now making their clamorous way up the stairs towards the suite.

The noise brought Henning to his senses. He stepped back and looked out of the window searching for a means of escape. Seeing a cast-iron drainpipe leading to the ground only one floor below, he opened the window to its fullest extent. He turned towards Sinead. Tears welling in his eyes, he uttered only one word as he stepped onto the window frame in readiness for his absconsion.

"*Schlampe!*"

In the hotel wing across the atrium, Hasofer watched intently the series of events that had unfolded before his disbelieving eyes. He watched Henning making his way down the drainpipe to the atrium garden as police entered the suite above him. He unscrewed his silencer and placed it along with his Lugar in his bag before turning on his heel, leaving his room and making his way to the door he knew to be at the bottom of the rear stair-well. It would lead him to the wooded area beyond, to his car, onwards to the docks at Belfast and to his beloved Rachael.

As Hasofer and Henning both separately made their way hurriedly through the foliage in the expansive gardens of the hotel to escape those who would apprehend them, a hurried knocking on the window of Joseph Kelly's car window woke him from a light slumber.

"Boss, come quick. The feckin' *Gardai* have all ran towards the hotel and the Brits are jumpin' over the wall to make a getaway by the looks of things."

Kelly and McCann together made their way the short distance back to their vantage point and saw the last of the British officers, pistol in hand, leap the low wall and walk hurriedly towards the car. Timpson sat in the passenger's seat, talking animatedly. Outside, crouched beside the bonnet of the car, Captain Carter-Hogg made ready to drive the vehicle once his last man arrived.

Observing the scene, Kelly was decisive. He stooped as did McCann, the better to steady his aim.

"Somethin's spooked them. They're all over the place. Once that last man gets in the car, shoot that fecker who beat on my poor niece. Him that's crouched beside the engine. Shoot him dead!"

Carefully in the black of the forest, McCann lifted his powerful Lee-Enfield rifle and set his sights on Carter-Hogg who, still on one knee, was busily gesturing his colleague to hurry towards the safety of the car.

It took a few seconds for the round fired by McCann to ignite the fine spray of petroleum which hissed under pressure from the metal container beneath the car. An inch to the right and the bullet would have struck Carter-Hogg, albeit in the buttock region. An inch higher and it would have buried itself harmlessly in the sill of the car. As it was, the bullet missed both and ricocheted from the road surface beneath the car causing a flashing cluster of sparks which began to ignite some heavy oil deposits underneath the chassis of the poorly maintained vehicle. As the occupants of the car turned momentarily towards the direction of the flash and noise emanating from the woods slightly to the side of them, the nascent flame beneath them reached the spray which fizzled from the tank and ruptured it, causing a rapid increase in volume as its contents evaporated uncontrollably. The instantaneous effect of the rapid and violent gaseous explosion sent thermally expanded, super-heated gases perpendicular to the surface of the roadway, fragmenting the various metal constructions supporting the shell of the car, blowing it to smithereens in a blinding orange ball of fire, shredding its occupants and sending them in portions and slivers to meet their maker.

Joseph Kelly looked on at the carnage caused by McCann's shot.

"Holy Mother of God...that was one hellofa shot, Martin."

McCann remained on one knee, still cradling his rifle, open-mouthed at the consequences of the discharge of his single bullet.

"I'd say that was quite a night's work, son. Most of our people are in internment. We've only a couple of hundred Volunteers fightin' the good fight. You're now my number one marksman."

He placed his hand on the tree trunk in readiness to lever himself from his stoop.

"If I let you loose on the Brits," he grunted as he rose, "this struggle'll be over in a couple of weeks."

Still McCann looked uncomprehendingly at his Lee-Enfield rifle.

Kelly struggled to his feet.

"Now let's go home."

## CHAPTER FORTY-NINE

Éamon de Valera stood beside Eduard Hempel at the graveside and awaited the concluding words of the priest as the coffin of Kurt Weber was lowered slowly into a grave at Glasnevin Cemetery by four Germans who had benefited from his investment in their Irish futures. Head lowered reverently, hat in hand, he cut an altogether different figure from the now retired German Envoy Extraordinary and Minister Plenipotentiary, Eduard Hempel who stood rigidly to attention. Gradually, the words of Gather McGrory prevailed over his thoughts.

"...I am the resurrection and the life. Those who believe in me, even though they die, will live and everyone who lives and believes in me will never die."

The priest said a silent prayer and paused before adding, "Thanks to the generosity of Doctor Hempel, tea and stronger refreshments have been made available in the rooms of the Church of the Resurrection just across the Finglas Road for those not familiar with the local geography. All are welcome."

Mourners began turning slowly towards the church and de Valera fell in with Hempel. They shook hands and walked together towards the gate, de Valera's officials keeping a discrete distance.

"Well, Eduard, I'll not manage the church as I've another burial this afternoon. One of the British Officers killed in the car explosion had Irish antecedents. A Mullingar man; Edward Timpson."

Hempel nodded his acceptance and replied.

"I've two funerals over the next few days myself... those killed by whoever was murdering our German immigrants. One yesterday, Geert Hirsch. Suicide they say. But somehow he had the same yellow Star of David placed on his chest as had the other two who were also victims."

"Most disconcerting, Eduard. Upsetting. My police officers are investigating as you know. Early days."

Stopping, he took Hempel's arm and gestured to a bench that was situated at the side of the path.

"Let's sit a moment."

The two men sat and de Valera removed his hat, lifting his face to the weak sun.

"This is all madness, Eduard. All this killing and maiming. Our young men and woman, the future of our countries, of this planet of ours...perished like so much discarded fruit. I must admit there are times when I fear for my own sanity. Maybe it takes old age to understand the futility of it all, don't you think?"

Hempel pursed his lips in agreement and nodded towards the open grave they'd just left.

"We celebrate the warrior abilities of someone like Kurt Weber too easily, perhaps. He was such a gifted man...a professor of history. He could have been a wonderful diplomat or a brilliant academic but I fear that while he was here in Ireland, he pursued covertly those ends you've just decried."

"Well, I can tell you that my senior police officers kept a close eye on him. Obviously you know he was close to that young woman Sinéad O'Grady who was found holding him in her arms when the *Gardai* rushed the hotel last week. We've assumed a romance given that he was naked and she was almost so. She's a member of *Cumann na mBan,* the women's movement that supports the families of members of Óglaigh *na hÉireann*, the IRA, whom we've imprisoned or who have fallen on hard times. So it's possible to surmise that your *Herr* Weber was not himself unfamiliar with the movement."

He shrugged his shoulders and continued.

"That said, we have no proof whatsoever that he was involved in anything other than investing in Irish businesses just as he claimed he was doing. It makes sense that he'd use an Irish go-between in his transactions... just unusual that he'd select this particular young woman and not someone recommended him by your Legation."

"So she was a member of *Cumann na mBan but not the IRA?*"

"We don't believe so. When she was questioned, she answered our questions which is significant as we'd normally expect a Volunteer to remain silent. She alleged that one Daniel Lafferty was working for British Intelligence and this too is in accord with our own information. She informs us that it was Lafferty who shot Weber and that he was tackled by the young doctor, Hermann Henning after Lafferty had shot at him. We found a bullet from Lafferty's gun wedged in the pages of notes he carried in his briefcase which gives some credence to her assertions. Henning then shot Lafferty in a fight with his own gun after he announced that he intended shooting Miss O'Grady. She claims to know nothing of the killing of the British officers outside the hotel and I'm told her denials have the ring of truth about them although it certainly wasn't us and looks to all the world like an IRA attack."

"You have O'Grady and Henning in custody?"

"Miss O'Grady is being held but I'm told she'll shortly be released as she's committed no crime. Herr Henning has disappeared but there will be no charges filed against him when we catch him supposing he remains on the Irish mainland as it seems he was acting in self defence. But it would be good to put them both on the stand and allow the matter to be concluded formally."

"And what of your investigations into the three Germans who were murdered?"

"Well, *Herr* Hirsch might have committed suicide but given the two subsequent deaths we've now established were murders, it would appear that he was the first to be killed by someone who targeted Germans that had served at a senior level within the Waffen SS."

"Lafferty again?"

"We suspect so. British Intelligence has a long reach and our central policy of neutrality does not find favour with Mr. Churchill. So if you ask me do I believe that that old rogue was capable of sending someone to Ireland to achieve what was not going to be possible by the trials at Nuremberg? Then I have to confess it to be a consideration. However, we remain interested in a young man who served Professor Weber. Name of Dietrich Naumann. He hasn't been seen since a week now but the young Irish girl, Freya Kerrigan who served you so admirably in the Legation confirms that he had been in touch with all of the three German nationals just before each was killed. We remain open to the possibility that he was working for a foreign power, perhaps Palestine, perhaps America...who knows. But he's disappeared off the face of the earth so we're investigating whether he's a fourth victim of this bout of killing or possibly the perpetrator."

"Jewish or American. You say?"

"Perhaps...and in one way I hope so and that he's disappeared, bringing an end to this episode. If he's been killed himself, it may be that other Germans will yet follow in his wake. We'll find out soon enough."

He placed his hat on his head signifying an end to the conversation and pointed casually to the graveside as the two men rose.

"Your man there, Kurt Weber. He seemed a good man. The stories coming from Nuremberg are hard to hear but his war record, so far as I'm guided by my officers, seemed not only to be heroic but humane, if that's at all possible."

"He could have made a historical contribution to the *Reich* had he remained at the front. The youngest General in the German army."

"Maybe so, Eduard. But he did good over here...in Ireland. And the future of the world going forward will depend not just on the great historical acts...but on the myriad unhistorical contributions that are made every day by ordinary people whom you and I will never hear of...people who bring up their families despite their poverty or lack of education...doctors and nurses who will only be heroes to their patients...those who make a small act of kindness that perhaps turns a low-life into someone who changes others' lives for the better."

He stopped as they approached the entrance to the Cemetery and faced Hempel.

"Eduard, you and I have been privileged...or condemned more like...to play a pretty significant role on the world's stage. It can be wearisome I know, but you have fulfilled your duties in an exemplary manner. No one could have worked harder to help me maintain Ireland's neutrality and I thank you from the bottom of my heart."

He squeezed the elbow of the German statesman in friendly parting.

"Until this unpleasantness is resolved, I hope you don't mind but I've doubled the *Gardai* contingent looking after your home in Dún Laoghaire. I've asked that they're discrete."

He smiled at his friend.

"Mrs de Valera and I send our very best wishes to *Frau* Hempel."

## CHAPTER FIFTY

# Liverpool, England

## 1950
## Epilogue

Sinéad O'Grady pursed her lips and blew smoke in a long breath from her lips as she casually perused the stories in that morning's Liverpool Daily Post. Atop the usual collection of theft, assault and football related stories was a bold headline announcing no end in sight to the warm front that had settled over the British Isles these last ten weeks. Other than Scotland which had endured its usual rainy summer, England, Wales and Ireland; both North and South, had experienced hot, dry and sunny weather unprecedented in the previous three decades. A drought was announced in several counties in the South of England and in Ireland.

The staffroom on the second floor of Sefton Hospital in Liverpool was empty other than an auxiliary nurse who, like Sinéad was engrossed in the morning paper. As Sinéad's right hand idly began the process of exchanging her lit cigarette for her cup of tea, she first turned the page and let out an involuntary gasp which momentarily alarmed the auxiliary who returned to her own newspaper once reassured that it was only the import of a story being read by Sinéad that had caused her to start.

Sinéad slowly manoeuvred the newspaper at an angle to permit more light from the staffroom windows to fall on its columns as her eyes took her further into the story which reported that a seventeen years old farmhand working on Kilmainham Farm in County Kildare had discovered dozens of gold ingots in the middle of a dried-up duck pond. The lead story on page two told breathlessly of how each gold bar was stamped with a Nazi *Swastika* and speculated how the consignment might have found its way to Ireland. The story also reported that each gold bar was possessed of a solid lead component but that nevertheless, the value of the find was substantial and while the State would lay claim to the treasure, the young man, one Sean O'Malley, would be given a not insubstantial finder's fee. When pressed, young Sean confessed to the journalist that he had had for some time his eye on a two year old chestnut mare he thought might be good at the racing.

*Well, I'll be damned,* thought Sinéad. *Kurt told me of the gold but not of the quantity.* She raised her head from the paper and stared hard at the wall, trying to compel an account of the conversation they'd had, wrestling it to the forefront of her mind. *He said if anything happened to him...there was gold at the bottom of a pond on a farm in County Kildare and although he wouldn't tell me the name of the farm, I'd know it as soon as I saw its name as I'd an association with it.*
She permitted herself a mild chuckle as she read on.

*Beggar me!..Kilmainham Farm...the name of the street I lived on in Dublin. He told me he'd renamed the farm when he bought it to permit me to recognise it.*

Her gaze fell absentmindedly once more on the newsprint almost to confirm her understanding wasn't misplaced, her mind racing. *Holy Mother of God, I could have been wealthy rather than scraping a living here in Liverpool...able to care for my family...able to travel...*

Her reverie was broken by a hand on her shoulder.

"Sinéad, we'd better get back to the ward."

"Eh, thanks Mary. I'll be along in a minute."

She drew long on the last end of the Woodbine, holding it tentatively between the tips of her thumb and two fingers, tightening her lips to permit her access to the last half inch drag of the remaining tobacco. That done, and with a great exhalation, she stubbed the resultant negligible stub in her saucer. Drinking the remnants of her now cooled tea, she stood and brushed some ash from her tunic before folding the newspaper and taking it with her. *Perhaps if I read it again when I get home I'd be better able to reminisce the conversation I'd had with Kurt.* She tucked the paper under her arm and strode purposefully towards Ward Fourteen where ten children, both boys and girls with various ailments, awaited her attentions.

The bus taking Sinéad to her one-bedroomed tenemental 'Tenny' flat, in Eldon Street, proceeded along Hornby Boulevard past Bootle Docks and signalled its manoeuvre to a bus halt to permit Sinéad to alight. Setting her down some hundred yards from her apartment, the bus coughed and drove on. Sinéad waited for a gap in the traffic but stood longer than was necessary at the side of the road, lost in memories of her last months in Ireland before the resultant court case in which she was but a witness saw her remove herself to the relative anonymity of Liverpool, just a ferry ride away across the Irish Sea. A taxi driving near to the side of the road passed sufficiently closely to Sinéad to nudge her back to the present and hesitating for a moment, she crossed and made her way to Eldon Street and home.

Now settled with another cup of tea, she removed a fresh orange and yellow pack of ten Wild Woodbine cigarettes from her bag and removed one, raising it to her lips and lighting it. Carefully, she took her copy of the Post and read first the short teaser article on the front page before turning again to the full story on page two where once more she devoured every word.

Folding the newspaper as carefully as she'd done when first she'd read the article in the hospital staff room, she took a deep pull on her cigarette and placed it on her saucer. She leaned her elbows on her knees and placed her head in her hands, kneading her forehead with her thumbs as she remembered the events of five years earlier; Kurt...Hermann...her execution of her dear friend, poor Seamus O'Leary. Slowly, silent tears appeared at the corner of her eyes and rolled free down her face. She shuddered involuntarily and gave way to deep sobs, catching her breath convulsively, gasping for air. Quietly at first, then louder she began to wail a high-pitched, keening cry of grief interposed with silent sobbing. She slumped to her side and rolled slowly onto the floor where she assumed the foetal position, still heaving with a pain she'd ignored since leaving her homeland.

# Haifa, Israel

"Ezra Hasofer" boomed Abraham Youdim M.S., PhD, Guggenheim Fellow and Professor of Applied Engineering as he announced the conferment of a Degree in Engineering on his slightly older star student.

*Technion*, the Institute of Technology in Haifa had been Hasofer's place of study since he'd returned from Ireland and his hard work had been rewarded. First in all subjects, he had been a popular student with both academic staff and fellow undergraduates.

Out in an audience shrouded in darkness sat his now wife, Rachael; their young son David being cared for at home by relatives in order to permit Hasofer's mother and father to join her in witnessing their son's success. Many other parents and spouses applauded Hasofer just as they did the other one hundred and twenty-three men and women who had been graduands until their names had been called by their head of department. Joy was ubiquitous in the university theatre and much back-slapping followed the announcement by the Principal that the ceremony was concluded.

"We're so proud of you, son," said Mr. Hasofer senior as his wife hugged the newly qualified engineer leaving his wife, Rachel to hover close by awaiting an opportunity to do similarly.

After some moments, Mrs. Hasofer relented and permitted Rachael access.

"I love you so much," she whispered in his ear. "You're the cleverest man in all Israel."

Hasofer hugged her tightly and breathed his response quietly.

"Perhaps now I can earn a wage that will allow us the second child you yearn for."

Rachael laughed. "First things first, my brilliant husband. We have a room full of our friends and family who are patiently waiting our arrival in the restaurant. They all want to hug the first man in all the generations of our families who has completed a degree course...and who had topped every exam he was set."

"Of course. But first I want to say goodbye to those who went through the same trials as I did to achieve the degrees we were awarded today. I'll only be a few minutes then we can set off. The restaurant is only half an hour from here. We'll get there precisely at one o'clock, the time we agreed."

Rachael embraced him one more time.

"The three of us will walk to the entrance and meet you there."

Hasofer smiled. "You'll recognise me because I'll be the one walking on air...a foot taller than everyone else."

## CHAPTER FIFTY-ONE

An evening of deep remorse, recurring bouts of tearfulness and eventually whiskey-induced sleep saw Sinéad awaken, still fully clothed, to a morning sun which lit her room brilliantly, causing her to shield her eyes. The ticking of an old mahogany clock on the mantelpiece told her it was six o'clock. Time enough for a cup of tea before setting off again to Sefton Hospital. Wearily she washed her face and upper body in cold water while the kettle whistled and boiled before dressing and pouring herself a cup of tea, decanting the soured milk she'd earlier hoped might yet be serviceable down the drain in her sink.

The bus journey to her place of work allowed Sinéad to read the story of Kurt's gold bullion in that morning's Post. No new information was incorporated in the story but more speculation was displayed about how it might have arrived in Ireland. This time, Kurt's name was mentioned *inter alia* as a German entrepreneur who operated from within the German Legation. It was obvious, though, that no one had any idea how the gold had arrived and journalists were merely repeating local rumours and adding their own when the imagination of the Kildare *indigènes* didn't live up to their ambitions for a sensational tale.

Listlessly she climbed the stairs to Ward Fourteen and smiled wanly at her friend Maureen's bright 'good morning' as she laid her newspaper and lunchbox to one side of the work surface next to the sink and removed her light cardigan. Her drooped posture and melancholic demeanour was soon discerned by Maureen.

"You okay, Sinéad? Your eyes are all red. You been cryin' darlin'?"

"Bad night, Maureen. I'm okay now."

Maureen placed her hand on her shoulder.

"You don't look okay, darlin'. When the doctors do their rounds they'll see straight away that you're not up to scratch."

"I'll be fine. Once I get out in the ward, I'll be fine."

She rubbed her forehead and squeezed her temples, willing her headache to ease.

"Do me a favour, Maureen. Can you keep any aggravation away from me this mornin'. I'm just a bit fragile today."

"Men trouble, Sinéad?"

Sinéad attempted a smile. "One way or another, isn't it always?"

Morning duties lifted Sinéad's spirits slightly as she engaged with children whose ailments were distressing yet who bore them with a fortitude that routinely left her humbled. She busied herself and forsook her usual tea-break to avoid the usual bright banter of her colleagues but couldn't ignore the frantic waving of Maureen who stood at the far end of the ward with the phone to her ear beckoning her towards the nurses' station.

Reluctantly, Sinéad walked past the five pairs of beds and waited while Maureen finished her conversation.

"Certainly doctor. I'll have her come over immediately. Goodbye."

Sinéad invited an explanation merely by lifting her chin and raising her eyebrows.

"The big boss wants you, Sinéad. Dr. McLean...the Hospital Administrator. He's asked me to get you to go to his office as soon as you've finished whatever you're doing!"

"Doctor McLean? Whatever can he want with me? My work's been good. Matron was very complimentary last week."

"Maybe it's a promotion. Everyone knows you've been great since you arrived here."

"I don't want a promotion," said Sinéad stubbornly. "I just want to be left alone to do my job."

"Well, he was quite pointed. Asked if he'd got the right ward. Asked if you were on duty and if you could be spared to come to his office. Didn't say why."

"The office block?" asked Sinéad.

"D'you know where it is?"

"I'd to go there when I started." She lifted her cardigan. "Jesus, Mary and Joseph. I could be doin' without this shaggin' malarky today of all days."

After freshening herself up in the staff toilet, Sinéad made her way over to the office block and presented herself in front of the receptionist.

"Nurse Sinéad O'Grady. I'm to see Doctor McLean. He phoned for me."

The young receptionist smiled.

"Ah, yes. You're expected. Just go straight in to Doctor McLean's office. It's at the end of the corridor. His name's on the door. Just knock and enter."

Sinéad walked along the passageway, trepidation building with each step. She reached Doctor McLean's door and after a brief pause, knocked timidly and entered.

The blinding sunlight in the office was in sharp relief to the gloomy corridor along which she'd just walked and involuntarily, she screened her eyes with her hand as she positioned herself in front of the silhouetted figure which stood tall at the window.

"Hello, Sinéad."

In an instant, Sinéad's hand moved from her eyes to her mouth, masking a cry which emanated from somewhere deep inside. Still her vision was impaired by the strong sunshine but it mattered little as her powers of recognition triggered a flood of tears and a weakening of her knees which caused her to stumble against a chair. Strong arms caught her and guided her to the chair as she turned her face upwards to confirm the identity of the voice.

Haltingly, her voice trembling, she asked, "Hermann, is it you?"

"Doctor Hermann Henning. It's been a while."

He knelt down on one knee so their faces were in proximity. For long moments he struggled to find his voice. Eventually, he removed Sinéad's hands from her face and gently drew his thumb across her cheek, sweeping the tears from her face; but still they flowed.

Sinéad began again to keen quietly as she'd done the previous night, this time shaking her head as if to signal her inability to cope with yet more emotional turmoil. Henning drew her closer only causing Sinéad to weep uncontrollably, unable to comprehend. Slowly,

Henning gathered her in his arms, bidding her to stand as far as her crouched posture allowed and tenderly manoeuvred her to a couch in Doctor MacLean's office where they both sat. After some while, Henning found his voice.

"Sinéad, I'm so sorry if I've caused you pain today. I promise you that was not my intention."

Sinead received this information with further silent shaking of her head. Eyes closed she lowered her chin to her chest and recommenced her distressed sobbing, her shoulders shaking.

Henning, now concerned, sought to soothe her.

"Sinéad, if I'd thought for a moment you'd be so upset, I'd never have set out from Germany. I came here to apologise for my poor behaviour five years ago...there hasn't been a day when I haven't thought fondly of you... and there have been *many* days when you occupied my thoughts for the entire duration.

Slowly, Sinéad wiped her tears on the sleeve of her cardigan prompting Henning to remove a handkerchief from his jacket pocket and hand it to her. Smiling, he lowered his head slightly inviting eye contact, attempting reassurance.

Gradually, Sinéad began to compose herself and she rose from the sofa. Henning followed suit, hands on her arms, still smiling his best comforting smile.

She rose tall, standing her full height and met his gaze. With one swift movement, her arm snapped back and she slapped him full across the face, bringing blood to the surface, immediately reddening his stinging cheek.

"*Go dtachta an diabhal thú,* Hermann Henning! You fecker! You feck off for five years and now you wander back into my life without so much as a by-your-leave with your best doctor's smile and expect me to...I don't know...to...well, what the feck do you expect me to....?"

Tears again began to roll down her face as Henning removed his hand from his pained face and opened both, palms downwards, fingers spread, to invite a more amicable conversation.

"I don't blame you Sinéad after what I called you when I left."

"And what was that mister doctor? What was it you called me?"

"There hasn't been a day when I've not regretted..."

"*Is Troid á an Saol*, she said sarcastically. Will you get to the feckin' point? What did you call me?"

"I lost my temper, Sinéad. I don't usually do that but when I saw you holding Kurt..."

"That's it, you called me a *hoor* or somethin'!"

Henning looked most disconsolate.

"Almost, I remember shouting...shouting '*Schlampe!*'...*slut* in German...but I didn't mean..."

"So you've come all the way to Liverpool to call me a...and how in God's name did you find me anyway?"

"Your Uncle Joseph. I managed to track him down in Dublin. There are still people at the house in Rialto who told him from me that I would wait in the Patriot's Inn until he had time to look in. It only took a few hours...."

"Never mind...so you've travelled over here just to tell me I'm a hoor and a slut, have you?"

"No, Sinéad...I came over to Liverpool to tell you that I love you and that I've been a fool. I tried to tell you many times when we lived together but I'm such a shy person. I came to the hotel that day to ask you to marry me but instead I found you...."

More tears ran down Sinéad's face but they were born of different emotions.

"Hermann...I'm in *bits*! Over the last few years I've developed a taste for Woodbine cigarettes and whiskey. Cigarettes to keep me awake...whiskey to make me sleep...I'm a bag of nerves. My mind won't let me sleep. I go over and over that nightmare. You don't understand. I'm not worthy of you. I felt that then and I feel that now. I didn't do anything with Kurt. Not that he wasn't trying it on...and I was drunk...and I know how it must have looked so I deserved you calling me names..."

"I was in shock, Sinéad. I'd just shot and killed a man. I'm a doctor. My duty is to preserve life and I'd just killed another human being."

"Hermann, he'd just shot at you...trying to kill you. That's what I told the court when I was asked to be a witness. They believed me because it was the truth."

"I know, but nevertheless...I killed a man...and ran away like a fugitive."

Sinéad reached out and wove her fingers through Henning's hair, forming a fist, gently shaking his head.

"Well, that's behind us now." She moved her palm down and caressed Henning's cheek.

"Sorry about the slap. I'm not having a good day... and now you appearing out of the blue"

She remembered she was in the office of the hospital administrator.

"...And how did you manage to use Doctor McLean's office?"

"We worked together remember?.. when I was a doctor here in Sefton. He was happy to..."

Sinéad shook her head as if to bring her back to the point she wanted to make.

"Anyway, is that *it*? You wanted to find me to *apologise* to me?"

"Partly, Sinéad. I wanted to ask you...if there is someone special in your life...Your Uncle Joseph didn't think so but he warned me that your beauty was such that you must have dozens of suitors."

Sinéad laughed.

"If only you knew, Hermann."

She wiped her tears with Henning's handkerchief.

"All the time you were in Germany thinking of me, I was over here thinking of *you*. I've never met anyone so kind, intelligent and tender. I decided long ago that if I couldn't have you...I didn't want anyone else. The main reason I'm working here in Sefton was to be closer to my memories of you."

"Then the second part of my visit to Liverpool is made easier."

Self-consciously, Henning knelt as Sinead stepped back, her hands covering her mouth in shock as a gradual confused appreciation of his action began to register.

"Sinéad O'Grady, will you do me the honour of being my wife? I have a ring...it's probably not the correct size... in case you say 'yes'. You would make me the happiest man in the world."

Henning's handkerchief was pressed into further service as a tearful but happy Sinéad nodded her agreement before composing herself.

"There's a condition, Doctor Henning."

She cleared her throat but still spoke tremulously.

"You'd never have found out about this unless you'd asked me to marry first...but are you prepared to be the father of a child?"

471

Henning had risen and stood holding Sinéad by the arms as he had done earlier when trying to mollify her.

"Of course, Sinéad. That's usually how marriage works, God willing."

"Well, it might work a bit quicker that you'd imagine."

Again she cleared her throat, preparing her next comment.

"When you and I spent the night together in my house in Dublin..."

"How could I forget..?"

"Well, you're obviously a very *virile* doctor because nine months later a baby girl appeared. Her name's Patricia...Patricia Henning Devlin after my sister's man... and after *you*.

Sinéad bit her lip, awaiting a reaction. Henning's mouth was agape.

"So I'm the father...I'm the father of...Wh..where is she?"

"*That's* why I'm in Liverpool. I might have been able to live with my notoriety in Ireland if I'd just been involved with shooting and general mayhem...but the single mother of a child? I'd have been strung up. I came over here to have the child and my sister Mary and her man Daniel are raising it as their own in Tralee. The child's only four but she thinks I'm her Aunt. I visit regular...and it breaks my heart every time I arrive and every time I leave my darling daughter...*our* darling daughter...and it's doubly hard when we're apart. Even my Uncle Joseph doesn't know anything about this...and he thinks he knows everything."

"And you're sure...?"

"Hermann! I've slept with one man in my life. One *time* in my life. That man was you. I was in love with you or you wouldn't have been able to sleep in the same bed as me. Kurt was persistent but other than a forced kiss when I was drunk, he never touched me, despite how it looked when you arrived...although I suspect he might have taken a bit of resistance that night, I can tell you."

She took Henning's hands gently from her arms and held them tight in her own as if she was preparing to dance a reel.

"Hermann, you're the father of the most beautiful little girl in all Ireland. She has your intelligence and grace. With any luck, all she has of me are my dark curls once she grows up...none of my nonsense, none of my tempers...although she's developing a mind of her own I must say."

Henning was silent as he digested the confusing welter of information Sinéad had just presented. Sinéad stood, anxious to embrace him, but wary... her eyes locked on his, trying to establish his reaction.

Henning took a pace backwards and sat on the edge of McLean's desk, pulling her towards him as he did so. Tears welled up in his eyes.

"I've been so stupid, Sinéad. I should have come looking for you years ago but I was so confused, I felt so guilty, so sacred of the authorities..."

He shook his head.

"This is madness! We must act immediately. I will speak with Doctor McLean and thank him for employing you in Sefton. If you are prepared to be married to a shy, confused, idiot of a doctor, we'll make immediate arrangements...and then...once you and I are married, we leave directly for Tralee and you can introduce me to our daughter. I'll get a medical practice or a hospital job in Ireland if the authorities have lost interest in me and

I promise on my honour that I'll devote every waking hour to making you and our daughter the happiest, most beloved young ladies on the island of Ireland."

More tears of happiness flowed as the two tearful lovers embraced and lingered over a kiss that had been some five years in the making.

## Haifa, Israel

The large room in Lev's Restaurant in Haifa was so full that many had had to stand at the rear and when Hasofer stopped thanking people, hauling his wife to her feet for a kiss to mark an end to his speech, it erupted in good humour. Friends shouted cheery insults and relatives applauded. It had been a good day for Ezra Hasofer; graduating from the new nation's most prestigious university, at least in engineering, and now being in the company of his dearest friends and relatives. He looked down at the now re-seated Rachel and thought that if only his son David had been old enough to attend and to appreciate his success, it would have been perfect.

The meal had been a great success and now those who remained were focused upon the consumption of quantities of wine. Small knots of people thronged the room and still the outbursts of laughter punctuated the ambience. Hasofer moved from group to group, making small talk, smiling and accepting pats on his back from everyone.

His eyes some time before had noticed a celebrant standing alone at the bar smoking a large cigar and drinking what looked like whisky; Scotch whisky if Hasofer was correct in his identification and his recollection of the stranger's preferences in alcohol.

Slowly Hasofer made his way from group to group until he approached the man at the bar.

"Your glass is almost empty," said Hasofer lightly. "Would you like another?"

The man smiled and nodded, finishing his drink in one smooth gulp.

"If you are who I think you are, that's a Scotch whisky...a malt whisky."

The smile broadened. "You are as perspicacious as Menachem told me you'd be."

Hasofer caught the barman's attention and gestured at the empty glass.

"Another one of these...and I'll have a glass of water please."

"Congratulations, Ezra. You have done exceptionally well."

"And I hope you know how grateful I am to *Haganah* for the financial support I've received. Also for allowing me to study during some difficult years for our new nation. You could easily have ordered me to return to the ranks. In all candour, I could not have refused. We were in great peril and I am nothing if not a patriot."

"Many young Jewish boys contributed their blood to the birth of Israel. But you would have been wasted at the front, Ezra. Your talents are much too sophisticated for the ugly confrontations against the Arab forces in the Sinai Desert or in Southern Lebanon."

"You have me at mild disadvantage," said Hasofer holding out his hand. "You know me to be Ezra Hasofer. Can I assume that you're Reuven Shiloah, the new

Director of the Institute for Intelligence and Special Operations? I've seen only a few photographs but I've heard so much about you."

"I am, although most people refer to the organisation I now direct as *Mossad*. I was appointed last year and I take a keen interest in our star performers. I hope you'll forgive me but I thought it appropriate to come along today on behalf of the State of Israel and congratulate you."

"I'm honoured. But for the past five years I've just been a student engineer."

"You have. And the State wishes to see you appointed in a significant role in some of our most prestigious projects where your talents might be most of use. We are in need of a new international airport to be built just outside Tel Aviv at Lydda, for example, and you would be able to play a significant role there. It would pay well," he added, as if the excitement on Hasofer's face didn't reveal his sufficient inclination to accept the brief whatever the financial rewards.

"I'm flattered."

"Top student in each of your subjects? It is *we* who should be flattered that you would consider applying your talents to projects that are important to us."

Hasofer smiled. "Your reputation as a man who is urbane and sophisticated is well deserved."

The smile on Shiloah's face fled as he took on a new seriousness.

"And, if I may say so myself, I also have a reputation for brilliance, ruthlessness and tenacity."

Hasofer sensed the new atmosphere immediately and mirrored Shiloah's stern gaze.

"You omit your fondness for good malt whisky!"

Shiloah tapped the end of his cigar against an ashtray. His eyes creased in the beginnings of a smile that didn't reach his lips.

"And fine Cuban Cigars."

Hasofer attempted a closure to the discussion.

"Well, thank you again for coming along to..."

"Before I leave, you and I must talk, Hasofer."

He checked to ensure that no one was able to overhear their conversation.

"*Haganah*, now *Mossad*, have been very generous to you. We have paid handsomely for your education and are prepared to continue this in ensuring that you hold a well paid job of national importance that will excite your interests and is worthy of your engineering talents."

"That debt was paid in advance when I took the mission to Ireland."

"That's not how we see it, Hasofer. In fact we take the view that you remain in our debt...although I must confess that in reading your files, I was most impressed by your performance in Ireland. Quite brilliant. A perfect execution of your mission but no hint of diplomatic repercussions. Completely excellent!"

Hasofer sighed loudly.

"Director Shiloah, I now have a wife and child. That changes things."

"I agree, Hasofer. Which is why you are *not* being given the task of travelling to South America leading a team of our agents in the search for Josef Mengele, the evil Nazi 'Angel of Death' who ran the gas chambers at Auschwitz. That task, for which you would be well suited, is expected to take some considerable time so because of my well-known reputation for compassion...

you forgot my quality of *compassion*...you are being set a much simpler task."

"And I have no say in the matter?"

"None whatsoever, Hasofer. Israel is the youngest nation in the world. Barely two years old. Born of bloodshed on every continent in the world. Millions of our people have been butchered. Our children...our *children*...have been gassed. Now, at last we have our own land. We control our own destiny. We have to be strong to...what is the name of your child...was it *David* I read on your file?"

Hasofer nodded.

"Then we have to be strong and strain every sinew to ensure that young David and all other Jewish children like him are not gassed or maimed or shot or starved at the hands of our enemies."

Hasofer sighed resignedly. "What would you have me do?"

Shiloah patted Hasofer on the shoulder affably.

"You *are* a true patriot, Ezra. The Mengele business has us worried because he may have changed his identity. We are aware that during the war, a Nazi doctor called Leonardo Conti was performing constructive facial surgery on Nazis who wanted to look more Aryan. Before the war, he left his medical activities and started organising the *Nationalsozialistischer Deutscher Ärztebund* in Berlin. A ruthless Nazi. And his enthusiasm for constructive facial surgery, we believe, is still being practiced...both on the most senior of men who seek to escape detention and return to the Fatherland to continue to promote the cause of Nazism as well as those who would seek to avoid our retribution. We believe there is now a network of medical practitioners who assist this process."

"And you would have me uncover these people?"

"Just one, actually. He was an associate of the German General that you were asked to dispatch; one Kurt Weber. He was actually present and defending the General when he was killed. He must have been sent to Dublin for a reason. It took us some time to surmise the Nazi motive but we think it was because he was in a position to alter the facial features of those Nazis who settled in Ireland. He disappeared for some years after Weber was shot but our investigations reveal that he has recently resurfaced in Dublin although he has just travelled to Liverpool in England."

"Doctor Hermann Henning?"

"The same!"

"Surely not! I never met him but I was told he was a humanitarian...a kind and talented doctor."

"Perhaps so, Ezra Hasofer, perhaps. However, when it comes to protecting the interests of our new nation, we don't take chances."

"And you expect me to track him down and interrogate him?"

Shiloah stubbed out his cigar and finished his whisky.

"No, Hasofer. I expect you to *kill* him. Do not fail us!"

## CHAPTER FIFTY-TWO

# The End

If you enjoyed *'The Patriot Game'*, why not try *'A Confusion of Mandarins'*, a 428 page spy thriller and *'The Kaibab Resolution'*, a 278 page novel dealing with gun control in the USA and its links with the Irish Republican Army. You can find excerpts, reviews and purchasing details at;

http://www.ronculley.com

Ron Culley's excellent books are read internationally. His audience is somewhat bifurcated...some preferring his pawky Glasgow humour, recalling tales of the city of his birth...others more partial to his all-action thrillers and works of historical fiction. Whatever your fancy, his web site keeps his avid readers up to date on new releases and occasional blogs as well as facilitating an exchange of comments and questions to the author.

A 437 page autobiography called *'I Belong To Glasgow'* (with a foreword by Sir Alex Ferguson) charts the development of this magnificent Scottish city in the 50's and 60's in what is a warm and witty account of Culley's youth growing up in a Glasgow just recovering from the war years as well as his transmogrification from a young boy expelled from school via public service to becoming an author. A second book about the city of his birth, *'Glasgow Belongs To Me'* is also available. Same web site as above.

Another work of historical fiction, *'A Terrible Beauty Is Born'* about the 1916 Easter Rising in Dublin is currently being written.

Ron Culley lives in the leafy suburbs of Glasgow, Scotland with his wife and family. The proud father of four sons and now three grandchildren, his *'Who's Who'* listing shows his hobbies as watching association football, irreverence, laughing out loud and convivial temulence.

# Author's Notes

1.  **Irish Free State/Irish Republic**
    In 1937, de Valera's government presented a draft of a new constitution to *Dail Eireann* which repealed the 1922 Constitution and came into effect on 29 December 1937.

    The state was named Ireland and a new office of President of Ireland was instituted in place of the Governor-General of the Irish Free State.

    A small but significant minority of Irish people usually attached to organisations like the IRA or *Sinn Fein* decried the right of the twenty-six counties to use the name Republic and continued to refer to the state as the Free State.

2.  **De Valera's Condolences.**
    De Valera and Joseph Walshe, Secretary of the Department of Foreign Affairs offered their condolences upon the death of Adolph Hitler to Eduard Hempel, the Head of the German Legation on May 2$^{nd}$, 1945, *two days* after Hitler committed suicide – not on the same day.

3.  **Charlie Kerins**
    Charlie Kerins was not executed in the summer months as is suggested in the narrative. On 1$^{st}$ December 1944

in Mountjoy Gaol, Kerins was hanged by British Chief Executioner Alfred Pierrepoint who was employed for the occasion. Huge public debate was suppressed by the government and many public protests preceded his hanging – especially in his home county of Kerry.

4. **The Nazis in Ireland.**
   In the aftermath of the Second World War, Ireland provided safe haven to a number of Nazi collaborators and war criminals. Protected by church and state, many made their home in Ireland or used it for a staging post for escape to America. Simultaneously, the de Valera Government refused asylum to many Jewish refugees.

5. **The Isle of Man**
   The British used the island as an internment camp, a major prisoner of war stronghold just as they did during the First World War. Various locations held prisoners and internees. Japanese, German and Italian nationals deemed to pose a security threat; British Blackshirts, Fascist sympathisers and Irish Republican Volunteers were all interned there. No one ever escaped from the Island.

6. **German Spies in Ireland**
   Irish neutrality permitted Germany to maintain an espionage centre within its Legation in Dublin. The Abwehr [German Military Intelligence] sent spies to Ireland and used Irish/German immigrants to encourage the IRA to sabotage Allied military targets in Northern Ireland and on the mainland. They were all unsuccessful.

7. **The German Legation, Dublin.**
   The German legation in Dublin was headed by Ambassador Eduard Hempel who had his radio transmitter confiscated in 1943 to prevent him from passing information to Germany. The Legation provided support to nationals and represented German interests. It was located at 58 Northumberland Road, Ballsbridge, Dublin and flew two large Nazi flags ostentatiously from its portals. A deployment of *Gardai* was always in evidence at its entrance to provide protection but also to keep an eye on visitors. It closed immediately after the conclusion of the war and did not reopen under the guise described in the narrative. The Legation had very few resources when its keys were surrendered.

8. **St Kevin's Hospital**
   St Kevin's Hospital was renamed St. James's Hospital in 1971.

9. **Jewish Immigration to Ireland.**
   There was some official indifference from the political establishment to the Jewish victims of the Holocaust during and after the war. This indifference would later be described by Minister for Justice Michael McDowell in 2003 as being "antipathetic, hostile and unfeeling". Post-war, Jewish groups had great difficulty in getting refugee status for Jewish children, whilst at the same time, a plan to bring over four hundred Catholic Children from the Rhineland encountered no difficulties.

10. **Petrol rationing.**

Rationing of petrol began almost immediately just after the start of the World War Two in October 1939. The official allowance for ordinary people with cars was eight gallons a month up to 10 hp; 12 gallons a month for cars 10 - 16 hp. For the first few years petrol was not too scarce but by the middle of 1941 things deteriorated and many private cars were taken off the road. The German Legation had supplementary fuel supplies. Doctors, priests and vets also received an extra allowance.

# Bibliography

1. Andrew, Christopher. **The Defence of the Realm.** (The Authorised History of MI5) Allen Lane, London 2009

2. Heraghty's, Tony. **The Irish War.** (The Military History of a Domestic Conflict) HarperCollins, London 2000.

3. Coogan, Tim Pat. **Ireland** (In the Twentieth Century) Arrow, London 2003

4. Fisk, Robert. **In Time Of War.** (Ireland, Ulster And The Price of Neutrality 1939 - 45) Gill & Macmillan. Dublin 1983

5. Keogh, Dermot & O'Driscoll, Mervyn. **Ireland In World War Two** (Neutrality and Survival) Mercier Press, Cork 2004

6. Ferriter, Diarmaid. **Judging Dev.** Royal Irish Academy, Dublin 2004

7. Girvin, Brian. **The Emergency** (Neutral Ireland 1939-45) Pan Macmillan, London 2004

8. Nolan, Aengus. **Joseph Walshe** (Irish Foreign Policy 1922-46) Mercier Press, Cork 2008

9. Delaney, Frank. **The Matchmaker of Kenmare.** Random House, New York. 2011

10. Behan, Brendan. **Borstal Boy.** Arrow Books, London 1958

11. Chappell, Connery. **Island Of Barbed Wire.** (World War Two Interment On The Isle Of Man) Robert Hale, London 1984
12. Wills, Claire. **That Neutral Island.** (A Cultural History Of Ireland During The Second World War) Faber and Faber, London 2005